Chief
An American Novel

Cole Strider

Chief: An American Novel

First Edition

ISBN-10: 1514644932
ISBN-13: 978-1514644935

This book is a work of fiction. The Ronopo and Mihote Tribes do not exist. Names, characters, tribes, cultures, organizations, places, events and incidents are either the products of the author's imagination or used fictitiously. Any resemblance to actual persons, living or dead, or actual entities or events is purely coincidental. All dialogue, as well as any opinions or philosophy appearing to be expressed, are also a product of the author's imagination.

Cover Design by Cole Strider

Cover Art Under License:

Black Hawk:	Dennis Crow / Beyondmascotart.com
Indian Chief (headdress):	Dennis Crow / Beyondmascotart.com
Feather (also on End Page):	Tribalium / Shutterstock.com
Hunting Arrows (selection):	Tribalium / Shutterstock.com
White House (selection):	Slobodan Djajic / Shutterstock.com
Assault Rifle (selection):	Grimgram / Shutterstock.com
Flag of the United States of America:	Gil C / Shutterstock.com
Realistic Red Maple Leaf:	OmniArt / Shutterstock.com
Chili Peppers on Paper (selection):	serazetdinov / Shutterstock.com

Selection from *Warrior Creed* by Robert L. Humphrey. Source: Kindle Edition of *Values for a New Millennium* by Robert L. Humphrey. Life Values Press 2012

Published by Cole Strider
Lewes, DE   USA

Printed by CreateSpace
Also available in e-book format

For You Know Who

I've told you many stories.
Now I've written one for you.
Thanks for sharing so many of your own
and for all the joy and laughter.

TABLE OF CONTENTS

FIRST WORDS

You asked me to tell you a story, so I made one up for you. This story is not historical fiction nor is it science fiction – but it does take place in a parallel universe, in a galaxy and solar system similar to ours, on a planet called Earth which is much like our planet Earth.

All of the people in this story are different than any people on *our* Earth. Some of the events described may resemble events here – but things are not the same amongst parallel universes.

This is a story of what *could* take place on a *different* planet Earth, in a *different* time, if *different* people were involved than people on *our* Earth. The outcomes of events may be similar or dissimilar.

It is, after all, just a made-up story.

CHAPTER ONE
Echoes of the Past

The chilling sound was the grotesque scream of something surely not human. Kogan Kichoba did not realize that it had emanated from his own throat. He was falling, head-first, into a seemingly bottomless abyss. The Elder turned his head hard to look up at the canyon rim from where he just launched. He saw a huge boulder bounce off the side of the gorge and hurtle directly towards him. His eyes darted downwards. A rocky peak was rising up beneath him, and he flailed frantically in a futile attempt to avoid it.

The boulder and the peak met, sandwiching and crushing Kogan's lower body into a bloody and gelatinous mass. His shriek of agony and terror echoed around him, the canyon's acoustics distorting the sound into an eerie likeness of evil and triumphant laughter.

The man and the boulder separated and resumed their downward plunge.

My penance at last, was his final thought before his mangled body bounced like a rag doll off another rocky spire – and the flow of life energy to Kogan Kichoba was mercifully shut off.

COUNTERPOINT I
GENESIS

"Is the enterprise laid out to the absolutely smallest level of detail?"

"Yes. It's all in The Master Business Plan. We have identified and retained the most elite team of experts ever brought together to design and execute this unprecedented venture. As is the case with any undertaking, there will be bumps in the road that are not possible to predict in advance. For any such deviations from the plan, our crack team and highly advanced computers will immediately improvise an alternate path. Any new path will be incorporated seamlessly into the remainder of the plan."

"If we succeed, this will be truly historic – and the payoff – astronomical."

"Without a doubt. Our team will be 100% dedicated to this project, ensuring success."

"What happens first upon initiation of the enterprise?"

"Phase 1 is the procurement of the initial funding from all sources – then recruitment, training, placement of personnel, and the laying of infrastructure."

"Excellent. It is my great pleasure to sign off on this. Let the grand venture begin."

4

CHAPTER TWO
The Mother Lode

Breeze Whitecloud gathered up the long, dark tresses of hair draped upon the now moist skin of her neck and shoulders. Some tendrils escaped her hands and cascaded down the neckline of the tank top that was stretched too tightly across her chest.

Everything in her very limited wardrobe was packed except for what she would wear tomorrow while traveling. Having no money to buy anything extra, she had scrounged up some old, undersized clothing left over from her preteen years, before her body took on its softness and curves. She did not find any spare undergarments, though, so today she had to go commando.

Wearing so little today doesn't matter, she thought. *Where I'm going, not a single soul will see me.*

There were multiple settlements totaling a few thousand people on the Ronopo (RON-uh-po) Tribal Reservation. The largest, most populous and developed one was referred to as "the village." In addition to many homes, the tribal government offices were there, as well as the reservation schools and the tribe's few commercial establishments. There was a wide variety of terrain across the expansive reservation, including large parcels of land that were barren and uninhabited. Breeze had risen very early to drive out to one such region in the southwest quadrant.

She knew it was risky to be searching in this quarter of the reservation, but she was here on her own time. The summer had drawn to a close, and tomorrow she would leave for her last year of college. As an Earth Science major, she had been an intern again for the Federal Energy Agency (FEA). The FEA supervisors told the interns not to explore on Native American tribal reservations. Those locations would only be pursued when there was agency funding for a joint exploration with the tribes.

Breeze knew that meant *never*. She also knew how much it could mean to the Ronopo Tribe, her people, if natural resource deposits were found on their land, and better yet, independently by a member of the tribe. The Ronopo would extract any resources in a manner respectful of the Earth, of sacred places, and of the creatures dependent upon Earth's gifts. Such a find could mean good jobs, a source of needed funds, and leverage that could go far to lift the Ronopo people out of their cycle of unrealized dreams.

Breeze knew not to get too close to the canyon edge, since sinkholes and rock-slides were possible hazards there. The Elder, Kogan Kichoba, had recently been approaching that very gorge when the ground collapsed beneath him, sending him helter-skelter to his death.

Using geological scanning instruments to ascertain the stability of the ground ahead of her, Breeze edged her old, Army surplus vehicle closer to the ravine. Then, even though she was still a distance from the rim, the equipment made it possible for her to inspect the canyon floor far, far below.

She heard the distant howl of a wolf which was a familiar sound in these parts. It made her smile.

After working awhile in the sweltering heat, her thin, tightly clinging top and shorts were plastered to her sweat-slick skin beneath. Since her tank top was too short, there was at least a little relief when a rare breeze found its way up underneath it. She twisted her voluminous hair into a loose puff on top of her head. Feeling a little cooler, she bent over the equipment again, leaning on her elbows and refocusing her attention on the readouts.

The howl of the wolf seemed closer now.

Disregarding it, Breeze continued the tedious process of electronically scanning the landscape. She was searching for signs that could signify the presence of natural gas or liquid gold – crude petroleum oil.

After spending an hour analyzing an area inside the canyon, she had found nothing of interest; so she refocused the equipment onto a section with different geological characteristics. A change in a readout indicated some sort of movement down there. Breeze picked up her high-powered, periscopic binoculars, adjusted them, and...

"Whoa! There's a man down there! How the heck... and uh... hmm... he's *very* naked..."

Breeze was beta testing experimental, electronic binoculars. With them she was able to see a remarkable level of detail despite how far away the man was. Then, even more startling than his presence down there, the man looked up and appeared to focus his gaze directly upon her. She knew that was impossible due to the great distance and the topography. She had only been able to pick him up via sensitive electronics and special, high-powered optics.

She wondered, *Is his attention being drawn in my direction by something I should know about?*

Breeze's instincts for self-preservation kicked in. Swiftly lowering the binoculars, she drew her 9mm pistol from the pocket holster in the gear pack by her side. She quickly surveyed the area around her. Then, she carefully scrutinized the vicinity – looking... listening... searching for any sign of danger.

I haven't heard the howl of the wolf for a while now, she realized.

It was rare for a wolf to approach a human; but if one were to suddenly appear and threaten her from more than a short distance away, the shotgun in her vehicle was within reach. She should be able to scare off any animal with just a warning shot.

She detected nothing of concern, however, so she re-holstered her pistol. Upon lifting the binoculars once more, she found that the man had moved out of sight.

It was common knowledge that there was no access to the formidable canyon, that it was not safe to hike or climb in, and that its only inhabitants were flora and fauna.

The man's presence down there certainly merited investigation, so Breeze called the reservation's Search and Rescue team and described her surprising discovery.

While waiting for them to arrive, Breeze continued to scan the area where the man had been. Her time there had not been completely wasted, as she had found some geological features that she could include in her senior thesis. Wrapping up, she recorded her observations and backed up her data twice, using two flash drives. She stowed one in her gear pack and put the other in her vehicle's open storage tray. There, she would see it and remember to copy the data to her laptop when she got home. Since she had been in an area where the FEA had not authorized her to work, she carefully deleted the data from the equipment before shutting it all down.

Although Breeze's sense of awareness had been heightened by her brief scare, she was oblivious that a vicious predator actually *was* watching her – waiting... calculating... salivating...

The rescue helicopter finally stopped hovering and rose out of the labyrinth of tall rock formations in the canyon. It landed at a safe distance from the rim, close to where Breeze had parked.

For a better view of the rescue in the canyon, Breeze was sitting up on top of a seat-back in her open-top Army vehicle. Her arms were draped over the roll-bar, and her hiking boots rested on the dashboard. Only now was her mind roused from pondering how a man could have come to be in the exceedingly deep canyon.

The rescue team disembarked with their now-clothed guest. The mystery man stepped away from the chopper and locked eyes with Breeze. He was an extremely striking young man with long black hair, dusky native coloring, a rugged face, and a powerful build. The clothing Search and Rescue loaned him was not large enough for his impressive proportions. Thus, the shirt was open and the top of the shorts unbuttoned, displaying the young man's sun-bronzed and well-defined chest and abs.

The intensity with which he looked at Breeze jolted her like a lightning bolt. She involuntarily sat up straighter as goose bumps washed over her. She saw his eyes drop down to scan the rest of her. His gaze halted on the way back up to her face – and she felt a hot flush rise in her cheeks. It was a shock of a reminder of what she was wearing, not having expected to see anyone today and having totally spaced it when she called in the rescue team.

Glancing down, she saw, to her horror, that her tightly form-fitting clothes, now wet with perspiration, were practically transparent in places. She crossed her arms over her chest but could not shift her body enough to hide the nakedness exposed through her shorts. She dropped down and stood where her vehicle partially shielded her from the man. Her lips parted, but she was speechless. When his eyes returned to hers, she felt as if his piercing gaze was physically holding her, motionless and electrified.

The members of the Ronopo Reservation Search and Rescue Team were Breeze's close, childhood friends. She knew that they would always have her back. One of them, Aspen Mijeesi, noticed Breeze's discomfort. Quietly and reassuringly, he said,

"Your secret is safe with us, Little Sister. And I have an idea to allay your concerns about the FEA ban on exploring here. You said that Birdie persuaded you to follow your instincts about this location on your last day. So it's really not a lie to credit her with finding this loner. Anyway, she deserves a commendation for the incredibly skillful way she piloted the chopper through that *devil's maze*. That woman really knows how to handle a joystick!" he said, winking. "What do you say we report that Search and Rescue found him during a routine patrol?"

While Aspen had spoken, and not skipping a beat, his eyes on Breeze's face the entire time, he had casually, yet expeditiously, unbuttoned his shirt, taken it off, and held it for her. Breeze gratefully slipped into it. The large shirt was a welcome coverup for her embarrassingly revealing attire. Despite her agitated state, Breeze noticed the pleasing, masculine scent Aspen's body had left on the shirt and felt comforted by it.

"So," Aspen continued, hooking his thumbs in his belt loops, "that energy agency will never even know you were prowling around in these parts."

"Thanks," Breeze managed to utter, her eyes tearing up. "On *two* counts," she added, looking up at the now bare-chested young man who was smiling kindly at her.

She finished buttoning up Aspen's predictably thoughtful offering. Nodding, she said, "That would work out well for all of us."

COUNTERPOINT II
PEEP-SHOW

"OK, guys, we need to pinpoint this perfectly. This must be precisely and cleanly executed with minimal collateral damage. We are, under no circumstances, to hit the area on the other side of the target. So we need to reposition and come from the other direction. Once we let it loose, unwanted attention could be focused on this location. So we need the first one to count, then we get the hell out of here. Remember, if we're caught, we're to say that this was a training exercise gone awry. Everybody got that?"

"Wait, Rob! There's a transmission coming through on the secure channel."

"PD-Alpha, do you read me?"

"I read you loud and clear, X-1," Rob replied.

"Your order is to STAND DOWN. Repeat, STAND DOWN. Do you copy?"

"Roger, X-1. Standing down."

"Your new orders are to document only, full detail. Do you copy, PD-Alpha?"

"Roger, X-1. The drone is documenting only, full detail."

"Hot damn!" Rob whooped. "Do you guys see what we're recording?!"
"On the big screen, Bozeau (BO-zo)! Let us see what you've got."
"Oh, Baby! Sweet!!"

Rob thought, *Later, I'm downloading some of this for me! Woo-ee!*

CHAPTER THREE
Golden Hawk

Kristal Parks was an African-American woman who had grown up near the Ronopo Reservation, interacting with the tribe throughout her youth. Her parents had imbued in her the boundless value of education, and she became a teacher, hoping to work on the reservation. The Ronopo had good schools, but they welcomed Kristal's additional contributions. She established a program for gifted students and one for those who needed extra help.

Like everyone else, Kristal was impressed by the newest member of the community, Dukon Chatan. He had been found in Rattlesnake Canyon, strong, healthy, and alone. He appeared to be between twenty and twenty-five and was an extremely fine specimen of Ronopo male. The tribe had welcomed him into their midst, giving him the nickname, Golden Hawk.

It was not surprising that he had gone undetected all those years in such a remote corner of the reservation. The canyon was far from any settlements, and there were well-known hazards that would hinder any safe entry or exit from the isolated gorge. It was more amazing that he had survived – apparently alone for much of his young life.

Golden Hawk's exceptional physique and athleticism were testament to having roughed it in the wild all those years. He was taciturn, but when he spoke, it was in limited Ronopo. He quickly learned to communicate in broken English, which was the language the younger generations usually spoke on the reservation. Eventually, he actually surpassed his peers in English language competency. He also showed considerable interest in Native American history and its significance in the history of the United States.

His quiet reserve and palpable intensity set him apart from the more raucous young adults of the tribe. It was difficult to gauge if his reserve was maturity born of a harsh and primitive youth or if it was something else. The fine-looking young man attracted much attention from the women and inspired awe and envy amongst the men.

When asked about his past, he told them that his mother had died giving birth to him and his father had perished in a rock slide when Dukon was just a boy. If pressed for more details, he shared a few but clearly resented the intrusive curiosity.

Some Elders speculated as to who his grandfather might have been – a member of the tribe who had left to seek adventure long ago. Kogan Kichoba, the many-decades-long Official Keeper of the Register, would likely have been able to shed light on this had he not recently died. Chief Bridgewater appointed Hunter Wya (WHY-uh), a smart but antisocial young college graduate, to replace Kogan. There was no immediately apparent place for Golden Hawk in the Official Tribal Register which required some expertise to read. Eventually, Hunter pieced together an intricate trail of links that definitively traced Golden Hawk's clan. It had been so difficult because there were no known members of his clan still living.

It was not unusual for tribal registers to bear in-depth scrutiny when seeking the name of someone who had become dissociated from a tribe. There had been a flap in the news when someone had allegedly, incorrectly claimed to be Native American. People wondered if that person had gained advantages reserved for people of special ethnic origins. Some members of that tribe were indignant that a claim to its grand legacy was professed by a person neither listed in their Official Register nor evidently documented elsewhere with them. They especially resented that such a lineage had apparently not been meaningful enough to that person to research it and reconnect before laying claim to such a proud heritage.

Forging a solid personal identity as a Native American Indian in the ever-changing world was understandably hard. Members of the Ronopo Tribe grappled with conflicting cultural, political, and economic forces. Interestingly, Golden Hawk's isolation from his people seemed to have rendered him more representative of the tribe's historical image. He confidently personified the ideal of the people who inhabited the continent long ago, before foreigners invaded, nearly effacing the slate of native America.

Gradually, Golden Hawk was accepted as a member of the community, but his cool intensity kept people from getting too close. Women tried to attract his interest but were not successful. He did ask about Breeze but did not know her name, referring to her as one of the Search and Rescue team. Breeze was now back at college; and thanks to her faithful friends, no one else knew that she and Golden Hawk had ever encountered one another. Thus, people assumed that he was inquiring about little Birdie Moonsong who piloted the rescue helicopter.

Golden Hawk did not connect any better with the men in the tribe, though he seemed somewhat drawn to Hunter Wya, the sullen, new Keeper of the Register. Kristal Parks suspected that he was attracted by Hunter's similar reticence, as Hunter was a bit of a lone wolf himself. Beneath Hunter's reserve, however, he possessed unusual worldliness from his mainstream college experience and some travel abroad. Given Golden Hawk's commanding presence, Kristal imagined how well he might leverage higher education. She resolved to help him to at least have a chance at it.

Golden Hawk frequently asked certain Elders to recount the old stories and to describe cultural rituals. Those men were pleased to impart their knowledge of the tribe's heritage along with countless anecdotes of times gone by. They were also glad to have a new ear for their old complaints about the disconnect between tribal needs, tribal sovereignty, and U.S. government involvement. As Golden Hawk began to understand the issues, he tentatively suggested alternative approaches which were likely different because of his outsider's point of view. Some members of the tribe, awed by the physically impressive and serious young man, were inspired by his ideas and youthful energy. They wondered if he might be the one to accept the baton and lead a resurgence for the Ronopo and other Native American peoples.

CHAPTER FOUR
In the Wild

Aspen had wanted to be a doctor. He dreamed of better access to quality care on the reservation. Working hard at college, he earned a scholarship to medical school. However, his father became ill, necessitating his return to the reservation. Thus, he redirected his coursework, earning basic certifications in Physical Therapy, Nutrition, and as an EMT. Back on the reservation, he studied with a shaman and incorporated some of the ancient knowledge and techniques into his occupational repertoire. He also volunteered his time, teaching healthy living habits in the reservation schools. With his knowledge of good health practices, he maintained his own body and mind as the precious vessels he understood them to be. He often walked, ran, or hunted alone early in the mornings in all seasons and weather conditions. He filled his lungs with fresh air and challenged his muscles and reflexes to keep them limber and strong. During the annual summer games, his conditioning paid off, as he always won the foot races.

On his solitary outings in the wild, Aspen also took time to gentle his mind, taking in the peacefulness found in the early morning quiet. He strove for balance in his life as he felt it was key to health and happiness. These habits contributed to Aspen being famously even-tempered, healthy, and physically fit; and his kind and giving nature was a pleasure to all who knew him.

On one predawn excursion, soon after Golden Hawk's rescue, Aspen observed him also out alone, walking in the direction of Rattlesnake Canyon. The two young men had not had much chance to interact since Aspen was very busy with his many commitments, including caring for his father and helping to support his family. Aspen approached Golden Hawk to extend his hand in friendship, but he seemed rattled by Aspen's unannounced presence.

"Please... excuse. I go... to great canyon... to give... respects... to my late father."

Aspen regretted having disturbed him on such a personal mission. He humbly apologized and departed, hoping Golden Hawk would regain his serenity to commune with his father's spirit. He thought Golden Hawk must feel so alone amongst a people he never knew and having no family or friends. Aspen cherished his connection with the people who had shared his life's journey. He dreaded the prospect that he could soon lose his own beloved, ailing father. There was a lump in his throat as he imagined himself in the future, making pilgrimages to his own father's final Earthly resting place. However, the images of this that appeared in his thoughts were snapshots of him, not alone, but accompanied by the dear family and friends with whom he was so deeply connected. Aspen vowed to make a greater effort to reach out to Golden Hawk.

CHAPTER FIVE
Choices

During his first year of integration into the Ronopo community, Golden Hawk made strides through parts of Kristal Parks' academic program. She had explained to him the value of higher education, and he had accepted her offer to help him become a college candidate.

To gain a better understanding of Ronopo ways, Golden Hawk joined the Tribal Council. He was a welcome addition from the younger generation. The other young representatives were: Aspen, Hunter, Fox – the Chief's son, and Sequoia – the only female, who was currently away at college. Each of these younger members served on a different Council committee to bring their newer perspectives to multiple issues.

After a year, Golden Hawk had fulfilled, at a *very* minimal level, the educational requirements to apply to college. This had only been possible by using an extremely modified version of what home-schooled students use to document qualification through life experiences and alternative education.

Not surprisingly, most of Golden Hawk's standardized test scores were low, except for English, for which he displayed a truly exceptional aptitude. His Ronopo language skill was so limited because he had lost his parents at an early age and had then been alone for years. Given his gift for mastering English, Kristal offered to teach him Spanish or to have an Elder work with him to augment his Ronopo language skill. He declined, however, and focused on studying English, achieving a remarkable command of the language.

Kristal Parks and Chief Bridgewater wrote college recommendations for Golden Hawk as they did for all who were willing and able to venture on to higher education. They highlighted his unusual life history, growing up in a canyon mostly alone. They added testimonials about his leadership potential which he increasingly displayed on the Tribal Council.

Golden Hawk was offered admission to an American Indian tribal college where he could receive an excellent higher education or vocational training while maintaining his cultural grounding. He was also accepted to a mainstream American university. Golden Hawk chose the latter as he wanted to experience U.S. culture off the reservation firsthand.

There was a modest number of college graduates on the reservation. One group that stood out was the circle of friends that included: Aspen, Breeze, Fox, Birdie, and Sequoia. They were close in age, the range spanning just a few years. Each was endowed with intelligence, honor, personal drive, and love of tribe and country. They were neither racist nor bigoted but modest and inclusive. They were realists, not idealists; pragmatic not melodramatic; and they invariably chose cooperation over conflict.

Back during their teens, several of the friends were lying on a hillock, looking up at the clouds and philosophizing. Fox Bridgewater proclaimed,

"We need to be the generation to take full advantage of opportunities on and off the reservation so we can improve the prospects for our tribe."

"Count me in!" Sequoia said. "I'm willing to make the sacrifice of sticking it out through extra school or training, because that investment will lead to more opportunities and better pay."

The others nodded in agreement. Then, chuckling, Fox waved his hand back and forth in front of Breeze's eyes.

"Earth to Breeze! Earth to Breeze! There she goes, ignoring us and staring while Blaze walks by!"

"Stop i-i-it," Breeze replied, laughing. She was lying on her side and had not taken her eyes off a young man who glanced in their direction as he walked by. The friends raised a hand in greeting, but he had already looked away.

Fox asked, "So, what exactly is it that you find so irresistible about him?"

"Just everything," Breeze said, flopping onto her back and looking up at the sky. "He's smart, he's attractive, and he has a really big heart."

Birdie raised her eyebrows. "Do you really know him well enough to tell? Methinks there be some *chemistry* involved here... you know, pheromones or older man appeal or something?"

"Breeze might actually be right about the big heart," Fox said. "I overheard my father saying something like that about him."

This talk got Sequoia daydreaming. She had a serious crush on Aspen who was a few years older than her. Lots of girls liked Aspen. It was clear that he regarded Sequoia kindly but as if she were a little kid tagging along with this gang. Aspen addressed his close friends by special nicknames. Sequoia was miffed that she didn't have a cool or meaningful one like "Bittybird" or "Foxer." He called her "Dear One" as if he were addressing a child. Of course, that status gave Sequoia freedom that the older girls would not dare exercise. Taking advantage of that now, she shouted, *"Rumble!"* and launched herself onto him. The others followed suit, piling on and wrestling, tickling each other and laughing – done with serious talk for the day.

Like many young people, some of the friends felt driven to experiment and to rebel against authority. They had a favorite hangout, a remote grove of trees, where they occasionally drank alcohol, though they didn't usually have money or access to alcohol or other illegal substances.

One time they had badly overdone a drinking game, and all of them were seriously drunk. A member of the tribe, considered to be a rather unsavory character, walked by and noticed that one of the girls was passed out under a tree. Her friends were in advanced stages of intoxication and did not even notice him. He crouched and shook the girl's arm, but she was unresponsive. Seeing that no one was looking in that direction, he scooped Breeze up and carried her off into the woods.

It was late when Dr. Paul Ben Whitecloud heard someone at his door. He opened it to a parent's nightmare. He could not immediately tell if Breeze was dead or unconscious. She was a sticky, malodorous mess and in the sweaty arms of a filthy person of questionable character.

"What have you done to my daughter?!" Dr. Whitecloud bellowed as he frantically took her and carried her inside.

The filthy fellow at the door sneered and left.

Dr. Whitecloud determined that Breeze was alive and had passed out from excessive alcohol. He lay her on her side with her head tilted as in the Bacchus Maneuver. If she were to vomit again while unconscious, this would help prevent her from aspirating any and choking on it. Breeze's mother went for Dr. Whitecloud's nurse to examine Breeze for evidence of rape.

When Dr. Whitecloud's initial shock passed, and he was thinking more clearly, he realized what had most likely happened. Leaving Breeze in the care of her mother and the nurse, he drove his pickup truck to the hunting cabin in the northwest quadrant. He found Breeze's friends quite ill in the grove of trees there. He helped each of them into the bed of his truck and locked the tailgate so no one would fall out. Then he picked up and bagged their liquor bottles and other trash, took it all with him and drove the kids home.

Breeze had not been raped, but the friends recognized that they had all made themselves more vulnerable. They had also rendered themselves less capable of exercising good judgment or self-control, being at risk of doing things they would never choose to do when able to think clearly.

After that unpleasant experience with alcohol, and recognition of what could have happened to Breeze or to any of them, the friends further moderated or quit their substance use. Fox had the most difficulty limiting himself, but with determination and the support of his friends, he succeeded. Aspen never used any "recreational" substances and had not been with them that night. He spoke privately to Fox and gave him a reason to quit "using" altogether.

Most of the friends attended a two-year, American Indian tribal college and then spent two more years at their state university to complete a bachelor's degree. Their experiences on and off the reservation combined to solidify their self-confidence in both domains. Still, they sometimes felt disoriented by the starkly contrasting lifestyles. On the reservation, life proceeded at a seemingly more natural pace than the frenetic buzz across so much of mainstream America. They cherished their Ronopo heritage and customs yet also enjoyed exposure to America's diverse cultural groups and lifestyles.

All of the friends had joined the ROTC to defray the costs of college, to acquire the skills and physical fitness offered through the military programs, and to serve their country. Most of them fulfilled their military service commitments through The National Guard or The Reserves.

Each of them had a family name in Ronopo or in English. As was customary, they also had one or more nickname or honor name. Every nickname had a history, and each of the friends sentimentally loved his or her own special monikers.

These young adults were excellent role models for people everywhere as to personal character, community involvement, and education or training. The tribe was very proud of them.

CHAPTER SIX
Storm Coming

There was a sound of distant explosions. Was it gunshots? Was a person clearing a dam in the creek? Someone pointed to a dark cloud in the sky far off to the west. It was either smoke from an explosion, or it was an approaching thunderstorm. Some women in the village brought in laundry from their clotheslines in case rain was coming. Granny Katiri, however, did not.

She stared at the dark cloud and sniffed the air. *That's no raincloud,* she thought. She shivered, thinking of the Ronopo legend of Kleenthupenee, a monstrous creature with an insatiable appetite. It was said to have descended from a dark cloud above the western hills. It had turned those lush hills barren and was believed to prowl there still, preying upon any living thing that came near. In Granny K.'s childhood, the remains of a pair of missing young adults had been found, cast out from those hills in unspeakable condition.

That night, Granny K. had difficulty falling asleep. She got up and inhaled the scent of the beautiful flowers that Aspen had brought her. He had come to check on her progress with the physical therapy regimen he had prescribed for her. Doing those exercises had almost completely eliminated the pain in her legs. She had bounced back and could walk with much greater stability again. She went out to her little porch and sat in her chair in the dark. It was relaxing to look up at the familiar arrangements of stars in the sky. She sniffed the air and nodded. *No rain, just as I thought.*

The sound of hushed voices floated to her ears. She knew that some of her peers had sleep troubles, but the voices were coming from the west; and her little cottage was the last one at the edge of the village. She peered into the night and saw the silhouettes of two men walking out of the scrub. She couldn't hear what they were saying, but she could tell that the voices belonged to younger men. As they passed by, she saw that they appeared to be carrying hunting gear. There were outlines of long guns and what looked like bulging game sacks.

I didn't see them this evening on their way west, so they must have gone out during the day. Hm... maybe they caused that dark cloud of smoke earlier.

She was glad that the younger generations still kept alive some of the old ways. Memories of hunting with her friends long ago drifted pleasantly into her thoughts. Now, enjoying these reminiscences, she knew that she would no longer have trouble falling asleep.

CHAPTER SEVEN
Spare the Rod

Hunter Wya had smirked to himself when Chief Bridgewater offered him the prestigious position of Official Keeper of the Register shortly after Kogan Kichoba's death. He knew he was very young to be offered such an honor, having only recently graduated from college. There he had earned dual degrees in Political Science and Chemistry. He accepted, of course. He made a perfunctory show of respect to the Chief, but followed it with a rude gesture behind the old man's back as he walked away from Hunter's bungalow.

Hunter's childhood had not been a happy one. He, his mother, and his sister had been frequent victims of his father's physical and verbal abuse. From an early age, Hunter was repeatedly battered and publicly humiliated by vicious beatings at home and even out in the village in front of the entire community. These violent acts were out of proportion for a child's missteps but were usually for no reason at all. They were the actions of a bitter, alcohol-impaired man just itching to take out his anger and feelings of failure on someone powerless to stop him.

Most people were appalled by Heega Wya's treatment of his family. Like many American Indians, the Ronopo tended to guide their children by example rather than to punish them when they made mistakes. Chief Bridgewater repeatedly attempted to persuade Hunter's father to enter a rehab program, but it was to no avail. Chief also worked to have the tribal law changed so they could force Hunter's father into a facility. Unfortunately, with Heega's cronies on the Council, as well as others who feared being pressed into rehab themselves, Chief was unable to muster the necessary votes.

A member of the tribe, Brother Ron Scott King, led the nondenominational church that some people on the reservation attended. He exuded vigor and toughness, likely attributable to his service in the U.S. Marine Reserve. Long ago, he had remarked that Heega Wya could benefit from immersion in Holy Water rather than his usual "Hell Water." A few men, including the fathers of Aspen and Breeze, had thought that was an inspired idea. They gave Heega a dunking in the creek, exhorting him to man up, do the work to fight his alcohol addiction, and behave with Ronopo decency. Unfortunately, Heega had blacked out and did not even remember that well-intended "baptism."

Chief had no choice but to involve the tribal police who jailed Hunter's father multiple times for domestic abuse. While jailed, a shaman worked with Heega and other addicts, using age-old detoxification rituals and medicines. This helped many people, but Heega Wya resisted. When out of jail, he insisted that Hunter's chronic injuries were from him fighting with his peers. The Wya family did not speak out against this violent man out of fear for their lives.

Hunter secretly despised Chief Bridgewater for his apparent weakness. He was the Chief! Hunter thought that he should have been able to force his father to behave with Ronopo dignity or leave. Hunter did not understand that the Chief did not have blanket authority and that his ability to act was constrained by the required consensus of the Council.

Hunter wretchedly envied his peers like Aspen and Fox who seemed to have been dealt all the right cards in life. That group of friends had always been openly outraged by Hunter's poor treatment and were supportive of him. More than once, Aspen had even tried to intervene, but Hunter's father had just struck Aspen, too.

Hunter could not escape his feelings of belittlement nor the shame he felt of his family situation. It was embarrassing, too, that he constantly displayed the visible evidence of the "bad kid" he obviously was, regularly appearing at school with new bruises and welts.

His mortification was most profound in the presence of Breeze Whitecloud. His heart had silently called out to hers for years. Since childhood, both of them had been serious students and advanced readers. He would often find her browsing or reading in the small library that Kristal Parks established. Kristal solicited free, extra copies of books from libraries around the country. She kept it well-stocked with world classics, works authored by Native Americans, and many of the latest, popular books, especially for kids and young adults. The library was a haven where Hunter felt safe and could escape the realities of his life by vicarious adventures through books.

Once, when he was eleven, Breeze saw him searching behind the books on a shelf. "Is there something back there?" she asked.

When he turned around, she smiled at him, and he felt like sunshine had just swept into the library, filling it with warmth and good feeling.

"No," he replied in his raspy voice, "I was just hoping that a book I'm looking for had fallen behind the others, 'cause it isn't where it should be. It's the next one in the series I'm reading."

"What's it called?" Breeze asked.

When Hunter told her, she pulled it out of the pile of books she was accumulating to take home.

"Here, take it. I've found other books to borrow. Besides, I know you're a fast reader, so it won't be long before I can have it."

Hunter looked longingly at the book.

"I don't want to make you have to wait to read it. You're a fast reader, too."

Breeze put it in his hand, saying, "I was actually looking for the one that comes right before this one in the series."

Hunter ran over to the returned books slot and stuck his arm inside it, blindly groping through the books in the rough wooden bin. Finally, his hand, with now scraped knuckles, grasped one that he had dropped into the slot when he came in.

"Here, I just finished it. It's really good. Vaal is next on the list to borrow it, but you know what a slow reader he is. You'll have a long wait. It isn't due yet, so you can just take it and return it when you're done."

"But if I lose it, it'll still be out in your name."

"I know you won't lose it," he said.

They both happily gazed at the hoped-for treasures in their hands.

Hunter thought Breeze was so warm and nice and wondered if she could possibly like him at all. She usually appeared to be absorbed by Aspen's every word – and didn't seem to even notice him. Nonetheless, he took the risk of asking Breeze's best friend, No See, if she thought Breeze would agree to be his partner in the required, Ronopo traditional dance classes.

What a mistake that had been! He wished he had never asked, because No See said that Breeze *disliked* him and was sweet on Aspen. Hunter's heart ached and ached. He was sure that No See would tell Breeze that he had asked about dancing with her. Breeze would then know that he liked her, embarrassing him all the more. Now knowing Breeze's feelings about him, along with the shame he felt of himself and his family, it was impossible for Hunter to accept invitations or gestures of friendship from Breeze's crowd.

Some members of the tribe, like the Elder, Kogan Kichoba, had adopted religious teachings different from the original Ronopo beliefs. Kogan would wag his finger and cluck his tongue when he saw Hunter, saying, "You surely deserve your father's punishments!" He quoted holy writings that said, "...spare the rod, spoil the child..." He asserted, "More children in the tribe need a rod to teach them obedience and respect!"

Of course, appropriate *behavior* can be taught – and best with words and by example – but genuine respect can only be *earned*. Abuse and neglect had certainly not taught Hunter respect. He seethed with inner rage which he, in turn, took out on younger boys in his small band of sidekicks.

Some children did not bear visible marks that would evoke a specter of abuse, but, contrary to cultural tradition, they were physically disciplined any time they did something wrong. They, too, had the pent-up anger and hostility that corporal punishment often brings.

Nonphysical correction would not only have taught right versus wrong – but also *self-restraint when angry*. Since children learn by imitation, corporal punishment set the example that, when angry, violence is acceptable.

Some of Hunter's sidekicks were neglected by young, single mothers who had not become mothers by intent. Some had not even had sex by consent. A few of them stoically accepted or even welcomed this unplanned change in their lives. Others had cherished different life aspirations, including further education, interesting work, or at least marriage and preparation *before* inviting the precious gift and serious responsibility of children. Some had wanted to prevent or stop their unasked for pregnancies and the unwanted children who would be born into dismal circumstances, changing their mothers' lives irrevocably whether they kept the children or gave them up for adoption.

Despite promises made by the U.S. Government in treaties long ago to provide health care to the tribes, access to even basic medical care, medicines and supplies was woefully inadequate. Pregnancy and childbirth presented additional healthcare challenges and risks. As for contraceptives, few in the tribe were able to acquire them.

It was the women and girls who were saddled with any inadvertent offspring – the burden for their support usually left to those single mothers or to the tribal community at large. Paying all of the consequent costs devoured the Ronopo Tribe's funds and stifled its advancement. The potential was also diminished for those accidental mothers to improve their own lives or to contribute to their communities, other than as reproductive vessels, often unqualified for parenting. Not surprisingly, it was then more difficult for many of them to attract a husband at all. This haphazard procreation perpetuated a cycle of poverty, as it generally does everywhere.

Some of the mothers, still just girls themselves, without capable family to help them, left their offspring to their own devices. Of course, that usually spells trouble, as it did for the kids in Hunter's rat pack. Hunter ruthlessly dominated this group of boys and influenced them to commit minor acts of criminal mischief. The tribe had a name for them that translated loosely as: *The Ronopo Bad Boys Gang.* Without the guidance of a strong family unit, many of them eventually became more seriously involved in crime or otherwise burdened their community and beyond.

In his early teens, Hunter was offered a construction job. He started working many hours performing physical labor when not in classes or doing homework. This job enabled him to help support his family since his father provided for them only sporadically. Fortunately, Hunter no longer had time for his band of young hoodlums.

Hunter dearly loved his older sister, Rozzi. But he felt betrayed and humiliated when she became one of those unmarried, teenaged mothers. She changed and withdrew from him. Worse yet, now that she was a mother, she had no choice but to abandon their long-shared dream to escape together, get college degrees, and leave their painful family life behind. They had fantasized about returning to the reservation, educated and independent of their father.

Once, when Hunter was fourteen, he had to force himself to go to school. He only did go because it was final exams. His father had been especially ill-tempered the night before, so there were horrendous bruises on Hunter's face and arms. His father had also thrown him against a cinder-block wall that morning, so a patch of hair on the back of his head was matted with a clot of blood. Hunter could not hide these stigmata that caused him such shame; so he ignored the looks from his schoolmates and focused as best he could on the exams.

Hunter noticed that Breeze did not seem to be herself. After the first exam, he saw her head into the washroom. As he passed by, he heard soft crying. He knew that she took her studies as seriously as he did but could not imagine her doing poorly enough for tears. He mustered up his courage and was about to knock on the door to see if she was okay when Sequoia walked up behind him.

Hunter hurried away, and Sequoia entered the washroom, finding Breeze in tears. Outside, as Hunter walked towards the library, he passed an open window and overheard Sequoia say,

"Please tell me what's wrong. Is it something to do with Blaze?"

"Mhm," Breeze replied, sniffling.

Hunter felt a stab in his heart, realizing that it wasn't the exams – something he could possibly comfort her about. It was boy trouble! He knew that Breeze had long been sweet on Aspen, and Blaze would be a good nickname for him, since Aspen was, by far, the fastest runner in the tribe. But Breeze was also often with one of her older brother's friends. Hunter didn't know him, so Blaze might be his name.

Feeling even more dejected than usual, Hunter continued on towards the library. He and Chief Bridgewater crossed paths.

"Hunter, I have been wanting to speak to you. I would like to offer you a place in my home. You do not deserve your father's violence; and we would truly enjoy having you with us."

Hunter's surprise showed in his face, but after a moment of visualizing that scenario, he responded bitterly, "Thanks but no thanks, Chief."

"I have not seen visible marks of violence on your mother or sister lately. I have hoped that meant that things are better for them. Now, if we could just get *you* out of that household..."

"Yeah, get me out of there, and this is what my mother and sister will look like!" Hunter said, pointing towards his face as he disrespectfully turned and continued towards the library.

Chief shook his head, feeling grief for Hunter. He was also in awe that Hunter was staying in his home to be his father's punching bag instead of allowing that to befall his mother and sister. Chief called out, and Hunter turned to face him.

"Do you know why we have always called our warriors 'Braves?' It is because they truly are brave – putting themselves in danger to protect others – just as you do. You are very brave, Hunter, and very inspiring."

Chief's astonishing words floored Hunter. He was completely unaccustomed to praise. He was proud of his top grades at school but received no recognition for that from his parents, so it seemed to have little value. He rarely had any reason to visualize himself as anything but a loser.

A tiny flicker of self-esteem that still remained in him was captured and nurtured just in time by Chief's words. Unfortunately, such gestures of support or encouragement from the Chief and other caring people faded into the background of Hunter's mind, as his daily life was so relentlessly filled with pain and abasement.

When Hunter turned sixteen, the handsome but irascible young man made plans to leave the reservation. He sought to broaden his horizons and find respite from his miserable family life. But first, there was something he needed to do.

A few weeks before his departure, having developed into a strong and muscular young man – though not a tall one like his father – he mustered all of his courage. Finding a suitable opportunity, he baited his father in public. He loudly excoriated him for the cowardly way in which he had treated Hunter's mother and sister over the years. He described multifold offenses vociferously enough to draw a crowd of observers. As expected, his father was shocked and enraged by the public humiliation of having his abusive behavior exposed in detail.

Grabbing Hunter by his hair, he promised him the beating of his life and punched him squarely in the face. But Hunter had long prepared for this. While his father retracted his fist to land a second blow, Hunter turned the tables on him. Hunter emerged from the encounter with only a black eye and a few bruises, but his father had to be hospitalized. He had a broken jaw, missing teeth, cracked ribs, broken limbs, testicular bruising, and a concussion.

As befitted this long overdue comeuppance, not a single person in the crowd of onlookers intervened on Heega Wya's behalf. Instead, there were numerous nods of approval.

After Heega was taken to the hospital, Hunter went to the appropriate tribal official and pressed charges against his father for his crimes against Hunter's mother and sister. He pressed separate charges for that day's attack on himself, to which many witnesses could attest. He concurrently filed for a protection order for his mother and sister. By reservation law, Heega Wya would have to move to a remote, outlying community on the reservation upon leaving the hospital. There, along with others like him, Hunter's father would be monitored by a probation officer of sorts and was never to return to the village again. Any infringement of this order would result in the severest penalties.

Tribal law had required that an adult family member file such papers. Heega had threatened Hunter's mother and sister, and there had been no one else to do it on their behalf. Only now, was Hunter old enough to qualify. Over the years, Chief had appealed to the Council to alter this requirement but had never been able to achieve consensus.

Before leaving the reservation, Hunter visited his father in the hospital. He was overheard telling his father that he would kill him if he ever harmed Hunter's mother or sister again. As Hunter departed, he swore an oath to himself,

One day I will return and more properly vindicate injustices of the past!

Now, years later, Hunter had the prestigious tribal appointment of Official Keeper of the Register. This gave him *somewhat* closer standing with those Elders who had so sanctimoniously approved of his abusive upbringing. His new position came with some power and privileges. He would be sure to use them both wisely...

As if this weren't good fortune enough, the awe-inspiring new member of the tribe, Golden Hawk, chose him as the one peer worthy of his attention. And then, Hunter's father passed on. Hunter wanted to start this promising new chapter of his life with a cleaner slate, disassociated from his ignominious father. He decided to see how he felt using the English version of his last name: Wolf.

At last, Hunter felt that the Great Spirit was giving him long-desired blessings. Things were looking up, indeed.

CHAPTER EIGHT
Honey

The drone operator, Robin "Rob" Bozeau, had waited for the others to leave and then downloaded a selection of photos from their recordings with the drone that day. It was "true love." At home, he printed out enlarged copies and taped a bunch of the sexy photos onto the wall near his bed.

"Hm, what shall I call you, my honey-skinned lovely? That's it! I'm going to call you *Honey!*"

When Rob returned to the base the next morning, he found that there was no other mission scheduled for the week. Operators were encouraged to train with the drone when free, as they needed a certain number of hours to keep their certifications current. The other guys chose to take the week off, leaving training for another time; but Rob could not stop thinking about Honey.

I'll just take the drone out for a spin and see if I see anything or any... body of interest.

He launched the now unarmed drone and scanned the area. No luck by the canyon where he had seen her the day before. He flew it over the settlements on the reservation, searching for her while being careful not to be seen.

I can look through people's windows with this thing, and I'm seeing some... interesting things – but not my girl. I guess I'll just have to wait for her to come out to play. I can always peep in those windows again if I get bored.

Piloting the drone away from the village, Rob practiced some quick turns and camouflaging maneuvers over unpopulated areas. He caught sight of an old Army vehicle tooling down the road.

Hmm, what's that up ahead? Could it be? Zooming in on the subject now... Yesss! It's her! It's my Honey! I gotta see where she's headed!

Rob followed the young woman all the way to her destination then turned around and headed back to the base.

"Wahoo! I know where to find her! We can be together after all!"

CHAPTER NINE
Energize

In addition to her degree in Pre-Engineering from an American Indian tribal college, Breeze earned a B.S. in Earth Science from the state university. Surprisingly, the Federal Energy Agency refused her job application even though she graduated with honors and had been a well-regarded intern with them over multiple summers. Had the agency somehow discovered that, on one occasion, she had explored in unauthorized terrain? She could not figure out how they would have known, though. She had deleted that site's data from their equipment before returning it. Of course, one of the two flash drives that she used to back up the data *had* been stolen. It was taken from her vehicle that same night along with some loose change. It was ridiculous to think that the stolen flash drive could have ended up at the FEA – but even if it had, surely they would have just admonished her to not work in excluded locations in the future.

Breeze had counted on her hard-earned standing with the agency as a stepping stone to obtaining work that was important to her tribe and to her country. She was disappointed by the rejection but simply set out on a different path. She accepted a university's generous offer that covered all expenses for a graduate program in Energy Resource Science to which she had previously applied.

Breeze hoped the future would bring more widely usable "green" energy alternatives. She might be able to help to make the energy conversion and storage technologies efficient and more effective. It was an area she would like to explore later. But Breeze clearly understood the national security imperative of *immediate* U.S. energy independence. That meant *responsibly* taking advantage of more of America's vast supplies of domestic oil and natural gas. Doing so would stop the flow of *billions* of U.S. dollars to oil-producing countries that harbored, funded, trained, and/or armed terrorists, *using those U.S. dollars*.

The Ronopo Tribe felt deeply the pain of the terrorist attack on 9/11. They had lost two members of the tribe who were in the World Trade Center on that terrible day. They had been there to significantly advance the tribe's economic interests. That tragedy had contributed to Breeze's career choice. She hoped to help expedite America's independence from hostile suppliers.

Clean-burning fossil fuel technology – and techniques for minimally invasive extraction of oil and gas were already available. Some American Indian tribes had demonstrated on their reservations how to access natural resources with little or no lasting impact upon the locations or upon the environment. Those good stewards of the Earth conscientiously preserved the sites while extracting the resources. They then restored the terrain to a desirable condition afterwards. Breeze had ideas that could advance the technology, but there was little government funding for fossil fuels-related research. Fortunately, some large, American energy companies donated money to support scientific research at universities. Breeze took advantage of that private funding and focused her energy on furthering developments in the field.

CHAPTER TEN
Venom

Blood dripped onto Shondee's hand from the small puncture wound in his neck. He didn't move a muscle. The gang's new recruit had pushed just the tip of his knife into Shondee's throat. Gang members behind the recruit jeered.

"Scared, choirboy?" they taunted, their voices echoing in the empty warehouse.

Shondee wasn't sure if they meant him or the recruit. He was terrified, but the kid with the knife looked calm. They were face to face, and light reflected off the kid's earring. Unlike the diamond earrings that most of the gang members wore, this kid's earring was metal. It was an odd, squarish shape with some kind of dog on it. Shondee didn't know why, but the sight of the dog comforted him a little.

"So, do him already!" the gang goaded.

Movement caught the recruit's attention, and he glanced at the wall above Shondee's head. He withdrew his knife and stepped backwards, yelling,

"There's a snake on the wall!"

The leader hooted, "The symbol of our gang appeared just for your initiation!"

The gang members all laughed but also took a step backwards... which was a big mistake. They stepped into shadows, treading on a swarm of slithering snakes, some boys slipping and sprawling on the slimy mass. Screaming, they grabbed at each other, colliding as they bolted pell-mell from the building. Outside, they tried to appear cool again while furtively checking themselves for snakes.

Sirens sounded, and the leader blasted, "Split up, and get out of here!"

Too late. The SWAT team was already there. The gang feared the snakes, but there was no place to run except back inside. Problem was, the warehouse door was now closed – and locked.

The police took away that elusive gang that had ravaged their hapless community.

Inside the closed-up warehouse, Shondee was confused. The recruit was laughing and saying, "Kids in city gangs should spend more time enjoying city parks. Then they'd be familiar with snakes like these and would know they're not poisonous. C'mon, it sounds like they've all left. I'll walk you home."

He put his finger to his lips, and neither of them spoke another word.

The next day, thinking of the recruit's earring, Shondee went to the city pound and adopted a big dog to accompany him on his patrols of his community. He decided to name his new companion: *Hero* – in honor of someone he would never forget.

COUNTERPOINT III
STATUS REPORT: HOUSE OF CARDS

"Recruitment? Where do we stand, and what results have our recruits achieved?"

"We created 'organizations for social change,' hiring or offering rewards to people who would champion certain causes. We located near schools and colleges to reach impressionable young voters. We put other branches in low-income locations across America, both urban and rural, to rally hard-working, low-income people, along with the ones who can't find work and those who don't want to work. These groups represent large, manipulable voting blocs. We had no trouble recruiting students, most who are still supported by parents yet are in the rebel-against-authority stage of life. As a result of our youth-targeted marketing, students vote for *our* candidates who promise to take even more from the 'rich' *supposedly* 'to give it to the poor.' "

"Go on."

"Naturally, the freeloaders are onboard, but the working poor are a tougher sell. They astutely question that if the government takes what richer people earn and give it to them, what would stop officials from taking what *they* have worked hard to earn and give it to others who haven't worked or sacrificed at all? We provided sound-bites for our activists, blaming Americans who have earned economic success for the failure of others to do the same. Separately, we finished grooming our special female task force. They are now being strategically placed for espionage and political scandals."

"Very good. Finance? What is the status of the financial strategy?"

"We have been creating the economic climate needed for our venture to succeed. As just described, our social activists have been elevating tensions over economic disparity in America. We identified institutional targets for them to blame, focusing first on banks. Our activists have been forcefully pressuring banks to make loans to people who the banks, justifiably, deem too risky since they are unlikely to repay the loans. Some of the unqualified borrowers are of religious or ethnic minorities, but most are of the majority ethnic makeup. Although the banks are using standard, sound business judgment when declining loans to high-risk borrowers, our recruits accuse the banks of *ethnic discrimination*. Most of the media happily report that the banks are discriminating against minorities, even though there are just as many people being declined who are not minorities. Banks certainly have some predatory lending practices that affect *all* ethnic groups, but we spin even standard, rational lending practices as *ethnic discrimination.* Many people believe us."

"That can only be successful because most American media, academics, youth, and others are obsessed with political correctness, which they value over the truth!"

"Exactly. Since the banks were coerced into making the high-risk loans and then started losing big money on them, some banks have been bundling the bad loans together with stronger ones and selling the bundles to save their banks from failure. This is not against current laws – and the *government* loan companies have been buying the bundles. In this way, we have gradually transformed a strong financial system into a fragile, economic house of cards."

"So, if the banks did not resort to this 'bundling', they would eventually go out of business because they cannot lend money and then not be repaid. Americans rely on banks for ATMs, debit and credit cards, home purchases, tuition and car loans, and business expansions to hire more people. If this were to continue, there would be no banks to provide for any of this."

"Precisely. Whenever anyone disagrees with our claims of ethnic discrimination, we publicly slam them as being *racist.* To avoid that negative publicity, some banks have just taken the questionable 'bundling' route to protect themselves in the short-run. The federal loan companies and their guarantor – the Federal Finance Agency – have continued to deteriorate as they purchase more and more of the weak bundles from the private banks. *And today,* as planned, the extremely wealthy patrons of our venture made large-scale moves in the financial markets—"

"Knocking down the fragile house of cards that the U.S. economy has become!"

"Correct. As expected, this is causing an economic crisis. The government will need to act to prevent the total collapse of the economy. Our protegees are in place to advise the U.S. President to respond with an enormous cash infusion. This will set the stage for the President's successor – and we *know* who that will be – to *continue* the newly-created federal deficit level. The new President will blame the predecessor for bringing it to that outlandish level but will then make it the 'new normal.' While the U.S. tries to recover from the collapsed house of cards, our network of well-placed public officials will ensure the maintenance *and increase* of the federal deficit and debt. This will be the economic climate in which our venture can *and will* succeed."

"Good work! Keep me apprised."

CHAPTER ELEVEN
Star Fire

Niki Katiri had always been restless. As a child on the Ronopo Reservation, she tired quickly of school while earning excellent grades. Hungry for new experiences, she felt an explosive need to burst out to something more challenging. She was unusually mature, and in college she participated in many activities, taking on mountains of responsibility.

Niki felt that the USA had been a fountainhead for the world in many ways but was pitifully behind when it came to having women in government and other leadership positions. Some time back, the U.S. had had its first female and first black Presidents. Niki thought there was a need for many more women in decision-making positions, representing the perspective of *half* the population. There were some female Governors whom Niki admired, and she thought about pursuing a career in government herself. She graduated college with a double major in Psychology and Economics and was now pursuing a Master's Degree in Government.

A few weeks into graduate school, Niki reveled in the change of pace and the fresh population of students and staff. She scanned the list of extracurricular activities and was glad to see that there was a club for Native Americans. She put that month's social event on her calendar.

"Breeze!!" Niki exclaimed upon arriving at the Native American Club social.

"Sequoia?!" Breeze replied with surprise and elation.

The two young women threw their arms around each other.

"Sequoia?" intoned a deep, male voice. "I thought your name was Niki."

Niki spun around, and both women froze. What Niki saw was an exceptionally attractive young man who was now staring past her, looking bemused, at Breeze.

"*Well,*" he said, "I believe it is the heroine who saved me from a life of canyon solitude."

Niki tried to interpret the medley of emotions in Breeze's rapidly changing expressions. Breeze paled, blushed and shivered, her pupils dilating and contracting like a light show. She displayed recognition but seemed agitated and confused.

"You're G-Golden Hawk," Breeze stammered in a whisper, staring glassily at the man she had discovered a couple of years back in Rattlesnake Canyon. "I-I... didn't know... that either of you were here at the university. Don't tell me that you've both been here since last year, too?"

Simultaneously, Niki answered, "No, I just started grad school here," as the young man said, "Yes, I'm a second year undergraduate."

Niki thrust her hand towards the intimidatingly striking young man and said, "Sooo, you are the renowned Golden Hawk! I'm Niki Katiri – but you seemed to know that already."

Now facing Niki for the first time, his eyes widened a little as he just stared at her for a moment. "We are... in a class... together," he stammered.

He took her outstretched hand and held it firmly – for a few beats too long. Niki could feel his increasing body temperature through his hand.

"I heard the professor call your name," he said, "and... I hoped you would be here tonight."

Niki's body temperature started rising along with his as she found herself powerfully attracted to this man. It was both delicious and unnerving.

After a highly charged silence, Golden Hawk addressed both women, breaking the smoldering tension. "Please, call me Dukon. I do not use that... other name... here."

"Ah," Niki said, "then you understand the reason for my two names. Breeze addressed me by the name she's used since we were children. But, like you, I don't use that name here."

The three of them continued their introductions while sampling the tasty finger foods provided by the university.

"So, at home, you go by... Sequoia... Katiri?" Dukon asked.

"Starfire," Breeze quietly corrected, "Sequoia Starfire."

"Sequoia Starfire," Dukon repeated, nodding approvingly. "As you are statuesque, I can see where Sequoia comes from."

Sequoia blushed. She was one of the taller females in the tribe but was more of medium height than tall. In any case, his words were clearly chosen to be flattering.

"I assume there is a story behind *Starfire?"*

Sequoia shook her head, shrugging it off with a wave of her hand.

Not seeing this, Breeze answered pointedly, "Yes, there is. The shaman singled out Sequoia at an early age as being very special: 'One who might be *Chief.'* When the shaman conferred this distinction upon her, she was given the name: Starfire."

Dukon looked at Sequoia appraisingly.

Thoroughly embarrassed and anxious to change the subject, Sequoia asked Dukon how he was enjoying the class they shared in common.

Abruptly coming out of his reverie, he looked at his watch and apologized.

"Forgive me, but I have another engagement. Unfortunately, I must leave."

Rising from his seat, he suggested that they get together again soon.

The young women watched the attractive young man traverse the room. They saw others turn to stare at him, too.

Sequoia looked at Breeze, and breathed, "Whoaaaaaaa!!"

Breeze nodded, her face unreadable, still focusing on the door through which Dukon just exited.

Sequoia marveled at the young man's eloquent command of English, especially considering how recently he had begun its study. She was also impressed that he had been admitted to a graduate level class while only in his second year of college. She smiled, thinking,

Some interesting possibilities have just appeared on the horizon.

CHAPTER TWELVE
Sweet Dreams

Dukon Chatan (a.k.a. Golden Hawk), the drop-dead gorgeous young man of the Ronopo Tribe, returned to his dorm room after going for a run. He pulled off his sweat-drenched T-shirt and reclined on a towel on his bed. His hands were clasped beneath his head, a shock of black hair displayed in each armpit. As his body cooled down, he quietly repeated a mantra he had created from various words he could remember his father saying when he was young.

"I shall never forget who I am, where I came from, nor the great destiny that awaits me. There will be many influences and many diversions, but I will stay true to myself and to the purpose that the Highest Power gives to me. I will make my people proud."

Unbidden thoughts of two such *diversions* plagued Dukon incessantly: Breeze, Sequoia: Sequoia, Breeze. Students and staff at the university flirted with Dukon relentlessly; but it was images of those two young women that were imprinted on his brain as if by a searing hot branding iron. Those imprints kept his young and restlessly virile body scorching with desire.

He was haunted by the memory of the first time he emerged from the canyon and saw Breeze. She was lounging provocatively atop her old Army vehicle. The brilliant light of the sun had penetrated her nearly transparent clothing, revealing much of the curvaceous body beneath and illuminating her delicate face. He remembered the tantalizing way that her face and body had moved and changed in response to his presence.

He then recalled his early impression of the dominant male in the rescue team, Aspen, who had begun removing his clothing while rapidly approaching Breeze. Dukon had noticed her trying to escape them; but Aspen was upon her in the next moment. Dukon had wondered what he was going to do with her. He had instinctively wanted to grab her himself and had begun moving to challenge Aspen. Fortunately, he did not get very far as the actual outcome was quite unexpected. There was so much that Dukon had still needed to learn and incorporate into the necessary new way of thinking!

Then came more recent memories – of the first time he saw Niki (Sequoia) in class. He had been instantly smitten. He had stared at her, helplessly entranced. He was mesmerized by her long, black eyelashes that seemed to extend all the way to her cheeks when she looked down. He watched her rosebud lips as she spoke aloud in her confident, sonorous voice when called upon. He was riveted when she licked her lips to moisten them, and a dimple appeared in her luscious cheek. Her golden skin radiated a soft, inviting glow, and her long, dark, silky hair moved fluidly at each turn of her head. He had imagined himself stroking that beautiful hair.

He had been oblivious to the entire lecture until she rose at the end. He had watched her long, athletic and feminine figure stride with commanding power from the room. He had found himself pulled to his feet by the sheer magnetic force of her. He had tried to follow, but flirtatious students, attempting to engage him in conversation, blocked his way. He could only watch as another young man lit up her million-watt smile and accompanied her from the building.

Now, Dukon was kneeling on the floor with his head bowed. After a time, he silently thanked his father's spirit. It had filled his mind with the peace of knowing that these beguiling possibilities would be decided for him by a higher power. And right he was – as that decision had already been made.

CHAPTER THIRTEEN
Data

Breeze was about to head to another remote location to do field work for her graduate school program in Energy Resource Science. Before leaving, she took a rare time-out from her research and studies to call home. Her mother caught her up on reservation news as Breeze had had so little free time since her senior year of college. In passing, her mother mentioned the confirmation of Golden Hawk's lineage.

A long time ago, Birdie had sent Breeze a message saying,

Hottie from the canyon was nicknamed Golden Hawk!

His clan identification was interesting news. That tickled something in the back of her mind. She thought of the data that she had collected from Rattlesnake Canyon the day she discovered him. She had only had time for a brief look at it since then. That quick review had raised questions in her mind, and she had wanted to analyze it further.

She now "reconstituted" the compressed and encrypted data and images that she had moved from her flash drive to her laptop. After another quick review, she felt that there were things that she should probably bring to Aspen's attention. She wanted to evaluate them a bit more, though, to be clearer about her conclusions and concerns before discussing them with him. Since she was about to go out into the field again and needed to prepare for her departure, Breeze set this aside to do when she got back.

When I return from the field in a few months, I'll get back to this analysis and contact Aspen then.

CHAPTER FOURTEEN
American Idol

Although Dukon's test scores had not identified him as a scholar, he had apparently blossomed at university and was going to graduate early. His participation in Student Council had been almost non-existent, yet he was idolized by the student body as the representative for the few Native American students there. It was his movie-star looks and increasingly charismatic manner that resulted in a breathless following. Students and certain staff pushed him into the limelight at every opportunity. Thusly, he gained purchase in the political arena.

Idealistic youths, as are found at most colleges, and the professors who encouraged idealism, basked in self-congratulatory ecstasy that they were supporting a member of a minority people. But as is so often the case, they became "champions" of Native American causes – without even bothering to learn what they actually were.

Not so far in the future, many of those students would leave college and have real responsibilities. They would no longer be coddled by their parents nor sheltered by the bubble that a college provides for its students and staff – including "free" access to all sorts of facilities that a college has. They would then be earning their own living and paying income taxes to fund the programs that elected officials decided to support, including ones that, if analyzed, might be seen mostly benefiting those officials and their cronies rather than the targeted recipients.

Other students would not become taxpayers, having no job and perhaps being dependent upon government handouts funded by the earnings of people with jobs. Some might become young parents, possibly single parents, having a child to support, as well.

Then living the experience – not just reading and discussing theory or being revved up by mob-energizing activists – they would likely find their youthful idealism evolving into something more like realism – as had happened to generations before them.

Some of the students would learn how some idealistic dreams *could* be brought to fruition – *but along with their costs to everyone.* They would see some of those costs reflected in their paychecks diminished by higher taxes to *pay* for the idealistic dreams or in Welfare allotments devalued by resultant price increases, eroding the idealistic dreams come true. They might then demand that elected officials apply tax dollars economically and to the most *needed* programs. They would tell their officials to honor promises, choose priorities, eliminate waste, and be accountable for their spending, instead of just taxing workers and their employers even more when the care-freely spent tax money ran out.

Overly-taxed employers would have to cut back employee hours and benefits, lay people off, raise the prices of their products and services and forgo expansion. This would offset the good of the idealistic dreams achieved. With fewer people then working, the government would have less income tax revenue to collect, eliminating the gains they had expected from raising the tax rates! Some officials would just promise to tax the rich even more. Then, as happens around the world, the rich would cut back on spending, not buying as many goods and services or they would leave, taking their money with them, no longer providing all their tax revenue and purchases that had previously supported their communities.

Some fraction of the former college students would come to question the difference between a *natural right* and an *act of goodwill* – and how much burden one citizen should be forced to bear for others, including for acts of goodwill for them – regardless of the choices those others make. And what about for non-citizens in the country? And for everyone else around the world? As the working and investing people's income would increasingly erode in support of more and more other people – keeping their *own* dreams – for which they had worked – out of reach, some would ask, *How free am I really?*

People from around the world enter America daily, legally or not, and feast for free at America's table of goodwill. This magnanimity is funded by the freely-given generosity of people through charities – or by the only money a government has – that which it forcibly takes from its citizens through taxes, including hidden "fees" that the government adds to gasoline and transportation prices and to phone, utility and other bills, raising their costs. Or the government borrows money, placing the nation in debt. When the lenders are foreign countries, the citizens of the borrowing nation can be placed *at the mercy and control* of the lending nations.

If money is taken from people who are earning their living and given to a *growing* number of people who are dependent – then, of course, the money will eventually run out. But until it does, some politicians may get into power or stay there by courting voters with promises to take even more from the earners and give some of it to *them*.

Since different people champion very different priorities, and since nothing is actually free, some idealistic dreams never can come true in the real, non-utopian world.

Sadly, few idealists recognize that many candidates manipulate and exploit them *in the name of* pursuing beneficial-sounding goals for humanity, while mostly serving themselves and their cohorts. They target well-intentioned idealists, using clever marketing techniques instead of the bland facts, to support a rise to power.

Thus, idealists represent an important voting bloc. They are vulnerable to peer pressure in favor of a candidate or issue that makes the voter feel "plugged in" or "politically correct." Being politically correct usually means euphemizing to be sensitive to certain people's feelings, but sometimes it actually means masking the truth.

If the idealistic students from Dukon's college examined the outcomes of programs that they had supported to help native peoples and other minorities, they would see that little improvement actually resulted. Meanwhile, many elected officials went into office with little money but left with much greater family affluence than their civil servant salary could possibly explain...

Despite Dukon's minimal involvement in Student Council, it was through that activity and interacting with its advisors that he learned the most *useful* things about mainstream, American political behavior and techniques.

CHAPTER FIFTEEN
Traffic Jam

"Where's my Mommy?" the scared little boy asked through his tears.

The man with the crazy eyes sneered, "Your Mommy *gave you to me* in exchange for some... *candy.* You know what I want you for? I like to do things to little boys. Things... that are gonna *really* make you cry!"

The little boy cowered on the mattress in the abandoned shack.

Bam! Bam! The little boy jumped at the banging on the door.

The man swore as he opened it. "I told you I'd be—"

No one was there. Much worse, the tractor-trailer that he had left with his comrade down the dirt road wasn't there either. The horde of women and children packed inside its trailer were worth a fortune in the black market for sex slaves. The husbands and fathers who had tried to stop them had all been unarmed. Those men were now lying in a shallow grave far away.

Frantic that the truck was gone, the human-trafficker stepped outside, looking around and yelling his comrade's name.

A noose fell around his head, landing in his open mouth. It tightened, and his head snapped back.

"Gahghhgh!"

He tried to reach up and remove it, but another loop had fallen around his torso. It tightened, pinning his arms to his body. The man was then yanked up into the air.

The little boy inside was wide-eyed. A different man jumped down from above and stood in the open doorway. He quickly scanned the interior then softly said,

"It's all right. I won't hurt you. And I won't let that bad man hurt you, either. There's someone here who wants to take you home."

The man stepped aside, and the little boy's aunt swooped into the shack and threw her arms around him. She carried him out past the smiling man.

When the little boy grew up, he became a law enforcement officer. Time had blurred the memory of most details of the incident. But one thing remained clear and everlasting in his mind. It was the image of dazzling light, reflecting off a smiling man's metal earring, gleaming like a bright, shining star.

CHAPTER SIXTEEN
Sunbeams

Sequoia awoke refreshed. Stretching her arms, she smiled at the early morning rays of sun just peeking into her apartment window through the curtains.

"I'll race ya!" she called out to the sun.

Kicking off the covers, she pulled herself out of bed, stripping off her sleepwear. She faced the spot where the sun's first rays glowed through a corner of the window. Then, as she had done for as long as she could remember, she commenced a Ronopo ritual of gratitude, greeting the gift of the morning sun.

Stretching her athletic body up until she stood on tip-toe with her fingers reaching high, she imagined that she could touch the sky. Then, slowly rolling her body down until she was crouched at the floor, her arms encircled her knees in a close embrace. With her head bowed and her long hair brushing the floor, she closed her eyes and whispered, "Thank you for this new day."

Holding onto her ankles, she slowly raised her hips, stretching her sleep-tight hamstrings. After a long, deep breath, she gracefully rolled back up, lightly tracing her fingertips along the front of her body. She stood in a strong, surefooted stance, her spine straight, head level, clasping her hands behind her. She turned her head all the way to the left, then back over to the right, acknowledging the domain that would receive the gift of sunlight throughout the day.

Then she extended her arms in front of her. Crossing them at the wrists, she swept her open palms up and out to the sides as if drawing an expansive arc of sky down to the horizon, her arms finishing at her sides. Then, raising her arms and moving her legs apart so that her body formed an "X", she turned her face up toward the sky and wiggled her fingers and toes.

After completing the ritual stretch, she felt energized, as always. She pulled on a pair of running shorts, a sports bra, and a long-sleeved top for the early morning chill. Humming softly, she plaited her hair into a thick braid and donned her socks and running shoes. She lifted her shirt and wrapped her security pouch around her waist. She inserted her phone, key, and pepper spray. She put her head through the loop of the lanyard with an alarm whistle given to all students, and she was ready to run.

Sequoia did not go anywhere without some sort of self-protection. She knew that violent incidents can occur *anywhere*. Then, as they say: "When *seconds* count, the police are just *minutes* away."

Sequoia started down the path, noticing that there were few people out and about so early. She let that be a warning to herself to be extra vigilant. She relished the energy and clarity of mind that physical activity gave her. She thought of the delicious tingle that she would feel in her muscles later. It would be a reminder of how good it is to be alive. She looked at the rising sun and mugged a face at it, miming her earlier challenge to a race. Breathing deeply of the cool, fresh, morning air, she jogged on.

CHAPTER SEVENTEEN
Chief Concerns

Chief Benjamin Bridgewater was an outstanding leader. He achieved many advances for his tribe, including getting the U.S. government to finally honor an important treaty. Long ago, he had also protected his people against an incursion from a group trying to lay claim to part of the Ronopo Reservation. He had allowed those people to temporarily reside on a remote parcel of land while he reviewed their claim. However, when those people displayed hatred and attacked members of the tribe, he rallied his warriors and sent the invaders packing.

On a personal level, he had inspired many of his people to persist in the pursuit of their dreams. He said, "In this country, there are always choices." He touted examples of American Indians, black Americans, white Americans, and other immigrants who had availed themselves of the myriad opportunities to improve their lives. He added, "But it is up to *us* to grasp a helping hand, pull ourselves up, and move forward. We are a people capable of doing anything we set ourselves to do."

Over the years in the Governing Council, Chief Bridgewater had successfully maintained a peaceful consensus process despite vastly differing opinions across the tribe. Recently, however, a rift was developing. Members of one faction had become hostile and were launching verbal attacks against members of the tribe. Some were shockingly disrespectful to Elders, such as calling Granny Katiri "Cuckoo Bird" after she spoke of seeing a tiny plane over the reservation. Chief knew that she had been nicknamed "Eagle-Eye" in her youth for good reason. He also knew that there was nothing wrong with her mental acuity. Fox agreed with his father that she had likely seen a drone that was being flown below normal altitudes. He had seen a drone in the vicinity himself.

People in the restive faction were advocating *violent* action to "better" serve the interests of the tribe. Such talk was worrisome. Violence would, without any doubt, be counterproductive. The Chief's amicable relationship with U.S. government had yielded many gains for the tribe during the prior decade. Yet, this one group focused only on wrongs of the past, totally ignoring the recent, productive collaboration with government and non-profit organizations. This posturing was divisive and unsettling to most people – but exciting to some.

The Chief admonished, "If divided, a community is weakened and more easily exploited. I ask you to remain patient since further advances are in progress. Let us not risk sabotaging that process.

Members of U.S. government in both political parties, as well as many citizens, support our objectives – though progress is slow. It is slow for many demographic groups, as the government deals with everyone's issues. But in this country, advances will not come through violence. We must continue to elevate our status through education and achievement, by instilling our traditional values in our young people, and especially through increased, peaceful engagement with tribal, local, and federal government. Elsewhere in the world, violent rebellion has not been serving the interests of any of the people involved.

In these uncertain times, we must remain unified. There are hostile parties currently threatening both American sovereignty and the individual freedom of all Americans, including Native Americans. Some threats come from outside the U.S. and some from within – possibly even from inside the government. Malefactors may stir up groups of people to violent rebellion, offering empty promises that cannot and never would be fulfilled. The pawns would suffer the violence, while the instigators – safely on the sidelines – would be the only ones to benefit.

We must stand together – within this tribe, with other Native peoples, and as stakeholders in the United States of America."

It came out that Golden Hawk had been the source of the unrest. Chief wondered: Was it due to his unusual upbringing or ideals inculcated in college? Was it excess energy of youth? Or was Golden Hawk seeking to satisfy a personal drive for power? People considered the young man to be attractive and compelling. Thus, they might be blind in their admiration and in their willingness to believe and follow him. Chief felt a sense of foreboding. History held examples of people judging a leader on a superficial basis only to find that they had been badly misled. He hoped that this was not in store for his tribe.

One day, some belligerent members of the Tribal Council visited Chief Bridgewater, asserting that "the people" thought it was time for a new leader. They claimed that the tribe wanted Golden Hawk to replace him. They said that he should agree to a special election.

Chief was surprised that a majority would want him to step down. It was also highly unusual for such a young man to be nominated to be Chief. Furthermore, the self-described "emissaries of the people" had made no mention of the two highly respected young men who had long been expected to succeed him one day and to likely work together. They were: his son, Fox, and Aspen Mijeesi.

Chief's personal wishes aside, this new hostility was extremely disturbing.

CHAPTER EIGHTEEN
May Day

In May, during final exams, Sequoia received a notice via snail mail about an impromptu special election for a new Chief. Unfortunately, her last exam was on Election Day.

Immediately upon finishing, she headed back to the reservation to cast her vote. She had a couple of text messages from Aspen, congratulating her on completing her first year of grad school and asking her to stop by as soon as she got home. She noticed that the messages did not even mention his and Fox's candidacy for Chief. Aspen had been in touch with her regularly throughout college and now grad school, always offering any support she might need. Aspen took care of everyone.

While on the bus between the university and the reservation, Sequoia was delighted by a phone call from Golden Hawk, inviting her to dine with him that evening after the election. She had not seen him at all at school other than at the first Native American Club gathering. He said that he had doubled up his schedule in order to graduate early. He told her that he had stopped attending the lectures of the class they had in common because of a time conflict with another course he needed as well. He said that he had watched the taped lectures when time permitted, instead.

While Golden Hawk was away at college, impressive stories about him at university had circulated on the reservation. To some members of the tribe, he began to symbolize great promise for the Ronopo people. In his campaign to become *Chief Golden Hawk,* he promised sweeping change that would elevate the circumstances of all Ronopo. He provided few details as to how this would be achieved, but the vision he put forth was extremely exciting. The pomp and style of Golden Hawk's campaign was like nothing the Ronopo had ever seen. Unfortunately, that included aspersions cast upon Aspen and Fox that planted seeds of doubt about those heretofore highly respected young men. The mudslinging was instigated by Golden Hawk, but it was Hunter Wolf who very effectively and innovatively ran the operation as his campaign manager.

As Official Keeper of the Register, Hunter was in charge of the "voter rolls." Despite his facility with technology, he arranged for *most* of the tribe's absentee voter notices and ballots to be sent to people off-reservation by *regular* mail instead of by express mail, email, fax, or social media. That meant that many members of the tribe, especially those in the military, would not receive their absentee ballots in time for their votes to count.

The apathetic youth on the reservation rarely paid attention to any elections. This time, however, the young women were all agog about the handsome and commanding new candidate – though Aspen and Fox had always been popular with that crowd. Girls dreamed of marrying a Chief. When false rumors spread that both Fox and Aspen were secretly engaged, it was not hard to believe. It was well-known that they were tight with the young women in their close circle of friends. Golden Hawk said that if he were elected Chief, he would choose a Ronopo wife, thus motivating single women and their families to vote for him.

The young male population was less enthusiastic about him as they felt competitive and were put off by the constant allusions to his superiority. They were far more likely to vote for Aspen and Fox ... if they bothered to vote at all.

There was a very last-minute addition of a referendum to be voted on: to legalize the use of the illegal drug, herocaine, on the reservation. No one could explain how it had gotten onto the ballot.

Chief Bridgewater, Fox and Aspen strongly opposed such a change, since people all across America already suffered much short and long-term physical and mental debilitation, as well as crime, thanks to drugs and alcohol. There was a terrible toll in highway and other deaths and disfiguring injuries caused by drug or alcohol-impaired people. And there was the problem of rape – by people under the influence – or of victims too intoxicated to thwart it. There would also inevitably be escalated drug-related crime as drug cartels, dealers, and gangs violently staked out and defended new territories.

This sudden wild-card addition to the ballot dramatically raised the interest of the young male set to vote – *and* shifted their allegiance towards the more "forward-thinking" Golden Hawk who did not oppose herocaine's legalization. The prospect of having another means of escape from the realities of a hard life was mobilizing. Thus, the young male voters came out in droves.

Sequoia's decision regarding the election was an easy one. As expected, Aspen and Fox had combined their names onto one ticket to co-lead the Ronopo Tribe. They promised a fresh approach that would accelerate the fruitful and harmonious progress of Chief Bridgewater's tenure. Although Sequoia was helplessly attracted to Dukon, she felt that he was an unknown quantity with only minimal, *if any*, qualifications to execute the myriad duties of a tribal chief. Common sense always prevailed with Sequoia, so without hesitation, she would cast her vote for Aspen and Fox. She knew with certainty that they would achieve great things for the tribe they clearly loved. Unlike Dukon, they had laid out a detailed plan and had already served and led in visible and tangible ways outside of Tribal Council.

One major innovation that they had proposed was to partner more with *state* government as opposed to federal. Even though many laws and treaties had been made at the federal level, the Governors had sovereign power in many areas. They also had a closer relationship and more tangible reasons to take care of the needs of the tribes in their states.

Sequoia felt that, despite Dukon's lack of experience or detailed plan of how he would serve the tribe, he would surely receive some votes because he was novel and attractive. There was no question in her mind, however, that the tribe would elect her two highly-qualified peers.

She was disappointed that Breeze was not present. Doing field work out in the boonies so often, Breeze might not have even received the mailed notice about the special election – just as she never seemed to receive Sequoia's messages asking her to chat or get together.

The two young women had not had time to catch up after the Native American Club reception at the university. Breeze had needed to leave the event right after Dukon departed. Sequoia wondered about Breeze's agitation at the reception.

Maybe Breeze is also attracted to Dukon. Her reaction to him was kind of strange, though. In any event, I want to let her know my own feelings so it's all out in the open.

Sequoia had some misgivings about dining with Dukon right after the election, which he was sure to lose. But not being one to run from an uncomfortable situation, she just looked forward to being with him again. Arriving at the reservation late in the day, she barely had time to vote and get ready for her dinner date. That meant that there would be no time to see Aspen until the next day.

Tension had grown throughout the day amid whispers of fraud and intimidation committed by Dukon's cronies at the poll. Sequoia witnessed some questionable acts herself but had no documentation to relay to authorities – some of whom seemed to be *involved* in them. So Sequoia just cast her own vote and left to get ready for her date with Dukon.

CHAPTER NINETEEN
Botnet Hack Attack

It was the middle of the night. The only light in the pitch black room was the ghoulish glow of computer screens. Pasty-faced guys with bloodshot eyes stared at their monitors. The floor was littered with empty pizza boxes and cans from caffeinated sodas and "energy" drinks. To eliminate power-related risk, all of their computers, and nothing else, were wired into the building's high-capacity electrical box.

"It's almost time!" said Nee-Ho, the leader of the group. "They've paid us *extravagantly* well for the work we've done so far. Now we have to finish it and launch the attack! Everyone get ready!"

"Hey, Nee-Ho, now can we know who the target is that we're about to take down?"

"Smurfius, this time, even *I* don't know who it is. All I know is that this is *really big*. When they pay us for this final act, we can all retire to the islands. *Islands of our own!*"

"Yeah! With gorgeous chicks to wait on us hand and..." The geek called Sci4 let that hang in the air while waggling his eyebrows and chortling gleefully.

"Really guys? You didn't figure it out?" sneered the one called Infinity. "Don't you guys talk to each other? *You* are the bot master. *You* wrote the code for the malware. *You* catalogued and infiltrated all the upstream routers. *I* coded the denial-of-service attack launcher. This attack is going to shut down Internet access for *an entire state!* And their recovery will take a looong time. Wanna know which state?"

"GUYS! There isn't time!" Nee-Ho yelled. "We're in countdown! Our timing was precisely coordinated with the others! We cannot miss our window! So SHUT UP, and get ready! On my mark..."

All of the computer monitors suddenly went dark. A couple of guys freaked out.

"Hang on," Nee-Ho said smugly. "My backup generator will kick on any moment..."

But nothing happened. No one could see it in the dark, but Nee-Ho's smirk had disappeared.

Someone at the back of the room struck a match and lit a sparkler. The guys spun around to look. Flashes of the sputtering light kept reflecting off the woman's metal earring.

"Duuude! There's a *woman* in here!" Sci4 exclaimed.

Each of the guys unconsciously checked that his fly wasn't open.

The sparkler went out. The room was dark again. The voice of the now invisible woman said,

"Gentlemen, consider yourselves hacked."

A piece of cloth and some clanking metal hit each of the guys in the chest.

The disembodied voice said, "You have two choices: 1) I leave here alone, and you can wait for your *enraged* employer's goons to come after you... Or 2) You put on those hoods and handcuffs, and I will take you to a place where your employer will never find you.

Frozen, Sci4's mind irrationally kept replaying the sound of her voice saying, "handcuffs..."

CHAPTER TWENTY
First Date

Sequoia took a luxurious bath. She scrubbed her whole body with a soft-bristled brush, leaving her skin velvety smooth. Then she stood in the tub and let the water drip off her body while she twisted her long, long hair into a thick rope, squeezing out the excess water. She stepped out of the tub and slathered her favorite, clean-scented cream all over her body. She massaged it in, turning her skin to satin. Granny Katiri made the cream out of natural ingredients and always resupplied her on her birthday.

She put on a silky, red sundress and walked to the little restaurant where she was meeting Dukon. She enjoyed greeting the villagers along the way. There was a crowd outside the restaurant. Sequoia spotted Dukon and instantly felt the almost paralyzing attraction to him as she had before. He saw her and beckoned to her to join him. He placed his hand on her soft, bare back and guided her into the restaurant. She felt a flash of heat run from his hand all the way through her. At their table in a private corner, Dukon regarded her intensely. She was still electrified by him, and she found it hard to speak.

"Aren't you going to congratulate me?" Dukon finally asked, smiling.

Sequoia realized that she had put the election completely out of her mind! She had been awash in the delicious anticipation of being with him tonight. Now, she thought that she must have misheard him. Had he asked her if she was going to offer him condolences? No... he had not. So, was he *joking* about congratulations for second place? His demeanor suggested otherwise.

"You mean...." she uttered. "Are you...?"

Her eyes were wide, and she was unable to find her breath or her voice.

He took her hand in his. Meeting her eyes, he quietly said, "Yes, Sequoia, I am the new Chief."

Sequoia gasped and choked a little, looking around the room as if to find confirmation and to hide the shock she was feeling. She withdrew her hand and coughed into it, turning far to her side, trying to clear her throat. She knew she had tears in her eyes. He had been elected Chief?! It felt so wrong! How was it even possible, personally knowing so many people who would never have voted for a man with no applicable experience for such an important job! She knew she had to shake this off – and quickly. She took some deep breaths and looked back at him with an unsteady smile.

"C-congratulations, Dukon. I... missed the final tallies while getting ready for dinner..."

She lost her tongue again and just stared at him, hoping that he could not perceive the shock and fear and disappointment she felt for the tribe. Shaking slightly, she lifted her water and drank some, trying to snap herself out of it.

"I will be a good Chief," he said reassuringly, "but I will need the help of someone smart, strong, and confident, like you."

Whoa! Is he offering me the chance to work in the Offices of The Chief?!

She blinked mid-sip and lowered her cup.

"I'm asking you to be my wife, Sequoia."

Sequoia's shock was now complete. She choked and spluttered, ejecting a cloud of the water she had just been sipping. She coughed in spasms and put her napkin to her lips as she turned away. Bending over at the waist, she tried to recover. In an instant, she felt a warm arm around her back and found Dukon squatting beside her chair. He placed his lips close to her ear and whispered,

"I am so sorry. I gave you no warning at all. Are you all right?"

The soft scent of her clean skin made him close his eyes and breathe her in. His warm breath on her ear and neck compelled *her* to inhale deeply. With that breath she regained her equanimity and looked him in the face. He took her hand again and held it, searching her eyes.

"Let me order you a drink."

Sequoia nodded, holding her napkin to her mouth. Dukon retook his seat and signaled the waiter. He ordered wine for Sequoia and a soda for himself.

"Sequoia, I knew from the moment I first saw you in class that I wanted to be with you. Then, after meeting you, I knew that I wanted to be with you always. I know this is not how it's done, but... I just... *know.* I don't expect you to answer me tonight. I certainly understand if you want to get to know me better. Are you willing to spend time with me to that end?"

Sequoia had never fainted in her life, but she felt as if she might now. Between Dukon's election as Chief and his marriage proposal, her psyche had been catapulted into an emotional maelstrom. Drawing from prior training, she looked down and breathed deeply, working to center herself. Finally, she looked up, and smiled bravely.

"I would enjoy getting to know you better... Chief... Golden Hawk."

Sequoia sat at the little table at Granny Katiri's house, sharing a pot of the herbal tea that she had brought her grandmother from off the reservation.

"My dear Sequoia," Granny K. said, "I know it is hard to ignore the voices of our hearts and the demands of our bodies, but this match does not feel harmonious to me. He is a stranger, and I am uneasy."

"Oh Granny, I understand your apprehension. I feel it too, but I am so drawn to him! And I cannot help wondering – is this a gift? My calling? I would be in a leadership position as the Chief's wife, being able to help especially the women of our tribe."

Granny K. nodded, studying her lovely granddaughter.

"And you would do that very well, Sequoia. I know that you always run towards, not away from, the most difficult challenges that life puts before you. I just feel an ache in my bones whenever I see the man. I was so sure that you would end up with that wonderful Aspen Mijeesi."

Sequoia had never shaken off what started out as a crush on Aspen when she was younger. As she grew up, she always found herself comparing the men that she met to him – and they never measured up. Golden Hawk was the first man whom she also saw as an ideal but in a different way. It was also plain reality that Aspen had never even asked her out. He seemed to care about her but no differently than he did for everyone else. Sequoia stared into her teacup as if it might hold the answer that she was seeking.

"Thank you for being honest with me, Granny. I will spend time getting to know Golden Hawk– *Chief* Golden Hawk, and then try to make a good decision."

CHAPTER TWENTY-ONE
The Heat is On

Dukon and Sequoia spent a great deal of time together. Most days, Sequoia helped him in the Offices of the Chief. They spent time enjoying recreational activities off-reservation and discussing their values. Sequoia tried to talk about more personal details of her own history and to ask questions about his, but it seemed ridiculously fateful that every time she started down that path, Dukon's phone would ring. Since he was the Chief, he always had to answer.

Dukon had Sequoia so fully booked, that she was unable to get together with her other friends at all. Aspen and Birdie had left her multiple messages. Sequoia knew that if there were something *critical,* her friends would contact her using a special code. The thick envelope that Aspen left with Granny K. was obviously the summer recreation schedules that he always circulated in May. And right now Sequoia did not have the time or emotional energy to deal with anything other than her courtship with the extraordinary new Chief of the tribe.

Dukon told Sequoia up front that he thought it best that sex not be involved while they got to know each other. He explained that, if Sequoia were to refuse his marriage proposal, he did not want the woman who did accept him to feel any discomfort about this very public courtship. Nevertheless, every night, when saying goodnight, Dukon held her and kissed her very passionately and seductively. He then always renewed his marriage proposal.

After several weeks, Sequoia felt that they had spent so much intensive time together, that it was the same as if they had been dating more conventionally over a longer period of time. She was still drawn to him like a magnet – the chemistry between them clearly explosive. Of course, spending so much time with a man to whom she was so wildly attracted was terribly sexually frustrating. It was obvious that he felt the same way. During their time together, she had not encountered anything of concern. Since they shared the same goal – a life of service to their community, they seemed to be a truly excellent match. Therefore, with only a few qualms, Sequoia accepted. Dukon then insisted that they not delay the marriage. Sequoia acquiesced but lamented the absence of her dearest friend, Breeze, who was unreachable somewhere out in the field.

The tribe celebrated the auspicious marriage of one of their favorite daughters to their dashing new Chief. The newlywed couple slipped out of the celebration and escaped in a chauffeured limousine that had been a surprise from Dukon, the first of many luxuries that he had arranged for their honeymoon far away. Dukon checked them into a resort on the water, and they were escorted to an extravagantly spacious, beachfront cottage.

The couple sat on their balcony in a loveseat glider, romantically looking out onto moonlit water. Chief Golden Hawk raised his bride's hand, lightly caressing her wedding ring with his lips. Then he pulled her into his arms and kissed her. Their pent-up desire for one another turned into a firestorm of passion, so they moved inside to a bedroom.

Dukon quickly stripped Sequoia down to her thong and guided her onto the bed while she finished unbuttoning his shirt. She pulled it over his shoulders and off, exposing his well-sculpted upper body. Dukon's eyes and hands hungrily explored the bare skin of his lovely wife's body. She slipped one hand inside his straining waistband, causing him to inhale sharply, while her other hand unbuttoned the top of his trousers. As Dukon reached to extinguish the light, Sequoia whispered to him,

"My husband... will you please try to be gentle this first time?"

Dukon stared at her, his eyes wide. "Sequoia! You're not....?!"

Sequoia nodded, smiling a little self-consciously.

Dukon looked stricken. Then taking her in his arms, he held her, squeezing her tightly and murmuring something that she couldn't quite catch. When he pulled back to look at her, she could see that he was completely discombobulated.

"A virgin already?" he whispered with surprise and tenderness in his voice.

It was rare for Dukon to use the wrong English word, as he had truly mastered the language, despite it being so recently foreign to him. Sequoia remembered how she, herself, had constantly confused the words: *already* and *still* when first studying Spanish. She was touched that he was emotional enough over this to be at a loss for the right word now.

"Yes, *still* a virgin," she replied.

"An American virgin?" he breathed with comical wonder on his face.

Sequoia had to say something, wondering if it was the guys on the reservation or at college that had given him such an expectation.

"Did you think that there were no Native or other American women – or men – who are still virgins at 21? You'd be surprised how many there are."

Dukon looked confounded and apologetic. He turned out the light and finished undressing himself in the dark. Sliding under the sheet beside her, he eased his arm underneath her. Pulling her close, he said, "I will be as gentle as can be, my lovely wife."

Sequoia awoke the next morning with the rising sun, feeling a warm flush and pleasant memories of making love with Dukon. She turned over and found that he was not there. After some time had passed and he still did not appear, she got out of bed. She began her ritual greeting to the morning sun, expecting that Dukon would enter shortly and join her in doing it. When she had finished, and he still had not returned, Sequoia put on a short, silk robe provided by the resort and went to look for him.

It was a large cottage, and it took her a few minutes to search the place. He was not on the balcony, nor in either of the bathrooms or living areas. Wondering if he had gone out, she went to check the only other room, the second bedroom, though she doubted he would be in there.

The door was locked. Bewildered, she knocked and then heard a noise from within. A few moments later, Dukon appeared at the door, wearing silk shorts and smiling with delight.

"Good morning!" he said stepping out into the hall. He closed the door behind him and wrapped his arms around her. "Did my beautiful wife sleep well?"

"Yes," she beamed. "Is everything all right? I didn't know where you were."

"Everything is perfect. After you fell asleep, I went to my bedroom," he said.

Sequoia was puzzled. "Your bedroom? Why would we not share the same bedroom?"

He smiled, "So my wife can have the privacy that a woman needs."

Sequoia mulled that over.

"It's a considerate thought, but I don't need a bedroom to myself for privacy. I would much rather wake up with my husband beside me."

Dukon's expression darkened, and he spoke in a decidedly more insistent voice.

"I want only the best for our marriage. Many couples sleep in separate bedrooms but share a bed when they make love. It is said to keep a marriage pleasing."

"Dukon, I don't—"

Dukon kissed Sequoia roughly, silencing her. He pulled her against him and continued kissing her as his hands slid across the silk of the robe on her back. He slipped her robe off one shoulder and sucked on her sweet skin. Breathing heavily, he ran his tongue up her neck.

The sensation caused Sequoia to close her eyes and tilt her head the other way. His abrupt kiss had at first felt aggressive, but now Sequoia began to relax. He moved his mouth back onto hers, kissing her heatedly while pulling her robe further off her shoulder. He fondled her breast, eliciting sighs of pleasure from her. He then drove his hands down her back to the hem of her short robe. Slipping his hands up underneath the robe, he grabbed her bare backside and pulled her hips tightly against his. Sequoia gasped and closed her eyes, feeling his hardness pressing against her in just the right spot.

Despite the touchy discussion of a few moments ago, Sequoia found herself succumbing to desire. With his hands still holding onto her backside, he lifted her straight up, and she wrapped her legs around his waist. Holding her close, he strode back to her bedroom where Dukon now introduced Sequoia to a bit more heated and vigorous sex.

Afterward, Dukon rolled onto his side with the sheet pulled just to his waist. He leaned on one elbow, tracing Sequoia's shapely lips with his fingertip.

Her mind had returned to the conversation outside *his* bedroom earlier. His view on the marital bedroom was strange, and the domineering tone of his last words, along with his rather aggressive kiss to shush her, had seemed hostile.

His voice brought her out of her reverie.

"You bathe first, Sequoia. While you dress, I will shower. Then we can go to breakfast, okay?" Dukon said, already shifting to get up.

Noticing that he was not *actually* consulting her, Sequoia just agreed since it was not an important decision. Dukon kissed her on the cheek then turned away and left the room.

Sequoia thought of how she would shortly be showering in *her* bathroom and he would be showering in *his*. Her gradually clearing mind realized, that although Dukon had spoken of *her* privacy, it was *his* bedroom that had been locked. Then, thinking of all the extra rooms, she thought that this wedding trip *had to* have been a gift from someone, as it was unimaginable how he could have afforded a place like this. Sequoia realized how very little she actually knew about the man she had just married.

CHAPTER TWENTY-TWO
Hawk Rising

Dukon spent long periods of time away from the reservation – now that he was Chief. He promoted Hunter to be his "Sous-Chief" and back-filled the position of Official Keeper of the Register with a crony of his from the Tribal Council committee on which he previously served. He left Hunter in charge of the mountain of issues that had to be dealt with daily. In spite of himself, Hunter was developing a healthy respect for what he now knew that Chief Bridgewater had dealt with and handled so well during his tenure.

Dukon usually even left Sequoia on the reservation since she needed to be on-site while establishing a clinic and a resource center for women, a project that was her brainchild. Aspen worked with her on the clinic as that had been a dream of his, as well. In her new role, Sequoia made many meaningful contributions. She succeeded in securing an amendment to tribal law that measurably protected women and children from domestic abuse. Elder Chief Bridgewater was pleased that Sequoia achieved what he had tried so many times to do. Going a step further, Sequoia initiated the building of a residential complex for battered women.

Her highest visibility project of all was a cluster of programs aimed at *forestalling* the development of domestic and substance abusers. Her program targeted to young adults was called: *"Get a Life. Have a Life. Save a Life."* She hired members of the tribe to create posters, leaflets, and short films. She funded this work with honorariums she earned giving presentations to schools and colleges outside the reservation.

She pointed out to students that, by day, they protest the lack of progress in reducing inner city violence; then, by night, they thoughtlessly indulge in illegal substances, the sale and use of which is the root cause of so much of the violence.

Her programs were so successful that other tribes began to implement them. Gradually, they were hailed across mainstream America as well. Sequoia's growing reputation, along with her prior coursework in economics and government, served her well in acquiring private grants and low-cost financing for her undertakings. Sequoia put her graduate school education on hold. She seized the opportunity to make a tangible impact now and would finish her studies later. She became a highly visible example of what a successful social activist can do. Her impactful work permeated diverse communities on and off the reservation, appealing to people's positive instincts and drawing them together to work productively as unified, fellow human beings.

Meanwhile, Golden Hawk immersed himself in re-working land grant petitions that the tribe had been long and passionately pursuing. He frequently met with other tribal Chiefs, hammering out negotiating advantages for them to use together. Sometimes his activities took him further afield, and he began to establish relationships with some U.S. government officials and other useful contacts.

Since no one in the tribe oversaw his work, his constituents were unaware that the "higher impact improvements" that their Chief was making to the land petitions resulted in shifting the benefits away from serving the interests of the Ronopo Tribe as a whole and more towards benefiting the few who were involved in making it happen. Completely consumed by fund-raising and networking, Dukon spent no time whatsoever on any of the issues about which he had promised the tribe swift and significant change when he campaigned for election.

Hunter and Sequoia managed many day-to-day issues of the tribe, working well together. Sequoia regularly sought the counsel of Elder Chief Bridgewater, and she consulted with Aspen and Fox on some issues. Hunter, however, was vehemently opposed to this and did not do the same.

More and more, as Dukon returned from his trips away, Hunter could see that he was changing, hardening, the weight of responsibility apparently showing its effects. One day, Dukon said he wanted to talk privately. He and Hunter drove to the barren southwest quadrant and walked there as Dukon spoke.

"Sequoia tells me that she consults with Elder Chief and his minions but that you do not."

Hunter clenched his jaw tightly, his eyes slitted with disdain.

"So your long-held opinions about that bunch have not changed?"

"No," Hunter curtly replied.

"How would you like to move up in the world and show up the others as the amateurs that they are?"

Hunter looked inquiringly at Dukon and waited for the imposing man to continue.

"You and I are a good team, Hunter. The people needed me to lead them, and you brilliantly arranged for it to be so. You are actually quite proficient at running the show yourself. I think we both deserve better."

Hunter eyed him with uncertainty.

"I am viewing a step up for me. Unfortunately, we both know that this tribe would not hand the reins to you if I were to leave. I have a shot at becoming the Chief of a new national organization representing all U.S. tribes, and I want to take you with me."

Hunter gaped at him. "You have got to be kidding. We've hardly been in these positions–"

"Not at all. I have accumulated significant political capital working on the land petitions. I've gained allies in other tribes and have persuaded them to collaborate with us in some enormously lucrative transactions."

"What kind of transactions?"

"There are outside investors interested in helping Native Americans to acquire more and better land. Our participation would be limited to trading a useless parcel of Ronopo land in exchange for shares in existing and *new* tribal real estate across the country."

"The Ronopo people will *never* agree to give up *any* Ronopo land," Hunter asserted.

"I am the Chief. The tribe elected me to serve their best interests. I am sure they expect my bold approach to do just that."

Hunter thought, *Elected you? As you said, I more or less made that happen...*

"The Council of Elders would have to sign off on such a deal. I can assure you that they will not."

"There are many ways to persuade a person," Dukon said, looking at his nails.

Hunter frowned.

"Don't look so worried. I already know that there are members of the Ronopo Council who will support anything that Old Bridgewater hates. My time in Ronopo Council committee was well-spent clarifying for them the bad hand that this tribe has been dealt, both by the U.S. Government and by Old Chief. It will be clear that those who participate willingly in these deals will not be left behind when the payoff comes. As for the others..."

Dukon shrugged and continued.

"Each of my allies in the Ronopo Council has people who will follow his lead. All of those people have others who will follow *their* lead, and so forth. People tend to be like sheep. For any who are undecided, it will be your task to help them understand that this is in their best interest."

"Will it be?"

"That depends on your point of view..." Dukon answered with a predatory smile. "Gambling on real estate is like gambling on any kind of investment. It certainly will be in the best interests of some of the participants – and possibly for all."

Hunter tried to imagine the conservative Ronopo people putting their land at risk.

Dukon continued. "How many in this tribe would not expect to be better served if their own Chief became head of a new national organization?"

"There are already multiple national organizations for American Indians. The tribes are not likely to support a new one and would not install you as Chief if they thought that you would be self-serving."

"That is not what they will think. Word is spreading across the tribes that a great champion of Native Americans is *rising*. People believe what the most persuasive leaders tell them is right and good and true. Even the Council doesn't need to know everything about my actions. The tribe elected a new Chief, and I have a new way of doing things. Sometimes it is best to take more control and provide less transparency."

Hunter looked suspiciously at Golden Hawk. "Just where is this *useless* parcel of Ronopo land that the tribe would be trading?"

Dukon opened his arms expansively and turned 360°, smiling broadly.

"Right here, Hunter. This and Rattlesnake Canyon."

CHAPTER TWENTY-THREE
Disclosures and Demons

Word was out that Golden Hawk was to be Chief of a new national organization in Washington, D.C. and that he was taking Hunter with him. By popular acclamation, and with Elder Chief Bridgewater's full blessing, Fox and Aspen were to become Co-Chiefs of the Ronopo Tribe.

Kristal Parks, the schoolteacher and founder of the library that had provided a safe and happy haven for Hunter for many years, asked him out to lunch during his final weeks there. After they had eaten in awkward silence, Kristal spoke.

"Hunter, I am very proud of you. We *all* are."

The perpetually cold and austere young man regarded her stiffly.

She continued, "There is a story that I wanted to tell you before you left. You know, no one is prouder of you than Elder Chief Bridgewater."

Hunter raised an eyebrow with a skeptical look on his face.

"Even though your father is no longer living, I don't think that Elder Chief would tell you about this, but I thought you should know."

Hunter now knitted his brows warily.

"You may not be aware that Elder Chief tried repeatedly to persuade the Tribal Council to change the laws to better help victims of domestic abuse. Unfortunately, your father had influence on the Council and prevented Chief from succeeding. So, when you were ten years old, and your sister was thirteen, Chief Bridgewater asked for my help in locating a placement for you and your sister off the reservation."

Hunter looked doubtful but then contemplative as he recalled the Chief's offer long ago for him to move in with the Chief's family to escape his father's abuse.

"Chief told me that he wanted only the best for you. The placement had to be at a first-rate, American Indian-run school for gifted students, where you and your sister could receive the education that your extraordinary minds deserved. Chief stipulated that there had to be a thoroughly vetted, traditional Native American host family with whom you could both live. I thought it was a wonderful idea, but I asked how it could possibly be paid for? Chief said that if we were unable to procure a scholarship or other financial aid for you, that *he* would take on a personal loan. It would be secured by a property abroad that had been given to him in gratitude for a life he saved long ago. This property was the only material inheritance that he could leave to his son. He told Fox that this inheritance might be put at risk to help someone in an unfortunate situation not of his own making. He did not tell Fox who it was. Fox agreed without hesitation, saying that he would gladly help another who needed it more."

Hunter looked down, astounded and humbled and more than a little ashamed. Snippets of memories popped into his head. He thought of the disdain and bitterness he had felt for so long towards the Chief for failing to deal with his abusive father in a manner satisfactory to him. He thought of the acrimony with which he had dealt with Fox and with others in the tribe, purely out of his own anger and envy. This thought conjured up flashbacks of Fox and Aspen from long ago:

"Hey Hunter, a bunch of us are gonna go play stick ball or lacrosse. C'mon!"

"Wolf-man! We're going night hunting later. Come with us!"

"Hunter, we're getting together tonight to play games like Gathering Stones and Sticks in the Fist. The girls are bringing f-o-o-d... Wanna come?"

Hunter suddenly saw with clarity that these people, *had* cared about him and his deplorable home life. And now they could end up on either the winning or losing side of Dukon's land trade deal. He was slammed with the realization that the responsibility for how he had handled himself as a result of his unfortunate beginnings, including his now complicit involvement with a possibly corrupt man, lay solely at his own feet.

"We did find a place for you," Kristal went on. "And due to your extraordinary test scores and academic records, a private venture capitalist offered to pay full freight at the school and for living expenses for both you and your sister as a gift with no strings attached. When Chief Bridgewater told your father of the offer, your father threatened to do terrible things to you and your sister if any member of your family even learned of it. So the Chief's hands were tied. He suffered great anguish over his powerlessness to do this for you. The risk of further harm to you and your sister was considerable, and Chief felt that he could not take the chance. Still, he did not give up on helping you. You have heard him tell the tribe:

'The path to health, happiness, and tranquility is a journey filled with work – work that tires us, work that engages us, work that fulfills us.'

Chief could not move you to a safer and more enriching environment, but when he attracted a private company to the reservation, he put you first in line for a construction job with them. He did that to keep you from the downward slide that idleness and unhappiness so often engender."

Hunter looked up at Kristal, the cold shield gone, new awareness and a little bit of humility in its place. After several moments, he rose from his chair, took money from his pocket, and quickly counted out enough to cover both lunches plus a tip.

"Oh no, Hunter, I invited you!" the older woman protested.

Hunter's next action was even more unexpected than the last. In a traditional gesture of respect to a tribal Elder, Hunter closed his eyes and dipped his head to her. Then, looking down, he said in his deep, raspy voice,

"Thank you, Ms. Parks. Thank you... *for everything.*"

Hunter turned and left the restaurant.

Kristal sat very still, remembering the boy whom she had done her best to foster and shield. She thought of the man he was now – educated and productive but still lonely and in pain. Then she needed her handkerchief, because she was weeping. She wept for what had just been confirmed without any doubt – that, despite his hard, protective outer shell, Hunter Wya Wolf did have feelings. And importantly, he had not yet withdrawn too far inside that shell to be reached. The visible effect that her words had had on him was confirmation of the critical importance of interpersonal communication. She regretted her belatedness in reaching out to him.

Hunter stopped in the washroom outside his small office and splashed cold water on his face. His dark, serious eyes regarded his reflection in the mirror, water dripping off his sharply-defined features. He thought of Ms. Parks' revelations regarding Chief Bridgewater and of the flashbacks he'd had of his peers' many attempts to be his friends, all of which *he* had rebuffed.

"Who are you?" he asked his reflection. *"Who are you really?"*

After some contemplation, he added, *"And what kind of man do you want to be?"*

Hunter and Sequoia spent long hours finishing work that needed to be done before they could depart to join Golden Hawk in his new position. Hunter tentatively consulted with Elder Chief Bridgewater on a few issues – much to the older man's surprise and great pleasure. Then Hunter guardedly ventured contact with Aspen and Fox to transition ongoing matters. He wasn't sure how they would receive him, especially in light of the role he had played, depriving them of being elected Co-Chiefs instead of Dukon. There was also his involvement in Dukon's land trade deal which, though not yet concluded, was causing considerable turmoil within the tribe.

To their credit, Aspen and Fox treated Hunter with courtesy and focus on the issues at hand. Hunter realized that, although they disagreed with Dukon's viewpoints and actions, and thus Hunter's alliance with him, they seemed to genuinely respect *him*.

Hunter found himself newly able to listen to their input. Gradually, he was even able to reciprocate, at least to a small degree, a show of esteem, which he had always felt for them beneath his bitterness and envy. For the first time in his life, Hunter felt like he was part of something truly important – a member of a respected team.

Even at college, Hunter had mostly been a loner, not joining in any activities. During the summers, when not on the reservation, he traveled alone, seeing the world via work offers and free programs that he found on the Internet. One summer, he enrolled in an extremely compelling recruitment program that resonated deeply with his inner turbulence and desire for action. While involved, he realized that the program was run by *terrorists*. He ultimately left, agreeing to consider a future with that organization.

Hunter stayed in minimal contact with a few acquaintances, but there were really only one or two whom he might call a friend. During those years, mostly away from the reservation, Hunter had ruminated at length about the roots of his inner turmoil. He had identified people who were at fault and had devised a plan to exorcise his personal demons. Now, in a position of power, and with some parts of that plan already executed, his developing new perspective spurred him to overhaul and redesign it.

CHAPTER TWENTY-FOUR
Acid Reign

In Washington, D.C., Dukon settled in as Chief of the new, national tribal organization. He now inserted Hunter's clauses into the land trade contracts, finalizing the transactions with the outside investors. There were, more or less, winners and losers. Dukon, Hunter, a few Ronopo, some members of other American Indian tribes, and the outside investors came out on top.

When Hunter had agreed to promote the land trade deal, there was a critical component of which he had been unaware. Since the members of the younger generation on the Ronopo Tribal Council were always placed on committees separate from one another, they each had detailed knowledge only of the segment of tribal business that their committee handled. Dukon had been on the committee dealing with tribal land.

What Dukon knew, that Hunter and most of the tribe did not, was that the residential privilege granted to each family was tied to the tribe's land as a whole. So, when a majority of Ronopo citizens were persuaded to trade Rattlesnake Canyon and the rest of the southwest quadrant for "shares of better land," they did not know that they were also parting with their rights to use the land on which their homes and businesses stood!

Elder Chief Bridgewater, Aspen, Fox, and others had adamantly opposed trading *any* Ronopo land for "shares" of land or for anything else. They had tried to explain about the homestead losses, but Dukon's allies in the tribe rebutted their interpretation of tribal law. Many Ronopo believed in their dashing, young Chief, just as Dukon had predicted they would. He recruited a few imposing members of the tribe to portray Elder Chief as senile and to suggest that Aspen and Fox only opposed this rare opportunity out of spite for not having previously been elected instead of Golden Hawk. No one seemed to have "standing" – whatever that meant – to question Chief Golden Hawk's assertion that certain initiatives, such as this one, could be consummated by a *majority* of votes instead of the usual, required *unanimous* consent.

All the common sense in the world from the well-known, proven (and thus boring) leaders in the tribe was no match for gambling on the dazzling and optimism-inspiring new Chief, Golden Hawk. It is no different than the way people gamble their money in a lottery or casino even though they know that statistics show that *they will not win.* The excitement of promised or hoped for good fortune often trumps common sense. Thusly, Golden Hawk had received the needed support from the Ronopo Tribe for both the land trade deal and in his campaign for his new, prestigious, and more powerful position in Washington, D.C.

As for the shadowy apparatus that had somehow yielded the support of the other tribes to elect him Chief of a new Native American organization – it had too convoluted a trail to be traced without an operation dedicated entirely to its unraveling.

While Dukon immersed himself in Washington politics, it was Hunter who listened to the ideas, needs, and grievances of the tribes.

Members of the Ronopo Council protested that Golden Hawk had not done anything positive for them – even as he had advanced his personal career in large part due to their support. They groused, "It was only his assistant and his wife who worked on our behalf! Then, after we helped him to become Chief of a national organization, not only is he doing nothing positive for us, it is looking more and more like he slung us a raw deal! Foreigners are wandering all over the reservation. They take photographs and spray lines of paint on the ground! When questioned, they just wave permission letters signed by former Chief Golden Hawk!"

Hunter placated them with promises to look into the intrusions of the foreigners. He exhorted them to be patient – that Golden Hawk would be better able to fulfill his promises as he settled into his higher position. While Hunter tried to reassure the people of their leader's commitment to their best interests, Golden Hawk's ruggedly handsome face was increasingly featured on magazine covers and in TV interviews for which he made time. The first black and first female U.S. Presidents had also been treated as big kahunas and had been featured widely as well. Yet again, it was Hunter who deflected the question:

How is Chief Golden Hawk working for us if he spends so much time being interviewed on TV, meeting with celebrities, traveling the country, and schmoozing?

The media did back-flips trying to score interviews with his lovely wife, Sequoia Starfire, but she always politely declined, saying that her work commitments had to take priority.

Despite being on the payroll of the national tribal organization, Golden Hawk was personally paid for his many appearances and interviews. He publicly stated that this significant income was going to be used for a good cause. He did not reveal that this "good cause" was a not too distant campaign to elevate him to the *very highest* position of power. And, *of course,* that would only be to enable him to "best serve the people."

CHAPTER TWENTY-FIVE
Inconceivable

Through book royalties, honorariums for speeches delivered on a tightly-packed schedule, and new land investment deals, Dukon and Hunter were *inconceivably* wealthy – far beyond anything Hunter had ever dreamed possible. Not that he had much time to enjoy it. His life was an endless cycle of work. Hunter took responsibility very seriously, and Dukon was not doing his job; so Hunter was doing it for him.

Hunter started his days before dawn in his townhouse, rising from his bed and warming up his muscles with dynamic stretches. Most mornings he did pushups and planks, jumped rope, and did chin-ups or pull-ups on a bar he installed in a doorway. His lean, muscular body showed the results of the physical labor of his youth and his regular regimen of exercise now.

He would shower, eat a quick breakfast while scanning the news, and be at his desk by 6:30 am. After working until 7:00 pm, he would return home, eat another unmemorable meal, listen to music, and read some of the classics, including American Indian stories that had been transcribed from storytellers of various tribes. Occasionally, he streamed a movie to his laptop. Then, he would get into bed, tired and lonely, only to start all over again the next day. He worked six days a week, and on the seventh, he always left the city and spent time outdoors to commune with nature. In this way, he satisfied his increasing desire to nurture the bond between the spark of spirit within him and the Great Spirit.

Hunter's social life was non-existent. He had never interacted well with people and did not accept social invitations. Sequoia tried hard to change that, but she only ever succeeded in scoring an occasional working lunch for him *with her.*

Hunter did not drink alcohol or use drugs since they damage the body and the mind – and he never wanted to lose his temper the way his father so often had. Neither did he want to impair his judgment or leave himself unable to defend himself if necessary. Besides, he found people who were intoxicated or high to be eminently boring or ridiculous; so he rarely went to bars or clubs.

He frequently thought of Breeze. He imagined how different his life could be with her as his companion. He simply could not succeed in engaging in social activities, let alone intimate ones, with the other women that he met. He tried, but those encounters usually ended the same way. He walked away – alone.

COUNTERPOINT IV
PREDATOR

"I only learn of this now? I thought your plan covered such details!"

"It's not an issue. I told you there would be bumps in the road. The computers found all points in the Plan that could possibly be affected. We created a workaround that takes care of the problem *and* provides an opportunity to gain leverage on another individual if we need it."

"Explain the mishap and how your team handled it."

"An outsider appeared to observe one of our developers with our primary asset before it was complete or ready to be unveiled. Our computers found only one solution: eliminate the outsider and not risk what may be the only opportunity *ever* for this venture. We had an armed drone in place, but we picked up a signal that *could* have represented audio/visual transmission from the outsider to an unknown audience. Obviously, we could not risk a drone strike in the U.S. being broadcast! We later determined that the signal was from the outsider *collecting* not *transmitting* data. We quickly seized that data, and our analysis showed that the person could not have actually seen our asset before we prepped it for public viewing. We adjusted our plan to eliminate any remaining risk. Our drone captured useful material to that end."

"Was that the full extent of the breach?"

"Local authorities came, but they saw nothing of concern."

"How difficult was it to acquire an armed drone?"

"Not at all. It is now legal for *anyone* to have drones, thanks to vigorous lobbying. Legislators were persuaded by the economic boost that drone-building and licensing would give to the states. Many officials will support anything, even if detrimental, as long as it brings in revenue. It only takes money to buy already armed drones or to have them modified – and as you know, we have *no* lack of funds."

CHAPTER TWENTY-SIX
Murder and Cheesecake

"Close the door and take a seat, Hunter."

Dukon was sitting in his office with a large envelope on his lap.

"I have the most critical and most *sensitive* assignment for you yet. As we have embarked upon my campaign for President of the United States, I need you to handle a detail that could otherwise derail my chance for success."

Hunter regarded his boss wearily. Dark shadows had become fixtures under his eyes. In the mirror that morning, he had even noticed a silver hair on his way too young head.

"There is a woman. She has been... *involved* with me during my travels over the past few years. The nature of our... relationship could be damaging to my candidacy."

Hunter glared at Dukon, unable to hide his scorn. "Even while Sequoia was–"

"Yesss, Hunter. Don't be so naive," Dukon snapped.

"Okay-y-y... so.... where do I fit into something like this?"

"I need you to get rid of her."

"Excuse me? Get rid of her? What does *that* mean?"

Dukon glowered at his assistant. "Do you not want to be Vice President of the United States?"

"What the–?! You have never suggested putting me on your ticket!"

"That's because I cannot put you on my ticket – for a whole host of reasons, not the least of which is your age."

Hunter remembered how, seemingly so long ago, when he was Official Keeper of the Ronopo Register, Dukon had "helped him to see" a credible path for Dukon's lineage. At the time, he made it sound like he was doing Hunter a favor. That it would be a great accomplishment to be credited with decoding the onerous Register while so young and new to the job. Dukon had tempted him with how that would elevate Hunter in the eyes of the community. Hunter thought of what an angry, young wretch he had been back then, so susceptible to manipulation. The prospect of being associated with the awe-inspiring big shot, Golden Hawk, was such nourishment for his desperately starving self-esteem. It seemed like such an innocuous deed at the time...

He then thought, *I didn't put anything in the Official Register that would provide an age for Dukon, but the credibility I gave him by falsely confirming a Ronopo family line for him was the crucial first step in making any of this even possible. Then, when he was Chief, and he promoted me out of that job to be his assistant, he installed a crony who just happened to later be one of the "winners" in the land trade deal. That crony then did provide "proof" of Dukon's age from the Register when it was required for his Presidential campaign.*

These thoughts made Hunter wonder for the first time if Dukon's ambition had been to become U.S. President all along.

"In addition," Dukon continued, "we would not likely be elected with a double Native American ticket. I will need an irresistible draw for Vice President. The person I have in mind is a woman. She is a youngish, pop celebrity and will be an asset to ensure our win. However, she will not be an asset to my agenda for this nation nor for us. Of course I don't want a VP so popular that someone might want to get rid of *me* and have the VP replace me. So, I... uh... know that she will not hold up under the pressure of the position. When she quickly steps down to enter rehab... I will appoint you, my Chief of Staff, as her successor. At that point, I will be able to bypass the age requirement and appoint you by emergency Executive Order. Someone could bring a challenge to the courts, but I doubt that they will dare oppose me. If they do, my Legal Agency will appeal and delay. By the time the courts get to it, our work will be done."

Hunter's head felt like it might explode. The prospect was sensational, but the suddenness of it caught him totally off guard. He didn't even know if he trusted Dukon. He had not liked his tone or insinuations, including saying "my" Legal Agency. He also wondered what he meant by "our work will be done."

"So... do you want me to make an offer so appealing that it would completely appease this 'other woman' you were involved with to keep her quiet? Maybe buy her an island somewhere?"

Dukon glared at Hunter.

"No? Okay-y... do you want me to *threaten* her with something?"

Dukon shut his eyes, squeezing the bridge of his nose between his thumb and forefinger.

"Hunter, if you want to be Vice President, you must get *rid* of her. *Permanently.*"

Hunter stood up, his face contorted with disgust and disbelief.

"You have unimaginable gall! I have done many things, but I am no murderer! I resign!"

Hunter strode towards the door.

"Not so fast!" Dukon roared. "I suggest you look at what I have in this envelope!"

Seething, Hunter halted at the door.

"Sit down, Hunter."

Hunter returned to his chair. Dukon removed a document from the large envelope and handed it to him. As Hunter read it, the blood drained from his face.

"Reporters were trying to dig up dirt on us in advance of the campaign, and they unearthed this Ronopo Tribal Police report that had previously been sealed – probably by old Chief Bridgewater. It was only through my... monetary intervention, that the reporters were persuaded to not publicize or pursue the evidence of your involvement in the death of the Elder, Kogan Kichoba. Your prospects looked grim. I learned that everyone knew that you hated the old man, and that you had it in for him. Then, next thing you know, after his death, what a coincidence! You were given his suddenly available, prestigious position as Keeper of the Register!"

"I didn't... kill him!" Hunter choked, his voice only a hoarse whisper.

"After his death, the tribal police found a note in your handwriting in his hut. It encouraged him to ascertain if a man sighted in Rattlesnake Canyon was actually his childhood friend – alive, not dead as presumed all those years. The police report even lists witnesses who saw you that day, heading in that rarely traveled direction. Then, there's *another* 'coincidence' that the reporters pounced upon. Your notoriously abusive father died shortly after you graduated from college and returned to the reservation– "

Hunter jumped to his feet, blasting, "These are lies! This is blackmail!"

"No, Hunter. It is evidence in the hands of the law. Are you ready to leave the luxury of your home and possessions here, go back to that dreary old reservation, and try to defend yourself against these charges? I assure you that without my continuing intervention, you will not succeed. I'm sure you understand that if you leave, my campaign cannot risk the exposure of my involvement in something like this. The choice is yours."

"Why are you doing this, Dukon? You're a superstar! Your worshipful paparazzi beg to join your team. You don't need me."

"You are exactly what I need. You have a brilliant mind, you churn out product like a machine, and you understand the Native American condition. All you have to do is keep doing what you do so well... and... handle this one little loose end...."

Hunter sat back down and put his head in his hands. After some time, he looked up and asked in a defeated tone, "Who is the woman?"

Dukon smiled.

"Her name is Breeze Whitecloud."

Hunter felt as if he had been kicked in the gut. He could not move or breathe. After several moments, he drew in a breath and swallowed. He looked at Dukon from under his brow.

"I don't believe you. You're married. Breeze would never– "

"Oh no?" Dukon snorted. Take a look at my little collection. Dukon removed several photographs from the envelope, and Hunter's mouth went dry. He could only look at them with his face half-averted, desperately trying to hide his pain.

No! Not Breeze! I don't believe it!

Hunter numbly glimpsed the cheesecake shots of her in various poses, very sparingly draped in provocatively diaphanous attire. In one photo, Dukon was half-naked with her. If Hunter hadn't seen the photos with his own eyes, and if Dukon weren't so obviously a babe magnet with his looks, his money, and his power, he would never have believed him.

Hunter got up from his chair and crossed the room, turning his back to Dukon. He said, "I find it hard to believe that Breeze would betray Sequoia. They were best friends."

Dukon wondered if he had been wrong about Hunter hating *everyone* in the tribe.

Hmm, if there is any chance that Breeze is an exception, I need to fix that...

"Well, she did betray her. Haven't you heard Sequoia complain that Breeze does not return her calls or emails? Why do you think that is?" Dukon sneered, "Breeze said that I was the first *real man* to set foot on the reservation and that the other women agree. I'm not surprised that they find Aspen and company a bit wimpy, but I was disappointed that she didn't think too highly of you either. I asked her – what about Hunter? I was frankly shocked at her harsh words. She said that you were... from a trashy, disreputable family... that you lacked class... and that you have a slut for a sister who got pregnant being easy with the boys."

To add something different to the emotional mix, Dukon added, "But Breeze *really* surprised me when she said she's pretty sure that you're gay. I hadn't sensed that, although I never do see or hear about you with any women. Breeze said that she, and other people in the tribe, thought that maybe you... had feelings for me. Are you gay, Hunter? That could actually help me to secure votes from the homosexual population and others, especially young voters."

Hunter turned and glared at Dukon, shaking his head at the suggestion that he might have feelings for a man whom he did not even like. He turned his back to Dukon again and thought,

It would be nobody's business if I were gay. I don't care what people think, and I wouldn't dignify any small-minded prejudices with an answer. But I wonder why Breeze thinks that?

The other words that Breeze used to describe him and his family would not stop echoing in his ears. Those aspersions started dredging up all the old feelings of shame.

"trashy... disreputable family... lack of class..."

Hunter's emotions dissolved into a feeling of total wretchedness. His shoulders sank. Deeply suppressed memories of pain and humiliation that he had worked hard to keep buried, resurfaced and began replaying over and over in his mind. He began to viscerally re-experience the burning degradation and mortification that had dominated his entire youth. Brutally assailed anew by the overwhelming shame and pain, Hunter felt increasingly and powerfully suffused with his old partner – *rage.*

He could not get Breeze's words out of his head.

"...a slut for a sister..." *My sister is no slut! A slut for a sister?!*

Dukon smiled as he watched Hunter's body language showing him becoming more and more agitated.

There, that should have erased any sentimental feelings he might have had.

He continued talking to Hunter's back.

"With the depressed economy, scientific research funding is harder to get than ever. So Breeze is blackmailing me for what she thought would be easy money. She could destroy our once-in-a-lifetime chance. The method will be up to you, but you must be totally discreet. I don't want to know any details – just that it has been done."

Now brimming with fury and resentment, Hunter turned around. His eyes were dark, and his face was filled with rage.

"Where is she?" he snarled.

CHAPTER TWENTY-SEVEN
Breeze in the Field

During the first two years of Breeze's graduate program in Energy Resource Science, she had done fieldwork with various professors. Those experiences helped her to focus her interests and to begin applying for grants to fund her thesis research. The field trips and long hours writing grant applications had left her little time for a social life. She was so busy that she was hardly even in touch with people back home. There were some issues that she had wanted to discuss with Aspen, but she had put them on the back burner while churning out the grant applications by their deadlines. Because of all her field trips, she arranged for her mail to be held at the post office. She usually only got junk mail anyway, so she rarely bothered to collect it.

Breeze's grant-writing efforts did not go unrewarded. She scored a small grant to work for a Principal Investigator at a remote, isolated location with a small team of researchers and cutting-edge equipment. Breeze was overjoyed at her good fortune. Out in the field, the work was slow and tedious, but the hypotheses they were testing were revolutionary. Breeze made a small but valuable discovery, and the Principal Investigator asked her to write a paper on it to submit to a scientific journal. This meant that Breeze's name might gain recognition in her field already! This kept her immersed and engaged, and time passed quickly.

Eventually, she came up for air and realized that months had passed. She asked her colleagues when they might be returning to civilization where there would at least be a cell tower or access to the Internet so they could communicate with the outside world. No one knew exactly when that would be. A truck arrived weekly, bringing supplies to the outpost, and Breeze always asked the driver if he had a radio or other means of communication she could use. They all only had cell phones, which didn't work out there.

Having been out of touch with the outside world for so long, Breeze felt that she had to reconnect with family and friends. She felt as far removed as if she had gone to the moon! So, she asked the next supply truck driver to take her back to civilization with him. She accompanied him on his long trip to Eastwood that evening, but Breeze never made it to the town.

The supply trucks never brought any newspapers, so during the trip, Breeze asked what was going on in the world. The driver gave her a couple of updates from the sports world, and that was the extent of their conversation. Eventually, Breeze noticed a corner of newspaper jutting up behind her seat. She asked the driver if she could pull it out for something to read. He told her to knock herself out.

Well, the news almost did knock her out! This old issue glowingly described the Chief of a new organization representing all U.S. native tribes. He was being eyed for a Presidential run in the near future. It said that he was previously Chief of the Ronopo Tribe! Chief... *Golden Hawk?!* Breeze thought this had to be a joke. But no, it appeared to be the real news!

He was elected Chief of my tribe?! And no one told me? I didn't even know there was an election! Oh... maybe they sent me a notice by snail mail, which I haven't checked lately. And I haven't been in touch with anyone for so long! I hope Chief Bridgewater didn't pass on! How long have I been away?! WAIT. What is THIS? His wife... Sequoia Starfire...?!

Breeze dropped the newspaper, completely in shock. She wasn't sure which was the worst piece of news. She turned her head towards her door and stared sightlessly out into the night.

I MUST talk to Sequoia right away! Oh, why didn't I contact Aspen while writing my grants?! I've been so absorbed with my research that I've missed so much! I have to tell them what I discovered on the reservation and what my analysis suggests! I'm not sure what it all means, but I have a feeling that it's important and that some of it might not be good....

The driver noticed Breeze's agitation. He kept glancing at her, wondering what was up. As he looked, he observed different things about her. Her soft-looking, deep-tan skin. Her pretty hair. Her lips. Her curves. They were now far from the research outpost, out in the middle of nowhere. The driver pulled over by the side of the road, shifted the gear into Park and killed the engine. Giving Breeze a once-over with his eyes, he said, "Such a sweet young thing you are." He grabbed hold of her left arm and leaned over to put his drooling mouth on hers.

Even through the fog of shock, Breeze instinctively leaned away from the man while rotating her left arm out of his grasp. She used her right hand to release her seatbelt buckle, then flung that arm back and opened her door. Holding onto its handle and pushing off with her feet, she launched herself backwards, headfirst, out the open door. She drew her knees into her chest and forcefully kicked out her left leg. Her hiking boot landed a solid blow in the driver's face. He fell back, howling with pain and anger. Breeze energetically retracted her leg as she had been taught in martial arts class. As she fell out of the truck, she pulled her legs up and over herself while maintaining a loose grip on the door handle. Completing the somersault, she let go of the door and had a rough landing – partly on her feet and partly on her rump. She reached in and snatched her gear pack from the footwell. Leaving her door open for the driver to deal with, she took off at top speed, shouldering the backpack as she ran.

"You'll never survive out here, you little BITCH!" the truck driver screamed, dabbing at his bleeding nose with a paper towel.

Breeze actually did know the basics of how to survive in the wilderness. Anyway, she figured that her chances were better in the wild than they were in that truck.

Fortunately, she had her gear pack. She kept running in a line perpendicular to the road, her way lit faintly by moonlight. She ran until the truck was long since out of sight.

Keeping her eyes in the direction of the road, she leaned forward with her hands on her knees. She gulped in air and rested her legs as her adrenaline slowed its flow. She mentally patted herself on the back for staying in shape out in the field, having jogged a few days per week. She also silently thanked Hanshi B, her martial arts master, for having instructed her so well in self-defense.

She heard an engine turn over in the distance, and she glimpsed the truck's tail lights moving away and disappearing into the night. As her breathing returned to normal, she scoped out the vicinity with her flashlight. She knew she was still far from civilization, but she checked her mobile phone just in case she had service here. No such luck. As expected, neither did her laptop pick up any wireless Internet connectivity. She moved closer to the road to set up camp for the night where she would be able to hear any cars that she could try to flag down. She wasn't worried about the truck driver, as she thought it unlikely that he would return.

She pulled a thin package out of her gear pack and tore it open. The blanket inside expanded as it was released from its vacuum state. She shook it out and laid it on the ground. Sitting down, she took her 9mm pistol out of its pocket holster inside her gear pack. She hadn't fired it in a while, but considering her vulnerable situation, she didn't think this was a good time to field strip it. She decided to just run a cursory function check. She eyeballed the vicinity again and saw no threat, so she released the loaded magazine into her lap. She flipped down the safety, and in one quick motion, pulled back the slide, putting the gun into slide-lock. The round in the chamber ejected, and she snatched it in midair. She set down the empty gun and reinserted the round into the magazine in her lap. She used her flashlight to inspect the pistol's barrel and chamber for any obstructions (not from the muzzle end, of course.) After checking the empty grip as well, she pushed the loaded magazine back into the gun, giving the mag a tug to be sure it was properly seated. She chambered a round and thumbed the safety back on. Then, she pulled two more loaded magazines from her gear pack. She tucked them into a pocket of her cutoff jeans shorts, positioning them for accessibility if she needed to reload her gun under pressure.

Breeze knew that she probably had a very long walk ahead of her. She would keep to the road; but if no cars came along, it could possibly take her days to reach a town. There were little intersecting roads that snaked off into the distance here and there, but she had no idea how often people traveled any of them. A supply truck would go back to the outpost this way but not for a whole week, and her water bottle would not last more than a day or two.

I must make sure that certain information gets to Aspen – no matter what happens to me.

She figured out what she needed to get into Aspen's hands and how to get it to him. It was tricky, and Breeze was limited as to what she could do. It took some time, but she finally finished setting it up, using her laptop. It had been a stressful day, and

Breeze was tired. Although it was early, she thought she should get some sleep before starting out on her trek.

Gazing up at the stars, she oriented herself. It was a clear night, so her only concerns were adequate warmth and predators. She set out her "watch-wolf," a small mechanical device that she had engineered back at the tribal college. Like a watchdog, it would emit a sound that would wake and warn her if any object of significant mass approached. She then unfolded a thin, metallic sheet designed to keep astronauts warm. When folded, it was more compact than a deck of cards. She wrapped it around herself and lay down on her blanket, using her gear pack as a pillow. With her "watch-wolf" and her pistol by her side, Breeze felt that she could safely sleep. Fatigue overtook her, and she drifted off.

CHAPTER TWENTY-EIGHT
Peeping Tom

Rob continued to stalk Breeze via the drone's camera whenever he wasn't working a mission. He was supposed to continue training, so he rationalized that following her was justified. He shadowed her to her research outposts and enjoyed spying on her. There were so few people at the outposts that he almost felt like he was alone with her. Of course, he was actually miles away in a secret, hidden control center, operating the drone by remote control. It was good practice, because some locations provided little cover for the drone, and he had to be creative to camouflage it.

Rob was watching by drone when Breeze left the research outpost with the supply truck driver. He had zoomed in enough to see that the driver tried to assault her. The drone wasn't armed, but he had thought about ramming the truck with it! Then he regained his senses, remembering the astronomical cost of the drone. Anyway, he saw that Breeze had gotten away. Using the infrared night-vision settings, he watched her set up camp by herself. He took note when she cleared and reloaded a pistol, displaying training and adherence to safe gun practices.

What a woman!

Peeper-creeper that he was, Rob thoroughly enjoyed using the night vision lenses to watch Breeze pull down her shorts and underwear when she needed to relieve herself. She thought she was alone in nature, but she actually had a grinning audience.

Rob couldn't watch everything she did since he had to keep moving the drone out of sight and earshot. He did watch her prepare her bed, however, which got him thinking...

Honey's location isn't that long a drive from the drone base camp if I put the pedal to the metal.

He decided to go meet the girl of his photos and dreams – in the flesh! He would be her hero! He was going to rescue her and drive her home. Rob was optimistic that Honey could first be persuaded to show her new boyfriend her gratitude right there at her isolated campsite...

He entered the coordinates of her location into his navigation device and rummaged through the duffel bag he had in his truck. He applied some scented deodorant that he kept alongside a pack of condoms and threw on a few other items from the bag. Then, all geared up, Rob sped off to meet "his girl."

CHAPTER TWENTY-NINE
Night Visitor

Breeze awoke with a start. Her little "watch-wolf" was howling. She saw a human form approaching her in the dark. She grabbed her pistol and yelled,

"Stop right there! I have a gun, and I *will* shoot you!"

"I think you're outgunned, Honey," the man chuckled, his voice sounding muffled as he continued to approach. Breeze was now able to see that he was holding a rifle. He appeared to be dressed all in black, with body armor, a thigh holster bearing a handgun, and a helmet with a tinted face shield – the reason for his muffled voice.

He said, "Stay on your knees and put down your pistol. Then raise your hands high, or *I'll* have to shoot *you*. There's no need for anyone to get hurt. Just do as I say."

Breeze complied, her mind reeling.

"Are you the truck driver? I didn't mean to—"

"Stay on your knees and shuffle away from your pistol. Then turn around so you're facing away from me. Keep your hands in the air."

He let go of his rifle, letting it dangle from its sling, while instantly drawing the pistol from his thigh holster. Clearly, this man was skilled with gun handling.

"*Thatta* girl... Now... put your hands on the ground so you're on all fours like a good little doggie. Remember, I'll shoot you if you make a move I don't like."

Breeze stole a glance over her shoulder and saw the man shift the slung rifle to his back. She didn't see it, but he then re-holstered his pistol. She sensed that he had gotten down on his knees directly behind her and was handling something. A distinctive odor reached her nostrils, and her brain flashed a warning to flee. As she started to make her move, the man grabbed the waistband of her jeans shorts and yanked hard. His other hand groped the front of her in the dark. He found his mark and clamped his hand tightly across her nose and mouth. The cloth in his hand bore the overpowering smell of chloroform. Breeze quickly passed out.

To the now unconscious young woman, the man said,

"Sorry, Honey, but you have to go someplace where it's unlikely that anyone will see what happens to you."

CHAPTER THIRTY
Late to the Party

By the time Rob reached the location of Breeze's encampment, she was gone! *Damn! How did I miss her?*

All of her stuff was gone, too. He ran back to his truck while scanning for her and saw a glow on the ground near the road. It was an open, metallic-colored laptop, glowing in the light of his flashlight. During the day, due to its placement, the sunlight would have reflected off it and easily caught the eye of someone driving by in a car.

Maybe it belongs to Honey!

Rob pressed the power button and it lit up. A message appeared across the screen:

NO SIGNAL - POWER LAPTOP OFF!
POWER ON WHERE INTERNET OR CELL SIGNAL AVAILABLE!
PLEASE HELP! $$$ REWARD INSTRUCTIONS VISIBLE WITH SIGNAL!
PRIVATE: XXX PHOTOS!

Please help? I'd better check if that's for real! And XXX photos? That sounds promising and 'bares' looking at! There might even be a monetary reward to boot!

Per the instructions in the message, Rob powered the laptop back off and placed it in the back of his truck. He didn't see any other items on the ground, so he climbed in and sped back to the control room.

Using the drone, he searched the area around the campsite but did not see Honey. He circled in a larger radius and spotted a rugged SUV speeding through the night. He zoomed in with the drone's camera and saw a man driving, with Honey, apparently asleep, in the back.

Who the hell is this guy, and what is he doing with my sweetheart?!

With the drone, Rob tailed the SUV. It left the road and drove across rough terrain to an isolated expanse of empty, flat ground where a small plane was parked in the middle of nowhere. The man carried Honey onto the plane and returned to his SUV. The plane took off immediately. The SUV got back on the road and headed towards the town of Eastwood. Rob followed the plane, and before he knew it, he was piloting the drone *offshore* over water!

Geez! Good thing I topped off its gas tank earlier!

When the plane finally landed on a small island, Rob circled with the drone.

CHAPTER THIRTY-ONE
Rendezvous with Fate

When Breeze awoke, she was lying on her side. Her wrists and ankles were bound, and her ankle bindings were tied to a metal ring in the floor. She could hear a low thrum. She pulled herself up into a sitting position. She appeared to be in the cargo compartment of a small airplane. There was a man off to the side, watching her. He was dressed all in black, including a ski mask and gloves, and his eyes were hidden behind mirrored sunglasses.

She silently lamented, *So, the incident with a man in black in the night was not a dream!*

She said, "I don't... think... you're the truck driver. What's happening to me?"

The man just shook his head. Later, he approached her, holding a dark hood. He crouched down and pulled it over her head.

Uncharacteristically, Breeze found herself trembling. The man put his hand on her shoulder, squeezed gently, then left his hand there. Breeze was surprised at the comforting gesture but feared that it was sympathy for something terrible that was going to happen to her.

She felt the plane descending. As it landed, the man untied her ankles and pulled her to her feet. Standing on her right, he held her arm which was still bound to her other arm at the wrists. He led his hooded captive towards an exit hatch.

Breeze knew that there was at least one other person with him – the pilot. She figured that if she was going to initiate an escape before the kidnappers were together – it was now or never.

Acting as if she had lost her balance, Breeze jerked her upper body to her left, away from the man, while actually remaining stable on her legs. As expected, she felt the man lean towards her to catch her. Now that *he was* off-balance, with his weight shifted onto one leg, Breeze used her right leg to sweep his weight-bearing leg out from under him. He fell backwards away from her.

The man had good reflexes, though, and as he fell, he grabbed her arm, yanking her down, too. He landed on his back next to a wall of the compartment, and Breeze tumbled on top of him. The back of her head and body slammed into the wall, knocking the wind out of her.

He rolled them away from the wall so that he was on top of her, then quickly shifted so that he was kneeling and straddling her. From this position of control, he pulled on her wrist bindings, raising her upper body. He propped her back against a wall behind her so she was sitting up. Still kneeling, he spanned her lap, pinning her to the floor. They both panted, recovering from the scuffle.

The man still did not speak, and Breeze was still hooded, so she could not see. She knew that he had taken off one of his gloves when she felt him reach up under her shirt. She inhaled sharply as his hand slid up the bare skin of her back. When he reached the clasp of her bra, he slipped his fingers underneath it. After momentarily stroking up and down underneath the clasp, he eased his fingers back out again and continued to walk them up her spine to her neck. He slipped his hand under Breeze's hood, running his fingers through her soft hair and stroking the back of her head. His other hand securely gripped her wrists lest she try to escape again.

Breeze sensed that this man was not molesting her. He seemed, instead, to be *examining* her head and spine for any injury from her impact against the wall.

There was something paradoxical about the intimate juxtaposition of the bodies of the two adversaries. They were recovering from a combative skirmish, yet the man seemed to be taking no advantage of his dominant position.

He removed his hand and put his glove back on.

Breeze wondered, *Am I being kidnapped for ransom? That would make no sense. Neither my family nor my tribe has much money. Could it be related to my recent research discovery? Not likely. Human trafficking?! I hope not!!*

Her thoughts returned to the newspaper article that she had read in the supply truck – and then to her observations in Rattlesnake Canyon that she wished she had relayed to Aspen sooner.

I hope Fox and Aspen received my message and can make sense of it. They should realize that I must be in serious trouble to contact them like that! Hopefully they'll figure it out – and in time to help me!

The plane came to a stop. The man pulled her to her feet again, walked her over to the exit hatch and opened it. Outside the plane, someone firmly grasped her other arm.

"Got her," a second man said.

The man inside let go. After walking her about a hundred yards, this man led her into a building. He pushed her down until she was seated on the floor against a wall. He tied her wrists and ankles to a wooden column beside her. He reached under her hood and stuffed a gag in her mouth. He tied it on and walked a couple of paces away.

Breeze jumped at the loud report of a gun. She felt a searing pain and frantically tried to break free – but her efforts were futile.

One more shot was fired and Breeze stopped struggling.

CHAPTER THIRTY-TWO
Helpless

By way of the drone's systems, Rob watched with helpless disbelief at what took place on the island. Through the windows of the building, he witnessed the entire scene of the shooting and then the dumping of Honey's body offshore, rolled up in a rug! He had even seen one of her delicate arms dangling from it.

He hadn't been recording, because he shouldn't have even been there, and he certainly didn't want photographic evidence of him stalking a young woman.

Rob watched numbly as the small plane left the island. Horrified and grieving, Rob did not follow. He returned the drone to the base and went home, trembling with emotion, not knowing what to do.

Rob tried to sleep, but he tossed and turned, dozing and having nightmares. He awoke with a start, remembering the laptop that he had found near Honey's campsite. He retrieved it from his truck. According to the instructions he had seen on the laptop, it should function now since he had both wireless Internet and cell phone service here.

He lifted the lid and pressed the button to power it on. The screen lit up with a flash of brilliant light but immediately went dark again. The laptop was silent, seeming to be off again. Rob saw threads of smoke rise out of its side, and he smelled something burning. He pushed the power button again and again, but nothing happened. The unit was clearly fried.

Rob's hopes were dashed for finding clues about what had happened to Honey. He also regretted not seeing the XXX photos. Agitated and confused, he lay back down on his bed and looked sadly at the sexy pictures of Honey on his wall.

CHAPTER THIRTY-THREE
Dropped Signal

Sequoia was back on the reservation for a dedication ceremony for "The Lodge," the completed safe haven for battered women that she had initiated when Dukon was Ronopo Chief. The next morning, she met up with Aspen for a very early breakfast before leaving the reservation to go back to D.C.

"Aspen, have you been in touch with Breeze at all? I haven't been able to reach her for so long! I can't believe I got *married* and she wasn't there! Do you... know something that I don't know? Or can you just tell me if you're not concerned? If that's the case, then I won't worry."

"Um, it's uncanny timing for you to ask that, but... Breeze... is off the grid," Aspen said tentatively.

"I know that her work takes her out in the field where there are no phones or Internet, but– "

"I don't mean *that* grid. I mean she's off *our* grid," Aspen said gravely.

Sequoia's face showed alarm. "Do you mean... she's on duty?" she asked hopefully.

Aspen shook his head.

"Are you telling me... Doesn't Fox have her?"

Aspen bit his lower lip and shook his head again, a deep furrow of worry between his brows.

"How long?" Sequoia whispered.

"She's been off the grid for less than 12 hours, but we only realized it a couple of hours ago. Fox was out prowling the nightclub scene off-reservation yesterday evening and didn't notice until he got back. He received an unidentified *Smoke Signals* message in the middle of the night which he thinks must be from Breeze. We're about to meet with members of SIGNAL from the other tribes in our region. If you can postpone your return to D.C., let's head over, and I'll fill you in. Fox is sending the *Smoke Signals* as we speak."

CHAPTER THIRTY-FOUR
Brain Storm

"Are we all here?" Aspen asked. He looked around the main room of the big hunting cabin in the northwest quadrant of the reservation.

Fox nodded to him. The call had been answered by *every* operative from the member tribes in that regional territory of SIGNAL – the Security & Intelligence Guard of Native American Lineage.

"Thank you all for responding, and so quickly despite the early hour. As you may have heard when you got here, Breeze Whitecloud *went off the grid* last night. We all know how serious that could be. But until we have irrefutable evidence that Breeze is... really gone... we are going to operate under the assumption that she is alive, that somehow her life-signs tracer is being blocked or malfunctioning, or that she may need help. We all know the statistics of how little time we have to find her, and alive, if there actually is foul play involved."

Aspen paused, obviously affected by his own words.

"We've already investigated recent locations where Breeze's transmitter was still active. A truck driver was giving her a ride from an isolated research outpost to the closest town. Apparently, Breeze left his truck en route after a negative interaction between her and the driver. Our evaluation suggests that the driver was not involved in her disappearance after she left his truck. Fox, please share what you've got with the group."

Fox stepped forward. "A number of hours ago, we received a message via my *Smoke Signals* app. It is likely that it was from Breeze, although it did not have her identifier. The message did not originate from her cell phone – nor from any phone. I have never yet found that anyone else could tap into *Smoke Signals,* nor have I ever received random communications. Since all other members of SIGNAL have been accounted for, everything points to this being from Breeze – even though it came *after* her life-signs tracer stopped transmitting. Proceeding under the assumption that it is from her, we need to figure out the meaning of her message."

"C'mon Fox!" Birdie exhorted. "You're the genius who works for the American Security Office! I bet you've never met a code you couldn't crack!"

"I'm really not a code-cracker for the ASO. I've done decoding, but only to inform my electronic systems design."

Readdressing the group, Fox continued,

"You all know how the *Smoke Signals* app works; a message is sent in bursts of one, two, or three characters at a time, using the encoding system you've all learned.

There is a message, but it's unclear. Since the Ronopo team knows Breeze well, we will continue to work on decoding it. If necessary, we will forward it to you to analyze, as well. Separately, we've been monitoring the activity of a *drone* that we picked up over our reservation some time ago. It is possibly related to Breeze's disappearance."

Aspen picked back up from Fox. "What I need from all of you is to exploit all networks and channels of information at your disposal, local and worldwide, for any chatter possibly relevant to Breeze's disappearance. Only communicate with other SIGNAL operatives via *Smoke Signals*. Report to Fox anything that might be even remotely related. I also need you to be on standby for a blitz to search for Breeze or to investigate drone ownership or other leads. Make sure all your gear is in top working order and that you are ready to make a sudden departure for an indefinite period of time. I have briefed my counterparts, the Commanders of the other SIGNAL regions. That's all I have for you now."

As the group stood up to go, Aspen gestured towards someone and called out, "Kiwi! May I have a word with you?"

Jon Kiwideekon was a tall, strapping young man of the Mihote (mee-HO-tay) Tribe, whose reservation was adjacent to the Ronopo Reservation.

He and Aspen performed a ritual hand greeting that they had devised as kids.

"I'm betting that I'm going to need you here in the village for bodyguard duty while some of us depart to search for Breeze," Aspen said. "Can you stay at my place tonight and possibly longer? If so, I'll fill you in when I get back there later tonight."

"You got it, Commander," Kiwi said with a nod of his clean-shaven head. He strode from the cabin with sparkling eyes and a hint of a smile, because a request from Aspen always heralded some kind of adventure.

After the other members of SIGNAL from nearby tribes had dispersed, Aspen, Fox, Birdie and Sequoia remained in the cabin.

Fox said, "There is no intelligible message using the standard code. The way the message appeared was:

DC RCM CZD C8

"Remember, this message seems to have *not* come from a cell phone. So, depending on what kind of apparatus Breeze – or whoever – used for sending it, there may have been constraints on how *long* a message they could send. In *Smoke Signals*, we can only send clusters of one, two, or three characters, but there is no limit to how many clusters can be sent. If this sender was limited to a certain total length, then the breaks between these groupings of letters could be arbitrary. If we assume that the spaces are not in the right places and run it all together, it looks like this:

DCRCMCZDC8

"At a glance, a word jumps out at me. How about the rest of you?"

"Circumcised?" Birdie chirped.

"Right. If we separate that out, the message then looks like this:

D CRCMCZD C8

"An obvious possibility would be that the sender is referring to someone who is circumcised. But it's hard to think of a context in which that would have significance. So let's keep looking for other possible meanings of the message."

Aspen noted, "Barring some minority groups, most American guys are circumcised, as are Yotish and Moscken guys almost everywhere. Sadly, it could refer to a female, but odds are that the reference would be to a male – if this is even about circumcision at all."

Birdie said, "Well, who do we know whose name starts with D? There's: Duane Yazzie, Dakirhan Isshak, Donni Good Iron..."

Sequoia said, "The way the letters were originally grouped, 'D.C.' could refer to Washington, D.C. – or it could represent my husband, Dukon Chatan. Those are his initials..."

The others looked at Sequoia, waiting to hear her verdict on that possibility, but Sequoia was now looking blankly off into space.

Aspen said, "Um, obviously that would be improbable, since we Ronopo don't do that. Most native peoples don't cut. Since Dukon was born and grew up in an isolated canyon, it would be even less likely for him." He gestured to Sequoia. "Mrs. Chatan? You're the one who can tell us for sure."

Sequoia's eyes had glazed over. Realization upon realization were dawning upon her, and she put her head in her hands. Aspen crossed to her chair and crouched down, putting his arm around her.

"I'm so sorry, Sequoia. I didn't stop to think what a private question that was to ask a woman about her husband."

"It's not that. It's just... How could I be so dense?!" she moaned. She looked up at the group. "Believe it or not, even though I'm married to the man, *I don't know* whether he is circumcised or not! But if he is and were *hiding* it from me, that would explain so much! It has always worked out such that I have never actually seen... I mean, he never walks around naked... and he never wants me to... Oh this is so embarrassing!"

"It's okay," Aspen said soothingly, giving her a hug. "Its *us*. You know that none of this will leave this room. We just need to find Breeze. If there is anything relevant here, then we need to know it. If it turns out not to be relevant, each one of us will wipe what you've told us from our minds. Okay, Dearest One?"

Sequoia nodded, feeling stronger.

"We have separate bedrooms. He says this is to give me the privacy a woman needs, but it's *his* room that is always locked. We have separate bathrooms as well."

Aspen said, "The day we rescued him from the canyon, I was lowered into the gorge to put him in the harness and send him up to the chopper. When I got down there, he was wearing a traditional breech-cloth that wasn't holding together so well, but his privates were covered, so I wouldn't have been able to tell."

Fox interjected, "We don't know that Dukon is circumcised; but if he is, the implications could be *colossal*. If he actually *isn't* Ronopo, then what the heck is he?"

Birdie suggested, "Maybe his mother was not Ronopo and she required it?"

Fox and Aspen said in unison, "No Ronopo man would let his son be circumcised.

Aspen added, "Medical studies do now document important health benefits of male circumcision that affect a man and his sexual partners; but those medical studies had not yet been published when Dukon was young."

Birdie asked, "How can you question Dukon's heritage? His lineage was confirmed in the Official Register."

"Yes, but look who confirmed it!" Fox said dolefully. "It was *Hunter,* and it wasn't right away. It was after the two of them became friendly. If we really go down the rabbit hole, Hunter has a degree in Chemistry. If it were necessary to alter the Official Register to *add* Dukon's family into it, and in a way that would make it look like old entries, Hunter would probably know how to do it. Now, they have risen together like a pair of superstars! But... despite Hunter's issues, it's hard to believe that he would perpetrate such a profound and consequential lie."

"Hunter may have been manipulated," Aspen said. "Considering that Dukon may attain the Presidency of the United States, this could be something *much bigger.* This could be... a conspiracy."

The room was silent as they ruminated over the possibilities.

Fox said, "If Dukon *is* circumcised, Breeze might have been... 'disappeared'... *because she knew.* I don't know how she would have known, unless she and Dukon were in a relationship, perhaps at university. This would also lend weight to the threat to her that we've been trying to chase down."

"What kind of threat?" Birdie asked.

"The drone that we mentioned at the meeting seemed to be monitoring Breeze's activity on a number of occasions. We figured it was likely just some pervert stalking her from afar. We thought it might have found her while planning to do target practice in the canyon – because that first time, it was *armed,*" Fox said gravely.

Birdie gawked at Fox. "An *armed* drone? It's bad enough to have an unarmed one watching you!"

"I know," Fox agreed. "There are so darned many law enforcement, commercial, and personal drones buzzing around nowadays. It's impossible to tell which ones are harmless, which ones are *merely* abrogating citizens' right to privacy in the name of unconstrained capitalism – *or voyeurism* – and which could be life-threatening! All it takes is money, so once drones were allowed, it became a piece of cake for evil-doers to start doing their evil.

"We have to find her," Sequoia whispered. "Maybe it's not too late."

"We need to talk to Hunter," Aspen asserted. "Other than you, Sequoia, he's our only high-level connection – except for SIGNAL Headquarters. And they have nothing for us on this. I think we have to gamble and let Hunter know that we're looking for

Breeze. If that message was about Dukon, Hunter may be involved and may know where Breeze is."

Sequoia said, "Actually, Hunter has not been himself lately. He does seem to be agitated about something."

Aspen looked pensive. "When we were working with Hunter in the final months before he joined Dukon in Washington, it seemed like he was changing – softening towards us. We all know that Breeze has been in love with Blaze – that is, Hunter, forever, but he never reciprocated. He didn't want to have much to do with any of us. It was unfortunate. And I had really wanted to recruit him for SIGNAL."

Fox admonished, "None of us can contact Hunter directly as his communications are almost certainly being monitored. Even you, Sequoia, would be unable to contact him cleanly. I think I need to send him a *Smoke Signal*."

The group looked quizzically at Fox.

"I know. He's not one of us and doesn't know about the app. Even so, I have a feeling that if I send a symbolic, pictorial *Smoke Signal* to Hunter's phone, even with no traceable phone number or other information, that he will figure it out and will come here. That guy has the most exceptional mind I've ever encountered. We've got quite a brain trust going here with the rest of us, so I mean *brilliant*. Since I feel certain that my *Smoke Signals* app is completely hack-proof, I think it's safe. If he doesn't figure it out, it'll be meaningless to him or anyone else. I'll make sure all traces of it disappear after he sees it."

Fox looked at Aspen. "Are you okay with this?"

Aspen nodded.

Birdie asked, "What about the remaining characters in Breeze's message, the C8? That sounds like a seat number or an apartment number."

"Apartment number..." Sequoia repeated. "C8 could be the number of a bungalow here in The Lodge complex for battered women."

She pulled out a notebook and leafed through her listing for the complex. Then she gasped and looked up at the others.

"Bungalow C8 is where Hunter's sister, Rozzi, lives."

CHAPTER THIRTY-FIVE
Secrets

Rozzi was always up early in the morning because of all she needed to do for her special needs child. Sequoia was politely noisy as she neared Bungalow C8, so Rozzi would be aware that someone was approaching. She waited a ways away from the door. She could tell that someone was looking through the peephole, and then the door opened.

"Sequoia!" Hunter's sister exclaimed, seeming oddly nervous. "It's... it's good to see you."

"It's good to see you too, Rozzi."

"Please, come in."

"How is your daughter?"

"Anata's all right, thank you. Would you like a drink of water?"

"Yes, thank you – if it's not too much trouble."

Rozzi brought two mugs of water. She was visibly trembling.

"I think I know why you are here, but I hope it is not what I fear most."

"What are you thinking?"

"That... something has happened to my brother."

"Oh! No, Rozzi, it isn't that, but Hunter *has* seemed troubled lately. Are you worried about something in particular?"

Rozzi looked down and didn't say anything.

"Rozzi, you and Hunter and I are clan cousins through the clan of our mothers. You can tell me what it is. I would always keep in confidence anything that you asked me to. Maybe I can help."

Rozzi looked at Sequoia with desperation.

"Oh Sequoia, Hunter called me recently – not from his own phone. He was more agitated than I have *ever* known him to be. He gave me the number of a bank account and said that he put it in both his name and mine. He said that if anything happened to him, the money in the account was for me and Anata. Hunter has already been very generous to me over the years, even when he didn't have much. Then, once he became well-off, he gave me enough money to pay for many things that help with my daughter's special needs. But those words of his have me terribly worried."

"Those *are* worrisome words. I promise that I will tell you if I learn of anything that could be related, okay?"

Rozzi nodded.

"The reason I am here is because Breeze Whitecloud is *missing*. She was last seen leaving a research site out in the wilderness."

"Oh no! That's terrible!"

"We're looking for any information that could indicate where she might be. Have you had any contact with her recently?"

"No, not recently. But back when she returned to college for her final year, she saw me on her way out of the village. She gave me something and asked me to keep it hidden for her. She said that if she did not come back for it, that I would know when was the right time to give it to Fox, Aspen, or you. I guess this is that time!"

"Yes!" Sequoia breathed hopefully. "What is it?"

"I don't know. It's in a sealed package with Fox's name on it. I'll get it for you. But... if you didn't know about it, what made you come to see me?"

"Breeze sent an enigmatic message to Fox, containing your bungalow number. I'm surprised she knew it though, since she left the reservation before we even built this complex."

"Oh, because of what I had of hers, I made a Harvest Celebration card and sent it to her after I moved into this wonderful haven. I didn't mention the item in it, I just sent her best wishes and this new address so she would know I was still here."

"Good for you and for your discretion, Rozzi. We're afraid that someone may be holding Breeze against her will... if not something worse. And... we're actually hoping that Hunter doesn't have anything to do with it."

"Well, let's hope that he does! Hunter would never let anyone hurt a hair on Breeze's head!"

"Why do you say that?" Sequoia asked with surprise.

"Oh, Sequoia. Today, I am giving away secrets entrusted to me. But this may be important for you to know, too. Hunter has *always* loved Breeze, and I mean *always* – since they were children. But he has invariably had reason to believe that she loved someone else. I can't imagine what could change his feelings for her; so, barring something unimaginable, I would think he still feels that way now."

Sequoia mentally processed this while Rozzi retrieved the package.

Poor Hunter and Breeze! All this time! And Rozzi's right. If Breeze's disappearance is due to a threat to her, and if Hunter still has feelings for her, it would likely be a good thing if he were involved!

Sequoia warned Rozzi not to communicate with Hunter for a while, since Fox believed that Hunter's phones and email were probably being monitored. Sequoia then sped back to the hunting cabin with Rozzi's permission to share their conversation with Aspen, Fox, and Birdie only.

Fox carefully opened the package. The group was pumped to find a *flash drive* inside. Fox plugged it into his laptop and eagerly accessed the files on it. They saw spreadsheets giving dates, locations, and rock compositions. There was an entry with geological data from Rattlesnake Canyon on the date of Dukon's rescue.

But was that it? The friends' shoulders sank.

Only Fox looked hopeful. He produced a gold-colored, oblong object from one of the many pockets in his cargo shorts. His friends watched with curiosity as he snapped this unusual gizmo onto Breeze's flash drive. He tapped away at the keyboard on his laptop. Then he waved his hand with a flourish as names of files and thumbnails of images filled the screen and kept on rolling.

"Did that data come from your flash drive or whatever that thing is?" Birdie asked.

"Nope," Fox replied smugly. "You have all just witnessed the effect of my *cloaking device.* It was a project of mine while studying electronics at the tribal college. I call it 'Buffalo Cloak.' I taught Breeze how to work it, and I'm pumped to see that she put it to good use. Without the key provided on a second device, like this gold one, any data that has been cloaked by my program will be completely invisible, inaccessible, and uncatalogued in the computer or flash drive directories."

Grinning and shaking his head, Aspen clapped Fox on the back, and the friends reviewed the files and images with high hopes. The data did not give any insight as to where Breeze might be, but the images confirmed, without any doubt, that Dukon was circumcised. The cutting-edge binoculars Breeze had been using at Rattlesnake Canyon had been able to capture *and record* a remarkable level of detail. The friends could see that Dukon had been stark naked when Breeze discovered him; so he must have donned the breech-cloth as the Search and Rescue chopper approached.

The binoculars had also recorded some strange and alarming images from the canyon that were only visible after Fox magnified them. The friends wondered if Breeze had another copy of this data or if she'd even had a chance to review and analyze it. If she hadn't, she might not have been aware of the other revelations and their possible implications.

So Breeze's message *had* been alerting them to the very un-Ronopo condition of Dukon's genitalia. The reason for her disclosure remained uncertain, but her coincident disappearance lent weight to its significance. Furthermore, Dukon's current pursuit of the U.S. Presidency provided *urgency* to ascertaining his true cultural heritage.

CHAPTER THIRTY-SIX
Smoke Signals

It was early morning, and Hunter Wolf stood in his office at the new, tribal organization in Washington, D.C. He was facing the picture window but seeing nothing. His brilliant mind should have been working on a host of tribal issues, but all he could think about was what he had done to Breeze. His thoughts were interrupted by strange sounds coming softly from his cell phone. It sounded like the rhythmic beating of drums! Even the phone's vibrations felt rhythmic! This was certainly not a ringtone or notification alert that he had loaded into his phone! There was a message, but it had no phone number.

That's strange, he thought.

He opened the message. There were no words, but there was a cartoon image of a cabin in a landscape scene. Animated orange, red, and yellow flashes that looked like fire appeared at the bottom of the screen. Small, gray shapes rose up from the fire and dissipated when they reached the top.

Hunter looked up, his mind churning. He looked back at the phone and saw several more shapes rise and fade away, leaving only the background scene. Then, a cartoon image of a fox appeared. It padded towards the cabin, stopped, and looked back at Hunter. It nodded then turned and continued on to the cabin door. The screen on Hunter's phone went blank. He checked the message history, but there was no record of the message at all.

Were those supposed to be... smoke signals? And a fox... hmm...

Hunter sat down on his office couch. The organization he worked for represented all U.S. native tribes. Smoke signals in a natural landscape scene could be characteristic of many of them. Did the fox symbolize wildlife in general? Or was this something closer to home? He put his head in his hands, closed his eyes, and opened his mind. He reached way back and grabbed hold of a memory from when he was twelve years old.

There was a lot of smoke coming from the dense grove of trees way off in the northwest quadrant of the reservation. He thought that the hunting cabin might be on fire, so he went to investigate. Approaching with caution, he found Fox Bridgewater using an animal-hide to cover and uncover a fading campfire, creating puffs of smoke in different shapes. Fox saw him and called out,

"Hey Hunter! Look! I'm making smoke signals! Wanna try it?"

Hunter started walking towards him, but just then, Aspen and Breeze came running from behind the cabin up the hill, yelping and laughing together. Hunter turned and ran away.

Hunter massaged his forehead, trying to banish the wave of emotions that had come with the memory. *Okay... Fox had a thing for smoke signals. He is now an electronics genius. There is no way he should have this phone number... but he is now an electronics genius. One of the graphics did look like the northwest hunting cabin on the reservation... But why? If Fox Bridgewater wanted to talk to me, why wouldn't he just call or send a regular text message? Oh... right. Phones here, including my cell phone, are likely being monitored. This must be really serious. Oh brother... I sure hope it isn't about Breeze's disappearance...*

Hunter left a note for his secretary, saying that something had come up and to please reschedule his appointments. Now that he was officially the Campaign Manager and Chief Advisor for a Presidential candidate, the Secret Service had assigned him a bodyguard. With a wolfish grin and a wink, Hunter told his bodyguard that he was off to a meeting with a woman and would not be needing him for a while. The bodyguard responded in kind with a wolfish grin and a thumbs up and stayed where he was.

The messenger bag Hunter was carrying contained some of the spare clothing he kept in his office. In a basement-level locker room, Hunter changed into jeans, a black T-shirt, and hiking boots. He put on his sunglasses, slung a leather jacket over one shoulder, and covered his longish hair with a cap of a local sports team.

There was some public controversy regarding the names of sports teams that referred to American Indians. Hunter understood why some American Indians felt that the names were disparaging while others did not and used those names for their own sports teams.

Hunter worried that, what *looked like* support for eradicating negative ethnic references, might actually be a camouflaged *exploitation* of American Indians to further the agendas of others, including driving a wedge between ethnic groups instead of fostering their peaceful coexistence.

Some minority groups garnered a lot of attention through their high-profile politicians, professional athletes, or entertainers. American Indians had those too but tended to leave a lighter footprint in so many ways. Some people might be only too happy to eliminate *all* high-visibility symbols of enduring ties to the *first* U.S. minority people, allowing other minorities to take precedence instead.

Certain special interest groups had recently been *very* well-organized to dominate the limelight and legislative attention, allowing critical issues of America's first minority citizens to be further marginalized. Now, savvy organizers were using the media and influencing politicians to favor *foreigners* over minority *citizens!* This was of justifiable concern for all Americans, and was especially worrisome for minority citizens – who would be the most adversely impacted.

Therefore, Hunter felt that if the highly publicized names of popular sports teams kept American Indians in the hearts and minds of America and beyond – despite possible efforts of other minorities' supporters to eclipse them – then that, at least, was a good thing.

Attired as he was, and with his buff build, Hunter looked more like a bodyguard than a bureaucrat. Trying to keep a low profile, he left the building through a service exit. He then grabbed a cab to a small, private airfield. He had brought lots of cash with him, so with a generous tip displayed, an available pilot with a "jet taxi" was happy to oblige his request.

CHAPTER THIRTY-SEVEN
Leap of Faith

To hide his true itinerary, Hunter took the "jet taxi" *most* of the distance but to an airport not close to the Ronopo Reservation. En route, he stuffed his cap into his jacket, since he did not want to advertise where he had just come from. He then took a prop plane to an airstrip near the reservation.

Now he was in really low-income country. Here, it would be even easier to pay his way with cash and no questions asked. He was glad to give work to the American Indian taxi driver who had no customers in sight nor likely to be coming. He had the driver take back roads and drop him about two miles from the hunting cabin in the northwest quadrant. That was where he expected to find Fox, and he didn't want to risk being seen by going through the village.

Hunter placed a generous payment on the console beside the driver and got out. He briskly walked the two miles to the hunting cabin, enjoying it immensely and finding his heart beating faster as he approached the familiar territory. He thought of how Dukon had described the reservation as "dreary." Despite Hunter's painful history there, he disagreed. He thought this landscape represented true beauty. The clean air, the quiet, and the purity beat the D.C. racket and stench any day.

Hunter looked ahead and saw smoke. Smoke *signals* to be exact. He nodded with satisfaction that he had been right.

There was no one near the smoldering campfire, so Hunter approached the cabin. He was about to knock when the door swung open, and there stood Fox, grinning like he was greeting a long-lost friend.

"I knew you would come. I knew that you would figure it out and come."

Fox, a few inches shorter than Hunter, clapped him on the back and ushered him inside. Sequoia, Birdie, and Aspen all looked tired but happy to see him. Aspen clasped Hunter's hand and gave him a nod of welcome. Hunter tilted his head inquiringly at Sequoia, surprised to see her there. 'Don't ask' was the obvious significance of her expression and the limp wave of her hand.

"You're looking good for a Washington bureaucrat," proclaimed tiny Birdie Moonsong, who stood on tip-toes to give Hunter a peck on the cheek. She did this as if they saw each other regularly and always greeted one another that way.

There was a fire in the fireplace and a cooler filled with ice and bottled drinks. Aspen offered the selection to Hunter who gladly took one. Hunter felt warmth, a sense of loss, and longing all wash over him as he recognized that this was what he could have been a part of over all those painfully lonely years.

Aspen, ever the leader, addressed Hunter.

"First of all, a huge thank you for coming. We really appreciate it and know what it must have taken for you to drop everything and come. So I'll cut to the chase. Breeze has gone missing, and we're worried sick that something serious has happened to her. We actually have reason to believe that that is the case. We are hoping beyond hope, that you can help us find her."

Hunter grimly studied Aspen's face and then glanced at each of the others, seeing the exhaustion, the desperation, and the hope in their faces. He looked down. He now knew that he was not going to say any of the crap that, from extensive work-related experience, he had automatically prepared during his flights. These young men and women with whom he shared so much history were genuinely good people. He wasn't sure he could say that about others with whom he had more recently become associated.

He thought, *Can I – should I – dare I – tell them the truth?*

Finally, Hunter looked up at the group.

"I'll also cut to the chase. I do know where Breeze is... and she is alive and safe."

Hunter watched Aspen, expecting to see the most emotion from him; but the group's collective gasp and quiet but jubilant gestures made Hunter realize that *every* person in this room loved Breeze, and that there was no way to compare how much that was felt.

Hunter then surprised himself by saying, "Also, I think Dukon may not be what he appears to be."

There was a murmur in the room as the others looked at one another, nodding.

"Looks like you're already on the same page," Hunter observed.

Aspen took on a severe tone. "Why are you telling us about Dukon?"

Hunter suddenly felt weary and looked at the group plaintively.

"Because I believe that there is something *really bad* going down, and that whatever it is, it needs to be stopped. I don't have much information. It's mostly happening outside my periphery. I'm trying to figure it out day by day." He paused. "Um... Dukon actually ordered me... *to kill Breeze.* I let him think that I would, but I hid her instead. I'm no murderer, and that sure isn't what I signed up for."

The others responded with shock – then gestures of relief and gratitude for Hunter's involvement.

Fox took over. "In a moment, we'll ask you where she is and why Dukon wants her dead. But first, we need to tell you what we know about a specific threat to her, because something happened today that might mean time is critical. Jump right in if you already know about this and can enlighten *us.* A few years ago, my monitoring picked up a threat to Breeze's life."

Hunter interrupted, "Your monitoring?"

"Yes, like how I tracked a plane, then a taxi, entering the area just before you arrived – but we'll cover that later. The threat... *an armed drone...* seemed poised to fire on Breeze, but then it went away."

Hunter looked shocked then frowned. He genuinely seemed not to know about it.

"A few years ago, you said?"

Fox nodded. "I captured its unique signature at the time and have continued tracking that particular drone's activity. It followed Breeze the next day when she returned to college. I was able to determine that it was not armed that time. It then turned around and returned to its base near here. That drone has had many sorties – only some of them near Breeze. Yesterday evening, it had an *offshore* round trip and then *again* in the middle of the night. I wondered if its offshore sorties could have been related to Breeze's location, because it didn't start going offshore until she disappeared. Just a while ago, that same drone, *now armed,* took off and left the area *again.* I tracked it leaving the continent, flying out over the water."

Fox showed Hunter a map on his tracking device, pointing to where the drone was right then.

"Please tell me that this *armed drone* is not near where Breeze is?"

CHAPTER THIRTY-EIGHT
Dumping the Body

After jumping at the first gunshot and feeling the instant pain in her arm, Breeze struggled to get onto her knees. Her arm scraped against the post she was tied to, and she felt another sharp pain, lower down on her arm this time. Because of the hood, she couldn't see; but she realized that there was a nail or something sticking out of the post.

A second shot was fired.

Breeze heard the thud of a body hitting the floor.

Are they shooting at someone else? Or did someone just shoot the shooter? Was it just the nail that gouged me before? I thought I was shot!

Footsteps approached, and someone pulled off her hood and walked away. It was still dark outside and there was no light in the building. Breeze could just make out a man and a woman rolling up a rug – with a person's arm sticking out! Breeze involuntarily cried out, but she was still gagged, so her cry was muffled. The man shouldered the rug and carried it outside, staggering under its weight. The woman was crouched low, not looking in Breeze's direction.

Who did they kill?! Am I next? Did they take off my hood so I would see what's in store for me? Why is this happening?!

Breeze heard a motorboat start up. After some time, she heard a big splash. The motor then grew louder as the boat returned. The man did not re-enter the building. Shortly, Breeze heard the plane take off.

After a couple of minutes, when Breeze could no longer hear the plane, the woman came over to her. Smiling reassuringly, the woman introduced herself while removing the gag and untying Breeze's bindings. Her name was Angela, and she assured Breeze that no one was actually killed. She said that it had all been staged. She told Breeze that the young woman in the rug was an experienced diver and was going to swim underwater to where she could surface without being seen. Angela explained that the man who just left was her brother. She said that he was helping Breeze's friend, Aspen, to hide her for her safety. Breeze was greatly relieved to hear Aspen's name. Unfortunately, Angela had few details.

Breeze wondered, *Did Aspen get my message?* She was grateful to be alive, but she wanted to know what this was all about!

CHAPTER THIRTY-NINE
WTF?

Rob knew that he could not just let this go. It was the middle of the night, but he returned to the base and sent the drone back to the island to record what he could of the scene of the crime. Circling the island multiple times, he did not see anyone nor anything useful to photograph. He zoomed in on the water to see if there was evidence of where her body had been dumped. He saw nothing except for a diffuse oil slick trail as from a motorboat. Heartsick, he followed the oil slick quite a distance, past other islands to a small island which seemed to be occupied. He saw a large cottage near the shore and dense trees across most of the island, ending at some rocky cliffs. Two people were visible outside the cottage.

To Rob's very great surprise... one of the people was Honey! She was talking to another woman outside the cottage, behaving as if nothing was wrong!

WTF? What did I witness earlier? Who was killed and dumped in the water?

Rob was enormously relieved that it wasn't Honey. He decided that the murder did not involve him and that there was nothing he could do about it anyway. So he put it out of his mind and decided to take a little holiday to the islands and finally meet Honey in person.

I'll go home and do some quick online research of these islands. Then, one more drone visit to scope out a vacation, and no more of this long-distance relationship!

CHAPTER FORTY
Direct Hit

After some solid hours of sleep that morning, Rob did some quick travel research. He wanted to go and scope out his island vacation while the drone was still available to him. So, in the early afternoon, he launched the drone. He didn't realize, until after it was airborne, that it was now armed.

Hm, it isn't on the schedule for any missions today. I guess I'll just have to be more efficient, since the fuel won't last as long with that payload.

When the drone reached the island, to Rob's infinite delight, its display showed Honey sunbathing in a bikini on the beach! Rob was mindful to not let anyone on land or water see the drone. He piloted it away from the beach, being careful of the trees behind the cottage. Once clear of the trees, he dropped the drone to a lower altitude to get a better angle for ogling her. He eagerly zoomed in, and... what did his eyes behold?

"Whoa ho! Is she actually unhooking her top? Am I feeling *lucky* today....?!"

Rob held his breath...

"Y-y-y-yessss! Toplessssss!"

She was now basically naked except for her teeny, weeny, bikini bottom. Rob could not resist filming her with the drone. He would just be sure to erase it after downloading it for himself. Without taking his eyes off the titillating entertainment on the screen, he reached to operate the camera, and... *KABOOM!!* A flash of fire was visible. Then the screen went blank, and the room went silent.

The drone had crashed and burst into flames.

Operating the camera had only momentarily diverted Rob's attention away from piloting the drone. But with his attention *mostly* focused on a topless, bikini-clad babe – that was all it had taken.

"SHIIIIIIIIT!!!!" Rob screamed, jumping up and holding his head, his mind blanked by shock and then filled with fear of the repercussions he was going to face. By crashing the drone, he had lost visual contact, so he didn't even know what he had hit, what was happening there, or if Honey or the other woman had been hurt *or killed* by the drone or its missiles.

Rob was frozen, trying to decide whether to call his superiors and get help to the island... or to flee... or what.

CHAPTER FORTY-ONE
Help Me

"NO!" Fox exclaimed, looking at his tracking device, which was now beeping. "Breeze's drone just disappeared from my tracker! I shouldn't have lost it unless it was destroyed! And... it could have been destroyed while taking out a target!"

Hunter was wild-eyed.

"That *is* near where Breeze is! She's on an island owned by my Aussie friend, Jonas George. How could Dukon, or whoever's pulling his puppet-strings, have found her? I made sure she had no way to contact the outside world so no one could trace *her* location!"

Sequoia said, "Maybe we need to involve law enforcement or even the military."

Hunter shook his head. "We can't use any government resources to help us, because we don't know who's with us and who's with Dukon."

The friends all noticed that Hunter had said, "us," aligning himself with them.

"I'm going after her now!" Hunter bellowed, turning to go.

As he reached for the door handle, he stopped and turned around.

Glancing at each one of them, he earnestly entreated, *"Help me."*

"You bet, Brother!" Aspen said, grabbing the cooler and pouring its ice-cubes into the fireplace, smothering the flames. "Finding Breeze is what this is all about!"

Fox said, "I have the location where the drone disappeared, but we can't be sure that's where Breeze is. The drone could have fired its missiles at a faraway target and then self-destructed where I have its last coordinates. So, how do we find *her*, Hunter?"

"I don't have immediate access to the island's coordinates! That was another layer of protection for her. We need to rendezvous with my friend, Jonas. He doesn't live on the island, but he can take me there in his small plane. You could follow."

Hunter dictated Jonas's address.

"Wait," he said. "How are you going to follow us? The Search and Rescue chopper could get us to where Jonas lives, but it's probably not licensed to go off-continent. If it isn't, it might draw unwanted attention and an unfriendly, military air escort! Jonas's plane only seats two passengers plus room for cargo. If it has a full cargo load now for his new business startup, there won't be room for any of you."

Aspen turned to Birdie. "We'll need to take Leapfrog. Is it primed?"

"Yes, but we'll need our other gear."

Aspen nodded and dealt out assignments.

"Birdie, you take the Search and Rescue chopper and get Hunter to his friend right away. I can fly Leapfrog. Fox and I will go get it now along with everyone's gear.

Sequoia, I want you on standby in the village in case we need you to coordinate more help. Even as the wife of a Presidential candidate, you managed a trip back here without Secret Service; so I've asked Kiwi to be your bodyguard. Fox, we have the address, but keep tracking Birdie in case Jonas has Hunter meet him elsewhere. We'll pick up Birdie wherever she takes Hunter to rendezvous with Jonas."

As they hustled out of the cabin, Hunter asked,

"If Jonas and I get ahead of you in his plane, how will you find us to follow?"

Fox bit his lower lip and lightly punched Hunter on the arm.

"Sorry, Hunter, but I stuck a tracer on you when you first came into the cabin."

Shaking his head and starting to run, Hunter said, "You guys are somethin' else!"

Fox and Aspen sprinted for the small, camouflaged hangar where they kept the aircraft that they nicknamed "Leapfrog."

Fox asked, "What additional help might Sequoia coordinate from this end? Other operatives? Or has someone from SIGNAL headquarters contacted you?"

"Negative, Foxer. There's probably nothing for Sequoia to coordinate from here," Aspen said with a sheepish look. "We mustn't forget that she may be about to become the First Lady of the US of A. We cannot risk her on an operation in the field!"

"Riiight, of course," Fox agreed. "Sometimes I forget she's with *him* and just think of her as our sweet Sequoia."

CHAPTER FORTY-TWO
Revelations

KABOOM! There was an explosion, and smoke was rising from the other end of the island. Breeze put her bra back on while hurrying towards the cottage in her bikini underwear, holding her shorts and shirt with her teeth. Angela was looking through binoculars in the direction of the smoke. Her dog, Bart, stood at her feet.

"What is it?" Breeze asked, zipping up her jeans shorts.

"I don't think it's a plane; but if it is, it's much smaller than my brother's. I can't see it clearly, but I don't see any flames, just smoke. Jonas was definitely not coming today, but he said he might come tomorrow. I hope someone doesn't need help. I would go investigate if your friend hadn't been adamant with my brother that we were not to leave this end of the island except to evacuate. He did warn us that someone hostile might come looking for you..."

Breeze grimaced, pulling her top over her head. "I'm so sorry if keeping me safe is putting *your* safety at risk."

Angela waved it off and said, "Maybe you should go back to the more hidden section of the beach in case someone does come. I'll stay here and go about my business. If anyone approaches, Bart will warn us by barking. Keep an eye and an ear in this direction."

"Will do! Your brother said he had to take our cell phones for our safety, but I'm glad he left me my pistol!"

"Definitely! Do you have reasonable capacity magazines, or at least extra mags and ammo? Having only a low capacity magazine could be fatal, especially if more than one aggressor approaches. If you don't, you can take my brother's pistol with you. Both of ours hold double-stack magazines, and we have several, high capacity mags for each of them."

"I'm good, Angela, but thanks! See you later!"

Breeze grabbed her gear pack and hustled back to the beach, mentally analyzing the situation.

Angela says that her brother, Jonas, became friends with Aspen one summer during their college years. She said that the two stayed in touch, and that Aspen asked Jonas to help him hide me from some sort of danger.

It was awfully strange, though, for a friend of Aspen to threaten me with guns and then chloroform me to bring me here! Why didn't Aspen just give Jonas a coded message, telling me to go with him? I hope it really was Aspen who arranged this...

If it wasn't, my SIGNAL tracer going dead should have alerted Fox that I was in trouble. At least he would have had the coordinates of my campsite from before I pried the tracer out of my navel, cut its tether, and disabled it.

Installing my tracer's microchip into my laptop was the only way I could think of to at least send a brief Smoke Signals message to Aspen and Fox. I knew somebody would eventually see my laptop and take it from where I positioned it by the road to reflect sunlight. My jerry-rigged setup should have worked – if someone found my laptop, and if they were motivated by at least one of the incentives that I programmed to appear on the screen. Promises of a monetary reward, porn photos, or the chance to help someone should have done it!

Once powered on in range of a cell tower or wireless Internet connectivity, my program would automatically use the microchip to send my Smoke Signals message and then kill the laptop. I still had my phone to use if I survived long enough to get in range of a cell tower. Of course, Jonas then took my phone away – supposedly so no one can track me here.

I couldn't risk sending that sensitive information via anything but Smoke Signals, and it HAS to get to Aspen whether I survive or not. I look forward to finding out if he did get it, and if my kidnapping is related to my message – or if it's something else!

The wrecked drone lay in a smoky heap at the far end of the island. It was seriously damaged when it grazed a cliff, shearing off one of its missiles which exploded as it fell away. Unfortunately... the other missile was still viable, and a breeze was fanning the smoldering ground cover underneath it. It took some time, but a flame finally burst forth from the embers and ignited wires that led to the missile like a fuse. The missile was pointed directly at the cottage with a clear sight line between the trees.

A couple of hours had elapsed, and Breeze felt that if someone were coming, they would have been there by now. As she got up to walk back to the cottage, there was a loud whistling sound and – Kaboom!! The cottage *exploded* and burst into flames.

With her gun drawn, Breeze moved stealthily along the beach, keeping her head down and scanning in all directions. She didn't see anyone hostile... but neither did she see Angela or her dog.

Avoiding the flames, she ducked into the smoke-filled structure, calling Angela's name. She heard moaning and tried to locate where it was coming from. Almost immediately, however, Breeze started coughing and felt woozy from the smoke. She had to get out of there. She remembered that it's best to get down underneath smoke, and that the heat at head-level can be hot enough to kill a person in seconds. She dropped to the floor to crawl the few remaining yards out of the cottage. Feeling light-headed and laboring to breathe, she actually wondered if she was going to make it.

In case the island was under surveillance, Hunter wanted to alter his appearance a bit en route. So, he left his jacket in the chopper with Birdie, and Jonas gave him his Outback cowboy hat to wear.

As the plane approached the island, they saw smoke and the burning cottage ruins. Jonas found his sister, Angela, lying on the ground several yards from the cottage. She was semi-conscious and bleeding with Bart barking and licking her face. Fortunately, she had been outside with Bart when the missile struck.

Hunter spotted Breeze weakly trying to get up from the ground on the other side of the cottage. He scooped her up in his arms, and walked briskly away from the smoking debris. She was coughing and blinking but with no visible injuries. Hunter yelled to Jonas that Breeze seemed okay and that Jonas should fly Angela to the hospital immediately without them. Hunter kept walking with Breeze until they were amid a dense stand of trees, well away from the fire.

Hunter knelt on one knee, seating Breeze on a tree stump so that her back was supported by another tree. She had stopped coughing but was weak from smoke inhalation.

"Are you okay, Breeze?" Hunter asked in his distinctive, deep, raspy voice.

"*Hunter??*" Breeze croaked, "Is that *you?*"

Frowning with concentration through soot and smoke-glazed eyes, she thought she must be imagining him.

Construing her tone and expression to be disappointment that it was him instead of Dukon or Aspen, Hunter replied, "I'm afraid so, Breeze."

Since they were shielded from view by the trees, Hunter removed his hat.

Physical shock set in and Breeze began shuddering violently. Hunter plucked her from the tree stump and pulled her body tight against his. He wrapped his arms around her and rubbed her back, arms, and legs, working to stop her reflexive convulsing. He sat down on the tree stump and cradled her in his lap, his arms bear-hugging her, his hands continuing to rub her. Gradually, her shaking became mild shivers, and then she was still.

Breeze pulled her head back a little, wiping soot from her eyes. Grimacing at the stinging sensation, she looked at Hunter. She was very confused that he was there. She saw concern written all over his face, and he saw distress all over hers.

Interpreting her grimace as distaste at him holding her, Hunter quickly stood up, separating their bodies. He still held her arm to be sure she was steady enough on her feet without his support.

"Sorry," he said. "I wasn't sure you were okay yet."

Breeze tilted her head inquiringly, not understanding.

He quickly clarified.

"I didn't mean to hold you any longer than you needed me to."

Breeze looked at the ground and replied in a heavyhearted and smoke-hoarsened voice, "I know, Hunter. I know. I'm totally confused why Aspen would send you, of all people, instead of coming himself. I'm sorry you got stuck taking care of me; but thanks for indulging me and holding me just this once when I really needed you to."

Fighting back tears, she looked up and saw the dark expression on Hunter's face.

"Are you mocking me?" he asked quietly, incredulous that she would do so.

"Mocking you?" Breeze chortled.

Hunter turned his face away, clenching his fists, his jaw muscle pulsating violently. Breeze reached out and placed her hand on his cheek, stroking it down to his angular jawline. He turned back to face her.

"Sorry," she whispered. "I've wanted to touch that majestic profile for more than a decade. I didn't mean to take advantage of the situation. It's just that... after all those years of wishing that you... I mean... you're here, and..."

She shrugged, smiling apologetically as a tear escaped.

Hunter fought his disbelief. Breeze seemed sincere.

"Breeze... you're not saying..." He looked at her intently. "I don't understand. You never even gave me the time of day. You were always following Aspen around, wearing your heart on your sleeve for him – anyone could see that."

Breeze gaped at him. "Aspen? Hunter, I've been crazy about... *you*... since I was ten years old!"

Hunter stared at her with incredulity as she continued.

"But you would never even look at me! And if you remember, *everyone* followed Aspen. He's a leader, a total doll, and a rock. Like everybody else, I respect and love him, just... not like *that*. Anyway, how could I give you the time of day when you avoided me as if I had smallpox? *Everyone* knows how I've felt about you. How could you possibly not know? I thought that was *why* you avoided me! They've teased me about you for more than ten years!"

"I don't believe this," Hunter said breathlessly. He swallowed hard a couple of times, his Adam's apple heaving conspicuously. Making himself vulnerable for the first time in a very long time, he huskily replied, "Breeze... I have *always* wanted to be with you."

Now Breeze's eyes were wide.

"Over the years, I overheard you talking about a guy you seemed to like, with a name I didn't recognize. So I thought that was your pet name for Aspen or that you had another boyfriend. I heard you and your friends say his name many times."

"Do you mean... Blaze?" Breeze asked.

He nodded.

"Oh Hunter, that was my nickname for *you*. Everyone teased me whenever you were around, because they caught me looking at you. That's why you heard it so much."

Hunter just stared at Breeze. Then, mustering his courage, he ventured,

"Do you... still...?"

With tears in her eyes, Breeze nodded.

Hunter stepped forward and wrapped his arms around her, bowing his head so that it rested on top of hers. They held each other, their minds reeling and processing what they both had just learned. Breeze felt euphoria, but her cheeks were wet with tears. Then she realized that those tears were not hers. She leaned back and looked at Hunter. He met her gaze with the pain and misery of his entire youth etched on his face in clear relief. He didn't try to hide it; he just looked at her as the tears streamed from his eyes. Breeze hugged him tightly, and now the tears on her face were her own.

"Well it's about time, you two!" they heard.

Looking up, they saw Aspen, Birdie and Fox down at the beach, grinning at them. The trio was all geared up with body armor, weapons rigs, and Aspen's EMT bags. They, too, had thought to conceal their faces, wearing helmets with partially lowered visors. A small, privately-registered, amphibious aircraft was beached a short ways behind them.

Hunter shouted, "It's a good thing she wasn't depending on you guys! What took you so long to get here?"

Birdie laughed, "From the air we saw that you had things... um... perfectly under control over here. So we went and checked out the smoky area on the other side of the island. As we expected, it was a crashed drone. We collected some components for analysis."

Aspen reminded them, "From what Hunter's told us, we still need to be careful to keep Breeze hidden for now."

Breeze cocked her head, wondering what he meant by that.

"Right," Fox agreed. "I've already remotely accessed equipment in my office at the ASO. I'm running probes to see if any satellites or government drones recorded anything from today's incidents – including surveilling any of us. Hopefully, the electronics we recovered from the crashed drone will indicate what *it* recorded – and who owns it. If I find evidence that Breeze could have been identified by anyone, I'll work on handling it."

Hunter raised his eyebrows at Fox. "You actually have clearance and authorization for accessing that kind of data at the ASO?"

"Of course not," Fox answered with a grin.

"Couldn't that be... problematic for you?" Hunter asked.

"Not likely," Fox replied. "According to human resource policies, all kinds of minorities plus women are in a 'protected class.' People now hesitate to question or criticize anyone in a protected class, because they're afraid they'll automatically be accused of harassment or discrimination. The important protection against *wrongful* profiling unfortunately has unintended consequences. If someone sees what I'm doing, they *should* question it – but they probably won't. It's a good thing I'm one of the good guys!" Fox winked. "Besides, I almost always work remotely and know these systems like the back of my hand. I designed some of them. So trust me, I know how to disguise what I'm doing."

Breeze turned to Aspen. "I cannot wait to hear why you sent me here and why *guns and chloroform* were necessary in the process!"

Aspen arched his eyebrows at Hunter and replied,

"Well, Breeze, you'll have to ask the man right next to you. He's the one who brought you here for your protection. We're only here as his backup today."

Breeze looked at Hunter with surprise. Then she covered her mouth with her hand, and whispered, "That was you on the plane..."

Hunter nodded and gently squeezed her shoulder.

"But it was someone else who collected you from your campsite. I knew that if I spoke to you, you would almost certainly recognize my voice. It's a long story, but it was important that you not know I was involved in hiding you. I'm sorry that it had to be by way of abduction. I had to pluck you out of there ASAP. I couldn't take the chance that you would delay by not cooperating."

Breeze raised her eyebrows, so Hunter elucidated.

"Breeze, Dukon ordered me... to *kill* you. I hid you from him instead."

"What?!"

"I'll explain his reason later," Hunter said, dreading the topic of her affair with Dukon. He added, "For the record, the guns used to threaten you at your campsite were not loaded."

With a look of chagrin, Breeze asked, "How did you even find me? Was the *truck driver* involved in this?"

"No. Tyson Carlson, the 'statistician' on your research team, is former military. I actually hired him to protect you. He had a hidden satellite phone. He informed me that you were leaving with a supply truck which he tracked electronically. He, Jonas, and I had to really scramble to nab you before you got to Eastwood. I couldn't let you surface and have Dukon possibly find out that you were still alive. When the truck stopped in the middle of nowhere, Tyson transmitted those coordinates to me. Then he geared up and... collected you at your campsite. He drove you to the closest place that Jonas and I could land his plane."

Breeze swallowed. "Okay... But why did you have Jonas tell his sister that his friend's name was Aspen, instead of giving your own name?"

Hunter glanced at Aspen apologetically.

"Even if I hadn't needed to hide my involvement and had explained the threat to you, I didn't think there was any chance that you would just go. Not with *me*. I also thought that you would feel more at ease if you believed that Aspen was behind it."

"Oh, Hunter," Breeze said, slipping her arms around him.

Fox cleared his throat. "Well, Hunter, you didn't need our help, but may we at least offer you a ride home?" He swept his arm towards the aircraft.

Hunter gave a nod and put the cowboy hat back on while slipping his sunglasses onto Breeze's face.

As the group climbed into the plane, Fox warned,

"Better buckle up! Birdie's driving! It'll be a short trip with her at the controls!"

CHAPTER FORTY-THREE
Blaze

They decided to fly Hunter to a small airport on the mainland where he could catch another "air taxi." Hunter would again take two circuitous flights back to D.C.

Fox and Aspen chatted with Birdie as she piloted Leapfrog. Meanwhile, Hunter and Breeze spoke privately in the rear of the aircraft.

"So... Blaze was *me* all that time?" Hunter asked, shaking his head.

Breeze nodded. "You were always the smartest kid in all our classes—"

"Wait," Hunter said, putting up his hand. "Excuse me for interrupting, but is a member of the renowned 'Brainy Bunch' bestowing that distinction on *me?*"

Breeze laughed and continued. "In a poem, I wrote something about... the 'bright flame of your intellect.' So the name 'Blaze' came to me as my nickname for you. After that, the whole gang started referring to you as Blaze."

Fox walked up just then. Overhearing the conversation, he grinned.

"Are you actually admitting to him that you nicknamed him 'Blaze' because you thought he was so *hot?*"

Breeze opened her mouth to say something but clamped it shut again as her face reddened. Fox winked, grabbed some bottles of water from the mini-fridge, and headed back to the cockpit.

"You wrote a poem about me?" Hunter asked.

"Lots of them," Breeze confessed in a whisper.

Hunter looked down. "I can't even think why you would have liked me at all."

"I always felt that you had a big heart."

Hunter looked skeptical.

"There are many examples. Once, when we were little, your sister, Rozzi, tripped outside the school and sprawled on the ground. Her doll got mangled, and she started to cry. You dropped out of a tree and fixed it for her."

Hunter looked pensive. "I had made that doll for her birthday. So, is that why you stopped disliking me so much?"

"What made you think that I ever disliked you?"

"Your best friend told me so."

"What?! Sequoia told you that?!"

"No, it was No See, the girl you used to be with all the time. Remember her?"

"How could I forget my friend, whom you chose instead of me, to be your partner in our required dance classes!"

Hunter looked rueful. "I was nervous about asking you to be my partner. So I asked No See if she thought you would say yes. She told me that you... *disliked me.* She said you wanted to be Aspen's partner but that *she* would dance with me."

Breeze closed her eyes. "No See knew that I liked you! My best friend betrayed me! And that kept us apart all these years? It's staggering how much power there can be in a lie. And direct communication, by either you or me, at any time over the years might have changed so much."

Hunter took a deep breath. "Breeze, you should know that I've done things I'm not proud of – especially with Dukon. I have... major atoning to do. I may have significant, but hopefully not *capital,* punishment coming. But aside from whatever the justice system hands me, I'm determined to make up for what I've done. I had no idea any of it could lead to things that have been happening. It's like I unwittingly triggered a cancer that subtly grew until it could be too late to undo the damage."

Breeze regarded him sympathetically but wondered what he could have done to merit capital punishment!

Breeze's words, "My best friend betrayed me," reminded Hunter that *she* had betrayed *her* best friend by having an affair with Sequoia's husband. Hunter had expected greater decency from Breeze. He looked at her from under his brows, having more discomfort with this topic. Checking that no one else was listening, he quietly said, "I... um... know about your relationship with Dukon. He told me about it."

Breeze looked puzzled. "Relationship? With Dukon? I have seen Dukon exactly twice in my life. The first time was— Hunter, I was the one who discovered him down in the canyon. I was checking a hunch that there might be oil or natural gas there. I saw him when he exited the rescue chopper, but we didn't speak. I was... too busy trying to hide, because... I had sweat right through my clothes, and I wasn't exactly decent. I was *so* embarrassed."

Wheels turned in Hunter's head. *Sweat through her clothes? The "cheesecake" photos Dukon had of her! But who could have taken them? Waiiit... the drone that Fox said was tracking her?! So Dukon really might be connected to that? And – there's possibly oil or natural gas in the 'worthless' canyon?! That gokka (demon), has been playing me all along!*

Breeze continued, "Then, during grad school, I formally met Dukon at a university social event. Sequoia was there too. I never saw him on campus other than that, and I've been doing research in the field almost nonstop since then. So... Dukon was telling you about someone else."

Hunter tipped his head way back, closing his eyes, his hands forming tight fists. He was half incensed at Dukon's profligate lies and half so very relieved that this one wasn't true. He took Breeze's hand. Gazing at her, he said, "I sure hope they don't put me away forever. It wouldn't have mattered before, but it sure does now."

CHAPTER FORTY-FOUR
Orders in the Court

When Judge Sara Breuer decided on a judicial career, she knew that there would be days when she would love her job and days when she would wish she hadn't gotten out of bed. She also believed that one day she would have a case that would truly break her heart. That day had come.

An eloquent young American Indian man stood before her. From what she had already heard, it was clear that he had been led down a crooked path when he was an impressionable, angry young adult – after having been the victim of significant abuse and neglect throughout his upbringing.

Yes, too many criminals everywhere had similar sad beginnings... the unintended and unwanted children... the ones then neglected or abused. It was a source of much dysfunction in societies around the world. But this young man, unlike many others with destructive early influences, had *chosen* not to continue on a path of decline. This young man had chosen to pursue a constructive future.

This defendant had allegedly been involved in fraudulent land deals. These charges were being heard in a court under U.S. jurisdiction instead of the more usual situation in which Native Americans are tried in the tribal courts. This was because there were foreigners and non-Native American U.S. citizens involved in bringing the charges of fraud. There was also a highest-order criminal charge being tentatively floated in relation to this case.

"Mr. Wolf, how do you wish to plead?

"No disrespect intended, Your Honor, but I would *like* to plead *Ignorance.*"

There was tittering in the courtroom, and Judge Breuer had to stifle her own smile.

"May I explain, Your Honor?"

"Yes, Mr. Wolf, continue."

"I am guilty of some things, Your Honor, but not of the charges being brought against me. I did not understand that agreements I wrote for the land trade deals did not stand alone but were provisions that would be incorporated by someone else into a larger agreement. The larger agreement contained clauses that fundamentally altered the effect of the deal on all parties. Therefore, Your Honor, to more appropriately answer your question, I wish to plead *Not Guilty.*"

The Judge had now heard all of the arguments. She had no doubt that this young man was being thrown under the bus by the powerful forces on both sides. He was a scapegoat for the offending parties and the sacrificial lamb to appease the "injured" parties who wanted their pound of flesh.

Judge Breuer had some leeway in ruling and sentencing, but she had to abide by certain parameters. She and her staff had combed the archives and all judicial resources, searching for a precedent or technicality by which she could let this man pay any debt to society that he actually owed without potentially facing the severest penalties.

This civil case was being heard in advance of his criminal charges, and Judge Breuer knew that the criminal charges could be completely dropped if this case went in Hunter Wolf's favor. What bothered her so deeply was that one of the charges was for Treason! This was because some of the parties to whom these lands had been traded were on the U.S. list of Enemies of America. Of course, the punishment for Treason was usually the death penalty.

Judge Breuer was not very religious anymore – not since the death of someone she dearly loved. A murderous, vengeful defendant had been enraged that his fraudulent activities had landed him in jail even though he was guilty and had been fairly sentenced by her. He sent a henchman to kill her, but Judge Breuer's loved one intervened and died instead. Though grief-stricken, she and her family courageously agreed to not let this deter her from removing miscreant scum from civilized society. The tragedy had, however, shaken her faith in the Almighty.

This week, she found herself praying once again. She was praying for Hunter Wolf. She was in this career because she had such a strong sense of right and wrong. She felt that justice was often not well-served; but this case bothered her more than most.

The Ronopo Elder, former Chief Bridgewater, had testified on Hunter Wolf's behalf. He vouched that Hunter had taken remedial action well before there were even any charges against him. Hunter had *personally* financed the restoration of property to every Native American involved – including those outside his tribe. He had given up all of his personal holdings and all of the funds in his bank accounts. His Washington townhouse was under agreement of sale, and he had incurred massive personal debt in order to restore the land to the tribes. Judge Breuer asked Hunter about this.

"Why did you put yourself in such personal financial jeopardy instead of allowing the case to move through the justice system so that all parties involved could pay their share?"

"Your Honor, land is sacred to Native Americans and is still crucial to the way of life for many who keep to the traditional ways. What little land there is in each tribe's jurisdiction, *must* stay within those tribes. I learned that the outside parties who acquired the land planned to move very quickly to carve up and develop land parcels that are the only home for virtually all of the American Indian families and tribes involved. If the transactions had not been rescinded *immediately,* I feared that it would be too late for those people to ever recover their homes and tribal properties. I also believe that none of the victims of this trade truly understood the risk that they were taking when they entered into the transactions. Even in my position, *I* did not completely understand it. I am hopeful that this case will continue through the justice system and that I may be at least partially reimbursed in the future."

Both U.S. and foreign complainants had asserted that Hunter *pressured* them into giving up their purchased lands after the deal was consummated. Some claimed that they had felt *physically* threatened by Hunter. (Indeed, Hunter's inner hoodlum had re-emerged and prompted him to bring to bear every manner of leverage, pressure and threats he could think of to ensure that things were set right.)

Thus, Hunter was facing both criminal and civil charges regarding those actions. The plaintiffs brought the charges even though they had been fully compensated for their financial outlays. They contended that the lands had already increased in value and that they should be compensated at a higher level than the price they originally paid. High-profile expert witnesses attested to this increased value, making it difficult to refute. Judge Breuer was pretty sure that these expert witnesses were being paid megabucks by the wealthy plaintiffs, likely committing perjury, and that the claim was baseless. But it was up to the defense to punch holes in the plaintiffs' case. Unfortunately, the defense team, with its limited resources, was no match for the powerful and munificently funded consortium of vultures bringing the charges.

Judge Breuer had reached the day when she would have to decide. She called a recess for lunch – and continued to pray...

After lunch, with a heavy heart, bolstered only by the knowledge that Hunter should have avenues of appeal, Judge Breuer reconvened the court for the afternoon session. A member of her staff whispered in her ear. She looked towards a private entrance to the courtroom and watched with intrigued wonder as a few very old men in special uniforms made their way unsteadily, but with dignity, just into the foyer of the courtroom. They were visible from the bench but not from the counsel table nor from the gallery. Judge Breuer read the notations on their uniforms and realized who these men were. They were the remaining living members of the famed heroes of the Global Wars – the American Indian Code Talkers – who had hailed from approximately twenty different tribes.

The Judge found herself rising to her feet out of respect. She had always been awed by the unique contribution those men had made, along with many other American Indians who had enlisted and fought alongside their non-native, fellow Americans. She was also aware of the continuing strong presence of Native Americans in the U.S. military.

A murmur arose from the gallery. People were wondering why the Judge was standing. She adjusted her robes, as if that had been her reason for rising, and retook her seat.

Behind the elderly men in the foyer stood a retired Four-Star General. He was the son of one of the heroes. The General beckoned to the Clerk of the Court who took a large envelope from the General and brought it to Judge Breuer.

Her prayers had been answered. The General had papers with an official seal from a highly classified Congressional Committee. The paperwork provided warnings to be given to the plaintiffs.

The plaintiffs were going to be required to undergo a financial audit to substantiate their claims. Furthermore, some of their current financial assets had already been frozen as it had been discovered that these U.S. assets were illegally in the possession of Enemies of the United States. Judge Breuer watched the claimants blanch as they read their individual documents. Then she asked each of them,

"Do you wish to drop the charges against Mr. Wolf?"

They all did. As required by the Congressional Committee, Judge Breuer quietly instructed the court reporter to not record who had delivered the paperwork and that all records from the case were to be sealed. She then happily remanded Hunter Wolf into the General's custody as ordered by the Committee. After waiting for that troupe to disappear into the private corridor from which they had entered, she adjourned court for the day. She silently thanked the Almighty for gracing her with this gift.

A very puzzled Hunter Wolf was led to the General, who said,

"Hunter Wya Wolf, I am General Brett Dark Horse. I am pleased to *finally* have you joining us."

Hunter looked at him quizzically. Out of the corner of his eye, he espied Aspen casually leaning against the exit door. He winked at Hunter while snapping his fingers and drumming one hand against the other in a rhythmic combination. Aspen gave a nod with a triumphant smile on his face. Hunter didn't know what those gestures meant, but he did feel with certainty that things were going to be all right.

CHAPTER FORTY-FIVE
Harvest Festival

It was Harvest Festival on the Ronopo Reservation. Garlands of flowers and leaves were strung everywhere around the village. The central plaza was packed with hundreds of happy and animated people. Table after table offered delicious, traditional food and drinks. The Ronopo Heritage Band was warming up. They would play the pieces that were performed annually to invoke sunshine, rain, and fertility for the crops – and good hunting and fishing for those who filled the meat and fish markets.

After the music burst forth from the band, the buzz of the crowd's high-spirited conversation continued as a lively background. Dancers in colorful, traditional garb performed well-loved routines, shadowed by joyful little children of the tribe. Elders took to the floor for some of the slow, interpretive dances, and the teenagers let loose, energetically demonstrating the latest dances of the times.

While the band was playing a contemporary set, two young women approached the spot where Fox, Aspen, and Birdie stood watching. The shorter, plump young woman asked Fox,

"Chief Bridgewater, would you dance this one with me?"

She was rewarded with Fox's sultry smile – the smile that made young women feel weak in the knees. Girls kept a competitive tally of those smiles. Fox had a bit of a "randy rep" around the reservation. It was whispered that he had many lady friends across multiple states and that he left the reservation so often to enjoy the pleasures of their company. Many a Ronopo girl hoped that instead of just smiling at her, he would blow into her ear. Word had it that if Fox Bridgewater blew into a young woman's ear, she was being offered the chance to get very lucky...

"You bet, Juicy," he replied, grabbing her by the hand and pulling her out onto the dance floor.

Many years back, when they were young children, a gang of boys known for bullying, were doing just that. Poking her, they were saying that she was ugly and fat.

Little Fox was there, and he was genuinely perplexed. He asked the boys, "What do you mean?" He placed his hands on the girl's very well-rounded upper arm and gently squeezed it. He turned to the boys and said, "She's tender and juicy! She looks good to me!"

The bullies looked at her a little differently then and shrugged and walked away. From that day forward, *everyone* called her "Juicy."

When they were older, Fox and Juicy dated for a while. They eventually went their separate ways, but to Juicy, Fox would always be her hero.

"Would you like to dance?" Aspen asked Juicy's overly-skinny friend who was still standing there. She nodded, blushing, and Aspen guided her out onto the floor.

"Finally!" a young man said, rushing up to Birdie. "I had to wait for the Chiefs to buzz off before I could steal a dance with you!"

Birdie joined him in the fun on the dance floor, agreeing to also grab a bite with him later.

In keeping with the theme of summoning fruitfulness and plenty for the tribe, the band started up a traditional number that some years nobody danced to. It was reserved for people who wanted to ask someone to be their special loved one. The dance floor quickly emptied out.

Then, an unfamiliar young man walked out into the middle of the circular floor. In accordance with tradition, he turned to the four points on its perimeter marking East, South, West, and North. A high-ranking Elder was seated at each location. The young man inclined his head respectfully to each of them, but when he faced Elder Chief Bridgewater, he made a slow and complete bow.

Like a ripple on the water, as recognition dawned, sudden quiet radiated throughout the crowd. It started close to the dance floor and spread all the way to the outer edges of the throng. Now, other than the strains of music, there was not another sound in the village plaza. Virtually everyone's mouth had fallen open in surprise.

No one – not a single person – had *ever* seen Hunter Wya Wolf participate in any festivities at this or any other social event. Early on, Hunter's cruel father had forced Hunter and his sister to stay home during events. Then, his father would take them to watch but would not allow them to participate in the fun activities. Later, Hunter's absence was just due to the dark cloud that always encompassed him. For him to be taking part in this particular dance was all the more astounding.

Breeze had kept a low profile since the drone crash on the island. Now, with special security measures in place, Aspen had given her the green light to attend the festival. She had not known that Hunter was coming to the reservation, so she had certainly had no idea that he was going to do this. When she saw him walk out onto the dance floor, tears filled her eyes.

The serious young man surveyed the crowd. Finding Breeze, he walked purposefully to where she stood. He bowed his head to her then stretched out his hand, his eyes asking her if she would join him. Beaming, she stepped onto the dance floor, nodding and taking his hand.

Then, Hunter did another thing that no one in the tribe could ever remember having seen him do.

He smiled.

He led Breeze to the center of the dance floor where he walked slowly in a circle around her. Then, standing before her, Hunter removed his beaded choker and ceremoniously placed it around her neck. Smiling at Breeze again, he led her in performing the traditional dance.

There were many sniffles and tears throughout the crowd. The adults who had so sorrowfully borne witness to Hunter's miserable childhood, including Chief Bridgewater and Kristal Parks, all cried with joy for him and Breeze.

"Wow!" Birdie said as she stood watching with Fox and Aspen. "Now that I've seen Hunter smile, and without all the bruises he always had on his face growing up, I can see why Breeze thought he was so attractive!"

Fox slowly turned to Birdie with raised eyebrows.

Birdie laughed. Leaning over, she whispered into his ear, "But no one is hotter than you, Chief Boy Toy!"

Fox leaned towards Birdie, cupping his hand to whisper back into her ear, but he softly blew into it instead...

Everyone continued to watch the handsome couple on the dance floor. When the dance ended, the crowd *roared* its approval, clapping and stomping and cheering. Interestingly, all present had been seeing their fellow tribesman, Hunter Wya Wolf, out there from beginning to end. It was not until it was over that the crowd remembered that, through an irregular series of events, this young Ronopo man had just become Vice President of the United States.

COUNTERPOINT V
STATUS REPORT: CROSSTALK DOUBLE-CROSS

"We have worked with the already one-sided media to ensure that they will be with us when we need them most. First, select news outlets will have *exclusive* coverage rights. They should object to this breach of freedom for all media, but they won't because they will enjoy their advantage over the excluded news services. The new Administration will even control which reporters are permitted to have coverage – and of which issues and events."

"...following well-established tactics of the most controlling governments."

"Yes. Eventually, *all* communications about meetings, real or embellished, will originate from the White House staff *only,* not from any independent media. The previously privileged but *now excluded* media services will squawk, but they will have little clout or support from their competitors. By then, there will be a strong *foreign* media presence in America – multiple foreign TV stations and radio outlets that will broadcast our desired messages. With foreign media broadcasting in foreign languages, Americans will not even be aware of the messages and instructions being delivered, 'hidden in plain sight,' to our people inside America."

"Excellent. So the propaganda machine and the attack commands delivery system will both be fully operational on time?"

"They will. On the financial front, we have made use of the new federal control over the banking industry. Under guise of consumer protection, our people embedded in U.S government have banks gradually restricting how much of people's *own money* they can withdraw. Now our plants on the Banking Committee succeeded in revoking the federal bank account insurance for consumers in the event of *any* catastrophe. When one does occur, which it will, and our wealthy patrons crash U.S. stock, bond, and currency markets again, Americans will have *nothing* but the small amount of cash they were previously allowed to withdraw. Businesses will not honor debit or credit cards as people will no longer have funds to pay the bills. So all Americans will be *wiped out* and at the complete mercy of their government!"

"While our assets will be safe, Western economies will fall like dominoes!"

CHAPTER FORTY-SIX
Special Force

Mason Aaron Workman was one of SIGNAL's *elite* operatives. These highly select, rigorously trained agents were SIGNAL's Special Forces Warriors. The few who successfully fulfilled the formidable training requirements were given the title "Brave." As they distinguished themselves and were promoted to lead other Braves, they were titled "Captain." The founder of SIGNAL, General Brett Dark Horse, had decided to use "Captain" instead of "Chief" to distinguish between a military leader and a tribal leader. Each of these elite operatives had a meaningful alias bestowed by the warrior's comrades. Mason Aaron Workman's alias was: Captain Lance Trueheart.

Lance grew up on a reservation in the South. In his youth, he spent significant time off reservation, working on nearby farms. Thus, when he spoke English, it was with a Southern accent. After graduating from a tribal college, a job relocated him to the Great Lakes Region. Lance was an engineer and a news junkie. He read Internet news sites from the far left to the far right, foreign news, and sites some people ridiculed as "wacko." More and more often, those "wacko" news sites were the first or *only* ones to cover important topics that the dying, mainstream (or so-called "legitimate") media conspicuously ignored or spun. Consequently, most people were blindly unaware of how uninformed they were.

Lance was both warrior and analyst. He cross-referenced select facts against a database he created of what he considered to be hotspots. His creative mind made connections most people would never think of. Being an engineer, he conceived of two possible threats related to electricity. The first was regarding reports that voting machines on Election Day were registering the *opposite* result of what some voters had entered. In virtually all cases, the error was in favor of one party. Officials asserted that it was a minor issue, and that the machines simply needed to be "re-calibrated." Of course, without a focused review of each location where this happened, there was no way to understand what would actually happen to votes already registered in the machine if it were "re-calibrated." No one had been allowed to investigate the problem during the election; and after the election, the problem could no longer be duplicated.

"What if we test the voting machines for their response to electrical changes such as a power surge?" Lance recommended to one voter agency. It turned out that the machines all responded the same way to power fluctuations – they changed every vote in the machine in favor of one particular party. There was no telling how many machines across the country had been compromised in this way. It was too late to learn if the results of that election would actually have been different than what was reported; but, hopefully, Lance's discovery would restore valid voting for the next election. Lance also recommended the purchase of American-made voting machines in the future.

The second issue bothering Lance was related to the Administration's push to centralize the U.S. power grid, as was proposed by a prior Administration. The current initiative might have inspired recent incidents – that were possibly perpetrated by hostile parties. A couple of major U.S. cities had experienced significant metro system stoppages, trapping hundreds of commuters for multiple hours. Top engineers could find no cause, and they were certain that computer hackers could not have done it.

Lance wondered, *What if someone hostile was testing linking a city's electrical system to a power grid outside the city? From such an external vantage point, an interloper could invisibly control systems for: mass transit, telecommunications, air traffic control, emergency responders, and electricity to the general public.*

Lance knew that centralization of power did not make sense. A power outage in just one part of the country could take down the entire country's electricity, communications, and emergency systems – region by region. Other countries had already experienced repercussions of centralizing their power grids, suffering widespread outages, causing chaos, destruction, and death. Dictators notoriously control citizens by centralizing power and communications and then shutting them off at their whim. The Internet was invented precisely to afford the security provided by *decentralization* – and no government control.

In the name of citizen safety, the National Protection Agency (NPA) had ordered companies to provide highly detailed information that would essentially allow the NPA to control Internet and *all* other communications systems "in an emergency." But if details of *all* the systems' blueprints, *now assembled in one place*, were leaked or hacked by a hostile party – as other strategic, classified information recently had – the ramifications could be devastating. Then, there were this Administration's newly relaxed immigration policies (which were in violation of federal law as with a prior President.) Now, to extend an olive branch to America's detractors, U.S. government agencies were being required to hire people of all cultural backgrounds, including *non-citizens*. Some new hires were discovered to have past or present ties to organizations hostile to America, but that didn't disqualify them! These hiring policies were even being implemented in positions of strategic importance such as national security, the military, the space program, the intelligence services – and jobs in critical infrastructure, including power grids, nuclear plants, railroads, airports, and dams! U.S. agriculture was already at risk, having so many undocumented laborers, some who were potentially not the innocent unemployed looking for work.

Given the now easy influx into the U.S. of potentially hostile parties, Captain Trueheart wanted to investigate. He wondered if his theory about invisibly linking city electrical grids was possible. One unexplained metro stoppage was in his territory and was recent enough that it might have traceable evidence. He obtained approval from his SIGNAL Regional Commander and set out to inspect power stations near where the metro stoppage had occurred. He grilled the personnel there for information.

The result of Lance's investigation was truly shocking.

"General Dark Horse, this is Regional Commander Annie Moosejaw. I am pained to report that Captain Trueheart is down."

"*All* the way down, Commander?"

"Negative, sir. He was severely electrocuted during an investigation. He is alive but badly burned and in a coma. Brave Jaimie Mendes was with him and halted the electrocution, procured medical aid, and brought back evidence that confirms the Captain's suspicions."

"Please send me your report via *Smoke Signals* along with Captain Trueheart's hospital location and family contacts. Thank you, Commander Moosejaw."

CHAPTER FORTY-SEVEN
Dance With Me

After they danced at the Harvest Festival, Hunter told Breeze that he would be returning to Washington, D.C. the next day.

"I'm about to meet with a Ronopo land official. After my meeting, will you have supper with me? I'm not really up for hanging out at the festival, though."

"I would love to, Blaze... I mean... Hunter."

Hunter smiled. "I don't mind if you call me Blaze. It's nice to have a nickname, especially one from you. With the festival on, there's no place I can take you out to eat. What do you say we pick out some tasty things at the festival and then eat at my place or in the tribal gardens?"

"Let's eat at your place. In the gardens, I think you would be mobbed by people wanting to ask the first Ronopo Vice President about Washington, D.C.! I'll go scope out the chow while you have your meeting."

Hunter caressed her face with his eyes, willing his hands to stay obediently at his sides. "Sounds good. I'll meet you over by the food stands in about an hour?"

She nodded. "See you then."

Hunter turned and walked briskly to the Ronopo Tribal Offices. Breeze saw two men in suits and dark sunglasses converge on him. Secret Service, of course. She noticed that the two powerfully-built men had American Indian features. She continued to watch the elegant young man as he walked away. He looked so fine. Having come directly from Washington, he was still in his suit trousers and crisp white shirt, its sleeves folded back above his wrists. The shine on his loafers showed through the streaks of dust picked up during the dance. She watched until he was no longer in sight.

In one hand, Hunter held the basket of food that he and Breeze had picked out from the festival. He opened the door of his bungalow with his other hand, allowing Breeze to precede him inside. His small abode was flooded with the soft rays of the setting sun coming through the window. Breeze was surprised at how fresh his place smelled as it had been unoccupied for a long time. There were newly cut flowers in a vase on a table, and Hunter laughed as he set the food down beside them. He motioned for Breeze to have a seat in an old but comfortable chair while he pulled two water bottles from a cooler. He handed her one and sat down on a milk crate across from her.

"I asked Rozzi for a huge favor – to just make sure my place was fit for human habitation since I would be sleeping here tonight after being away for so long. As usual, my sister went the extra mile and cleaned it – and brought flowers to boot. She's such a great girl."

"I've always thought so, too."

Hunter's face turned serious. "Well, *you* did something amazing for her."

Breeze was taken aback. *He knows about that?*

"When I was sixteen, Rozzi finally told me... that she was raped when she was thirteen. And that it was by an Elder, a friend of our father – that awful Okoma Goshicon. That *monster* was the cause of her pregnancy. She told me that one person witnessed it. You."

Breeze looked down. The memory brought on cascades of chills and revulsion.

Hunter continued, "She said that you came to our house to drop off a home-cooked meal from your mother to my seriously abuse-damaged mother. Rozzi said that you saw the assault through the window. She said that my father was passed out and that Okoma did not see you – but that you and Rozzi made eye contact. She said you ran straight to the warning drum in the village center and pulled and pulled on its rope, broadcasting the drumbeats through the loudspeaker system. I remember how everyone came running out of their homes and businesses thinking there was a fire or other emergency, since that is the ONLY reason the warning system is ever to be activated. Firemen left their jobs to get their gear, everyone ran for their weapons, and medical personnel grabbed their kits."

Breeze closed her eyes, remembering.

"So, there you were in the village center, surrounded by highly agitated adults asking you what the emergency was. You were dumbstruck and didn't answer. Rozzi was thirteen and I was ten. So you were what, eight or nine years old? Rozzi said that Okoma stopped assaulting her and ran outside to see what the emergency was – but it was too late."

Hunter shook his head bitterly. Then he looked at Breeze and his expression softened.

"It was ingrained in every kid in this village that there would be dire consequences if we ever touched that drum. I remember how your father punished you. I was so glad that he didn't beat you! I bet that your father has *never* hit you – or even your brothers – in your whole lives, has he?"

Breeze shook her head, feeling awful knowing what Hunter and his sister had so frequently endured at the hands of their father.

Hunter solemnly asserted, "If I have children, I will never, ever hurt or humiliate them." He paused before continuing, "I remember that your father made you apologize to every adult member of the village there. You then had to spend one hour working for each of them to make up for the time they had lost responding to a false alarm and for the agitation you had caused them. Such a reasonable punishment. Of course, no one could believe that *you* had misbehaved! And here you had done it for Rozzi."

Breeze looked at the floor, tears running down her cheeks. Hunter tipped her chin up and wiped them away.

"Rozzi and I are grateful that you were so brave and that you didn't tell anyone. It was because I knew this about you, that I realized Dukon was lying when he said you had called Rozzi a slut and said that she had gotten pregnant by being loose with the boys. It wasn't much of a mental leap then that other things you *supposedly* said about me and my family were more of Dukon's lies. He was trying to enrage me enough to... I still can't believe that he thought I would *kill* someone. I guess my rather... brusque disposition and my history of being abused made me seem like a good candidate for uncontrollable rage. Of course, he didn't know that you were one of the very last people that I could possibly hurt."

Sniffling, Breeze asked him if he had any tissues. He pointed her to his bathroom. When she emerged a few minutes later, she found that he had closed the curtains, turned on some music, and set the table.

"I didn't mean to cast a pall over our *first date,*" Hunter said, smiling.

Breeze shook her head and laughed. They sat and ate the delicious Ronopo foods from the festival and caught up from when they had seen each other last.

After their meal, Hunter washed their dishes, and Breeze dried them. He turned to her, and said with all apparent seriousness,

"I've danced with you once now, at the festival, but I have a lot of making up to do for us not being partners in our grade school dance classes."

They both laughed.

"So... may I have this dance?"

There was a slow song playing, and Breeze nodded, following Hunter to the open space in the seating area. He held her in a somewhat formal position, so she took a step closer to be more completely in his arms. They were now moving to the music with his lean, hard body and her curvaceous softness in full physical contact. They both felt the inevitable response from Hunter's body. He looked at her uneasily.

"It's okay," Breeze whispered, gazing up at him.

Looking at the face that was so positively beautiful to him, Hunter bent his head and kissed her.

Nothing – absolutely *nothing* in his life had ever felt sweeter than this. He was holding the young woman that he had loved for so long, and kissing her, knowing that she loved him too. He held her and continued kissing her, no longer hearing the music nor moving his feet in time to it. He found himself kissing her cheek and her graceful neck, both he and Breeze now ravenously exploring each other with their lips and their hands. Kissing one another deeply, their passion ignited. Hunter pulled back.

"I should take you home before—"

"We don't have to stop."

"Breeze... I don't want you to think that I used the Harvest Festival dance for this reason. I want you to never doubt that I asked you to be my special loved one... *because I love you.* It was not to get you to have sex with me."

Breeze's hand reflexively went to Hunter's choker around her neck.

"I *know* that you love me, and it's not just this. I feel it. Actually, I've always felt it. I just could not reconcile the way you avoided me with the magic that I sensed between us. And... *I love you, too, Hunter.*"

Hunter smiled sadly.

"I did not assume you would... My intention was only to tell you and the tribe that I love you and hope to make you mine. So... I did not get anything to protect us."

Breeze studied his face. Then she said, "Not to worry, Blaze... I'm carrying."

She reached into her native-woven shoulder bag and pulled out a box of condoms. "Of course we don't have to make love. But just so you know, I'm on the pill too."

Shaking his head, Hunter kissed her tenderly and then very passionately. He whispered in her ear, "Breeeeeeze... are you sure... you want to play... with a *Ronopo Bad Boy?*"

Breeze let go and leaned back, blinking at him with wide eyes.

He had a devilish look on his face.

The next thing Breeze knew, Hunter's leg had swept hers out from under her, and he was pulling her to the floor. He landed on his back, and she tumbled on top of him. Holding her tightly against him, he rolled their bodies, pinning her back to the floor.

Smiling roguishly, he said in his deep, raspy voice,

"Let's try this a little *differently* this time..."

CHAPTER FORTY-EIGHT
Confession

When Golden Hawk was elected President of the United States, along with his baggage-ridden, pop celebrity Vice President, it was truly *historic*. This was the first Native American Indian President in the history of the United States – and the first female Vice President.

However, not long after the inauguration, just as Golden Hawk had "predicted" to Hunter, the Vice President needed to enter drug and alcohol rehab for issues that had plagued her in the past when under stress. It was clear that she could not be relied upon in this high-pressure job, so she had to step down. President Golden Hawk quickly appointed his Chief of Staff, Hunter Wolf, as the new Vice President.

There was immediate backlash, because Hunter was surely not even close to being 35 years old. However, the Official Keeper of the Ronopo Register (one of Dukon's cronies) affirmed that Hunter had *just* turned 35, even though he looked much younger.

No member of the Electoral College nor any journalists were permitted to infringe upon the sovereignty of the Ronopo Tribe and look at the Register themselves. The media and members of the party in power vociferously labeled anyone who suggested that Dukon or Hunter could be lying – as racists. Ronopo Co-Chiefs Aspen and Fox, as well as Elder Chief Bridgewater, would not have opposed an independent verification of the Register. However, before Dukon had left his position as Ronopo Chief, he had quietly managed to have it codified into tribal law that the Official Keeper of the Register, not the Chief, had the final word on all decisions regarding the Register.

In addition, following a precedent set by a prior Presidential candidate, a judge had sealed all of Dukon and Hunter's college and other personal records prior to the start of Dukon's campaign.

Hunter was furious. He felt completely blindsided by this deception. Dukon had told him that he was going to issue an Executive Order to temporarily allow the emergency appointment. He had *not* informed Hunter that he was going to thrust him into a position of passively committing perjury. Hunter knew that *he,* not Dukon, would be held accountable if the truth came out. Dukon could simply claim that Hunter had deceived *him* and had "cooked the books" back when the Ronopo Official Register was under Hunter's control.

Hunter wondered if Dukon was doing this to set him up for removal at his convenience. Dukon's previous attempts to give him a criminal record had failed. First, Dukon had expected Hunter to murder Breeze. Then, he maneuvered Hunter's neck onto the chopping block, instead of his own, in the trial for the tribal land deals. The rescue Dukon had promised Hunter had never come during the trial. Hunter knew that it was the intervention of puissant secret forces outside of Dukon's ken that had saved him from a possible death sentence.

Although it was ground that had previously been trod by other candidates, there continued to be concern about the inability of the People of the United States to validate a candidate's eligibility in accordance with the Constitution. Although this question had been regarding Hunter's age, his and Dukon's U.S. citizenship as members of the Ronopo Tribe also had not been verified by the Electoral College due to tribal sovereignty over their own official register of names.

While the debate raged on, the White House simply went ahead and swore in Hunter Wolf as Vice President of the United States.

A few days after the swearing-in, Hunter told Dukon that they needed to talk – privately.

"What is it?" Dukon asked as they walked in a White House garden.

"You and I need to come clean with one another."

Dukon regarded him warily. "What are you talking about?"

"You lied to me."

Dukon cast a look of impatience at him.

Hunter said, "And I lied to you."

"We don't have time for this!" Dukon responded irritably.

Hunter ignored him and continued, "Back when we launched your campaign for President, you asked me to take care of a 'loose end' for you. You were concerned that it could adversely affect your ability to win the election. As requested, I reported to you upon its completion. But... I lied. I had not carried out your request."

Dukon's eyes grew large and dark.

"You asked me... to permanently get rid of... the *only* woman I have ever loved."

Dukon's eyes flared with alarm, and Hunter began to tell a partially fabricated story that he had prepared.

"Out of my own pocket, I anonymously funded a small research project for Breeze. She investigated a remote, geologically unusual location out of the country. She was completely unaware that she was *in hiding* there. She was accustomed to working alone and having no contact with the outside world for long periods of time. So having no phone or Internet service was not unusual to her. She had no knowledge whatsoever of my involvement, and obviously, she did not adversely affect your campaign."

Hunter *had* funded Breeze's small grant – with his own money and under a false name. To deflect suspicion away from her, he had stipulated that she and two other people were to be involved. One was a researcher already working for the Principal Investigator actually receiving the grant. The other was to be a "visiting statistician" who was really a bodyguard that Hunter had hired to keep Breeze safe and to covertly contact him by satellite phone, if necessary.

Hunter had exacted an oath from the Principal Investigator to protect the research by not identifying the data, the work-site, or the personnel involved to anyone or on any computer. Also, the personnel were to be sworn to secrecy – "to prevent getting scooped by another research team." Any failure to comply with those terms would result in a loss of the funding.

Breeze unwittingly disrupted her protective arrangement when she left the outpost with the supply truck driver. Hunter's man on-site had immediately informed him, and Hunter had scrambled, getting his friend Jonas to help him abduct Breeze and take her to Jonas's island.

Hunter continued with his story. "Breeze concluded her research and has just returned. And... she has accepted my proposal of marriage."

Dukon's lip curled back like a snarling dog.

"Now, about your lie to me. You got me on board to become Vice President with your promise to issue an emergency Executive Order to handle the issue of my age. Instead, without my consent, you put me in a position of passively committing perjury. I feel that my now precarious position is an indirect threat to me – by you. Also, since you are a man who would order the murder of a woman who might harm his career aspirations, I can only assume that you might order the same for me.

I have long suspected, Dukon, that you have someone providing you extraordinary financial, as well as other types of support that have made possible your meteoric rise to the Presidency of the United States. You are now in a position to repay this patron or patrons in all kinds of ways. This is something that the public would probably only recognize if they were looking for it, and even then only upon careful scrutiny. Your past record has been consistent. In your previous positions your priorities and actions basically only benefited you, your cronies, and some unexpected outsiders. You never focused on your constituents' critically important issues that, during your campaigns, you promised to address.

The fact that you asked *me* to get rid of Breeze, when you seemed to already have shady contacts – and personal funds that grossly exceed what you have earned – not to mention inordinate amounts of campaign funds from unidentified sources – made me wonder if you were setting me up. Why else would you have needed *me* to murder her?

I don't know what your agenda is now that you have attained one of the most powerful positions on Earth. You basically have carte blanche around the world and unlimited funding by simply putting it on America's 'tab.' Who can stop you?

Upshot? I want Breeze, my sister, myself, and the rest of the Ronopo Tribe, to be safe from any 'accidents' or other misfortunes. How do I dare make such a demand? It's simple. This gizmo that I wear on my belt every day is not a cell phone, but an old-fashioned recording device that I use to keep myself organized. I automatically turn it on every time that we meet. I have recorded every business-related conversation that you and I have had. Then, once I have my tasks scheduled based on those conversations, I generally delete the recordings – just not all of them. Those that I kept, including the one of you threatening me with trumped up charges back on the reservation and telling me to get rid of Breeze, are in multiple, safe hands to be broadcast worldwide if anything happens to me or people I care about."

Dukon's silence and dark expression seemed likely confirmation of Hunter's accusations.

"Oh, and Dukon," Hunter added offhandedly, looking at his watch, "in approximately two minutes, a press release will be aired, announcing my engagement to Breeze Whitecloud. It will also publicize a prior discovery by her, now confirmed, of a massive petroleum oil find on the Ronopo Reservation – in Rattlesnake Canyon. So, since I supposedly killed Breeze, and since the oil discovery will cast a new light upon your land-trade partners' undisclosed, *actual* interest in Rattlesnake Canyon, I will let you go. I imagine that you have some explaining to do... to someone... somewhere."

COUNTERPOINT VI
STATUS REPORT: UNDOCUMENTED & UNDERCOVER

"How many fighters do we have in place?"

"About a hundred thousand. We have been sending them across the lax U.S. borders. Then, some of our people embedded in U.S. Administration used their budget calamity as an excuse to release thousands of illegal aliens from detention, *including ones who had committed other crimes.* Some were our fighters. They are now recruiting other criminals from the prison release to join us."

"Status of our fighters? Where are they and what is their capability?"

"They're almost ready. We have some in every state. Battalions are encamped on federal lands closed off to the public 'for budgetary reasons' or 'to prevent unauthorized oil drilling endeavors.' We have been conducting terror training on-site. U.S. Intelligence seeks our training camps abroad, oblivious to those in their own backyard!

We offered rewards to some legal immigrants and others if they would demand rights for *illegal* immigrants. It worked, also scoring *U.S. driver's licenses* for our fighters, for which they use false names from nations south of the border. That vastly improves our hand, because with driver's licenses, they have the appearance of legitimacy since a driver's license is like a passport there. They can now drive vans loaded with fighters, explosives, destructive chemicals, etc. And they can drive vehicles into crowds, killing people randomly, claiming lost control.

The government auto company cheaply sells us what we need to mobilize our people, including self-driving cars! Soon we will take possession of the weapons, ammunition, and armored vehicles that the federal government has been buying. We sent our people there empty-handed and are supplying them with everything they need once there – mostly funded by the Americans themselves! Our fighters have even been given Welfare benefits and cheap cell phones as if they were citizens! We give commands to our fighters via those phones; and they will use them to detonate bombs as well. The federal government gave the service contract for those handout phones to *non-U.S.-owned* phone companies. *One of those providers, a company from Eurinatia, is working with us.* Though they *appear* to just piggyback off the American phone companies, they have been quietly building their own cell towers. Soon, they will have a complete service structure of their own in place. Moreover, our Eurinatian phone carrier does not come under the jurisdiction of U.S. law enforcement. Thus, no localities will be able to halt cell service to stop detonation of bombs as they did once before. When we terminate the Americans' phone service all across the country, *our people* will still have service through our *non-U.S.* cohort!

In preparation for however long this operation might take, our people on the inside made accusations that voter I.D. laws were attempts to keep *minorities* from voting. Instead of organizing local governments, students, and non-profits to help citizens obtain the needed I.D., our community agitators organized angry protests. So, with no I.D. required, many of *our* people were able to vote! Many Americans are more concerned about looking politically correct than they are about *anti-Americans* voting for policies that will hurt Americans! Since no I.D. was required, our recruits voted multiple times, using the names of people physically or mentally incapable of voting as well as dead people still listed on the election rolls. We have now been able to use the new driver's licenses to actually *register our foreign fighters* to vote! You don't have to be an American citizen to live – or even vote like one!"

"This is going well! What is our financial status?

"Our global partners provided funds as promised. Then, although U.S. law requires their Senate to pass a budget, they did not and suffered no repercussions. The federal legal agency is, instead, busily suing states that are trying to protect themselves from illegal immigration even though the feds are not fulfilling their legal obligation to protect them. The legal agency is also harassing opponents of the party in power. Thus, they are 'too busy' to bring charges against the Senate or the President, even though they have broken the law multiple times – as happened under a prior Administration. Certain members of their Congress keep forcing the U.S. debt ceiling to be raised, so there has been no limit for the budget items that *we* want. Our people in various federal agencies placed orders for weapons and ammunition, so no one would see the enormous amount coming from a single purchase point nor to a single point of distribution. We acquired other arms through an operation that reaped thousands of weapons. Thanks to media reports, it was viewed as just a government bungle."

"Ah, the power of the press!"

"Yes. The remnants of the media-for-the-masses report what the Administration prefers, and ignorant Americans do not challenge their President. Many people are not free to speak against their rulers or to vote them out. They live in fear of *death, torture, or disappearance forever into prisons of horror.* In America, they *do* have that freedom, yet many citizens do not speak out against their minority President, because *they* live in fear of... *being politically incorrect!* They take freedom for granted. Once we take over, they'll have *none* to take for granted! Any Americans we allow to live will do as they're told. Thus, they will always be politically correct!"

CHAPTER FORTY-NINE
Stung

The night was still. The only sound was the soft rustle of leaves stirred by the breeze. The man thought it was ridiculous having to stand watch this deep in the national park. They had long since lost any law enforcement that could possibly have been tailing them. They were so far off the beaten path, that the only thing they should have to worry about here was bear.

This wasn't the man's usual line of work. He much preferred trafficking girls. He wasn't going to get to use any of this merchandise; but he always got to do whatever he wanted with one of the drugged up, kidnapped girls that he transported for sale into sexual slavery.

He drew the last toke of his joint before using his shoe to grind the tiny twist into the soil. He heard a rush of air like the whoosh of a stronger breeze kicking up. Then, he couldn't breathe and just keeled over like a dead tree falling in the forest.

A woman placed her soft-clad foot on the man's back and forcefully yanked out her arrow, wiping it clean on the man's shirt. A hundred yards away, there was an identical whoosh and, with just a wheeze, another man fell quietly to the ground. Both bodies were dragged into tall weeds, disappearing from sight.

A stag suddenly rushed through the trees. It ran alongside a dark green van parked between the spots where the now-fallen sentries had been posted. The two dozing men inside the van startled awake.

"Shee-*iitt* man! That scared the life outta me!"

"Look, it stopped over there. What's it doing?"

"I dunno, it's too dark to see."

"*Whoa!* There's more of 'em!" the man said, recoiling from his door as more deer raced past. Those deer stopped near the stag and were prancing about and eating something. The men continued to watch what they could see of the boisterous bustle in the dark woods. They were oblivious that this noisy diversion masked clandestine goings-on with the cargo in the back of their truck. Eventually, the animals ran off, and the two men drifted back to sleep.

In the morning, they wondered why their comrades standing guard had not come to waken them and take their turn sleeping in the van.

"It's creepy that Rico and Mani aren't here."

"Gimme those binoculars. I should be able to see 'em if they're still out there."

After searching, he looked apprehensively at his partner. "Nada," he said.

"We better check on the goods."

They walked around the van and opened the rear doors. The cargo looked undisturbed.

"You think it was a wild animal that got 'em? Or maybe they got ambushed by our buyers – and they're coming for us next!"

"We were supposed to trade shifts hours ago. If the buyers wasted 'em, they woulda gotten us by now, too..."

The men eyed their surroundings uneasily.

"Reporting in, General," a female voice said over the phone.

"Go ahead, Captain Thunderstrike."

"We followed the straw purchasers from the gun shop to their hiding place in the national park. We know that the government group conducting the sting instructed the gun shop to transfer the lot without unsealing the crates. We unsealed them and found that, except for a couple of rifles near the top of each crate, the serial numbers on all the others had been filed off. And, sir, the rifles without serial numbers were not the *semi*-automatic kind that citizens can generally buy, often misrepresented as 'assault rifles' just because they look like them. These were *actual* assault rifles – *fully automatic*. We brought a couple of the rifles back with us, and the lab confirmed that there were no tracers of any kind on them. So, except for the few that still had serial numbers, there actually would have been no way for the government agents to track the rifles as they say they planned to do."

"Hm... without serial numbers, any deadly consequences from the use of those weapons also could not be tied back to the sting operation and blamed on the government."

"True, sir. We tagged many of the weapons with invisible tracers and mixed them in with the untagged ones. There is something else, sir. One crate in the van did not contain rifles. It held... *shoulder-fired missile and grenade launchers.* We don't know if those were acquired via the government sting or if the straw purchasers already had those in their truck from another source. We tagged some of them, as well."

The General was silent for a few moments. "This gun-running operation may be connected to something even worse than the fiasco of a prior Administration. Mission casualties?"

"We had to take out two of their armed sentries. We already knew from past experience that when the party who hired the straw purchasers would arrive to pick up the load, they would kill them instead of paying them. That is exactly what happened to the other two men. We fingerprinted the four casualties, and, as we had suspected, those four men were all on the *human* trafficking most wanted list, as well. My own team remained intact – with just a minor injury to my animal handler, Brave John Gentle Paw."

"Good work, Captain. When you next check in, I will apprise you of the path that your trace-enabled weapons have taken."

"Captain Thunderstrike, two rifles *with* serial numbers that you tagged were found near the southern border at a scene of violence against U.S. landowners. *A couple* of your other tagged ones were tracked into Mexico, but those rifles stayed close to the border. According to our Mexican SIGNAL operatives, those are *not* known cartel locations. We have also learned that *most* of the rifles tagged with your tracers *stayed in the U.S.* and were transported further *north.*"

"That is an ominous finding, sir."

"Yes. Although the news reports state that this *botched sting* resulted in massive numbers of rifles getting into the hands of drug cartels across the border, *we* know that most of the *tagged* rifles are still here in the U.S. Thus, it is likely that most of the untagged ones are as well. Since we know that the government sting program had multiple other operations go awry, there could be a staggering number of weapons being amassed here in the U.S."

"Do we know who has them, sir?"

"Not yet. They could be in drug cartel sites on *this* side of the border, but it may not be drug-related at all. We are following the weapons to determine their final destinations. We are also investigating the possibility that a person *embedded in the government* is involved in selling government-purchased guns – or distributing them for free – via 'botched stings.' Also, the few weapons found at the border could have been *planted there* as deliberate *disinformation.* Those few rifles may have been *decoys* to deceive the public and law enforcement, into believing that the rest of those weapons went into Mexico and are not still on U.S. soil. Therefore, no one would be expecting them to be here and used in the U.S."

"Sir, that possibility makes it all the more frightening that the government is trying to disarm citizens and disallow personal body armor. If dangerous people are acquiring large numbers of assault weapons here – and citizens were to have *no weapons* to defend themselves... Even if the sting rifles did make it south of the border – if they end up in the hands of people intending to attack Americans... This places additional urgency on securing our borders and ascertaining the identities of undocumented people already here. May I acquire the data that shows where the tagged weapons currently are? I'd like to look at the geographic distribution and discuss it with Captain Lightfoot, if I may."

"Certainly. I will send you the access codes via *Smoke Signals.* Your mission to tag weapons with tracers enabled us to collect extremely high-value intelligence for SIGNAL. Excellent work, Captain Thunderstrike – as always."

CHAPTER FIFTY
Green Games

Spokesmen explained that the Administration was stonewalling the exploitation of U.S. oil and natural gas in order to reduce climate change on the planet. They could not answer, "Why, then, is the Administration giving extravagant grants to *other nations,* supposedly to help *them* to *increase* oil production on this very same planet?"

Environmental activists had labored long and hard and had successfully secured many U.S. regulations. These rules required that energy resources be extracted and refined in a much more environmentally responsible manner in the U.S. than was being done in some nations whose expansion U.S. taxpayers were apparently now financing.

Meanwhile, federal funding for green energy development in the U.S. mushroomed as it had under a previous President. Breeze Whitecloud and her colleagues noticed that most of the funds were being funneled to certain, private energy companies and not to public research institutions. That could mean that select shareholders, chosen by certain public officials, could personally profit from a business funded by taxpayers! Seemed shady and like a recipe for a possible cycle of corrupt pocket-lining between corporate officers and the elected officials who had granted them the funds!

One company that had received significant federal grant money had made an enormous loan *to a political party* and subsequently *forgave* the loan! That basically amounted to a huge, camouflaged contribution of money taken from all taxpayers and given to one political party! How could that possibly be okay? And might such financial support have affected the outcome of that election?

Most important of all, although green energy certainly should be pursued, it should not be prioritized at the cost of continuing to fund murderous, oil nation terrorists, giving them lots of money *and time* they needed *NOW* to infiltrate and get into position all across the countries with lax borders – until it would be too late to stop them from their evil, barbaric intentions.

The Ronopo Tribe felt victimized by their former Chief, Golden Hawk, yet again. Like many other Americans, the Ronopo unemployed would have benefited enormously by the well-paying jobs that expanding oil and natural gas production on federal lands would have created. President Golden Hawk was even delaying permission to the Ronopo Tribe to develop the oil field Breeze discovered in

Rattlesnake Canyon on their own sovereign reservation! And this was despite their well-documented, Earth-friendly development plans.

There was justifiable concern about the impact of the economy on Native Americans and, especially, the lack of improvement promised to the Ronopo by their former Chief. They said, "The unemployment rate of American Indians is astronomically high, even compared to the high rate of the general U.S. population and other minority groups! *Illegal intruders* are receiving preferential treatment over us despite the fact that we are *U.S. citizens!"*

Still serving as Dukon's intermediary with the tribes, Hunter conceded,

"Some politicians are looking for new sources of votes. One camp has already counted on the votes of American Indians and other minorities – rightly or wrongly. Courting *foreigners* with offers and promises could yield them a significant crop of *new* votes. Yes, supporting more dependent people would drag down the economy even further for everyone. And, yes, not addressing unemployment and adding lots of needy newcomers to the poor end of the income spectrum *increases* economic disparity. I am working to get rid of the *fudged* unemployment rate statistic. I don't know if the President will allow it, but I intend to replace it with the *actual* percentage of people who are able to work but who are on government or tribal assistance instead. That much larger number, which is *not* reported to the public, is the true measure of our unhealthy economy and reflective of what you all are suffering."

All across America, the increasing numbers of unemployed people were now available and more vulnerable to calls from agitators to participate in riots and protests. Some people were *paid to be agitators* and some were paid to *participate* in riots! Instead of proper, peaceful protests, they destroyed personal and public property and impeded family affairs and work for people who still *were* employed. Such disturbances also diverted law enforcement away from more dangerous criminal activity.

Aside from the effect on America's economy, by continuing to purchase oil from hostile countries instead of exploiting America's own, the U.S. was indirectly a financier of global terrorism. This was something that leadership had the power to change – but did not. It was sickening to know that by now, North America could have choked off the lifeblood feeding the world-darkening plague of terrorism.

The new federal policies did nothing to help America's two most pressing problems: national security and the economy. The only beneficiaries seemed to be America's *enemies* and American *wannabees*.

CHAPTER FIFTY-ONE
Cherry Blossoms

Hunter and Breeze had a beautiful, traditional yet secular Ronopo wedding.

Like many scientists, Breeze was agnostic. She had neither blind faith nor disbelief in a Creator. Nor had she been indoctrinated that any one religion's teachings were "the correct beliefs." She formed her own opinions about all things – based both on evidence and on how her human spirit guided her. She had been raised with traditional, good values regarding right vs. wrong, personal responsibility, and compassion for all.

Hunter felt that his spirituality was a purely personal connection between him and the Great Spirit.

All that said, they both felt blessed by Heaven and Earth in this marriage; and after the joyful event, Breeze moved to Washington with Hunter.

Sequoia invited Breeze to lunch and a self-guided tour of Washington's famed Cherry Blossoms. At lunch they recounted favorite moments from the wedding.

"Breeze, your father definitely took the prize for the most shocking revelation during the storytelling!"

"I cannot believe he kept that secret from us all these years! Even my mother didn't know that it was Hunter who brought me home the night we all nearly got alcohol poisoning in our teens! Can you believe that he carried me all the way from the northwest quadrant on foot?! Of course none of us had money for a car back then. Hunter walked miles most days to and from that construction job he had. He must have already been exhausted from his day of physical labor! He told me that when he saw that I was unconscious, he was afraid to leave me there. He thought I might die before he could bring my father to me, since none of you were in any condition to help me. He couldn't call for assistance, because none of us owned a cell phone yet."

Sequoia nodded. "Boy, was Hunter ever embarrassed! He did not see that story coming!"

"How about the part where my father went to see Hunter and apologized for the way he had received him at our door?"

"It was amazing that Hunter refused the gift that your father tried to give him back then as thanks for what he had done. It made me want to cry that all Hunter asked was that your father *promise* not to tell anyone that it was he who carried you home."

"Hunter must have been so afraid that we all would label him as a 'squealer' for letting a parent find out that we were drinking. In actuality, he may have saved one or more of our lives."

Sequoia nodded. "Your father was so funny, thanking our ancestors for allowing promises to be released at a marriage. That secret was clearly a painful burden. He wanted people to know the goodness in Hunter but could not break his promise!"

They finished their lunch, contemplating the story. Then they were ready for their stroll. They set out, flanked by Secret Service at a distance respectful of their privacy.

"How are you holding up, Sequoia?" Breeze asked quietly. "It must be really hard knowing that your husband is involved in something shady – at best. I've worried about your safety ever since I learned that Dukon ordered Hunter to kill me! If Dukon had given that order to anyone else..."

"I'm not really concerned about my safety. You were a threat to Dukon's aspirations. You figured out that Rattlesnake Canyon likely had a valuable oil field in it; and he had already been conniving with others to swindle our tribe out of that wealth. His track record has shown him accumulating wealth at every opportunity – and without regard to the damage he causes others in the process. I don't think he sees me as a threat, so I'm well-positioned to keep an eye on him."

Breeze nodded, still looking worried.

"As for my relationship with Dukon, it was never what I expected to have in marriage. As you heard, it was a sudden, high-pressure, whirlwind courtship before I decided to take the plunge and marry him. I can't say that I've gotten to feel much closer to the man than I did when I was dating him. We've spent a great deal of time apart over the last couple of years with his rapid job changes and all his travel. When we're together, we never talk as spouses or lovers normally do. He discusses work with me and clearly values my input, but he really only talks to me when others are present. Sometimes I catch him looking at me... almost wistfully. From the start, I felt that the physical chemistry between us was mutual. He makes time for sex, but immediately afterward, he's off to answer a call or to shower, or he says he's tired and needs to go to sleep – *in his bedroom.* So, there is no pillow talk whatsoever. Believe it or not, he knows nothing about my family and has never asked me about them."

"Really? That is odd."

"Thankfully, I've had much fruitful and fulfilling work. The marriage certainly gave me the opportunity to accomplish things I might otherwise never have been able to do. But it's been so lonely. I feel as if my extreme physical attraction to him and his intense and seductive courtship were cruel tricks, luring me into an empty lair."

After a pause, she said, "You and I have always said that we want children."

Breeze smiled and nodded enthusiastically.

"Well, considering everything, I am grateful that Dukon and I have not had any."

Breeze squeezed her friend's arm and whispered sympathetically, "Perhaps your continuing journey will lead you to happiness – which you so richly deserve."

Sequoia smiled, appreciative of her friend's optimistic words.

COUNTERPOINT VII
STATUS REPORT: LAMBS TO THE SLAUGHTER

Americans will soon understand what their forefathers knew. People with weapons subjugate people without them. It's laughable. The primary premise upon which America was born was freedom of the individual from tyranny. Their Constitution specifically locked in the right for citizens to have defensive weapons in order to prevent *exactly what is about to happen to them!* It is going to be the height of entertainment to watch."

"What has our involvement been in bringing about their disarmament?"

"Our co-conspirators have been pushing globally for worldwide disarmament. Some of the high-ranking American officials whom we helped to elect, are supporting it. Most nations, even if they sign it, will certainly not abide by it, but the Americans will! We then... capitalized on a rare, mass shooting of children. The usual suspects in government and the media focused on this along with other sensationalistic events with small numbers of deaths. They overlook the fact that children in their inner cities die in those numbers *every day* by criminals and gangs who obtain their weapons *illegally, ignoring all laws*. New laws will not stop them either. Kingland is a perfect example. No guns are allowed there, yet violent crime has risen dramatically since guns were outlawed. By contrast, gun violence in the U.S. has *declined* year after year without new laws. The gun-control advocates don't admit that *most* deaths occur by *other* means. The vast majority of U.S. murders are by a blunt instrument like a baseball bat or a hammer – not by guns. And on average, *25 children are killed every single day in America... by cars!* Yet, they focus on the *rare* incident of 20 children killed by a severely mentally ill person, because it is shocking, and people want *emotional* satisfaction. Our people exploited that to lobby against gun ownership."

"Very good. While focusing on this, other social issues, and scandals that your people have kept thrusting to the forefront – as planned – their Congress has been successfully pressured to respond to those instead of focusing on their national security or economic situation."

"Exactly. We helped to usher in people whose actions will allow us the freedom to install ourselves and forward *our* agenda. Soon, any surviving Americans will live by

138

our rule of law. They will understand too late how some citizens and politicians tried to stop the weakening of America that will now allow us to take control."

"I presume that our first moves will be where we will meet with the least resistance?"

"Yes. Some states banned rifles, even *semi*-automatic ones, with which people might have stood a chance against our fighters with our *fully automatic* ones. The masses incorrectly believe that the letters in the model number of a popular rifle stands for 'Assault Rifle' when it is just letters from the name of the company that invented it. That false sound-bite has worked effectively and is repeated often by ignorant or complicit people pushing for more gun control. As hoped, other states have banned *all* firearms. Our First Wave attack will begin in those states.

On other fronts: a partner nation drills tirelessly, using the replica they built of one of America's largest cities. An automotive plant that the American government paid for *abroad* has been turning out armored vehicles that will be delivered to U.S. ports for us during the First Wave. The federal, across-the-board budget cuts are forcing their military to reduce spending in ways that leaves America most vulnerable, including cuts to their National Guard and divisions that control airspace and critical infrastructure. They have even given special exemption from normal airport screening to *certain foreigners*, including ones from nations whose terrorists have attacked Americans! Their mainstream media lackeys do not report such things, so accounts released by news services that *do* publish them are called the 'musings of paranoid conspiracy theorists.' In short – *the performance is about to begin."*

"We will be watching with great expectations!"

"You will not be disappointed. This has been choreographed such that it will be a thing of *epic* beauty."

CHAPTER FIFTY-TWO
Epiphany

Dukon entered the Presidential apartment in the White House, and was clearly startled to find Sequoia there. He had ordered his dinner to be brought to the rooms. Sequoia just happened to learn of this and added herself to the dinner order.

"Sequoia! I thought you had a meeting this evening. I wasn't expecting to see you at dinner."

"My meeting was canceled, so I can dine with you after all."

Dukon seemed flustered and like he was searching for an excuse to escape this unexpected close encounter with her. She quickly offered words to quell any fears he might have.

"I'm tired. I'm glad the meeting was canceled. A quick, quiet dinner with you and then an early bedtime is what I need tonight," Sequoia said, yawning.

Dukon appeared to be mollified by this. Smiling a bit weakly, he approached and hugged her. In a wifely gesture, Sequoia took his jacket from him. She could tell by the weight of it that his cell phone was in one of its pockets. She hung it on the back of a chair away from the dinner table. Then she sat down and uncorked the bottle of wine that she had requested. Dukon took his place at the table, and Sequoia saw his eyes dart over to his jacket that was now out of reach. She immediately engaged him to divert him from retrieving his phone. Handing him a platter, she asked,

"How was your day?"

"Busy and stressful, as usual," he answered, helping himself to some lamb chops and passing the platter back to Sequoia.

"Anything of interest?" she asked.

"*No.* Just budgeting arguments. Definitely *not* of interest," he said, rolling his eyes and scooping up a forkful of couscous from his plate.

Sequoia prodded him a bit, but getting more than a few words out of him was like pulling teeth. She saw him glance at his jacket again. She imagined that he was willing his phone to ring to rescue him from having to converse with her; but it didn't ring. Sequoia wondered if her long-held suspicion was correct – that Dukon had always *caused* his phone to ring whenever she began to discuss personal things. She had thought it might be to prevent her from asking him something he did not wish to discuss. Obviously, he could not do that if the phone was not in his hand. She distracted him again.

"Have you thought about us having children?"

Dukon looked taken aback. "What is there to think about? When... the Great Spirit decides to bless us, we will surely have children. I *have* been disappointed that we have not yet received that blessing. Perhaps you should be seen by a doctor."

"Have *you* been checked by a doctor?" Sequoia asked, feeling bad if he had done so without discussing it with her first.

He started shaking his head with what looked like derision.

Now, Sequoia was taken aback. *Why would he think the problem could only lie with me?*

Seeing her expression, Dukon abruptly looked down and answered, "No, but of course I should do the same." He then conspicuously focused on his dinner, and Sequoia felt chills run up her spine.

"Dukon, do you realize that you and I have never even discussed *if* or when we would have children? There are many things we have never discussed that engaged or married couples really should."

Dukon stood up, wiping his mouth with his napkin, clearly about to go get his cell phone. Sequoia rose from her seat and blocked his path.

Dukon responded irritably, raising his voice.

"It never occurred to me that it was a *decision* or something that we would attempt to *control.*"

Sequoia rejoined, "It never occurred to *me* that we would not engage in responsible family planning – especially since we *both* have goals of accomplishments in addition to raising a family. Given our mutual attraction from the outset, and how *physical* and *seductive* your good-night embraces were while waiting for my answer to your proposal, I started taking birth control pills in case we were to lose control. Since you have not yet found time to discuss plans for our future, including having a family, I have not yet stopped taking them."

Dukon's mouth dropped open and his face turned red with anger. He stepped menacingly towards her, raising his hand.

Sequoia shrank back and yelled, "Dukon!"

He raised his other hand as well and placed them both against his face, that possibly being all that he was doing when he appeared to raise his hand to her. He dragged his fingers down his face and glared furiously at her.

"Why didn't you tell me?" he snarled in a low voice, remembering that bodyguards outside the apartment might hear raised voices.

"When have I had the chance to tell you? *Every time* that I try to bring up anything personal, your cell phone rings, abruptly ending our conversation. Not to mention how much time you've spent away and out of touch with me! Anyway, I'm young. I have many childbearing years ahead of me. What's the hurry?"

"I expected to have a child with you by now," he said resentfully. "Did you actually never intend to have children?"

At those words, her testy demeanor deflated. Her tone became one of emotional anguish.

"No, but after September 11th, I did wonder if I should bring a child into this now very different world. I–"

"The world is becoming a much *better* place since September 11th!" Dukon hissed.

Sequoia reeled with shock, blinking, unsure of his meaning.

"It was a wake-up call to the West! The people who died in those *towers of capitalist greed* represented the worst of affluent America!"

Sequoia's eyes and mouth were wide open with horrified disbelief. Dukon responded disdainfully to the expression on her face.

"*What.* Why should you give a damn about those... *white Americans,* anyway?"

On the verge of apoplexy, Sequoia slapped Dukon's face with all her might. She hit him so hard that the brawny man spun sideways, needing to take a step to regain his balance.

His voice came out in a low growl. "How *dare* you strike me!"

Sequoia screamed, "How dare YOU *laud* that horrific and *cowardly* act of barbarism! *My parents* were *killed* in those towers that day!"

Dukon froze, dumbfounded, staring at Sequoia as she continued to scream.

"They were working with a group of philanthropists to establish a private entity that would self-finance American Indian-owned enterprise! It was another step forward, to help foster culturally desirable business opportunities wholly devised, owned, and controlled by the tribes! This was to further reduce our dependence upon government promises which some politicians use to *exploit* us, tethering our voting bloc to *their* agendas! They manipulate low-income citizens, and now court new immigrants just to get their votes, using social program promises that are mathematically impossible to keep! *Foreign countries* are even trying to seduce the tribes with suspicious offers! My parents' initiative would have enabled more Native Americans to advance *themselves!* Tribes would have had the financial independence to buy more land or negotiate leases, and to have the choice to return to a life of the old ways – or not! And yes! They were *mostly* white Americans who were helping to make that possible! You BIGOT! Are... are you actually *sympathetic* towards that *dastardly* act of EVIL?!" Sequoia finished at a fever-pitch.

Knocks at the door reminded them of the Secret Service outside. Dukon went to the door and woodenly assured them that all was fine. Sequoia staggered towards the door, feeling as though she needed the sight of another human being to re-ground her reeling psyche. She let the bodyguards see her overwrought expression before Dukon closed the door.

Dukon turned and looked past Sequoia, as if in a trance, with blank, glassy eyes. After a few moments, he spoke in a whisper, almost as if he were not speaking to her.

"How is it possible... that I did not know... that my wife's parents died there?"

Sequoia could not speak as she struggled to regain her equanimity. She just stared at Dukon, trembling and swaying, gripping the back of a chair for support.

Dukon's consciousness seemed to return. Life reappeared in his eyes. He seemed to refocus on Sequoia as if reminded of her presence. Looking contrite, he said in a soft and chastened voice,

"I won't even ask for your forgiveness. You are so very right. I allowed my responsibilities as Chief to take priority over learning more about you and discussing important things. It was partly because I was already certain that you were the one for me. I did not give proper attention to what I might not know or what you might want to discuss. I am... so very sorry about your parents."

Sequoia was unmoved.

"And, *of course,* I did not mean what I said about 9/11. You have unfortunately witnessed how the budget discussions have strained my patience, pushing me beyond rational speech. I was thinking of some Congressmen's *towering* greed, and that led me to a completely inappropriate comparison to that deplorable act of terrorism."

Dukon approached Sequoia. He placed his hands on her shoulders and said, "I am so sorry, Sequoia. So very sorry."

Her breathing ragged, she just kept staring at him. Then, tears began to flow from her eyes.

With a look of true remorse, Dukon guided her to a comfortable club chair. He sat down in it and gently pulled her onto his lap. Stroking her hair in silence, he held her.

COUNTERPOINT VIII
HOPE

"This mistake represents a CRITICAL failure in The Business Plan. How is it possible that you not only selected a Native American tribe with a connection to 9/11 but also chose a relative of the victims from that tribe to be the President's wife?! The President will never be able to bring her on board with us! He still doesn't even have children by her to use as bait. How did you not know about the 9/11 connection?!"

"It was a fluke due to the custom of Native Americans having multiple names – coupled with bureaucratic incompetence typical of federal government. The tribe had bestowed an additional surname upon Mr. and Mrs. Katiri as a tribute to the significant contribution they were making for American Indians. They gave them the honor name: Hope. There *was* a couple, a Mr. and Mrs. Hope, on the list of people killed at the World Trade Center on 9/11, but there was no link tying that name back to their Ronopo name. We have found that the Katiris legally registered the new name, but it was mishandled by the U.S. government."

"Our analysts are working to identify the risks this could pose to the venture. For your sake, let us HOPE that it does not adversely impact the outcome!"

CHAPTER FIFTY-THREE
Smackdown

Sequoia was on the reservation for business involving her substance abuse programs. She dispatched her Secret Service agents to watch points of entry to the village, assuring them that she was safe on the reservation with her tribe.

Aspen asked her to meet with him when she was free.

"It's good to see you, Sequoia."

"You too, Aspen. How is your father?"

"About the same, thanks. Is everything all right in D.C.?"

"Define 'all right'," she said with a wry smile.

Aspen's expression grew serious.

"Sequoia, your position as First Lady makes you particularly vulnerable. Although you have Secret Service protection much of the time, I'm concerned about your safety if you should need to defend *yourself.* I don't suppose you have much opportunity to practice your self-defense or other SIGNAL training drills?" Aspen asked.

Sequoia hung her head. She knew that she had fallen down on that obligation to which she had pledged her dedication long ago. She did work out in a White House gym, but it was not the caliber of conditioning that SIGNAL required. She had the uncomfortable feeling that Aspen knew of her recent fight with Dukon, and that that was the reason he was raising this concern. She looked at him guiltily.

"I didn't think so. I cannot imagine how you would have time. You are often involved with your domestic and substance abuse programs when not immersed in other First Lady duties. Your presence is required in the Washington social scene; and, of course, you have a husband who places demands upon your time as well. Nonetheless, I wouldn't want you to be in need of skills that have become rusty. It would have been perfect if you and Breeze could have practiced together, but that could attract notice, so obviously you can't do that in D.C."

Aspen crossed his arms against his chest and looked at her intently.

"Since you're not heading back until tomorrow, how about spending some quality time with your old Regional Commander up at the hunting cabin this afternoon?"

Feeling like she had let down a favorite teacher, Sequoia nodded in agreement. Then she quickly turned away. Aspen's demeanor had caused her to experience his suggestion as an intimate proposition. She did not want him to even possibly detect her long-suppressed attraction to him. Years earlier she had discounted her strong feelings for him as being just the product of a young girl's crush on a very popular older boy. And here she was, again having waves of the now-forbidden feelings. Great! This was even more to feel guilty about! Although she was married to a man who was universally viewed as exceptionally attractive and impressive, she felt the hollow ache of her unfulfilled need for warmth and caring. It was a need that was perhaps deeper for her due to the tragic loss of her parents, and one which Dukon hardly satisfied.

Ha! So much for the demands that Aspen thinks my husband places on my time!

She went back to Granny K.'s little house and changed into suitable athletic attire.

Aspen and Sequoia left the parked truck, and walked up the hill to the hunting cabin. They abruptly stopped talking as they both noticed the foxtail hanging from the door handle. They looked at each other and smiled, shaking their heads.

"For goodness sake!" Sequoia exclaimed softly. "Is Fox still coming to the hunting cabin for his trysts? He has his own cottage now! I don't think I want to be here to see who he comes out with!"

Aspen covered his mouth, stifling laughter. He beckoned Sequoia away from the cabin, far into the grove of trees. Standing next to a tree he said,

"Okay! Pick-a-Tree!"

"Oh no, Aspen! I haven't climbed a tree in years!"

"Well you're about to or I'm going to demote you! On three! One, two, three!"

Up they both went, each in their own tree. Sequoia surprised herself, moving strongly and agilely up through the branches. Aspen reached the top of his tree first, but Sequoia held her own. She felt a rush of pleasure along with the adrenaline. She was proud – and relieved – that she still had it in her.

"Excellent!" Aspen said. "Now you know that you still have that means of escape or concealment as an option. A slow descent, now, please. I don't want to lose the First Lady to a fall from a tree!"

Sequoia started to climb carefully back down. Looking at the ground, she saw that Aspen was somehow already below her, ready to spot her if she were to fall.

Dang! He still moves like lightning! she thought.

She dropped to the ground on her own, smiling with exhilaration and self-satisfaction.

Just then, the cabin door opened, and Fox came out, conversing quietly with Birdie. Aspen let loose an ear-shattering howl, and Fox and Birdie both jumped a mile. Although they had been taken by surprise, they both instantly regained their equanimity and took cover. Embarrassed that they had been caught off-guard, Fox lobbed a salvo back at Aspen and Sequoia.

"So, it's your turn in the cabin, huh? Well, let's hope the President doesn't hear about this!"

Aspen shot him a scorching scowl, and Fox put his hands up in surrender.

"I didn't mean any disrespect... not to *you,* that is, Mrs. Chatan," Fox said with his signature smile.

Sequoia was relieved that it was Birdie who was with him. She knew that Birdie and Fox were close but also dated other people. She gave them each a hug.

Fox said, "The signal-deflector is on, so you can speak freely here in the northwest quadrant. Let me know when you leave, and I'll shut it off."

Birdie and Fox trotted off, laughing and tossing the foxtail in the air in a snatching match.

Inside the cabin, Aspen and Sequoia dragged the thick mats from the storage closet and laid them out on the floor. They moved to the center of the mats.

Without preamble, Aspen said, "Okay, I'm a threat. Take me down."

Sequoia thought, *Hm, which approach should I practice first?*

Aspen wanted to remind her exactly what hesitation could mean for her. He charged her, pushing her shoulder back while moving his leg behind hers. He smoothly swept her leg up in the air, sending her backwards towards the mat. Not wanting to chance her being injured in the fall, he caught her and quickly lowered her onto her back. He spread out his frame over her, pinning her arms, but not allowing his body to rest against hers.

"Okay. I got the best of you. Now what are you going to do?"

Sequoia wanted to start over, so she said, "Yield!"

"Not a chance. This man's got you where he wants you. You'd better do something about it – and quickly."

Sequoia struggled to free her arms, but he wasn't giving her any slack. She didn't want to knee him in the groin, but she tested her leg positioning to see if she could flip him. Aspen allowed more of his weight to press her against the mat, now pinning her legs as well.

"C'mon, Starfire!" Aspen exhorted. "Do something!"

Sequoia felt her adrenaline rushing, and her pique rising. She wriggled and jostled and tried to free some part of her body to use against him. She gritted her teeth and grunted with effort, her frustration growing. She could not budge him. Although he was slender, he was deceptively strong. She stopped struggling. Aspen remained alert, expecting that it was a ruse to get him to let down his guard – a tactic of which he heartily approved. Sequoia did not make a move. He waited, but she still did nothing.

"Well? Are you giving up?"

"Yes! I'm giving up."

"Really," Aspen said, frowning. "What if this were for real?"

"It isn't for real. Give me a break."

"No. By the looks of it, you've already had a long one."

Irked by this barb and by the fact that she obviously *had* lost her edge, Sequoia let her body go slack, clearly signaling that she was not going to engage.

"Are you actually quitting, Sequoia?"

"I need a chance to practice."

"This *is* your chance to practice! Are you going to do this in D.C.?"

Her annoyance was clear, and she didn't move. Aspen took it in, his face now losing its characteristic warmth. He turned his head away, closing his eyes. He inhaled deeply and exhaled audibly. Opening his eyes, he slowly turned back to look at

Sequoia... and she felt chills go up her spine. Alarm bells went off in her head at the expression on his face. Her danger meter shot up into the red zone... *with Aspen??*

He spoke in a harsh, unrecognizable voice. "Okay-y-y. Have it your way!"

Sequoia froze. She was momentarily paralyzed by Aspen's shocking transformation. He swiftly swept both of her arms up the mat and over her head. Just one of his large hands easily clasped both of her wrists. He clamped his other hand over her nose and mouth. Sequoia could not breathe. His eyes bored into hers with no hint of playfulness or any indication that this was still a training exercise. She tried to shake her head to loosen his hand from her face. Her eyes widened, feeling panic as he showed no sign of letting up. Desperate, she managed to turn her head, dislodging her mouth from his grasp. She wheezed and gulped in air.

"W-what's the matter with you?!" she croaked.

"DEFEND YOURSELF!" he boomed. "You're a SIG-Op in an important position, so act like one!"

Sequoia opened her mouth to berate him, but Aspen clamped his hand back over it. She frowned angrily but took none of the actions that SIGNAL trainers had drilled into her for years. Aspen shook his head with disgust and removed his hand from her mouth.

"Still not enough for you?" he asked, glowering.

He pressed the full weight of his body against hers and used one knee to push her legs apart. Sequoia's eyes blazed with shock at what he was doing.

"STOP IT, Aspen! I'm married – and to the President of the United States!"

Ignoring the implicit belittlement, he shot back, "You made a commitment to *me* long before you got married! Now *honor* it and *defend* yourself!"

Trying to hide the shame she felt, she turned her head away and remained rigidly still, sure that he would now put an end to this.

He tilted his head which caught her attention. With a threatening look, he said, "I'm warning you for the last time."

"I'm not doing this, Aspen! Let me up!"

He shook his head with resignation.

"I'll have to take that as submission, Sequoia. Remember that I warned you."

His free hand shot up under her shirt, roughly pulling it up and exposing her sports bra. His hand grazed her breast in the process. Sequoia screeched with indignation, and Aspen brusquely clamped his hand back over her mouth, mindful not to bruise it.

Sequoia finally got it. Aspen was going to take this as far as necessary to make her act. Now she was furious. Undulating her body violently, she was able to lift his body slightly. It gave her just enough leeway to draw up one knee and slide it into his groin. It wasn't a forceful jab, but he knew she was there. As he shifted to protect himself, Sequoia channeled all of her anger and frustration into a monumental, full-body thrust, accompanied by a shriek of effort and ire. She succeeded in just pitching Aspen onto his side and then immediately rolled out of his reach. They both jumped to their feet. Sequoia's eyes were full of fire as she advanced on him.

"How *dare* you!"

She slapped him and then slapped him again. He let her continue to slap him, knowing that she needed to do it. And, of course, he *had* provoked her. But he had achieved his objective – he had gotten his operative to shake off her rust and defend herself. Sequoia became more worked up as Aspen just stood there, barely flinching as she slapped him. She felt her hand clench into a fist; and instead of slapping him again... she punched him.

Aspen's face displayed a flash of surprise as he partially dodged the blow. Then he grasped her hands, threading his fingers through hers. With gentleness back in his face and softness in his voice, he said, "*That's* my SIG-Op. Good job. Good job, Sequoia." He looked into her eyes. "I am sorry. I had to inflame you into practicing defending yourself. I just don't want anything to happen to you, Dear One. Okay? Truce? Friends?" He cocked his head and smiled beseechingly. "Forgive me?"

Sequoia started to cry. Aspen put his arms around her and bear-hugged her. He rocked her for a long time while she cried herself out. They both knew that punching Aspen had been Sequoia's release of much more than indignation over a fairly mild, mock assault – which was part of all SIG-Ops' training, both male and female. Finally exhausted, Sequoia looked up and said in a whisper,

"Thank you, Aspen. I can't believe I punched you. *I am so sorry.*"

Aspen hugged her again, rubbing her back vigorously.

"You go wash up," he said. "I'll put the mats away."

During the drive back to the village, Aspen felt Sequoia staring at him. He smiled at her and returned his eyes to the road. When he looked again, he found her still staring at him.

"Okay, let me guess. You're wondering how far I would have gone if you hadn't defended yourself?"

Sequoia nodded.

With his eyes on the road, Aspen replied, "Well... when I was lying there on top of you, I had to ask myself that same question. There was a lamb bleating into one of my ears..." He gave her a sidelong glance, then looked back at the road. "... and a *wolf howling* into the other!"

Aspen flashed her a "just kidding?" smile, and Sequoia started laughing. He stopped the truck and turned to face her. They could still speak freely, without fear of audio or video spies, thanks to Fox's signal-deflector.

"Sequoia, I would *never*... cross the line. If you had not responded when you did, I was going to grab the waistband of your pants. If you did not react to that... I would have been done.... and... very disappointed in you." He placed a hand on her shoulder. "There's something else that I want to set straight. Back in the cabin, when I really began to 'attack you', I saw genuine fear in your eyes."

"It *was* genuine fear! I have never seen you like that! You were terrifying!"

"Well that was the point. You were obviously way too comfortable with me to feel like you needed to defend yourself. That exercise gave you a taste of how you might feel and what your physical responses might be in a real world attack." He smiled kindly at her. "But I need for you to know, that all of that was purely for the purpose of training. You never, *ever* need to be afraid of me. Okay, Dear One?"

Bathed in the warmth of these characteristic words from the Aspen she had always known, Sequoia smiled and nodded. He started the truck back up.

"Had enough of me for today, Sequoia? I turned down Granny K.'s invitation to join you two for an early dinner. She gets to see me all the time, and I was sure you would want some private girl talk with your grandmother. There is one more thing, though, that I would like to do with you since you're here so infrequently. After your dinner, may I have you for a couple more hours? I want to take you into the woods... Um, hm... considering our last hour together, that didn't sound quite right."

They both laughed. "There was a time when you were the top shot in the tribe. As you know, shooting skill degrades without practice. I'd like to see how well you now handle a rifle, a shotgun, and a handgun. We can skip the bow and arrows this trip."

Sequoia's eyes sparkled. She loved target shooting, both stationary and in motion. She *had* been missing it and had wondered how much her skill might have declined. So, although she felt drained from their physically and emotionally intense encounter, she agreed to meet up with him again after dinner.

When Sequoia saw Aspen's face a couple of hours later, she had to quickly cover her mouth to hide her guilty burst of laughter. Despite Aspen's best efforts back at his cottage, a black eye had already appeared where Sequoia had slugged him. Seeing her mirth, he narrowed his eyes playfully at her.

Over the next two hours, Sequoia got to brush up a little on her still impressive firearm handling and shooting proficiency. Now, Aspen and Sequoia were both more at ease knowing that, if necessary, Sequoia still knew how to handle herself.

CHAPTER FIFTY-FOUR
Ramrod

The media positively fawned over President Golden Hawk. He was touted as having vision and courage to push forward even in the face of his detractors who tried to place a *monetary* cost on his proposals. *Selfish* people asked, "How will we pay to support the ever-growing number of government dependents?" and, "With the USA so deeply in debt, why are we still giving enormous sums of money to foreign governments, including some dangerously hostile ones? How does this help the *U.S.* economy and the vast number of *Americans* still unemployed so long after the onset of the recession?" They criticized federal officials for putting the needs of non-Americans before the needs of the U.S. citizens whose interests they had sworn an oath to serve.

The party in power in Congress followed the example of a prior Congress. They used loopholes to circumvent the usual debating and exchange of alternative viewpoints that is supposed to be part of creating well thought-out, collaboratively constructed legislation. This resulted in laws that were supported only by that party – and by the Executive Branch – which is supposed to be *checked and balanced* by the Legislative Branch of government.

A couple of leaders of that party exploited technicalities to ram legislation through without any agreement – or sometimes even the presence – of ideologically opposed members of Congress elected by the people of their districts. Fittingly, the public nicknamed those Congressional leaders: "The Ramrods." Whenever the Administration wanted something controversial to be quickly signed into law, they laughingly said, "Just give it to The Rods."

Of course, the majority of citizens objected to this circumvention of the legislative process intended by The Constitution. Some lawmakers almost seemed to be serving a master and could possibly reap rewards themselves afterward, intentionally or not.

President Golden Hawk succeeded in getting a child safety reform bill introduced. Everyone knows that child safety is important! Few knew what was in the bill, but that was unimportant compared to getting some safety reforms quickly into place for children! There were many pages of edicts, new taxes, and new or enlarged government agencies that, under the President's command, would control the lives of Americans even more.

Congress was completely overwhelmed, trying to read and understand this gargantuan bill while also responding to a blizzard of special interest issues, bills, and scandal investigations, not to mention their own re-election campaigns. Thus, it was a total surprise to them when The Ramrods suddenly brought the child safety reform bill to the floor. Many members of Congress were not even there to vote. The Ramrods got it passed and President Golden Hawk quickly signed the omnibus bill into law.

This caused even more chaos. Consequently, hardly any members of Congress even noticed, let alone were able to provide resistance, when President Golden Hawk quietly issued an Executive Order. It provided a temporary waiver of all Constitutional minimum age requirements "so as not to discriminate" against youth in government leadership positions. The Executive Order stated that Congress should formally act on this using proper protocol *after* resolving more pressing issues currently before them.

President Golden Hawk then acerbically asserted to Hunter Wolf that he should no longer feel "threatened" by him. If Hunter's true age were to come out, the Executive Order made Hunter's age irrelevant. Golden Hawk also gave Hunter a document, signed by him, to set aside in case he needed it. It said that the Ronopo Keeper of the Register had made a *mistake* about Hunter's age. In the document, the President took full responsibility for the "accidental misrepresentation."

Hunter gave Dukon a circumspect response, hiding just how appalled he was at this President's "progressive" tactics.

CHAPTER FIFTY-FIVE
Up a Tree

Sequoia had certainly noticed that Dukon's published daily calendar bore little resemblance to his actual activities. She thought she must have been naive to believe that a President actually had accountability to the people who elected and paid him to serve them. Or maybe Dukon was just running rogue, doing whatever he pleased and answering to *no one*. Sequoia ignored the rumors that his calendar was altered to cover for unrecorded visits from gorgeous, young women. She figured that type of gossip was inevitable.

Today, Sequoia had nothing on her calendar. She had verified it with her assistant. It was truly a free day! She started it uncharacteristically – by sleeping in. She then indulged herself, staying in her long, satin nightie. She took her cup of coffee to the breakfast nook with windows overlooking a private garden. When she went back to the kitchen to refresh her cup, she stepped into the hall to check the thermostat. From there, she saw that Dukon's bedroom door was ajar. She called to him, certainly not having expected him to be there. She stood just outside his room and called again.

She felt a bit creeped out since Dukon *never* left his door open. She was worried when he didn't answer, and she hoped that someone *else* wasn't in there. She warily stepped into the room and looked around. It seemed unoccupied and orderly with just some books and papers sticking out from under his bed. She peeked into his bathroom and closets but saw no one.

This was a rare opportunity to snoop on Dukon for SIGNAL, but she felt uneasy. She had been advised to err on the side of caution so as to maintain Dukon's trust. In case he had video surveillance in his room, she called his name again as she crouched to look under his bed. Closer to the floor now, she got a better look at the books and papers under there. She felt her eyes widening at what she saw, but her training kicked in and she maintained a bland expression.

Suddenly having a very bad feeling, she stood up and headed for the door. As she exited the room at a rapid pace, she marched right into Dukon who was running towards the room. He glared at her with steely, cold eyes.

"Dukon! You scared the life out of me! You never leave your door open, so I thought you were here! Then I got worried when you didn't answer me!"

He entered his room and looked around.

"Snooping, Sequoia?"

"For goodness sake! Is there something for me to snoop for? Your door was open; you didn't answer my call; I went in to be sure you were all right – and that no one else was here. Is there anything strange about that? What's the big secret? I'm your wife!"

Dukon exhaled forcefully. "I did forget to close my door. I left in a hurry this morning and just came back for something I forgot. My day is not off to a good start."

"I'm sorry to hear that. Do you want a sympathetic ear?" Sequoia asked earnestly.

Dukon noticed that Sequoia was still in her nightie. His eyes roved down the length of her and back up again.

"No. But there is something else that I want."

After Dukon left, Sequoia dressed and walked in their private garden. Her mind was in turmoil. She was disconcerted by what she thought she saw in Dukon's room. She sent a brief *Smoke Signals* message to Aspen, emphasizing that she was unsure of what she had seen. Her recent trip to the reservation had made her long to be back there again. She resolved to call Breeze to meet for lunch. Then, walking beneath the flowering trees in the garden, she felt a strong urge to climb one of them. So she did.

What a view met her eyes when she emerged from the top of a majestic Giant Cherry Tree. It was breathtaking and spirit-nourishing. She breathed in the floral-scented air around her as she scanned the panorama visible from her perch.

A moment later, the peace was shattered by the hue and cry of Secret Service agents who saw someone in a tree near the President's apartment. They came running from all directions with firearms drawn. Sequoia threw her open palms into the air and waved energetically, shouting, "It's me, the First Lady! Mrs. Chatan! Sequoia Starfire!"

Dukon was *not* amused, but Sequoia thought it was hilarious. She could laugh about it since she hadn't gotten shot out of the tree! She mirthfully related the story to Breeze when they got together for lunch a couple of hours later. They both thought that the most surprising thing was that it wasn't already in the news. Where were the headlines: "First Lady Up a Tree!" or "Sequoia in Washington's Cherry Tree!" or some other such poking of fun? Strangely, it never did make it into the news.

Sequoia later thought, *Highly classified and dangerously strategic U.S. information has recently been leaking to the public at an unprecedented rate; but a funny, harmless, slightly embarrassing story that the President didn't like was successfully quashed from reaching the public. Go figure.*

Sequoia did receive a *Smoke Signal* about it though – and SIGNAL had not learned about it from her or Breeze. SIGNAL had acquired information that *someone* was extremely concerned about her episode in the tree and another incident in the Presidential residence that morning. There was reason to believe that there was now an *imminent* threat to the lives of both Sequoia and Breeze... *from inside!* Accordingly, SIGNAL arranged notification to the White House, saying that the First Lady's grandmother had been hospitalized on the reservation. Sequoia and Breeze were instructed via *Smoke Signals* to depart the capital *immediately.*

COUNTERPOINT IX
BOMB SQUAD

"Our Asset has made his first real mistake. We need to quickly clean up behind him. We cannot take the chance that the First Lady saw something incriminating. She also has been with the wife of Vice President Wolf today and could have communicated to her what she saw. And now – it is too coincidental that the First Lady's grandmother was hospitalized today, requiring the First Lady and Mrs. Wolf to return to the reservation where our reach is very limited. The cleanup must not be delayed!"

"We're already handling it. Earlier today, after learning of the possible exposure in his room and the meeting of the two women, we marked them both for immediate elimination. While we were planning their demise, the White House received notification about the grandmother. The First and Second Ladies made plans to fly out right away, so we've arranged for them to perish together in an *accident* en route. Our people embedded in the Secret Service have worked it out. As usual, the First Lady will have three limousines to choose from with two Secret Service agents in each. Every limousine will have one of *our* people in it – all of them ready for martyrdom. The First Lady's limousine will pick up the Second Lady before heading to the airstrip. We should have closure very shortly."

CHAPTER FIFTY-SIX
Airborne

Grant Tomachichi was a Native American who loved to fly. His true bliss was to skydive from as high as possible, plummeting at dizzying speeds towards the Earth. He would pull the ripcord of his parachute at the last possible moment or stretch his bungee cord to the limit. He fearlessly leapt from bridges, mountain tops, helicopters, and airplanes. He accrued to his credit an extraordinary number of jumps and an exceptional level of expertise. Thus, it was not surprising when he was recruited to join an elite Special Forces corps of the U.S. Military. Clandestine insertions from the air was among that unit's many skills. Given Grant's tendency to "dive-bomb," pulling up at the last minute like a raptor grabbing its prey before soaring skyward again, his fellow soldiers gave him the nom de guerre: *Toma-Hawk.*

Although he was a formidable adversary, Grant was more protector than aggressor. Soldiers assigned to work with him felt both privileged and especially safe in his company. Many referred to him as the *gentle giant.* The meaning of the honorific was clear as Grant was not a physically large man. Like many of his fellow American soldiers, he felt that he was part of a force of "peace through strength." He subscribed to the *Warrior Creed* written by a U.S. Marine – especially the famous words,

> *Wherever I walk, everyone is safer.*
> *Wherever I am, anyone in need has a friend.*

There were some nations ruled by dictators who had complete control over their citizens and over all wealth. They did not want their people to have the freedom of democracy nor a capitalist economy through which the motivated would have a chance to work towards a comfortable life. Those rulers had the ability to mitigate the rampant unemployment and desperate poverty in their nations. But to do so, they would have to relinquish some of the nation's wealth which they stole and hoarded and used to buy luxuries for themselves. Instead of giving up some of the wealth to use for public services, they cleverly channeled the people's malcontent, revving them up and fomenting hatred *directed at other people.* The tyrants thusly diverted attention away from their personal use of the wealth which belonged to all of the people and from their lack of action on behalf of their people.

Some such leaders exploited the power of religion to fabricate reasons to target innocent civilians of different faiths or cultures. They funneled their people's anger – that should have been directed at *them* – into a supposedly "righteous cause" – turning the poor, the unemployed, and the confused and restless youth into terrorists. They offered payments to the families of people who would take up arms against the innocent or blow themselves up. Of course, those who died were unable to see if payments actually reached their families or if the money was later seized by warlords. Meanwhile, the powerful leaders lived long and sumptuously, thoroughly gratifying themselves, while the terrorists died off – as planned.

The mission of Grant's military was to stop evil people from invading, harming, or subjugating peaceful people. The goal was noble, but the intended positive outcomes were sometimes elusive. Grant was constantly in situations where his only choices were to kill an enemy, be killed himself, or let a fellow soldier die as they rooted out tyrants and terrorists or defended hapless victims. Grant also saw how the trauma of war could affect good people, sometimes driving them to uncharacteristic acts.

The painful memories of deeds that Grant had witnessed and performed were only partially buried in the dark recesses of his mind. Sleep provided little escape from his mental torment, as nightmares plagued him incessantly. He took some solace in knowing that all he had done had been initiated out of good intent. Soon he would fulfill his final mission for the military and leave that calling. He would seek help and hopefully find some manner of peace within his life and within his mind.

It might have helped to soothe Grant's anguish and guilt if he had recognized that every day, *civilians* around the world were responsible for many more deaths than those caused by the soldiers of democracies. Civilians perpetrated many violent crimes. Some committed bad acts in a fit of rage or under the influence of a compromising substance. There was drug-related, gang, and other violence, including teenaged mobs committing crimes out of boredom and lack of empathy or moral values. There were frequent, fatal or maiming car accidents, including catastrophic crashes caused by drivers of mass transportation. There were serious work-site incidents, sometimes due to inadequate safety inspections – or because management was forced to hire or retain certain people whether vetted and qualified or not. Unlike the casualties of Grant's military, the civilian-caused deaths and injuries did not even have an *intended* positive objective.

Grant's current assignment was fairly low-risk. It was to go into a situation from the air with a small team after a training drill. What made it precarious was that it was a joint exercise between the U.S. and an only recently and tenuously stable Central American nation. In addition, unarmed, young aid workers there from around the world were unaware that this drill was going to take place.

Colonel Winer, made it clear to the Special Ops unit placed under his command that they were, under no circumstances, to engage with force upon any parties *appearing* to be hostile.

"Remember," he said, "this is only a training exercise, and the foreign soldiers are our allies. Any stray gunshots from the 'attackers' will be an *artificial* display using blanks. The aid workers will be 'defended and rescued' by that country's security forces, not by us. You will go in afterward solely to shake hands with our recently established allies who will be the 'heroes.' Is that clear?"

Grant asked, "Sir, could there actually be hostile parties involved, given the varying levels of acceptance of outsiders by the different cultural groups in that country?"

"Negative, soldier. Operation Dove of Peace was initiated and carefully designed at the highest levels. A camera on this aircraft will record the events as they unfold – for distribution to the media. This operation will be a perfect demonstration of the Administration's efficacious program of diplomacy vs. force in this previously volatile nation. It will back up the push to cut military spending and will validate the brilliant, global teamwork of this President and his Foreign Relations Agency. They are taking a prior President's work to a new level."

"Sir, isn't cutting U.S. military capability risky until after diplomatic success is shown to work reliably across different regions? Especially since nations that oppose the free world are *building up* their military and nuclear capabilities?"

"No, soldier. The point is to show that American military strength is a backwards approach to peace. We need to cut our military might to show that we truly seek peace. We also need to rely more on other nations to protect themselves as well as Americans on their soil. This demonstration will show how to attain peace without arrogant U.S. military intervention. The prearranged 'attack' will be quelled and the aid workers rescued by that nation's security detail. It's a good exercise for the foreign military."

The other commandos looked at one another during this exchange.

"This President promoted me from a pseudo-military position where my voice was ignored to this position of military leadership. I believe that with his bold vision, he knows what needs to be done better than military brass who always believe that military strength, not respectful deference keeps people safe."

Grant thought of a small nation in Oprika. Having no military, it was constantly invaded and its people murdered, raped, kidnapped, and enslaved by Oprikans from bordering nations pursuing that country's valuable minerals. Diplomacy was not saving them despite *decades* of attempts, including the unfailingly fruitless actions of an international committee. The constantly shifting balance of power between that nation's government and various warlords, both domestic and from surrounding Oprikan nations, was clearly determined solely by who had superior weaponry and the financial resources to supply it.

The radio crackled. The special operative embedded with the aid workers was the only one there who knew of the impending drill. He broke radio silence.

"We have two people down!! This is no freakin' drill! They're using LIVE FIRE! I need backup NOW! Bring in air support! The security force can't protect the young aid workers! Somebody must have leaked the plan to hostile parties!"

Grant spoke up. "Sir! My team is ready! We can drop in and pull the trapped kids out before the hostiles even know we were there."

"Stand down, soldier. We have no authorization to go in. Those calls for help could be a test to see if we disobey our orders and engage."

"With all due respect, sir, we can *see* significant firepower in play down there! They are *not* shooting blanks! My team can at least extract the aid workers! Can't we *get* authorization?"

"No, soldier, we cannot. We have been forbidden to get involved until afterward. With the help of the United States, this nation has just found a fragile stability. The U.S. cannot now be seen using military force in their territory. It would be an embarrassment to that nation's government."

"Sir, won't your superiors want us to defend American and other unarmed civilians against a real attack – let alone one that was initiated by politicians as a performance? They placed people unnecessarily at risk without their knowledge or consent. Sir, let us not have an outcome similar to a violent debacle in Moscken territory years ago! If we just let the hostiles *see* this aircraft they might flee."

"Soldier! You are out of line! My commanders put me in charge, and I am going to follow the orders they gave me. I am sure they know what they're doing. Besides, they are not to be disturbed as they are now involved in something else."

COUNTERPOINT X
MATH

"How many people survived the Central American fiasco and know what actually happened?"

"∧∧∧∧∧∧∧"

"You're breaking up, so I can't hear you. Can you hear me? Whatever the number is, get rid of them. The Administration does not need to be involved."

"∧∧Yes, sir ∧∧∧∧∧∧"

CHAPTER FIFTY-SEVEN
Pounce

Heath Brian Mills raked his fingers through his short, blond hair, rolled his head to loosen up his neck, and cracked his knuckles. He hid himself deep in the shadows since his light skin and hair made him easy to spot. The alcove was a perfect location for an ambush. If they ambled past him individually, he would snag them like a coiled cat pouncing upon an unsuspecting rat. If they weren't alone, he would turn on the charm and draw them in together.

He saw a long, dark ponytail swinging as one rounded the pillar... alone. She appeared to be anxiously mouthing something, perhaps a silent prayer, while straightening her jacket as she walked.

She never even saw him. He did his thing and dragged his limp prey into the shadowy alcove. His long fingers darted beneath her clothing, and his brain registered: *Jackpot!* Just to be sure, he stabbed her with his fountain pen. He got what he wanted from her, then stood up and waited for another to come.

CHAPTER FIFTY-EIGHT
After Math

There was much confusion about what had happened in the deadly disaster in Central America. The mainstream media did little more than to regurgitate the vomitus of changing stories spewing from various federal agencies that were or should have been involved. A prior Administration had been equally inept in its handling and reporting of a serious incident. Officials were now tripping over themselves and the Administration with conflicting stories that made no sense. There was no evidence of any responsible leadership.

Nowhere did the media report that the tragedy had been set in motion for purely political purposes. Its expected success was intended to affirm the policy of diplomacy vs. military strength which was being advanced by one party to justify military cuts. Instead, it was a devastating validation that in the real world, military *strength* keeps people safe. Assailants generally attack the most vulnerable victims – not those most capable of repelling an attack.

There were also no reports in the news about the deaths of *all* of Grant Tomachichi's Spec Ops commandos present during the foreign catastrophe. They each died in separate *accidents* very soon afterward. These were people who would have been questioned by Congress about the fiasco. The fact that they were Special Forces was Classified information, but the sudden, coincidental deaths of eyewitnesses to the disaster should have been reported to the public as such. Perhaps the lapse by the media was because more than one of the few, remaining, true investigative journalists had recently died under unusual circumstances after publicizing an imminent exposé of powerful public figures. *Was this really happening in America?*

It was internally reported that Grant's team all had high blood-alcohol levels at the time of their accidental deaths. Grant did not believe the deaths were accidental or unrelated. In fact, one way in which his team had bonded over time was by sharing stories as to why all of them *never drank alcohol – and despite the traumatizing nature of their work, never would...*

Not long after the deaths of Grant's brethren warriors, he, too, disappeared while hiking in the canyon where his love of flying had been born.

"Captain Lightfoot, Captain Grant Broadwings has disappeared without a trace since his last, controversial assignment with the U.S. Military. Considering his reports to SIGNAL about that disaster and its aftermath, there is a real chance that foul play is involved. I would like you to investigate. His disappearance represents a great loss to SIGNAL and should not go unexplained."

"Yes, General."

CHAPTER FIFTY-NINE
Fried Ride

Dukon numbly acknowledged Sequoia's need to go to the reservation to be with her grandmother who had been hospitalized. He accompanied her out to a waiting fleet of White House limousines. He told her that he had to attend a fundraiser and that he would join her on the reservation, only if necessary, upon her request. He said that he had urged Hunter to accompany her and Breeze but that he had declined to go at this time. Dukon was unsmiling, but in bidding her farewell, he looked into her eyes for a long time and gave her a surprisingly warm hug. He then got into one of the limos with his usual entourage of Secret Service and decoy limousines and departed.

Knowing that she had a possibly *very* imminent threat, Sequoia cautiously eyed the three remaining limos with their dark-tinted windows. She did not recognize any of the Secret Service agents standing by them. Wondering how she should choose, she stalled by rummaging in her handbag. While doing so, she heard a sound that was music to her ears. It was a distinctive, rhythmic, finger-snapping and hand drumming combination. She held her cell phone to her ear as if listening, and casually scanned the agents standing by the vehicles. One man was looking away yet clearly identifying himself to her, as his hands were drumming a unique, SIGNAL salute. Anyone else would have just seen a man mindlessly fidgeting while waiting.

Her choice made clear, she walked towards that limo. Upon getting closer, however, she saw that the Secret Service agent had blond hair and light skin, giving her pause. *Not likely SIGNAL* – as all operatives had to be of majority Native American Indian blood for security reasons.

He opened the rear door for her, and she warily looked inside. She nearly cried out with relief, because there sat Kiwi in the back seat. Sequoia climbed in beside the brawny man and nodded formally as if acknowledging a Secret Service agent she hardly knew. The blond man slid into the driver's seat.

In silence, they swung by the Vice Presidential residence. Kiwi held the back door open for Breeze, then he moved to the front passenger seat. For a while, no one in the limo spoke, as all of them were feeling the tension of the high-alert situation – not all for the same reason. During the drive, Sequoia noticed that both Kiwi and the driver seemed to be intently watching the two decoy limousines. She assumed that Kiwi was on the alert for any sign of aggression from those vehicles. Still unsure about the driver, who was raking his long fingers through his short, blond hair, Sequoia hoped that his interest was the same.

The tension in the limo was palpably reduced after the two decoy limousines peeled off and went in different directions; but Sequoia noticed that her limo then changed course, taking them along an unfamiliar route.

"We don't seem to be headed towards the usual airfields," she remarked.

Kiwi turned in his seat to reply face-to-face. He tilted his head towards the driver.

"Heath, here, is taking you to a secure airstrip just outside the area, Mrs. Chatan."

Now having eye contact with Kiwi, Sequoia looked at him meaningfully. She slid her eyes towards the driver. Kiwi made a facial sign of acknowledgment. If it had been anyone other than Kiwi, Sequoia would have been making contingency plans for escape. She knew that Aspen trusted Kiwi with her life, and she trusted Aspen's judgment implicitly.

Shortly, they exited the highway where there were signs for fast food joints and gas stations. In a highly irregular move, Heath pulled into a drive-thru food queue behind an Army van. Many military vehicles were entering and exiting the lot. Two Army vans pulled up behind them in the queue. Breeze and Sequoia looked at each other tensely. When the van ahead of them moved forward, their limo pulled up so that it was now completely obscured by the overhang and the solid walls along both sides of them. They were further concealed by the three Army vans that were sandwiching them from in front and behind.

The driver-side doors of the three vans opened. The drivers stepped out onto their running boards and gestured and shouted to each other about the food orders they were picking up. Their name labels identified them as Patrick, Alexander, and Spencer.

Heath opened his door, bent down, and slid out of the limo. Crouching, he opened the back door on his side along the wall of the food joint. Kiwi gestured to Breeze and Sequoia to get out and crouch as well. Staying low, Heath opened the rear doors of the front van and ushered the women inside. While switching vehicles, they had been completely shielded from outside observation by the Army drivers who were still standing with their doors open, discussing their takeout orders. Heath returned to the limo and helped Kiwi with something in the front passenger footwell. Then he climbed into the van with Breeze and Sequoia.

Kiwi went to the back of the limo and opened the trunk. To the women's great surprise, he lifted out a groggy man bound with wrist and ankle restraints! Kiwi placed him in a rear seat of the limo, seat-belted him in, and shut the door.

Patrick, the driver of the Army van behind the limo, stepped off his running board and opened the sliding side door of his van. He helped Kiwi remove *two more people* from the limo's trunk, one at a time. One was a woman. They carried them to Patrick's van and placed them inside the open side door. All three people taken from the limo's trunk were wearing standard Secret Service attire. Kiwi handed Patrick a sack and joined the others in the back of the front van, pulling the doors closed behind him. In the semi-darkness, Sequoia saw Heath extract a device from his pocket. The hair prickled on the back of her neck. He held it up, and Kiwi nodded in acknowledgment.

Their van driver pulled up to the pickup window, and after receiving the ordered food, drove them out of the parking lot. Instead of taking them back onto the highway, he turned onto what felt like a dirt road. Everyone in the back of the van remained silent. Kiwi pulled out a multipurpose tool with scissors and pantomimed to Sequoia and Breeze to snip a lock of their hair for him. The women complied, and Kiwi put their locks into a small bag that already had some hair in it.

He then accessed a compartment in the side of the van, pulling out Army apparel which he distributed to all of them. The men turned their backs on the women, and the women faced away from the men. All four of them changed into the fatigues. Kiwi gave them each a cap, and the women put their long hair up under them. They all pulled down the caps, concealing their faces as much as possible. They put their own clothing and personal items into a sack that Kiwi held open.

Soon, the van stopped and the back doors opened. They were in an airplane hangar on a joint Army/Air Force Reserve base. Heath climbed out, manipulating his device. Kiwi also got out and beckoned to the women to move behind protective cover inside the hangar. The Army van that had been behind them at the drive-thru pulled in beside them. Patrick got out and opened the rear doors of the van. The two people that he and Kiwi had taken out of the limo trunk were still confined by restraints but were now more alert as they looked uneasily out the rear of the van.

Sequoia and Breeze saw their White House limo enter the driveway a few hundred yards away where it stopped near a small jet fuel storage tank. Heath pressed a button on his device and the tinting faded away on the rear passenger window facing them. They could see the man that Kiwi had put in the back seat who was looking their way and also seemed alert now.

Heath nodded to Kiwi and the women and solemnly said, "Here we go."

He pulled a cell phone from his pocket, and he and Kiwi waved "Bye-Bye" at the limo. The man inside it began thrashing about, struggling to get out of his seat. Kiwi turned to the two prisoners in the van next to them. They were looking with horror from Heath to the limousine. Heath lifted the cell phone and pressed some buttons.

The limo *exploded*. Breeze and Sequoia jumped at the eruption of fire and debris. Metal and body parts soared amid towering flames before raining back down again. Sirens sounded on the base, and within seconds, a fire truck and other vehicles rushed to attend to the conflagration.

A Reservist, who looked Native American, rapidly approached them. Kiwi handed him the bag of hair clippings. The young man sprinted towards the burning limo, pulling on firefighting gear as he ran.

Patrick got back into his van, turned it around and backed the prisoners towards a small Air Force jet in the hangar. David Bryan, the Commanding Officer of the base had received orders about prisoners who were to be transported elsewhere. He helped to carry the two struggling people onboard while U.S. Air Force Pilot Daniel Andrew Brown, climbed into the cockpit.

Heath slipped away, unnoticed by the others who were focused on the pandemonium outside and the quiet prisoner transfer inside. Heath scanned the hangar to see if he was being watched as he stealthily made his way to a small, privately-registered plane in a back corner.

CHAPTER SIXTY
First American Pride

A fighter pilot was leaning against the small plane. Noting the name "Lyle Fortin" on the man's bomber jacket, Heath casually drummed part of a rhythm with his hands. The other man completed the rhythm with his own hands and sauntered away. Heath then walked all the way around the plane, examining it carefully. He removed something from his pocket and pressed it onto the underbelly of the plane. He cautiously opened the cabin door and climbed inside. A couple of minutes later, he returned to the group.

"It's time to go," he said, turning and striding back towards the plane.

Sequoia and Breeze were still in shock from what they had witnessed. They numbly followed Kiwi onto the plane. Heath climbed into the cockpit, radioed for clearance, and taxied out onto the runway.

After takeoff, Kiwi used hand signals to question Heath if they were safe from listening devices. Heath nodded. Gesturing towards him, Kiwi said,

"Ladies, I am honored to introduce you to *Captain* Null Moonbow. Captain, this is Sequoia Starfire Katiri Chatan and Breeze Whitecloud Wya Wolf."

The women's eyes grew large. Kiwi's emphasis indicated that this man was a *SIGNAL* Captain. Captain Moonbow turned his head and nodded. Sequoia noticed that, upon closer inspection, his face looked less Caucasian.

"It's a pleasure to meet you both," he said, refocusing his attention forward. Chuckling, he added, "I have to admit I'm glad for a break from the Washington detail. Keeping up with dyeing my roots has been a real bear. I've colored my hair many times but never for this long."

Kiwi smiled gladly, passing his hand across the top of his own clean-shaven head.

Neither Breeze nor Sequoia had ever met a SIGNAL Captain! Many SIGNAL operatives had heard of the legendary Captain Lightfoot and the equally illustrious female, Captain Thunderstrike; but, as a rule, the code names of the Captains were not revealed. The acclaimed warrior operatives sometimes did kill people, but they much more often put their own lives at risk.

This Captain's alias fittingly alluded to the camouflaged aspect of moonbows – the much more muted, moonlit counterparts to rainbows, often perceived as being white. His code name reflected his less distinctively American Indian facial features and his skill at disguising himself.

Sequoia ventured, "Are we allowed to know what just happened out there?"

Captain Moonbow nodded, so Kiwi elucidated while the Captain piloted the plane toward a SIGNAL safe house on the reservation of the Mihote Tribe – Kiwi's people.

"SIGNAL operatives embedded in the Secret Service intercepted a communication. The President was arguing with an unknown party. He asserted that *he* had made a mistake not the First Lady. The caller *reminded the President of his place* and asked if there was any chance that the First Lady could have seen something that she should not have and then spoken of it at lunch with the Second Lady. President Golden Hawk said that there was. The caller replied that, in that case, both women were to be eliminated immediately."

Breeze and Sequoia looked at one another. Sequoia was pretty sure she knew what it was that she should not have seen in Dukon's room. She only hoped that she would be able to provide enough detail of value about it to SIGNAL.

Kiwi continued, "SIGNAL Command feared that the threatened 'elimination' could happen very quickly. We did not know how or where it might take place; so SIGNAL provided a scenario that would be irresistible for the hostiles to use. We could then control the situation and keep you safe. Accordingly, SIGNAL sent a wire to the White House regarding your Grandmother, Sequoia. It would be natural for Breeze to accompany you to the reservation. The probability was then high that they would plan to assassinate you once you were together en route to the airstrip or in the air – because one fatal incident, instead of two, would arouse less suspicion with the public."

The Captain nodded.

"Captain Moonbow has been embedded in the Secret Service White House detail. He went directly to the garage where he could intercept the agents heading there to drive you to the airport. He assessed each agent as a likely threat or not by reading their body language for signs of anxiety. He let the ones who were likely non-threats continue on their way, but he picked off three potential hot potatoes. He temporarily neutralized them by giving them each a Bear Claw Pressure Greeting, causing them to black out."

"A Bear... *what* did you call it... Greeting?" Breeze asked.

Sequoia leaned forward, also eager to hear. The Captain smiled at their enthusiastic interest.

"The Bear Claw Pressure Greeting is a hand combat technique that originated with Native Americans of Mexico. Ask your Regional Commander about it."

Kiwi continued, "Captain Moonbow chose well, as each of the three was wearing an explosives vest. He injected the suicide bombers with a short-acting sedative and a mild nerve agent, temporarily paralyzing their vocal chords and extremities."

Captain Moonbow interjected, "I spoke to each of them before giving them the nerve agent. I asked who they worked for and how many people were involved. The woman spat in my face, and the two men babbled what sounded like insults in a foreign language." He gestured to Kiwi to continue.

"After redirecting a garage security camera away from our limo, I joined him and moved the three incapacitated terrorists into its trunk – hogtied and *sans materiel*. The Captain had already taken a transponder from each of them, which their superiors were obviously using to track them. Captain Moonbow carefully disarmed the terrorists' bombs, and I put them into a sack in the front passenger footwell. The Captain inspected the limo itself for armed explosives and jammed the limo's computer – which all new cars have nowadays – so that no one anywhere could possibly control the vehicle but him. Meanwhile, I had SIGNAL Communications tap into the White House system and call the Secret Service for one more agent to drive to the airstrip. Captain Moonbow and I replaced the other two hostile Secret Service imposters – all three of whom were in the limo's trunk."

Kiwi gestured to Sequoia. "Before you came out to the limos, the Captain hit up the three remaining Secret Service agents for chewing gum. He took that opportunity to reevaluate those agents as possible terrorists. You then recognized Captain Moonbow's signal and chose our limo. I could not be the one standing outside of it since my posting here was not with the Secret Service, and the other agents might have questioned who I was. En route, the Captain and I carefully watched the decoy limousines. Although the other Secret Service agents were not wearing bombs, they could have posed a different kind of threat. If there had been any sign of aggression from the decoy limousines, I would have 'fallen' out of our limo with the sack of explosives."

Sequoia shuddered at the thought that explosives, though not wired, had been with them during the limo ride. "How brave of you to even contemplate that, Kiwi!"

He laughed, "Good choice of words. I'm not a Captain... but I *am* a Brave."

"Congratulations!" Sequoia and Breeze exclaimed simultaneously.

Kiwi smiled and continued. "SIGNAL then tapped into Secret Service communications again and directed the other two limos to go to the usual airstrips, as decoys. We headed towards the Army/Air Force Reserve base, where the SIGNAL Regional Commander for this area had arranged for help starting at the nearby drive-thru. Before joining you in the back of the Army van, Captain Moonbow re-connected some of the explosives in the limo. I gave the rest to the SIGNAL Reservist in the van behind us. The limo windows were at maximum tint so no one could see inside. The SIGNAL Reservist driving the van that we were in placed an order for himself and, supposedly, one for the limo behind him. He picked up both orders from the food window and drove us to the base. The Captain was driving the limo remotely from the back of our van, using the device that he had linked to the limo's computer. Then, at the entrance to the Reserve base, you saw the Captain light up the explosives in the limo. At that moment, I disabled the three transponders."

"So... that man in the limo was aware of what was about to happen to him and was responding to your waves when...?" Sequoia trailed off.

"Sequoia, those three terrorists *volunteered* to go on a one-way trip today – and to take you and Breeze with them – *involuntarily.* They intended to *murder* you. One of them got to go on that trip but didn't succeed at taking you with him. I'm also sure that he and I have a difference of opinion as to where his spirit ended up after the explosion." The Captain nodded, and Kiwi continued, "With the help of a SIGNAL Brave on the Reserve base, Jesse Firebird, along with a bit of extra jet fuel, there will be very little left from the explosion for anyone to identify. That's why you did not need to leave personal items in the limo, or worry about dental record checks, etc."

The women nodded.

"The President's associates will surely send a forensics team to conduct a DNA search. So Brave Firebird distributed your hair clippings, along with some from the terrorists, around the site of the explosion where they would pick up traces of soot and explosives. So, depending on how the President and his associates decide to handle this, you ladies may be seeing your obituaries in the news."

Sequoia observed, "There seem to be a lot of American Indians in the U.S. Military – and quite a few of them with SIGNAL?"

Captain Moonbow nodded. "I believe that American Indians have had the highest proportional rates of participation in the U.S. Military of any ethnic minority."

They all felt a surge of pride.

"As for SIGNAL participation, I believe there is a higher level near Washington, D.C. these days..."

Breeze asked, "What about the other two suicide bombers?"

"They are en route to an appropriate location for interrogation. Separately, a SIGNAL Reservist is taking the disabled transponders and the remaining explosives to a special Intelligence lab, not under the Administration, for analysis."

Sequoia asked, "Kiwi, aside from this specific incident, how is it that you have been posted here, outside of our regional territory?"

Kiwi replied in a stage whisper, "Let's just say that Aspen may have... um... overstepped the bounds of his authority a bit...?" He grinned and added dramatically, "He sent me here under threat of... *unspeakable* consequences if I let anything happen to you."

They all laughed.

He added, "Just so you know, Breeze, the Vice President has been apprised via *Smoke Signals* that you are alive and well – and in excellent hands." Kiwi winked.

"Thank you, Kiwi and Captain Moonbow. Clearly, we are in the best of hands."

CHAPTER SIXTY-ONE
Been There, Done That

The full Ronopo Council was present for a specially convened session. U.S. Vice President Hunter Wolf was on the reservation to face this tribunal and receive a sentence for the crimes he had committed against the Ronopo Tribe. Although his trial in the U.S. Judicial System had replaced any action by the American Indian Tribal Court System, it did not excuse him from being judged and sentenced by his own tribe.

Co-Chiefs Fox Bridgewater and Aspen Mijeesi led the session. The atmosphere was tense, and the young Chiefs exhibited none of their usual congeniality.

Fox read the charges. The list was long, because it named each member of the tribe who had been misled by Dukon's land-trade deal brokered by Hunter. In addition, Hunter was charged with creating a fraudulent lineage for Dukon in the Official Ronopo Register. Hunter also volunteered a confession to dishonorable election tactics back when Golden Hawk was elected Chief – tactics of which he was now deeply ashamed. All of the charges were serious.

Despite his highly elevated position in U.S. Government, Hunter took this tribunal very seriously. He felt true remorse for his deeds and would have liked nothing better than to relive that part of his life – very differently. He mused about the gifts of maturity and perspective and thought it a shame one did not receive them earlier in life.

Having never felt acceptance by his tribe, Hunter fervently wished for a clean slate and a place as a member in good standing. He thought that surely some of the positive recognition had been directed towards him when he and Breeze danced at the Harvest Festival and then when they married; but he needed confirmation and closure. His most dreaded punishment would be banishment and the loss of a place with his own people.

Fox began reading the preamble to the sentence which would be a standard penalty from the Ronopo Code of Law. Hunter had never, ever seen Fox look so distressed. This gave Hunter good cause for alarm, because precious little rattled Fox Bridgewater. Finally, Fox just stopped reading, mid-sentence, and looked at Aspen who seemed a bit wan himself. After a meaningful exchange of eye contact between the Co-Chiefs, Aspen asked Hunter if he would please leave the room and wait to be called back in.

Hunter was finally asked to return. He looked at the faces around the room. No one met his eye, but the tension seemed palpably reduced. Aspen addressed him.

"Hunter, this tribunal has agreed that regarding the land-trade deal, you have made all necessary reparations, so there will be no further penalty on *those* charges."

Hunter gave a grateful nod.

"However, there is a clear punishment outlined in our law for the very serious crimes of tampering with the validity of our deeply venerated Register of tribal lineage and with the integrity of our elections."

Aspen stopped speaking. He looked down and took a deep breath. Hunter glanced around the room. Each person looked away...

"Hunter, this section of the Code is very old. The penalty for this type of crime – well... the penalty is..." Aspen looked incredulous, "...it's... a public flogging."

Aspen and Fox looked openly aghast.

Okay. Hunter got it. Everyone's consternation was not just because of what the penalty was – it was the incredible irony of it in regard to Hunter's personal history. He closed his eyes, nodding his head. Then he bit his lower lip and shook his head. He opened his eyes and faced the Chiefs.

"Hunter, there was unanimous agreement on two things. The *second* one was that you could not get away with *no* penalty. But the *first* thing that everyone on this Council agreed to was that... this particular punishment... well... *you've... been there, done that.*"

Hunter closed his eyes and dropped his face into one hand. Shaking his head, he started to chuckle quietly. Then he lifted his head and began laughing out loud. Soon, everyone in the room was laughing with him. With that, something amazing happened to Hunter. He felt a cleansing – a purging of all the pain and shame that he had carried for so long. His fellow tribesmen were clearly showing their solidarity with him, and it felt incredibly good.

After a bit, Aspen resumed. "Since there is not something in the Code that would apply as a substitute, this Council decided to defer to Elder Chief Bridgewater. Elder Chief says that he has reached a decision and will now share it with us."

Hunter watched Elder Chief rise with great dignity. He instantly felt the weight of authority of this man who had been his Chief for all the years he was growing up. Chief had also been, in many ways, the positive aspects of a father to him, though Hunter hadn't always realized it.

Elder Chief spoke. "Hunter Wya Wolf, you have committed grave crimes against the people of this tribe. But you have also brought us enormous pride. The corrective actions you took represent the ideal of how to compensate one's fellow man or woman for wrongs committed against them. You gave up all of your material possessions and took on massive personal debt at great risk. You restored the homestead rights of everyone involved in the land-trade deal even though that burden did not belong to you alone. The world would be a much better place if all people behaved thusly."

Despite Hunter's high political position, he felt fierce gratification that he had earned the respect of this great man.

"In addition, there are no words that can adequately describe the gift of the personal role model that you have provided your Ronopo family – this tribe – as well as to people everywhere. It is not only that you rose to your recent and current important offices, despite the very difficult circumstances of your early life; it is much more by the manner in which you have acquitted yourself within those highly visible positions."

Elder Chief 's eyes bored into Hunter's. But... you committed crimes for which there must be consequences. As that decision has fallen to me, I have chosen the compensation that you will make to your tribe. Hunter Wya Wolf, as you have sworn to abide by the sentencing of this tribunal, it is now your solemn duty to fulfill your debt to this tribe... by providing it... " Elder Chief paused, "...with children – Ronopo children of you and your esteemed wife, Breeze Whitecloud. I can make such a demand that affects not only you, because a little Birdie told me that your wife *does* want children. And Hunter... the sooner, and the more, the better! I'm ready to be a Grandfather!"

In an effluence of great surprise, the entire Council erupted in high-spirited laughter. Hunter flushed and felt pervaded by a whole spectrum of emotions, including relief, redemption, gratitude, and a truly special feeling – that of belonging. He bowed his head to Elder Chief. He was then touched, noticing that Aspen and Fox now looked possibly even more relieved than he felt, himself.

Hunter was also honored that Elder Chief implied that Hunter's children would be like grandchildren to him. Hunter saw Fox, the Chief's own son, give his father a rather sheepish look for not having provided him with that status yet himself.

Elder Chief put his hands up, asking for quiet. He added,

"Hunter – please also give my apologies in advance to your wife – for the *diligence* with which I know you will fulfill this obligation. This tribunal is hereby concluded."

The room was again filled with laughter and the sounds of the group rising. Every person approached Hunter and offered him a personal acknowledgment of fellowship and goodwill. Hunter Wya Wolf reciprocated – with heartfelt warmth and gratitude.

CHAPTER SIXTY-TWO
Rigged

"Hey, Yuk (yook)! I'm picking up some funky readings here. I have something approaching slowly from the southwest. Are you getting this too?"

"Aye-aye, Stone. I'm watching it as well."

"Its size could make it a whale or a sub. You getting any read on its structure?"

"Negative, Brother. It's still too far away."

"Any communiqués or hailing signal?"

"None."

"Well, the tanker ship is still taking on oil from the storage tank out here away from the ice fields. I'm going to let them know that we're monitoring something questionable."

"Good idea, Stone. I'll try a 'ping' and see if I get a response from the object."

When Breeze Whitecloud's brother, Stone, began CSPI at college – the U.S. Coast Guard's counterpart to ROTC – he knew that he would find his bliss at sea. Upon completing his two-year Associate's Degree in Pre-Engineering at the American Indian tribal college, he was accepted to the rigorous U.S. Merchant Marine Academy. He worked hard there in pursuit of attaining a prestigious position as a Ship's Officer. Now fulfilling his initial service requirement with the U.S. Coast Guard, he was stationed along the northern coast of Alaska. Up there, his team had lots of interaction with their Canadian Coast Guard (CCG) counterparts. The two nations' Coast Guards worked well together, feeling a mutual bond of respect and camaraderie. Together, they kept an eye turned westward and southwestward where less friendly nations lay.

Although they had never met in person, Stone had become tight via radio contact with an American Indian in CCG Search and Rescue who hailed from Canada's Yukon province. Since there were many, diverse, indigenous tribes across the Americas, each having their own distinct customs and languages, it was not surprising that Stone could not pronounce the man's tribal name. Stone simply nicknamed him "Yuk." Likewise, Yuk could not pronounce Stone's tribal name, so he was glad that his friend was nicknamed "Stone."

Like many of the personnel who worked these waters, Stone did not bother to wear the uncomfortable, new life jackets except during drills or inclement weather or in the event of a threatening situation. Under the present circumstances, Stone thought it prudent to wear it. He grabbed the recently-issued, replacement life jacket. It was not American-made like the old ones. It had actually been made in a country hostile to America and was of lower-quality. The old, perfectly serviceable ones had apparently been traded to that hostile country's navy in exchange for the new ones. This barter was supposedly part of a new foreign trade partnership.

Stone slipped one arm into his new life jacket while handling the radio with his other hand.

"Ahoy, Promised Land oil tanker! This is the U.S. Coast Guard Arctic Shark. Do you read me?"

Stone's life jacket hung off one shoulder.

A female voice responded. "Halloo, Arctic Shark. Reading you loud and clear. Is this my favorite *non-Indian* Indian, Stone Whitecloud? This is Ship's Captain, Saji Gandhi."

"Well, if it isn't my *least* favorite *non-American* Indian!"

"Now, now, Stone," she laughed. "Just brush up on your online chess. When I'm back this way next month, if I lose, maybe I can move up a rung or two on your 'least favorite' ladder," she countered good-naturedly.

"Ha! I'm going to teach you a game called Playing Leader. My Native American friend from Canada taught it to me. Chess may be in your blood, but this game came from the natives of my continent. You won't stand a chance!"

Captain Gandhi laughed.

"Hey, listen up, Saji. My red maple buddy and I are tracking something heading slowly this way. It could be a submarine or a whale, but it's still distant and strangely hard to identify. If it's a sub, we should have received communiqués. We've both radioed our bases, and as of yet, neither we nor the Canadians have gotten anything on it. It's still pretty far south of us, but I wanted to give you a heads-up before we pursue radio contact. Stay tuned and be on alert. FYI, I'm idling just within your penumbra."

"Where are you? I can't see you. Are you still working shifts alone in one of those tiny boats? Do those U.S. budget deficits still have you guys down to skeleton crews? Must get lonely out there..."

"Yeah, and I'm embarrassed to admit that the President and I are from the same tribe. He should be providing compelling justification for allowing any cuts to security forces with the ongoing threats to the free world. They're even taking our best national defense equipment and sending it abroad, leaving us with less effective equipment for our own country's protection! The President doesn't seem to be trimming his *own* budget any! But hey, how could I be lonely out here when I have you and Yuk, and the sun, the moon, and the stars to keep me company?"

"Ah, Stone, you always make me smile. Thanks for the warning, my friend. As I'm sure you can hear, I sounded the alarm on the ship. It'll serve as a drill if nothing else."

Stone turned to slip his other arm into the life jacket and caught a glimpse of the monitor.

"WHOA! MAYDAY! MAYDAY!!" he shouted, switching the radio to broadcast on all channels. "Incoming projectile! Promised Land, prepare for impact! Yuk! Incoming!"

Stone rammed his other arm into his life jacket while he raced towards the stern of his craft.

"Ya'ii Ya'ii Ya'ii Ya'ii MAH-pay!!" (Sun, Sun, Sun, Sun, Water!!) yelled young Aspen Mijeesi as he swung the vine as far out over the river as possible before letting go and falling into the deep water below. He dove down to the river-bottom to pick up proof that he had gone all the way down.

Not all of the boys shared Aspen's fearlessness, but they weren't going to let it show. Most of them just didn't push the vine to its maximum distance over the water. One after the other, they took the plunge and quickly swam to shore with something they had picked up from the river floor.

There were two brothers in the group, the Whitecloud boys, who, like Aspen, had no fear as they flung themselves through the air and dropped joyfully into the deepest water. Aspen smiled to himself as he had noticed that the other boys had limited their swimming distance from shore and the depth of the water into which they submerged.

Aspen also noticed when Lota'yomasun Whitecloud was overdue to resurface. He shouted to the fathers who were back amongst the trees, setting up to teach the boys other survival skills. Then, Aspen took off, grabbing the vine and flinging himself far downstream. He made himself the first panel in a human fence to intercept the boy in case he was drifting underwater with the current.

The fathers were in the water in a flash. Some dove in from the riverbank to search for the boy where he had gone under. Others followed Aspen's lead. They grabbed the vine, launching themselves quickly to the point further downstream where they lined up across the river, treading water. They formed a barrier of stalwart bodies, probing arms and legs, and faces in the water as they searched for the missing boy. Some stayed on shore and scanned the area to see if Lota'yomasun might have reappeared elsewhere.

Nothing. No sign of him at all. The sad truth had to be accepted. The boy must have drowned. In shock, the grief-stricken fathers and boys left the water and gathered on the riverbank in silence.

A boy's head suddenly popped up out in the river. Then it started gulping air and wheezing. It yelled, "I found a cave! I found a cave! Come see!"

Dr. Whitecloud plunged back into the river and swam out to where his young son was treading water. He held him, giving the boy a chance to rest and breathe.

Numerous adults dove down and found the boy's "cave." It was in particularly deep water, and all of the men had had to resurface quickly for air. There was a small, rocky hollow, but there was no place within it to get air! That suggested that the young Whitecloud boy had held his breath that entire time. This called for repeat tests at a later date. It turned out that Lota'yomasun Whitecloud could hold his breath for an exceptionally long time.

Fittingly, he was given an honor name, extolling the unusual capability. But it was the nickname that his friends gave him that stuck. They called him "Stone" because he had gone into the deepest part of the river, dropped all the way to the bottom, and then stayed there... like a stone.

The torpedo hit the underwater oil reservoir far below the Promised Land tanker ship, causing a catastrophic explosion. It destroyed the reservoir and part of its feeder pipeline as well as a section of the ship docked above it. Two members of the ship's crew were killed, and a few others were injured.

The shock wave tore apart Stone Whitecloud's small Coast Guard craft that had been on the water nearby. Stone sustained mortal injuries as his body was tossed like a toy a hundred yards across the dark and frigid sea. His poorly-made life jacket failed to hold him, and the unconscious and dying young man sank down into the glacial Arctic waters... like a stone.

CHAPTER SIXTY-THREE
Till Death Did Us Part

Sequoia and Breeze were in hiding at the SIGNAL safe house on the Mihote Reservation after the attempt on their lives in Washington.

Sequoia asked Kiwi to discreetly summon the shaman who was a SIGNAL operative. She had the shaman put her in a trance and take her mind back to her brief scan of Dukon's bedroom when he had unintentionally left its door open. She hoped to recover detailed images of what she had seen and registered in her memory. She also hoped that this actually was what had been so compromising as to set in motion an attempt to kill her and Breeze.

After working with the shaman, Sequoia sent a *Smoke Signals* message to Aspen. He lauded her ingenuity in thinking to work with the shaman who would shortly bring Aspen what she had transcribed while in the hypnotic trance.

Naturally, Sequoia felt emotional turmoil knowing that she had been an intended assassination victim and that her own husband had been involved. Despite his participation in some shady intrigue, Sequoia had believed that Dukon truly loved her. The shaman privately performed a ritual recognizing the change in her life harmony. He performed purification and spiritual healing rites for her as well.

Breeze was a great comfort to Sequoia, but the young women's roles were soon to be reversed. Sequoia then needed to comfort Breeze when they received the devastating news of the death of Breeze's brother, Stone.

Stone had been extremely well-liked. There would be a huge outpouring and sharing of grief and support amongst the members of the Ronopo Tribe. Adding to Breeze's profound sorrow, she and Sequoia still could not risk leaving the safe house on the Mihote Reservation. That meant that they would miss Stone's burial and mourning ceremonies. Once again, Breeze felt that, even though she was relatively close to home in physical distance, she might as well have been on the moon.

CHAPTER SIXTY-FOUR
Real Slick

Saji Gandhi, Captain of the Promised Land oil tanker, gave a solemn report to the few members of the press selected to meet with her.

"I am deeply saddened that two members of my crew were killed and that three others were wounded in the explosion. The human cost on the Promised Land would have been even greater, had it not been for U.S. Coast Guard Petty Officer Stone Whitecloud. He warned us of an approaching submarine and then of an incoming projectile. His initial alert gave us time to sound the ship's alarm and to start emergency procedures before a missile was fired at the oil storage tank. Very sadly, this selfless and courageous young man lost his life while saving others."

Saji grew concerned when the news accounts did not report that a missile had been fired by a submarine, causing the explosion. Instead of calling it a possible act of war or terrorism, the media was calling it "a workplace accident!" They said it was likely due to inadequate maintenance of the oil storage tank, and there were calls for greater regulation of the oil industry. What's more, Stone Whitecloud was not mentioned at all.

There were nothing but stories about the corporation that owned the Promised Land ship and the oil conglomerate that owned the undersea, oil storage tank. Federal officials were debating which of the two was to blame for the oil still spewing from the damaged pipeline and from the tanker ship. All the media talked about was who was going to pay and how much. More than ever, the mainstream media had become oddly silent on too many truths of public importance.

Saji Gandhi was suspended during the inquisition. She was under investigation for possible safety violations on the ship. She knew that the allegations against her were false; yet, she never "played the gender card," whining that they were being made because she was a woman. She understood that there were other reasons and that the *facts* would exonerate her. She was barred by a U.S. court order from speaking to any news media; so she was unable to inform the particular news services that she knew would publish *all* of the facts. She decided to lie low when not under summons for the case; but there were a few questions for which she hoped to find answers, even if just for herself.

"U.S. Coast Guard Station ANWO-1. Taylor Vazquez here. How can I help you?"

"Good morning. I was a friend of Petty Officer Stone Whitecloud, and I was hoping that I could speak to a member of his crew."

There was a pause.

"Certainly. I am sorry for your loss. We are all mourning the untimely passing of a good man and friend to many. Please hold."

Shortly, someone else picked up. "This is Chief Petty Officer Robert John Houston. Stone was a member of my team."

"Hello, Chief Houston. We've spoken before. This is Captain Gandhi from the Promised Land tanker ship."

"Captain Gandhi. I'm sorry for what you've been through and for what they're putting you through now."

"Thank you, Chief Houston. I am so sorry for the loss of Stone Whitecloud – for all of us. He and I were speaking right before the explosion. I was hoping you might have the recorded transmissions from that day. I want to clarify what was reported just before the disaster – and I had hoped to hear Stone's voice one more time."

"I'm sorry, Captain, but we were informed that the blast triggered electromagnetic feedback that wiped our systems clean of all data from that day. And ma'am, I know that I speak for the whole team when I say that there is nothing any of us wouldn't give to hear Stone's voice again. Better yet, we would like to have been there to assist him. He might not have died if he had not had to work a solitary shift in a small craft. And that was because neither the President nor his Senate complied with the law and produced a viable budget. They just sat back and allowed across-the-board cuts to go into effect."

"It is truly unconscionable. You have my deepest condolences, Chief. Please give my sympathies to the rest of the crew as well."

A concussion wave wiping out the system data for that day? Pretty unlikely. I think someone is misleading this Coast Guard base. Okay, one more call to make.

"Canadian Coast Guard Station NW-1. This is Karl Yannick Greff. May I be of assistance?"

"Hello, I'm trying to get in touch with a Search and Rescue crew member who was on duty at the time of the undersea oil tank explosion. I do not know his name. I only know that he is of Native American heritage from the Yukon Province."

"Oh... I regret to tell you. We... lost him that day."

"Oh no! I am so sorry! Please forgive me for asking, but do you know if his transmissions from that day were kept?"

"We do keep them, but there were apparently no communications at all that day."

"Well, thank you anyway, and I am truly sorry for your loss."

No communications, eh? Stone told me that he and the Canadians were in contact with each other and with both of their home bases. Hmm...

Captain Gandhi wrote in her journal:

~ What is taking American President Golden Hawk so long to make a decision?! This is an easy one! Many U.S. allies have offered immediate help! (Some non-allies have also made propositions...) Prior Presidents have already dealt with such a situation. One was a spill involving an oil rig, and another involved a tanker breach.

Considering what was learned from those incidents, this delay is inexcusable! The oil piping is still spewing 50,000 gallons of oil per day, and my ship is still leaking oil! This *can* be contained. Resources should be on this NOW! Even if it takes awhile to close off the feed, there are many state-of-the-art, U.S. and foreign skimmers and storage vessels available *right now* to get that oil out of the sea and into storage tanks! The longer the President waits, the more damage will be done to wildlife, ecosystems, populations, and industries along the coasts. And talk about a lost opportunity for global cooperation and for a boost to the ailing economies of U.S. allies! Now the President has banned offshore oil pipelines and oil rigs as he says there is too much risk. The oil-drilling licensees will have to stop right when America needs to be liberated from buying oil from hostile nations! With America's money, extremists from those countries wreak violence on so many nations, including mine!

Since I know that there was a missile involved, I can think of three possibilities: an *inside job* that is being covered up; accidental friendly fire; or it was from an outside party, and someone in government is hiding what was possibly an act of war! ~

After President Golden Hawk *finally* chose which countries could participate in the oil cleanup, there were many questions about just who was aboard those foreign ships that arrived and what exactly they were doing out there.

Also, the decision was so long in coming, that the cleanup was taking place during storm season for the region. That meant that the skimmers and other oil cleanup ships had to frequently dock in U.S. harbors with their crews taking shelter on shore. The Administration instructed the Coast Guard and on-shore law enforcement to *not* surveil the foreigners nor to make them feel in any way as though they were not trusted. It was therefore unknown if the people who entered the U.S. on those ships were the same people – or even the same number of people – who left on them...

Much later, investigations would lead to a grim discovery. Hostile parties had capitalized on the President's long delay in granting permission for coastal cleanup. Under the concealment afforded by the heavy oil slick, the villains had constructed underwater missile and mine-launchers to be controlled remotely in the future.

CHAPTER SIXTY-FIVE
Retreat

An Army/Air Force Reserve Base near Washington D.C. reported to the press that a car had crashed into a jet fuel tank, causing an explosion. The report did not mention that it was a White House limo, and it said that no occupants had been identified.

The limo had been so thoroughly incinerated that the President's *special* forensics unit was only able to collect substantial DNA belonging to one suicide bomber. They retrieved nothing but singed hairs matching the DNA of Sequoia, Breeze, and the other two terrorists.

In an "unrelated" press release, the White House reported that the First and Second Ladies had gone to an undisclosed location, not on the Ronopo Reservation, for a private, American Indian retreat. The spokesperson said that they expected the women to be away for at least a few weeks.

SIGNAL Command believed that meant that the DNA recovered from the limo had not completely convinced Dukon's alliance that Breeze and Sequoia were dead. Since all three terrorists were missing, the alliance might also be wondering if they had all truly been in the limo or if two might have defected or been captured.

Sequoia and Breeze continued to stay off the grid and out of sight. SIGNAL leadership conferred and pondered about who would make the next move. All SIGNAL operatives, though not informed of the true status of the First and Second Ladies, were placed on high alert for any intelligence regarding a mysterious alliance with Washington, D.C.

They waited and they watched.

CHAPTER SIXTY-SIX
Crypt

A SIGNAL Regional Commander in Canada tasked a SIGNAL Brave named Roy Strange Day with investigating the Promised Land tanker disaster. The brilliant young special operative ingeniously found, extracted, and decrypted ghost images of computer files not fully erased from a Coast Guard database. The files documented that the U.S. and Canadian Coast Guards *had* been analyzing the presence of an unidentified submarine near Alaska. The files also documented Stone Whitecloud's warning to the Promised Land and to CCG of an incoming projectile. This information confirmed that there had been an attack, possibly an act of war against the United States, that was being covered up and not investigated.

SIGNAL intelligence analysts questioned who would have reason to cover it up? One theory pointed to members of the U.S. Administration who were trying to shut down the fossil fuels industries like a previous Administration had. If the public were led to believe that the oil tanker disaster was a destructive *accident* caused by the *oil industry,* they might support this Administration's efforts to stop harvesting America's own oil.

It seemed counter-intuitive, however, that the U.S. Administration would foster policy that would *harm* the U.S. and other nations. It was certainly important to pursue renewable energy, but the U.S. needed a great deal of fuel to power its economy until new green sources were readily usable. Not exploiting the United States' own oil reserves would ensure the continued flow of billions of dollars to oil nations that supported terrorism. Although that was not logical, the intelligence community was increasingly investigating if insurgent or foreign saboteurs might be embedded in U.S. Government. If that were true, it could explain how incidents such as this one were being "swept under the rug" and hidden from the public.

CHAPTER SIXTY-SEVEN
Trojan Horse

"You wanted to speak with me, Captain Lightfoot?"

"Yes, General. As you know, when Captain Trueheart emerged from the coma caused by his electrocution, he was moved to a SIGNAL safe house. I have been spending time with him there as he continues to recover. Thankfully, his mind is fully intact despite the coma. Captain Thunderstrike and I enlisted his help to analyze the movement of the botched sting rifles that we are tracking inside the U.S."

"I am glad to hear that you have taken the initiative to boost Captain Trueheart's convalescence and to foster his possible return to operational status."

"Certainly, sir. Captain Trueheart is a great asset to SIGNAL. He, Captain Thunderstrike, and I found that most rifles stopped being transported once they reached U.S. federal lands. We discovered that all of those destinations are tracts that President Golden Hawk's Land Controller closed off to the public and barred from natural resource exploration."

"Hm... closed-off federal lands... If that is the primary destination for most of the weapons *lost* by the feds, that introduces the possibility of government employee complicity."

"Yes, and sir... we traced the remaining rifles... to American Indian reservations."

The General inhaled audibly. "*That* is distressing, Captain."

"Yes, sir. Some Native Americans might *possibly* stoop to illegal gun-running as a result of our exceptionally high rate of unemployment. Or tribes could be being *misled* if someone in government were making false promises in exchange for participation in a supposedly legitimate, secret operation. Questionable *foreign* governments have even cozied up to some tribes recently. It is most likely, though, that no Native Americans are involved, and that intruders are storing weapons in remote areas of reservations without the knowledge of the tribes."

"That is plausible and certainly preferable, Captain."

"Sir, we came up with another, purely hypothetical scenario since many smuggled weapons are staying within the U.S. and since SIGNAL is already tracking threats at the highest levels. An enemy of the United States – possibly even embedded within U.S. government – could be building *a legion of fighters* to engage in an attack from *inside* America. The thousands of guns purchased by many federal agencies, along with the government's continuing purchases of massive amounts of ammo and protective armor could be used to arm such an internal assault."

"Yes... an infiltrated U.S. government could simply put it on the tab of the U.S. taxpayers – who might be the intended *targets* of such an attack."

"Sir, considering the recent, worrisome changes in American policy, including foreign policy, we came up with even *more* alarming hypothetical scenarios."

"Let's have it, Captain Lightfoot."

"President Golden Hawk has repeatedly lauded the uprisings that happened a long time ago in countries where people had no ability to elect their leaders. Those were called 'Arab Spring' initiatives. Captain Trueheart, known for his imagination and his way with words, conceived of a chilling possibility – that someone could be plotting something they might call an *'Indian Summer'* in the U.S. He suggested that this would not be to topple the President, though, but to conquer the entire United States."

General Dark Horse was quiet while digesting this.

"Such an uprising could potentially happen *soon* – possibly even this summer or in the fall during traditional 'Indian Summer.' It could be before the next election or Congressional turnover, since the balance of power might shift away from the Administration and back to The People. Captain Trueheart suggested that 'The Fall' might be chosen for an attack because of its witty-but-woeful double-entendre."

"I see..."

"President Golden Hawk has quoted former politicians, saying: 'You can't change government from the inside.' Whoever is behind the gun-running could be fomenting change from *outside* government, organizing violent uprisings *inside* the U.S."

"Go on, Captain Lightfoot."

"If internal uprisings were coordinated with an assault from *outside the U.S.* by one or more hostile nations... perhaps ones with whom the President and his Cabinet have recently cultivated relationships, there could be a Global War on U.S. soil, with all of America's enemies fighting not only us, but one another as well, vying for territory and dominance."

"Hm. The military budget *was* cut, and the most effective equipment for national defense is being taken away from National Protection troops and being sent abroad. Federal government has grown exponentially and is certainly in chaos, making it more ripe for the picking. Also, unidentified people have not only been allowed to cross U.S. borders, but the *federal government* has been transporting them all around the country. If any of them were terrorists..."

"Sir, this shows how an expansive, multilayer government could be like a Trojan Horse. Hailed by some as a progressive advance and gift to the people, it could actually be concealing instruments of sweeping destruction, intentional or not. If the fabled Trojan Horse had been *transparent*, the nation conquered and destroyed by its contents would never have embraced it and been deceived."

"Captain Lightfoot, I will discuss the *possibility* of these scenarios with our agent, 'John,' amongst the small cadre of trusted partners in Congress sworn to secrecy about SIGNAL. I will find out if any such machinations are already under suspicion and being probed. In any case, it appears to be time for SIGNAL's first ever *All Hands Operation.*"

COUNTERPOINT XI
STATUS REPORT: BATTLE PLAN

"Where do we stand on enabling the takeover?"

"The recent initiatives that will ensure the success of our incursion are:

1. *The disarming of American citizens* so they will be helpless against our well-armed fighters who will attack from inside and from outside America. We have almost completed building and training our armies on their closed-off federal lands.

2. *U.S. acceptance of hordes of undocumented – thus unidentified – foreigners –* even though their officials know that some 'terrorists' already slipped into the country. Our agents in the Administration are transporting our young fighters and suicide bombers, hidden amongst the clueless foreign pawns, to all states, under guise of humanitarian actions. No one has accounted for who has entered the U.S.

3. The government-ordered prison *release of hundreds of illegals even though they had been imprisoned for committing crimes.* Some were our fighters. The government justified the action by the budget crisis which, of course, they had a hand in causing.

4. *Foreigners who have entered America illegally can actually obtain driver's licenses* in some states! And they're not even *International Driver's Licenses!* In America, a U.S. driver's license is like a passport, providing an appearance of legitimacy. Our people can now drive vehicles loaded with fighters, weapons, toxins, and bombs. We have already tested having drivers 'accidentally' drive into pedestrian crowds killing and maiming Americans.

5. *Welfare employees hand out free or cheap cell phones to our undocumented fighters* who have gotten into the country. Our warlords use the phones to communicate with our soldiers. Some fighters will use the phones to detonate bombs! *Importantly – the federal government awarded the service contracts for those phones to multiple NON-U.S. companies!* When we take down all U.S. communications – *we* will not be affected. Our people will still be able to communicate *and detonate bombs,* since they will have service provided by the Eurinatian phone company owned by one of our associates! The U.S. government is even funding cell phone text-messaging in foreign countries in the name of freedom. That allows anti-Americans to detonate bombs, which they otherwise could not afford to do! Like other American programs,

they give it *a name that sounds progressive and benevolent*, like the Internet Freedom initiative which actually gave *control* to individuals in government! The masses believe those false names and never read the actual wording of the laws.

6. *Diminished protection of America* since the U.S. Administration let military budgets suffer severe spending cuts, even as our partner nations expand military *and nuclear* capabilities. The cuts caused reductions in personnel and equipment in their National Guard, Coast Guard, airport security, and northern and southern Border Patrols. Protection was further diminished by deploying many National Guard units abroad. Now, in response to our global attacks and epidemics, the Administration is further depleting their military resources. Our advisors also scored changes to the U.S. Military Rules of Engagement, resulting in much greater risk and casualties to U.S. fighters. This has helped to discourage others from enlisting. We have also incited attacks on U.S. civilian police, diminishing *their* numbers and discouraging new police recruits. People there will have little police protection when they need it most.

7. The Administration's *enormous handouts of money to other countries* which no American watchdogs are able to oversee. The U.S. public has no idea what the recipients are doing with that money. Of course, *we* know what they're doing with it!

8. Our activists in the U.S. rallied special interest groups to *overwhelm Congress with so many demands that Congress has felt unable to focus on national security.*

9. *Permitted presence of commercial and personal drones* as well as for law enforcement inside the U.S. will enable us to perform surveillance and to carry missiles and chemical and biological weapons. They'll also interfere with air and ground traffic.

10. We successfully tested *instigation of riots.* Mobs enthusiastically take to the streets, setting *other people's* cars and homes on fire and robbing and vandalizing other people's businesses. We will use these 'resources' in our assault. People in the mobs don't know that instigators are being *paid* to be there. Riot mobs will block law enforcement from getting close enough to protect rioters or others from our fighters. And the commotion and destructiveness of the riots will do part of our job for us!

11. Last but not least, our agents in the U.S. Administration allowed *the collection and storage of massive amounts of personal data about all American citizens* by both government and private entities. Acquiring much of the data, we identified individuals' political ideology; medical vulnerabilities; finances, weaponry and other possessions; as well as their means of communication – all which we have used in our planning. *Most importantly,* this tidal wave of data has completely overloaded their Intelligence analysts *who can no longer filter through it to focus on their actual enemies.*"

"Very good! The Plan is running smoothly. Our success is assured!"

CHAPTER SIXTY-EIGHT
The Price of Peace

It was highly unlikely that anyone would find Captain Grant Broadwings once he decided to disappear. He believed that he was next on a hit-list of witnesses who could end the rise of certain high-level people seeking yet greater power and riches. Grant's Airborne Spec Ops team had started dying off before being able to testify about the tragic U.S. operation in Central America. There had been other incidents where the lives of U.S. fighters seemed to have been traded for political capital benefiting certain people. A previous, high-profile military initiative had ended with another elite band of heroes being all but handed to the enemy on a silver platter. Many questions still lingered about that incident.

Captain Lightfoot compiled a tome of evidence that did suggest foul play was involved in the deaths of Grant's Spec Ops team. His investigation also led him to believe that Grant was alive and operating under his own power. He toyed with the idea of leaving Grant alone, allowing his true status to remain secret. He knew, however, that he might then inadvertently leave a man behind who would choose an alternate path if he had assistance.

Despite the odds, Captain Lightfoot did locate him. Being an elite special operative himself, he knew that it was extremely risky to track and approach a Captain who felt that he could trust no one. Nevertheless, he selflessly pressed on.

Captain Lightfoot did not foresee that his courageous recovery of Captain Grant Broadwings would prove to be his own final mission for General Dark Horse.

Upon his return to "civilization," Grant Tomachichi provided eyewitness testimony for the Congressional investigation into Operation Dove of Peace, the disastrous mission in Central America. Afterward he was advised to change his name for his own safety. This highly decorated, elite warrior veteran gave it careful thought. He chose his new name, Louis Kraig Thomas, in honor of a fallen Special Forces hero.

Before venturing out under his new identity, he visited his tribe. He was received there with an intensely meaningful, hero's welcome attended by everyone on the reservation. There were multiple ceremonies and purification rituals to help purge the toxic effects of war from his spirit. Grant felt measurably cleansed and healed by these powerful and caring attentions. All who were there expressed their admiration and appreciation for his service, and he received many job offers from members of his tribe. He wished that all of his brethren American warriors were received at home this way. He knew that Americans hold their warriors in extremely high esteem, but that non-Native American veterans did not receive this special cleansing, healing, and reintegration support. Too many received little recompense after having protected Americans and the American ethic to aid others fighting for their freedom.

Grant knew that he could not stay on the reservation as he might still be a target. Henchmen would likely seek him there, potentially endangering others in his tribe. When he was younger, he had fantasized about following in the footsteps of the first American Indian astronaut. Grant mused that outer space would be a good place for him now.

He set out to construct a whole new life. He hoped to bring to other veterans, and also to himself, some salve for the enduring wounds that war inflicts upon body and soul. Using his new name, Louis Kraig Thomas, Grant began making regular rounds, meeting with veterans in hospitals and in physical and mental rehab centers. Grant brought much solace to the fortunate recipients of his attentions with his gentle demeanor and genuine empathy from personal experience. He mostly listened to the veterans. All of them had stories that they needed to unload to a willing ear attached to an understanding heart. In this way, Grant soothed his own spirit while, yet again, giving of himself to help others.

Having inspired Vice President Hunter Wolf, Grant sometimes joined him on his visits to Native Americans in prisons. Hunter especially interacted with the Ronopo criminals who had started down their ignominious paths while associating with *him* in his childhood gang of hoodlums. He felt remorse and some culpability for his influence on them in their early lives.

Hunter knew that just one strong mentor influence can change the direction of a person's life to a positive one. Though he hadn't realized it when he was young, Hunter had been fortunate to have several. Elder Chief Bridgewater, a caring schoolteacher, and a few supportive peers and their parents had all helped to keep his struggling conscience alive. Elder Chief had shown such wisdom and compassion in securing a job for Hunter. That job had consumed Hunter's availability to associate further with the other unguided boys on their path of moral decline. However, as the Chief had often reminded the tribe, people always have choices; and the responsibility for which path a person decides to follow is ultimately *his or her own.*

Hunter encouraged the incarcerated men to truly accept accountability for their offenses and to work to better themselves. He offered his assistance to any who would do that and also find some way to compensate the crime victims or their families.

Thusly, Vice President Wolf brought peace to his conscience, using his highly visible position to be a positive role model and mentor. He never lost sight of how others had helped him to alter the evolution of his personal identity and, thereby, the course of his destiny.

CHAPTER SIXTY-NINE
Commander's Honor

"What?! *The Commander-in-Chief of SIGNAL* is coming *here?!*"
"Yes! After all these years, he's decided to retire. He's visiting every region to personally thank each active and retired SIGNAL operative and to honor each Regional Commander. We'll be convening in our usual meeting place. I just received a *Smoke Signal* about it, so you should have one too."
"Yup, here it is. Who's taking his place as Commander-in-Chief?"
"I don't know. I think it would have been Captain Lightfoot if he hadn't—"
"Captain Lightfoot?! You mean he's real? I thought he was just a legend – the totem of the Special Forces Warrior Operatives. Those Captains and Braves do so much more than just gather and analyze intel!"
"Hey! Don't sell short the intelligence work the rest of us do! Our work is critical to national and local security. We take risks, and our Regional Commanders shoulder *a lot* of responsibility."
"I know. It's just that Special Forces Warriors go through such extensive training – stuff like special warfare, technology, languages, and emergency medical procedures. They constantly work out to stay in top condition, and they take much greater risks than we do. They put their lives on the line and give up having a normal life. With the sacrifices they make, they really are the stuff of legends."
"True. Hm, maybe our new leader will be Captain Thunderstrike! According to the stories, she has some amazing feats under her belt! It's also rumored that she and Captain Lightfoot were lovers."
"Wow, yeah! It would be totally cool to have her in command!"

Fox Bridgewater was responsible for choosing the date and time of the General's visit to each SIGNAL region. He based the schedule upon a maximum window of time when no satellite would be directed at each location. He coordinated signal-deflection, monitoring, and transmission-jamming equipment for each gathering. He also implemented new anti-drone measures – including the use of some trained birds of prey and dogs! It was an intensified version of what he had designed and installed in each region for their general meetings. He would disable it all once all participants were safely away.

There was a respectfully hushed buzz in the large hunting cabin. The operatives reconnected with their comrades from other tribes while the awe-inspiring General Brett Dark Horse made his way around the room. He introduced himself and his wife, Lori, of many decades, to every SIGNAL member there. He thanked each of them, discussing their personal participation in that important partnership amongst the tribes. He placed a unique, hand-made honor bead threaded on a thin leather cord, around the neck of each operative. When he had completed the rounds, he asked for everyone's attention.

"I now want to honor your Regional Commander with special emblems for his distinguished service to SIGNAL. Since an operative from your region was recently promoted to Chief of Government Operations, a top-level post that reports to the SIGNAL Commander-in-Chief, it would be fitting for that new officer to make the presentation. Chief Starfire?"

Sequoia was delighted to have that honor. She stepped forward, wearing a silver, SIGNAL Chief's emblem on a chain around her neck. Everyone clapped and whooped in recognition of her impressive promotion.

For the ceremony, two operatives provided ambiance with hand drums and a wooden wind instrument. Aspen pulled his traditional tunic top off over his head. He looked so dignified and serious without his usual sunny smile. Lori Dark Horse handed Sequoia a set of four black armbands. Two of them were adorned with an embroidered white, feather quill, and the other two were embroidered with a gold arrow. Those two symbols represented both facets of the security organization's work.

Lori Dark Horse was mostly deaf and mute, so Hunter stayed by her side since he was facile in more than one sign language. He had learned them so he could communicate at least a little bit with his niece, Anata, who had many disabilities. For this part of the ceremony, Lori only needed to use illustrative hand gestures to describe to Sequoia what to do.

Deeply suffused with the solemnity of the ceremony, Sequoia approached Aspen. She wrapped the larger armbands around his muscular upper arms and slipped the others onto his wrists.

Lori Dark Horse was now holding two red sashes, one long and one short. She handed the shorter one to Sequoia, again with descriptive gestures. Sequoia stood behind Aspen, feeling as though this tall man had somehow grown a foot taller. She reached up and around him to place the sash against his forehead, tying the headband in the back. She then accepted the longer sash. Standing in front of Aspen, she tied it around his waist, angling the ends to the side over his traditional, deerskin breeches. She stepped back, and Aspen bowed to the General. Everyone else in the room also bowed, clapping their thighs in a noisy salute to their Regional Commander.

During the commotion, Lori Dark Horse placed a small metal bowl on the table and poured some clear liquid into it. She lit an aromatic candle beside it. When the noisy acclamation subsided, the General addressed the crowd.

"Now, many years after establishing the Security & Intelligence Guard of Native American Lineage, which has included most of the tribes of the United States, Canada, and Mexico, I am handing over the reins of this very special organization to a new Commander-in-Chief. It is my pleasure to announce that I will be succeeded by the highly accomplished Captain Lightfoot.

There were exuberant whispers amongst the crowd at this resolution of the *myth vs. reality* debate regarding Captain Lightfoot. For those who had already believed that he existed, this put to rest the rumors that he had recently been killed during a high-risk mission.

The operatives were exhilarated at the prospect of being led by such a colorful leader, long-regarded amongst them as a superhero. Though they had all heard of some of his reputed, extraordinary exploits, they knew that few would ever actually meet him, perhaps not until his retirement, as was the case for most of them with General Dark Horse. Just knowing that they would have Captain Lightfoot at the helm filled them with a renewed sense of purpose. It was a reaffirmation of the value of the cause to which they had pledged their service.

While the crowd reveled over this, the General removed an ornament from his ear lobe and dropped it into the metal bowl of liquid. The crowd became quiet, watching. Lori Dark Horse placed the tip of a twisty twig into the candle's flame, lighting it afire. She then touched the glowing tip to the liquid in the bowl which ignited. A brief plume of fire consumed the liquid, then self-extinguished. With a carved, wooden spoon, Lori scooped the ornament out of the bowl and onto a soft cloth. She wiped the ornament carefully with the cloth and gave it to the General.

He held it up and loudly intoned, as in making a toast, "To Captain Eagle Lightfoot!"

He then said, "Chief Starfire, would you also kindly decorate Captain Lightfoot as the new Commander-in-Chief of SIGNAL?"

The General handed her the ear ornament while gesturing towards Aspen. Gasps were heard throughout the cabin as understanding dawned.

Sequoia turned and faced Aspen, her eyes wide with astonishment, tears threatening to spill from them. Aspen stepped closer and looked down at her so that only she could see his eyes. He gave her a gentle but unmistakable look of warning. Sequoia immediately understood and blinked hard. The tears in her eyes beat a hasty retreat, not *daring* to show themselves in the face of this man's silent command.

The ear ornament that Sequoia held was in the shape of a feather quill pen, with a white enamel finish over yellow gold. Crossing the feather was a shining gold arrow.

Aspen sometimes wore an eagle feather hanging from one earlobe, since his family name, Mijeesi, meant *Eagle*. Now, instead of an eagle feather, he was wearing a gleaming, silver ear ornament in the shape of a winged foot. Aspen turned his head and Sequoia placed the SIGNAL Quill and Arrow ornament through his other earlobe before stepping away from him.

Aspen thrust his fists high, and turning his face skyward, he howled loudly. He began a rhythmic, chest-beating, vocal, and foot stomping ritual that Ronopo and many other tribal Braves once did before entering battle. *All* of the operatives in the room knew it and answered in kind. The hand-drummer kicked up the beat, and the crowd generated a thunderous and exhilarating commotion that shook the cabin.

Finally, Aspen extended both hands back in the air, his fingers spread wide.

The cabin went silent. With that, the now-emotional General proudly proclaimed Captain Eagle Lightfoot the new Commander-in-Chief of SIGNAL.

After more noisy recognition, Aspen raised his hands again for quiet. He spoke to the group, extolling the General's many accomplishments. He lauded General Dark Horse's foresight in establishing this clandestine partnership among the tribes so long ago. He told them that the General had changed the organization's name more than once as protection against security leaks.

"I want to remind you all that this cooperative has always been completely separate and autonomous from any U.S., Canadian, Mexican, or tribal government jurisdiction. This affords us special freedom and cover to perform our important work for the security of our tribes and of our respective nations. There are very few in these nations' governments who are aware of our existence; and those few are trusted conduits for the exchange of high-value intelligence."

He motioned for the group to be seated, and all sat down on the floor. He recounted a few of the now unclassified, but heretofore unknown stories of SIGNAL glory involving the General – and his wife, Lori, who had been one of the very first undercover operatives.

After the storytelling, Aspen announced that Phoenix Kiwideekon, Kiwi's sister, of the Mihote Tribe was taking over his position as Regional Commander of that SIGNAL territory. He also told them that Fox Bridgewater would now be sole Chief of the Ronopo Tribe. The plaudits for these announcements concluded the gathering.

Most of the Ronopo operatives had yet another stunning surprise while watching the General and his wife being escorted from the cabin. Amongst the retinue of distinguished retired operatives, who had been inconspicuous in a corner of the cabin, were: Elder Chief Bridgewater; Aspen's father, who was very weak but infinitely proud of his son; and Granny Katiri. As she exited, Granny K. turned towards Sequoia and winked, snapping and drumming her knobby old hands in the singular SIGNAL salute.

The throng departed, but the circle of friends remained to congratulate Aspen and Sequoia. Aspen told them that he and Captain Thunderstrike had *both* been selected – to be Co-Commanders-in Chief of SIGNAL – but that Captain Thunderstrike had not accepted, saying that she preferred active field duty over administrative command.

Aspen also said that he had invited Fox to be considered to replace him as Regional Commander but that he had declined.

Fox shook his head. "I think it's better for the partnership if no one tribe dominates the leadership positions. Anyway, now that I'll finally have Aspen out from underfoot here..." he said, grinning, "I have some ideas that will fully demand my attention."

When the group broke up and headed back to the village, Aspen noticed Sequoia walking by herself from the grove. He called out, "Sequoia! Are you walking back? I'll walk with you."

She and Breeze were still "off the grid" in the Mihote safe house, so Sequoia was relishing this opportunity to walk outside, shielded from detection, thanks to Fox's extraordinary security measures. In addition, *all* operatives at the gathering had taken a Pledge of Silence – to deny having recently seen *any other attendee* whom they would not normally see.

Sequoia was trying to center herself after the emotional maelstrom of the gathering. Aspen had always seemed larger than life to her, but this was over the top. She had recently experienced some imposing facets of his personality that were shockingly new to her. Now, revelations of his extraordinary alter ego left her feeling awestruck and very, very humble. She walked along in silence with him.

Noticing her reticence, Aspen said, "That was pretty overwhelming, wasn't it... *Chief* Starfire?"

Sequoia looked at him and nodded, smiling but not speaking.

"Are you okay, Dear One?"

Sequoia took a moment to answer.

"I... feel overcome with sadness, Aspen. You're leaving us, and I cannot imagine the reservation without you on it. I suppose I'll still be in contact with you in my new SIGNAL role – but it just won't be the same here. Is SIGNAL headquarters far away?"

"SIGNAL headquarters is wherever its Commander-in-Chief lives. I am considering several locations that I've seen in my travels."

Sequoia nodded.

"The decision won't be entirely up to me, though. The woman in my life is choosing it with me."

Sequoia stopped walking and looked at him, feeling bittersweet.

"Oh, Aspen – *congratulations.*"

Sequoia was happy for him but found herself needing to hide the unexpected jolt this caused her. It felt like yet another personal loss, another void. She, too, had long heard the rumors of romance between Captain Lightfoot and Captain Thunderstrike, but, of course, she had never even had an inkling that Aspen was Captain Lightfoot.

"Lately, I've been learning so many things I didn't know about you!"

Aspen grinned, shaking his head and tousling Sequoia's hair before starting to walk again.

"I'm leaving the day after tomorrow for a few days," he said. "I want to look over a possible location not too far from here that I've never seen at this time of year."

Sequoia nodded, looking down, definitely not wanting him to see that, yet again, her eyes were filled with tears.

The two continued along in silence for a little while.

Then, still walking, Aspen put his arm around her and said,

"Sooo.... will you go with me...? See if you like this place...?"

Sequoia stopped walking and looked up at him.

Stroking her silky hair, he softly added, "...my very Dearest One?"

CHAPTER SEVENTY
Run

The stocky man with the black hair and beard looked down over his glasses at the small Mexican woman who looked very young.

"You are the new pilot? I am to entrust millions of dollars in cash and merchandise to *you?"* he said in unusually accented Spanish.

"Yes, sir," she replied in crisper, Mexican-accented Spanish. "I have flown many runs back and forth across the border for others."

He turned to his assistant and snarled,

"Who allowed a *female* to be here? Is she our only pilot?"

"We need multiple pilots for our current schedule, sir. We have new and larger orders since some American states legalized one of our products. She brought the money pouch here from the last order on her flight today. She flies well, and nothing was missing."

The stocky man stroked his beard while looking her over. He was thinking of a very different use for her.

"When do you need her to fly?" the stocky man asked.

"Tonight and then later this week."

"All right. You're dismissed."

He turned back to the young woman. "How is it that a girl learned to fly?"

"My brother taught me. He is here with me."

"You remind me of... the child brides back at home," he muttered, giving her a sidelong stare.

She smiled meekly back at him, masking the light bulb that had lit up in her head and stifling the shiver that went up her spine. She thought this man might have just given away something very unexpected and possibly of great significance. She figured that she was probably safe with him right now because they needed her to fly tonight. After that... was questionable.

"I really don't need anyone to accompany me on the flight," she told the armed guard a couple of hours later.

"The boss says you do for now."

Birdie sighed. That meant she was unlikely to have an opportunity to communicate her suspicions to Aspen. It would just have to wait – and she would have to decide if she should risk being with that creepy man after tonight's run.

As Birdie had feared, the guard never left her side throughout the round trip that night. She returned to the drug cartel's compound and went to where she and the other Mexican "mules" were being housed, watched by armed guards.

There were no restrooms or even portable toilets for them. All of the "runners" had to use an open hole in the ground – watched by male guards. She had to awkwardly hold a towel wrapped around herself as her only screen from their eyes when she had to go. So there was no opportunity to send a message to Aspen from there either.

She lay down beside a sleeping Mexican SIGNAL operative who was also undercover there and supposedly her brother. He opened his eyes and she used some hand signals and body language to indicate that something might be afoot. Since there were guards watching them now, she would have to find an opportunity in the morning to elaborate further.

CHAPTER SEVENTY-ONE
New Digs

Fox was visiting Aspen at his new location not far from the Ronopo Reservation.

"So, Aspen, how long do you think Birdie will be on duty?"

"Unknown, Foxer."

"Ballpark? Like... multiple days?"

"I really don't know. It could actually be weeks or even months."

Fox's mouth fell open and he stared at Aspen.

"This must be really big."

"Yes."

"While I was away, Birdie left me a message, saying that she was going 'wheels up' and would call to hang out when she got back. I couldn't tell from the message if she was on duty for the National Guard or for SIGNAL. I checked the Guard roster and saw that she wasn't on it."

Aspen nodded. "I needed an outstanding pilot quickly, so I tapped Birdie."

"So... this is going directly through you and not through our new Regional Commander? Does that mean it's inter-regional?"

"Foxer, I am so accustomed to discussing everything with you, but I can't say anything more about this." Aspen grimaced. "I'm already missing that, Buddy."

Fox put his hand up. "I understand completely. Your new job as Commander-in-Chief puts you in a very different position."

Aspen nodded ruefully.

"All right, Brother. I'm gonna head out. I really dig your new location, but don't be a stranger back home, ya hear?"

"You can count on that, Chief."

CHAPTER-SEVENTY-TWO
Flee Fly Foe Funk

Birdie was wakened very early by a kick to her foot by a heavily armed guard.

"El Médico wants to see you right now," he said brusquely.

Birdie exchanged a glance with "her brother" and went with the guard, thinking, *I wonder why a doctor wants to see me?*

She was led to another small building, into the private quarters of the stocky boss she had met the day before.

"Buenos días," she said respectfully.

He gave her a once-over but did not reply.

"You are a medical doctor?" she asked in Spanish.

"Si...." he replied with a little smile. Then, looking her up and down, he said, "You are not needed for a few days, and... I thought of you when I awoke this morning."

Ewww, Birdie thought. She knew where this was headed and wanted to redirect the conversation.

"Was there something wrong with my run last night?"

"No, apparently you did fine despite being female."

He was pouring himself a tiny cup of thick, dark coffee. He did not offer her any.

She wanted to keep him talking as long as possible.

"Females are involved in many types of work – including in business and in government."

He turned from pouring his coffee and looked hard at her.

"Are you involved in that big project with the governments?"

Birdie looked down, wondering what he meant.

"I-I'm not supposed to talk about it," she said.

"So... " he said, pondering this. "You are to be one of the millions who go... *to Occupy America?* The United States of America?"

Birdie froze. She knew that she had just hit paydirt. She kept her face bland and looked up at him.

With a cruel smile he said, "They don't need millions plus one. You will be staying here and serving me. Where is your brother now?"

Birdie was alarmed. She now feared not only for her self but also for the Mexican SIGNAL operative posing as her brother. El Médico might see him as a threat to be eliminated, since a brother might try to protect his sister.

"He left this morning. Only I was going to stay."

"Good. We will find another pilot to replace you before the next run."

He scanned her with his eyes and then spoke much more gruffly.

"Go wash yourself!" He pointed to a small washroom. "In there."

Birdie was scared. She had uncovered something really big... *and* she was in a horrible predicament. She knew that if she resisted this man, he or one of his men would probably just kill her. It wasn't likely that she could escape; and she couldn't kill El Médico, because she didn't know if he was important to the mission.

She dreaded the heinous fate before her. Her SIGNAL training had prepared her for this possibility – but it could not prepare her for the reality. She hoped that Aspen would be able to conjure up a rescue for her without jeopardizing the mission, but she knew that it might not be possible. Birdie prayed for strength.

There was cell phone service on the estate, so behind the closed washroom door, she would send a quick *Smoke Signals* message to Aspen. It might be her only chance, as El Médico would likely take her cell phone from her – possibly as soon as she left the washroom. She knew it was safe to transmit, because Fox was certain that *Smoke Signals* could not be intercepted by any means.

El Médico grumbled at her through the door to hurry up. She turned on the water, and in code, she quickly punched into her phone:

OCCUPY AMERICA PLOT
Boss – El Médico – not Latin American? Moscken?
Brother must leave NOW

She added an S.O.S. for herself:
I have WOUNDED KNEE.

CHAPTER SEVENTY-THREE
Bird in a Cage

A few days had passed since Fox visited Aspen's new residence.

"Aspen! Welcome home! To what do I owe this pleasure?"
Aspen looked grim.
"Fox... I felt that you deserved a heads-up since you and Birdie have been especially close friends for so long."
Fox's smile disappeared, and he felt chills go up his spine.
"Birdie is... in serious trouble on the mission... and... possibly worse."
"What?! What kind of trouble?"
"She may have been made, but it seems more like an unrelated case of sexual enslavement by a sadistic man with the opposition. She's been seriously brutalized. We know where she is, but we cannot extract her."
"Fill me in! I'll leave right now!"
"I can't send you, Fox. Aside from Birdie's circumstances, the mission is proceeding exceptionally well, and we *cannot* jeopardize it. This is way bigger than all of us. And Birdie is part of why the operation is so successful."
"Aspen!" Fox cried out imploringly.
"I know, Foxer."
Fox looked at Aspen with condemnation.
"Certain risks are a given, but SIGNAL operatives are not supposed to be put into life and death situations except for Captains and Braves. Birdie did not sign up for life and death!"
"Actually, she did. I carefully explained the risks of this mission to her. I even made her sleep on it before deciding. We did not expect her to be at high risk, but she knew that just being on this mission could be deadly for everyone involved. It was a gamble she was willing to take for such high stakes."
Fox closed his eyes. He was remembering recent conversations with Birdie in which he repeatedly teased her as being cowardly.
Could Birdie possibly have taken on this mission just to prove herself otherwise? No, she wouldn't do that... would she?
"What did you mean, when you said her condition could 'possibly be worse' than being in serious trouble?"
Aspen gripped Fox's shoulder, and his voice was hoarse.
"We may have already lost her."

Fox stared at Aspen in disbelief.

Aspen whispered, "I have an *outstanding* SIGNAL Captain working the mission. He's checking on her."

Aspen's phone vibrated.

"I have a message from him now." He read it and said, "Our Birdie's still alive, but barely. She's lost a lot of blood. The Captain thinks... he thinks she can't possibly last much longer."

Fox roared, "Can't *he* help her?! He's a *Captain* for crying out loud!"

"Careful there, Buddy," Aspen said, putting his hand on Fox's shoulder and looking around to see if anyone might have heard. He softly said, "The Captain has been working to gain the trust of a person in power there. That relationship may lead to an opportunity, but that takes time... and Birdie just may not have enough time left."

Fox angrily shrugged Aspen's hand off his shoulder.

"You made her remove her life signs tracker and tracer."

Aspen nodded.

"If you hadn't, her deteriorating condition would have been clear sooner!"

"We could not risk them finding electronics on any of our people."

Fox pressed him again. "If the SIGNAL Captain is focused on the mission, then why not send me in just to get Birdie out?"

"I want her out too," Aspen said emphatically. "This is the most difficult thing I've ever had to do! But I cannot insert someone new at this point without risking the mission. This is one of the few situations in which I cannot send someone *from here* mid-operation."

"You mean... she's out of the country??"

Fox took Aspen's silence as confirmation and hung his head, feeling helpless anguish for their dying friend.

CHAPTER SEVENTY-FOUR
Sacrifice

Fox went to the woods near Birdie's isolated cottage, carrying his most-prized and irreplaceable possession. It had been a special birth gift to him as the son of a Chief. It was a magnificent, ornate, and exceptionally well-balanced, wooden bow. It had been fashioned by hand by the master craftsman, Potay Oora, who was now too old to practice his bow-making trade. There were few bows of this quality or beauty.

Fox went to the ceremonial tree of the woods. At its base, there was an arc of sharp, metal spikes pointing upwards. They were used for many purposes such as holding candles or symbolic offerings of food during religious and cultural rites.

Fox laid his bow across the spikes. He knelt before it and bowed his head, calling upon the Great Spirit to watch over Birdie and to protect her. In Ronopo, he implored the Great Spirit to not take Birdie into the hereafter anytime soon.

"Great Spirit, I, Sinota Fox Bridgewater, ask you to accept this offering of my finest bow as a symbol of the protection that I would give to Litanni Darting-Hummingbird Moonsong if I were able. I must entreat you for this favor instead. I understand that there is an order of life and that you preside over its balance. I pray that my offering and sacrifice will satisfy you and that the universal equilibrium will be maintained."

The bow was certainly an offering apropos to a supplication for protection. Fox knew that the Great Spirit would not want him to sacrifice any life in exchange for Birdie's with the hope of maintaining the universal balance.

He lifted a large rock and smashed it down upon the bow. The bow did not shatter as expected. Instead, its strong, yet flexible wood accepted the spikes. The bow was driven down, impaled along its entire curved length. Fox hoped this was a good omen. He tugged at the bow and found it immovable, so he left it there and went to Birdie's cottage nearby.

Fox had to know where she was suffering, so he searched her cottage for clues. He saw the outer packaging of two birth control pill packs in her trash. She had obviously prepared for a long absence and was protecting against indiscriminate pregnancy. He looked through her clothing and noted that warm-weather items were the sparsest. He found a contemporary Spanish phrase book on the shelf of her nightstand. From these clues, he deduced that she was in Central or South America – likely involved with surveillance or a strike on a drug cartel.

Fox went home and remotely accessed ASO satellite data from the day she messaged him and the next day. She would not have flown directly from the reservation. She would have been transported to an airstrip somewhere where she would be provided with a small plane or helicopter to fly. He searched satellite footage of the Ronopo Reservation and the area immediately surrounding it on those two days.

He found a departure from the reservation to a location that then had a couple of flights take off towards Central America. He was able to identify one flight as being a large plane and the other – a small plane. Bingo! In order to pinpoint her destination, Fox matched up footage of Birdie's flight from different satellites. He then hacked into a different database and researched who and what were located there. He found that Birdie was in one of the most dangerous places in the world.

He could not shake the thought that he might have driven her to accept this mission with his relentless teasing.

Did I bully her? Is she now going to die because of it?

Fox thought of the blood oath that he and his friends had sworn as preteens – to always have each other's back. He vibrated with emotion. Regardless of their *pledge* to SIGNAL service, they were not upholding their *oath* to one another. Birdie's friends were leaving her to die.

Fox returned to Birdie's cottage and locked the door. Now his mind and eyes were in hyper-focus. He stared at her religious cross on the wall. He looked at the many framed photographs of all of their friends, laughing, sharing, and growing together over the years. There was an old picture of just him and Birdie. It reminded him of their romance back in their teens.

Fox was seized by rage and anguish. He roared – a sound that morphed into a yowl of lament. Shaking with fury, Fox grabbed his razor-sharp knife from his belt sheath. Seizing a handful of his long hair, he slashed through it with his knife. He repeated this again and again. Uttering a guttural sound with each slash, he realized the potency of this mourning ritual. Hyperventilating – a pile of black locks lying at his feet – he knew that this was not enough.

Fox's fingers feverishly flew across the keys of Birdie's laptop. He pulled up some Internet pages and reviewed the note that he had composed for his family and friends. He had left the note displayed on his computer in his own bungalow. He was frequently off-reservation, so no one would go in and see it until it was way too late for anyone to interfere.

He gathered some things from around Birdie's cottage. Laying one of her towels on the floor, he knelt upon it while folding a washcloth into a wad. Looking skyward, he murmured some words in Ronopo. Then whispering, "For you, Little Bird," he clenched the wadded cloth tightly in his teeth and took the knife to himself.

CHAPTER SEVENTY-FIVE
Higher Remorse

When Aspen left the Ronopo Reservation after telling Fox about Birdie's situation, he struggled with renewed waves of remorse. He had steeled himself earlier against the heartache of almost certainly losing Birdie, a lifelong friend. He had dreaded telling her best friend – Fox – who was his best friend, too.

He stared at his cell phone for a long time, thinking of his duty as Commander-in-Chief of SIGNAL and his obligation to act rationally not emotionally. Of course, had he known the true make-up of the opposition involved, he would never have sent a female operative.

Arriving at a decision, Aspen punched in a *Smoke Signals* reply to the SIGNAL Captain on Birdie's mission.

CHAPTER SEVENTY-SIX
El Capitán

The Captain presented himself at the mansion and was told that the mistress of the house was not available. The servant handed him an invitation to the early evening soiree that would start shortly. He could meet with her then.

The Captain took advantage of the intervening time, taking a stroll around the estate. Multiple armed guards followed, watching him. There was a variety of buildings on the expansive property, and the Captain wanted to investigate some more closely.

There was a small, round, adobe structure with its door wide open. The guards who were following him halted at a distance but continued to watch him. The Captain stepped into the entryway of its sole, circular, rank-smelling room. There he encountered a grisly sight. There were multiple stretchers tilted upright against the walls around the room. Each one had a human form bound to it with leather strapping. Each person was in a different state of brutally-inflicted injury. Some were missing body parts. Others were just bloody messes. Some of the victims were unconscious, but others moaned or cried. The Captain guessed that they were arranged in this way so each would witness the torture of the others, adding to their terror and misery.

One stretcher was tilted against the wall a bit ahead and to the right of where he stood in the entryway. He saw a small arm dangling from it, bearing many bruises that almost hid a tattoo – of a hummingbird.

He stepped into the room, and to the right, he saw three guards sitting on stools under an open window. His gaze focused on the eyes of the man he assumed to be the head guard. The man looked startled and stared at the Captain, taking in his fine, military Captain's uniform. The guard hastily buttoned the lower half of his wide-open shirt as he approached the Captain. He muttered under his breath, "El Capitán?"

The Captain exhibited the conspicuous air of a man in charge. He sized up the other two guards, each of them shrinking a little under his withering gaze. The Captain slowly pivoted, scanning the circle of victims around the room. Lastly, he faced Birdie whose eyes were swollen shut. She looked unconscious, bloody, and bruised.

In brisk Spanish, the Captain said to the head guard, "Some of these people look dead already. Do you not give them enough water to stay alive for the work that is to be done?"

The guard clearly resented the Captain's criticism. He replied,

"We do as El Médico commands, but he will not be back until later tonight. I will have my men give them another water ration, if that is your wish, *Capitán.*"

The Captain gave a single, curt nod.

The guard eyed the Captain. "I was not expecting you—"

"Well you should have been, Carlos," the Captain interrupted, reading from the name label on the man's shirt. "Was it not you who sent for me?"

"Perhaps..." the guard said disdainfully.

The other guards, gaining moxie from the head guard's boldness, approached with their hands on their holstered guns. The Captain saw this in his peripheral vision and slapped the head guard hard, then again with the back of his hand and then again. The guards stopped approaching.

"That was a yes or no question, you insolent goat!" the Captain snarled.

The head guard fumed but saw his men advancing again. He noted the gun on the Captain's belt. He knew that a gunfight would not end well for anyone, so he halted the aggression, raising his hands in submission.

"I beg pardon, Capitán. My mistake, Capitán."

The Captain seized a long, loose, leather strapping strip from the stretcher beside him and began coiling it in his hands. He turned his fiery eyes upon the other guards. They retreated backwards across the room. The Captain lifted the limp arm of the tiny woman with the hummingbird tattoo and let it drop again. He strode over to a male victim and felt for a pulse. Shooting an icy glare at each of the guards, he secured the coiled leather strap around the knife sheath on his gun belt and left the building. The head guard tried to follow him out while finishing buttoning his shirt, but the Captain pointedly slammed the door in his face.

CHAPTER SEVENTY-SEVEN
La Bella Señora

The Captain straightened his cap and entered the mansion after superciliously handing his invitation to a guard at the door. He strode forward several paces. With his head held high, he scanned the crowd of socializing men and women. The splendor and festivity was in stark contrast to the squalor and misery not far away on the estate.

It did not take long for his eyes to be drawn to La Señora, the beautiful mistress of the house and head of the drug cartel that her husband had wrested from another gangster. Her husband was later killed during a skirmish with intrepid Mexican Marines.

The Captain found that La Señora's eyes were now firmly planted on him. He elegantly crossed the room, walking to her as if he owned the place and were approaching a guest. He had the bearing of a completely self-assured man, an august presence amidst the people in the room.

Now this is someone! La Señora thought, watching his approach with pleasant anticipation.

The Captain stopped in front of her and removed his cap. He inclined his head slightly, not dropping his eyes, keeping them fixed on hers. His face displayed no deference, warmth, or arrogance. He simply conducted himself in the manner of a nobleman introducing himself to someone of his own class. In Spanish he said,

"Señora. Capitán Rodrigo Morales – at your service."

She heard in his accent the Spanish of her youth – the language spoken by descendants of Spaniards who had settled in South America. The man's rich skin coloring suggested that there was indigenous blood somewhere in his lineage. She mused that it had been a good combination.

"Good evening, Capitán Morales."

La Señora had been angry when one of her men informed her of this man's hotheaded interaction with one of her guards earlier. She had intended to berate him. However, she'd had no warning that he would be so classy – or so attractive – so she toned it down.

"I understand that you wasted no time, slapping around one of my best guards and threatening a thrashing for the three of them there."

Her eyes dropped down to his belt where the neatly coiled leather strap hung at the ready.

"He is a good man, Señora, but he was out of line. I believe we have come to an understanding now."

While speaking, he had replaced his cap upon his head, punctuating his statement by giving it a firm tug. The Captain showed no emotion, simply appearing to be confidently in command – and still he kept his eyes on hers.

La Señora was accustomed to men lewdly lusting after her, which she despised. In contrast, this man held her gaze with a self-controlled intensity that caused heat to flare inside her. She liked a man with self-control and discipline. She liked that a lot.

The calm was suddenly shattered by the sound of an explosion in the room followed by people screaming. The Captain instantly drew La Señora against him. He moved her across the room, away from the sound, shielding her from that direction with his body. Meanwhile, everyone else in the room seemed frozen like deer in the headlights, including her bodyguards and another man in military uniform. By the time anyone else had even reacted, the Captain was holding La Señora behind a stone pillar, his other hand firmly gripping his drawn pistol.

It had only been a collision between a waiter and an unruly, drunken guest who was now escorted outside. Servants rushed to clean up the broken dishes and the stack of metal trays. The Captain re-holstered his gun and let go of La Señora's arm, but he remained standing well inside her personal space. This gave her the sensation of being pinned against the pillar by him. His eyes were locked on hers. They dropped down to her lips before moving slowly back up to her eyes. The Captain then smoothly took a step backwards, restoring decorum.

La Señora was heated by the adrenaline rush from the sound of the crash and the swift movement across the floor; but the real heat she felt was from having this attractive man's body pressed against hers. She had also noticed how good he smelled. She was more than intrigued.

"I was told, Capitán Morales, that you came here at the request of the guard whom you struck today. I trust his judgment, but I wish to become acquainted in detail with your background. Please attend a meeting in my parlor in... a quarter hour?"

"As you wish, Señora."

"Have you been provided with accommodations yet, Capitán?"

"No, Señora."

La Señora instructed a servant to prepare a guestroom for him *in the mansion.* She then dismissed the Captain. She watched him take only water from a waiter and walk the room, constantly scanning. This man made her feel very, very safe.

CHAPTER SEVENTY-EIGHT
Mucho Gusto

The Captain was shown to La Señora's parlor. It was a luxurious room attached to her boudoir. It had a meeting table and chairs, but La Señora directed him to a comfortable club chair across from a chaise lounge where she now arranged herself. He noted that the double doors to her boudoir were open, displaying her luxuriant bed. It became obvious that no one else would be attending this meeting.

La Señora asked the Captain about his personal history. He responded crisply and satisfactorily. She had long felt out of her element there and was desperately lonely. This very classy Captain would be a welcome associate. After questioning him, she was fairly sure that he had been born into a good family and was well-educated. However, she hoped that she might see more conclusive evidence that he was of an upper-crust family like her own.

La Señora unbuttoned the top button of her corset-style, bustier top. The Captain kept his eyes on hers. He asked her some questions about her preferences in security protocol. Then he delicately asked about the procedures and disposal regarding the victims in the torture room. After answering with clear distress, she entreated the Captain to speak no more of those things.

She pulled up her flowing skirt to liberate her bare legs, arranging them in an alluring pose as the Captain watched. She saw greater intensity in his darkening eyes. She returned to questioning him about his past and shared some details about her own.

While speaking, she slowly undid more buttons on her tightly form-fitting bustier, alternating between buttons at the top and ones at the bottom. Her actions were now obviously for the Captain's benefit. Accordingly, he watched each time she undid another button, exposing a little more of the naked curves beneath.

There was now only one center button preventing La Señora's top from flying all the way open. She arose, and the Captain courteously stood as well. She went to her bedroom door and looked at him invitingly. To her dismay, the Captain turned and headed for the exit. When he reached the door, however, he locked it. La Señora smiled with relief and admiration for his caution.

The Captain strode briskly to where she stood, taking her by the elbow and guiding her into the boudoir. Still holding her arm, he closed the double doors and locked them as well. He led her closer to her bed. Looking at her intensely, he unbuckled his gun belt and laid it on a bench at the foot of the bed. Then he took off his jacket and covered his weapons with it. As he moved towards her, he unbuttoned his cuffs and the top of his shirt. Placing one arm around her waist, he drew her hips against his as he dexterously undid the last button of her top. Slipping his hand inside it, he kissed her heatedly.

La Señora unbuttoned the Captain's shirt, revealing his muscular upper body and a silver cross on a chain around his neck. She smiled, thinking it a good companion for the one she was wearing herself.

The Captain did not disappoint the beautiful Señora. His serious manner deliciously complemented his seductive savvy as he slowly and skillfully gave her pleasure. He made sure that La Señora was well-gratified before moving to take his own pleasure.

She was surprised that this austere man had a brightly-colored condom. She looked down and reached to take hold of him, but he caught her by the wrist. While she tried to read his eyes that were holding her gaze, he put the condom in place with his other hand. Then he took her hands in his, so that they stroked it on together, his hands very deliberately dominating hers.

La Señora had succeeded in glimpsing what she had hoped to see. This man was circumcised. Most of the men surrounding her were from Central American families, amongst whom circumcision was not prevalent. It was not a common practice in South America either, except among a certain stratum of very wealthy, educated people. Thus, this pointed more definitively to a lineage like her own and sealed her belief that she could trust him.

Some other men here were foreigners of a religion who, like Yotish people, were usually circumcised. But she had no stomach for the men here at all. To the outside world, she was the putative head of the drug cartel, *but these men were actually holding her prisoner.* She and her private militia had been helpless in the face of the invaders' more powerful and plentiful weaponry. Those men brought to this land that bestial brutality and disregard for human life rarely found amid civilized humanity. Unfortunately, it was still prevalent amongst fanatical extremists of their denomination.

Some people believed that religions were more alike than different; that most people actually worshiped the same Creator and just venerated others with different rules, rituals, and names for them. Since different peoples spoke different languages, the sacred words were, not surprisingly, translated differently within each culture.

Some malevolent extremists in power persuaded the more lowly to kill all who did not observe the exact lifestyle or religious rituals that those leaders demanded. They encouraged their fighters to die while murdering peaceful people – supposedly in the name of the Highest Power. Of course, this just brought the *ringleaders* more power. They, thereby, deprived their brainwashed pawns of living fully and happily their own Earthly lives that were gifted to each of them by their Creator. Meanwhile, their overlords did enjoy all the pleasures of a long and full Earthly life, which was meant to precede any afterlife – for everyone, not just the powerful.

It was actually by the actions of extremist Mosckens in Central America that the drug cartels became notorious for beheading people. La Señora wondered why the world did not see that obvious connection as those hostile beings eyed the United States from that closer, yet more camouflaged vantage point. It also gave them greater access to the profitable drug trade – a source of funding in addition to Moscken petroleum oil which made possible the terrorists' barbaric, genocidal pursuits worldwide.

The extremists had been concerned that one U.S. political party might cut off the billions of dollars that were financing their activities. That could have happened since the U.S. had enough fuel sources of its own that, if tapped and combined with purchases from friendly nations, could have freed the U.S. from buying *any* from countries supporting terrorism.

That party had the perfect candidate to strengthen, secure, and revitalize America for *all* Americans. However, because of that party's true, but relatively boring facts instead of catchy propaganda; a lack of huge contributions from anti-democracy donors; little media coverage; and attempts by a few highly visible members of that party to impose their religious beliefs on everyone – they had not won the elections.

The person who was elected President prohibited the exploitation of available domestic energy resources. Thus, the massive flood of dollars financing terrorism had not been shut off.

Afterward, while La Señora rested contentedly, the Captain went into the bathroom. He scrutinized the room for any sign of a hidden camera. Satisfied that he was truly alone behind a closed door, he privately exposed his painful secret. He inspected the base of the condom and confirmed that there had been no leakage. Then, gritting his teeth, he gingerly removed the condom – which was filled with blood. He washed thoroughly and made certain that there was no more blood to come nor any traces left behind. The Captain put in place some protection against further bleeding before pulling on his shorts and trousers. He then returned to the bedroom to finish dressing.

La Señora reached for his hand, pulling him down to sit on the bed beside her. Having decided that she could trust him, she told him the truth – that she was a prisoner there – and not actually head of the drug cartel. The Captain learned that she loathed the man called "El Médico." She revealed that he was anything but a doctor. The nickname was a gruesome joke, as he was the torturer. Apparently, there was not even any "value" from his brutality aside from him satisfying his sadistic, and other, appetites.

La Señora's narrative clarified for the Captain that El Médico, as well as certain other men there, were not from Mexico or even from the Americas at all. The Captain offered his assistance to her since she was a prisoner of those men and loathed what they were doing.

She looked plaintively at the Captain. "If anyone confronts them... I and those close to me will pay a price. I have already lost my sister," she finished in a whisper.

In the name of caution, the Captain asked her how many men there were of that ilk and where they were stationed.

While he finished dressing, La Señora invited him for a late supper the next evening. He inclined his head in assent. She lifted her phone and gave instructions that Capitán Morales was to have free rein and should no longer be accompanied on the estate.

The Captain tipped his cap and left her.

CHAPTER SEVENTY-NINE
Desperado

The Captain went directly to the torture room, armed with valuable information and no longer followed by Security. The same three guards were there. The head guard informed him that one of the victims had died. The Captain apprehensively checked the pulses of all of them, including Birdie. All but one man were weak but still alive. The guard also said that El Médico was apparently sleeping off excessive drink from the early evening soiree and had not yet returned. The Captain realized that El Médico was the drunken guest who had crashed into the waiter and had then been escorted with a large platter of food to his quarters in another building.

The Captain asserted to the head guard that the little female was now also dead and that he was going to remove the two bodies and take them to "the pit." He engaged the head guard to help him place Birdie into a body bag, such as they had, so he could drag the bodies by himself without attracting notice from anyone who should not see the disposal process. The head guard stared at the Captain, knowing that Birdie was not yet dead, but he complied. The Captain directed the subordinate guards to put the dead man into another bag.

While those guards struggled with the man's corpse, the Captain communicated further with the head guard. The Captain quietly said that if he were to be waylaid by desperadoes while taking the bodies to the pit, then he – the head guard – should take his place, personally guarding La Señora – on *his* recommendation. The guard indicated that he understood. He described where the pit was, cautioning the Captain that he might encounter other, more menacing guards under a different supervisor's command. The Captain acknowledged the warning. The two men had conveyed as much with their eye contact and body language as they had with their words.

The Captain stepped outside for some air while the head guard helped his subordinates with the dead man. The Captain then dragged the two body bags out into the night.

There was a commotion outside the building housing the Moscken contingent. El Médico had come flailing outside, choking and grasping at his throat. One of his men tried the Heimlich maneuver, and another man smacked his back a few times – both to no effect.

The men were then agape, as they saw small nodules appear all over El Médico's neck. They began to grow outwards like fingers as El Médico gagged and clutched at his throat. A cluster of bones – the ribcage of the roasted rabbit from his dinner – was increasingly protruding from inside his throat as he hawked and gasped and grabbed at it. A man stuck his fingers into El Médico's mouth, trying to pull out the bones lodged in there. He could not reach anything, however, and El Médico bit him savagely. The man screamed and yanked his hand away.

El Médico choked and wheezed and fell to the ground, flopping like a fish out of water. His eyes bulged out of their sockets as his face turned redder and then bluish. He was grappling at his throat, exacerbating the situation, as some of the bones then punctured his throat and popped all the way out through his skin. For the bones to have been that sharp, he must have first cut off the tips, perhaps to suck out the marrow from inside them. That would explain why they were stuck fast and could not be coughed back up.

Blood and other fluids spurted from these holes in his throat as his men looked on with horrified fascination. El Médico continued to emit ghastly, gurgling pleas for help amidst his convulsions. Someone tried to push on one of the bones from the outside, but that made El Médico gag even more. His men did not know what else to do.

It looked like something out of a science-fiction movie in which an alien creature comes bursting out of its host. El Médico must have been getting a small amount of air as this grisly performance went on for some time. Finally, El Médico, the torturer, succumbed – very fittingly suffering a gruesome and painful death.

His men had witnessed that he died from choking on rabbit bones. One man had even recorded it with the video camera in his phone. The greedy El Médico had not shared his food platter from the soiree. What's more, he had been drinking alcohol. They thought that he must have been sucking the last bits of meat and marrow from the whole ribcage and that he had sucked too hard, causing it to lodge tightly in his throat. It had obviously been the glutton's own folly. Clearly, no blame could be laid on anyone else. It was not as if someone had *forced* the rabbit's ribcage down his throat...

There was thus an open position on the estate that might never be filled. At least for now, there was no torturer on the premises. Those who had suffered or died in agony at El Médico's hands had been avenged... by the ribcage of a roasted rabbit.

With all attention drawn to the bunny bone commotion, the Captain met with no resistance as he briskly absconded with the two body bags. He pushed the dead man into the pit and slid Birdie out of her bag. He stripped down to his shorts and stuffed his uniform and cap into Birdie's empty bag before tossing it into the pit. After buckling on his gun belt, he hoisted the dying little SIGNAL operative onto his shoulders. He bound her to his body with the long, leather strapping strip that he had snagged from the torture room for this purpose. Now, if necessary, his hands would be free for his gun and his knife. Creeping quickly through the night, avoiding the roads like a desperado of yore, he hoped that he had not been too late.

CHAPTER EIGHTY
Faux Foes

"It is time to reverse the public perception. They must see us as adversaries again."

"Ah! No more détente? That is too bad. I was beginning to enjoy it."

"I think we will enjoy our future situations much more. Do you not agree?"

"I am just glad that it is you and not I who will be the goat!"

"I will not be the goat! I will blame my predecessor and the lawmakers. It works every time."

"I am enjoying the distraction I am causing by flexing my military muscle."

"*Yes* – while our cohorts bombard the tiny nation and battle at its borders! I may need you to agree to halt your *overt* military actions since there is one more election I might need to win to carry out *The Plan*. Your cooperation will show the efficacy of my diplomacy and help persuade voters to keep my regime in power. But hopefully, *The Plan* will be consummated well before that election. Also, I have opened our border with your little ally near us. Your people can now inconspicuously infiltrate from there. Soon, I will invoke our military draft and will send *all* fighters *away from the homeland* 'to help' with the conflicts and epidemics abroad. Some soldiers will be exposed to diseases requiring quarantine, thus keeping them away longer. Conversely, we do not permit anyone to be quarantined *inside* our country!"

"It is pathetic, but certainly no surprise, that you need me to make you look good. I make no promise as to what I will do for you or when. How are the other global players going to know the timetable for their entrance into the grand finale?"

"I have sent well-disguised emissaries, friends, and travelers, to convey my true intentions and timing to the other involved players around the globe. I will see you in... *The New World!*"

CHAPTER EIGHTY-ONE
Blood Oath

Birdie began to regain consciousness. Her purple, puffy eyes were still swollen almost shut. Through the slit of one eye she could just make out a Mexican guard sleeping in a chair near her. She realized that she was horizontal, which meant that she had been moved. She hoped that El Médico wasn't going to punch, kick, and viciously rape her again. She turned her head so she could look at her surroundings. The pain of the movement caused her to emit a small peep. At that sound, the guard's eyes flew open. She cringed, closing her eyes again.

She heard a quiet utterance that *sounded* like, "Birdie." She almost opened her eyes again before dimly remembering SIGNAL protocol. She mustn't respond if someone actually had said her name. Had she been made? Had they *personally* identified her as well?

Then, sounding like the whisper of a distant wind, she thought she heard, "Little Bird...?"

Now, there was only one person in the whole world who called her that. She opened her eyes. The vision was fuzzy, but she saw an indistinct face that did look Fox-like.

"Fox?" she whispered weakly through her bruised and swollen mouth.

There was a muffled reply that sounded far, far away.

"Yes, Birdie! Yes, it's me."

The hazy apparition put its head down, making a choking, sobbing sound, whispering, *"Thank you, Great Spirit. Thank you."*

Birdie realized that she was likely dreaming this as she slipped in and out of consciousness.

Eventually, she awoke to the sound of another voice. Now, she saw a man who looked like Aspen. His face was more in focus. He crouched down, taking her hand. He pursed his lips and lowered his head. It was difficult to look at her in that condition. Aspen felt terrible guilt that the lives of life-long friends had been, to a large degree, in his hands.

He quietly said, "You done good, Bittybird. Real good."

"Was I... was I made?" she whispered.

"No, they never knew. You accomplished your mission. *Well done.*"

She managed a weak smile. Then she tried to look around and said, "Fox?"

Aspen looked down again and swallowed, shaking his head. He rose to his feet and turned away. A shadow crossed his path.

Birdie thought she heard the faint words,

"Roll up your sleeves, Aspen. They can't take blood from me any more. Birdie needs blood, and she can use your type."

Aspen stopped a nurse in the hall. "Where can I give blood for this patient?"

The nurse pointed down the hall. Aspen turned to Birdie.

"I'm going to give blood for you, Birdie. I'll be back to see you later."

Birdie closed her eyes. When she opened them again, the Fox-like man was back at her bedside. His eyes were moist.

"You're gonna make it, Little Bird. I was so wrong to tease you, calling you cowardly. I knew you were brave long before what you did on the mission."

She smiled weakly. "What happened to your hair? I didn't recognize you with it cut short like that. I thought you were a guard."

She stretched out her hand, and he lowered his head, but she couldn't seem to reach it.

"Are you going to let it grow back?"

He smiled nostalgically. "Some things can come back... "

CHAPTER EIGHTY-TWO
Birds and Bees

Birdie thought, *This isn't the smartest thing to do, but what are the odds of me needing a gun tonight? Hardly anyone's around. Besides, I'm all healed and strong again. Thankfully, my brain swelling and internal damage were not permanent. I finally got the thumbs-up today from both the doctor and the shrink for all activities.*

Fox would have had a fit if he were here to see me cleaning all of my guns at once. It's such a safety no-no. But I hardly have any cleaning solvent left, and I don't have money for ingredients to make more. The dirtiest parts of all three guns are soaking outside in what's left of it, and I'm almost done cleaning the other parts. Then, just a touch of oil, and I'll reassemble them in no time.

Fox is off-reservation... again. Maybe it's a checkup for his injury that happened while I was away. He hasn't wanted to talk about it. I'm glad he's okay. I hope he hasn't actually been going away to be with one particular woman. I've been so lucky to be one of his "special" female friends over the years. Of course, because of my... trauma in Mexico, my doctor's orders did include no lovemaking until today.

Birdie heard something outside. Then, Bam! Bam! Bam! Someone was banging on her door.

"Who is it?!" she called out assertively.

There was no answer. Birdie was stark naked, because one time she had ruined her favorite knockabout dress and her nice, matching underwear when she spilled dirty gun cleaning fluid. Now, she always cleaned her guns in the nude. She looked through the peep-slot but saw nothing. She could hear someone walking around the outside of her cottage. Her shutters were closed and barred from the inside, so they couldn't see her, but she couldn't see them either. She grabbed her soft, homemade, tube dress, pulled it over her head, and wiggled into it. She called out again,

"Who is it?!"

Birdie had one of the really old cottages. She had chosen it for several reasons: It was far from the village center, it was close to one of the woods on the reservation, and it had very few neighbors. This provided more privacy for Fox to be discreet when he chose *her* to stay with. The windows had no glass, just shutters and handmade screens. She'd had a skylight cut into the roof, and it was open now to let out the fumes from the gun solvent. Birdie thought she was hearing someone removing her window screens. Then, her rear shutters started creaking, and she could see that they were being pushed inward.

She loudly called out, "WHO IS IT? I HAVE A GUN, AND I WILL SHOOT YOU IF YOU COME THROUGH THAT WINDOW! THE TRIBAL POLICE ARE ON THEIR WAY!"

Birdie grabbed her cell phone and hit speed dial to actually call the police... but there was no service... again. *Crap!* Her shutters were bound to give way if pushed hard enough. So she stepped into her moccasins, strapped on her thigh sheath, and slipped her knife into it. Now she wished that she hadn't disassembled all of her guns at once – and left some parts outside!

Okay... I know exactly where he is. I hope he's alone, 'cause here goes nothin'!

Birdie cautiously opened her door. To the right, she knew that her only neighbors were not at home, and it was wide open in that direction with no place to shelter or hide. To the left were the woods. It was very dark out, and it would be even darker in the woods. She knew her way around in there and figured she'd be safe up a tree or in one of many good hiding places. Birdie could run like the wind and now fled fleetly for the forest.

She was almost across the empty flatland in front of the woods when she heard the sound of running footsteps behind her. She sprinted harder. The footsteps grew closer, and she caught a whiff of men's cologne. She raced to the tree that had a beehive in it. Knowing that there were sharp, metal spikes pointing upward around its base for ceremonial uses, she jumped before reaching the trunk, stretching for the lowest branch.

She didn't make it.

"Oof!"

The man had thrown his arm around in front of her, and she slammed right into it. He let out an evil chuckle as he drew her tightly against him with just one arm. Facing away from him, she reached for her knife, but his hand got there first. He unsheathed it and tossed it away from them. Birdie felt nauseated by the man's cologne. Fox never wore any. He always smelled good from the all-natural soap Granny Katiri made. Now, Birdie could smell alcohol on the man's breath, and his free hand was fumbling with his shorts.

No! No! No! Never again!

She thrashed violently, kicking and elbowing him as he suspended her above the ground. Lurching forward energetically, she caused him to take a step closer to the dangerous, metal spikes. She punched backwards over her shoulder and connected with his face, but he only emitted a grunt. She started to scream, but he clamped his hand over her mouth. Birdie pushed off with her feet from the man's thighs, launching herself up towards the low tree branch. He grabbed her arm, rotating her around back into his grasp. His hands landed on the outsides of her thighs. She was now facing him but could see nothing in the dark. Her legs were slippery with sweat from her sprint, so she slid downwards in his hands. Her feet were headed for the sharp spikes on the ground. As she dropped down, her dress rode up. She hoped the man could not tell that she had nothing on underneath it. As her feet were about to land on the sharp metal spikes, the man seized her at the waist and hoisted her firmly onto his hips. Moving away from the tree, he drawled in a low and throaty voice...

"Oh-h-h, Little Bird. You need to brush up on your self-defense skills."

"Fox!!!" she shouted, *furious.*

Still holding her on his hips, Fox walked several paces to where a bit of moonlight was filtering through the tree canopy. He dropped to his knees and placed Birdie on her back on soft moss, pulling her dress back down for her. Now, in the moonlight, she could see him. He was leaning on his forearms over her. He was grinning. She was not.

"No underwear, Birdie? I saw the jar of gun solvent outside your cottage. Were you gun-cleaning while naked again? *That* is a mental picture that I *really* love. Wanna clean my pistol?" He winked.

Still beside herself from thinking she had been chased and then caught by a rapist, Birdie blasted him. "You have alcohol breath! Is that why you're wearing cologne? Or was the cologne for someone who *likes* it on you?!"

Fox abruptly stopped smiling and sat up on his heels, swallowing hard.

"Whoa, Birdie. You've never said anything like that before."

Instantly wishing that she hadn't, she looked at him anxiously, distressed that she might have crossed a line. "I know. I didn't mean it."

"I think you didn't mean to *say* it. But you wouldn't have said it if you hadn't meant it."

Birdie sat up and put her hand on his. "Please, forget it. I'm sorry."

Fox looked pained. "You know, Birdie... I never asked you to be my girl or anything–"

"I know, Fox – I know," Birdie broke in. She spoke rapidly, hoping to undo the damage. "I didn't mean to suggest that your relationship with me was exclusive. We're... *special friends."*

Fox winced, closing his eyes. "I hate that phrase."

Birdie's heart sank, realizing that she had now stuck her other foot in her mouth. "Fox... I just didn't mean to imply that I think you owe me anything – or any explanation. I don't know why I said that. I love being with you when you are with *me,* and I... I just miss you when you're with... when you're away. That's all. I guess I was just freaked out by the home invasion and having a stranger chase me."

Fox's shoulders sank and he sighed, shaking his head. "In all this time, I did not know that you felt this way. You and I have shared a lot of good times over the years... not really being... together." He covered his face with one hand. "I did not want it to be this way. I've been ready for a change for a long time. What you just said confirms how far *beyond* time for a change it is." He looked at her sorrowfully.

Birdie closed her eyes as she felt a wave of overwhelming sadness envelop her. Long ago her mother had warned her not to get too attached to Fox.

"Litanni," she had said. "It's nice that you had a date with Fox Bridgewater; but you shouldn't turn down the other boys, hoping that Fox will ask you out again. He is

220

the son of a Chief and may be Chief, himself, someday. Fox is attractive in many ways. He can have any girl that he wants, and they all flirt like crazy with him! You may not be a beauty, but you are attractive in your own way. So many boys ask you out! Maybe you should get to know some of the other boys better."

Birdie had thought, *I couldn't care less if Fox were a Chief or a – whatever! I just love everything about him. I'm not going to give up my chance to be with him just because he's going to end it someday.*

She opened her eyes and saw that Fox was looking at her expectantly. She swallowed and said, "Whatever you want, Fox."

He nodded. "I want to give you a token from me. Something special."

Birdie thought, *You've already given me something special, Fox. And the only 'token' I had ever hoped for was your beaded choker, taken from your neck and placed around mine by your hands. But I did know that was a lot to hope for.*

Fox stood up and reached into a deep pocket of his cargo shorts.

"I was trying to get this out of my pocket when I was holding you next to the tree, but I fumbled it with all your squirming!"

So it wasn't what I said! He came here planning to end our 'special' relationship! He had a farewell token with him, and he said that he's wanted a change for a long time! Ouch!!

"Stand up and close your eyes."

Birdie complied, willing her eyes not to leak any tears.

He bent down and put it on her. "Okay, open your eyes."

Birdie opened her eyes, and her jaw dropped. What she saw was a magnificent, lavish, silver necklace. Suspended from the wide band of supple, silver strands that she could feel around her neck, was an inverted silver triangle linked to an upright silver triangle below it. The top triangle had a shining blue gemstone mounted in its center, and the lower one was resplendent with a luminous green one. A gleaming, silver fringe dangled from the bottom triangle. Birdie was overcome by its beauty in the moonlight; but it was tarnished by her sadness at why she now owned it.

"It's... magnificent," she whispered. "I'll cherish it forever."

Now tears did fill her eyes, and she smiled at him. "But Fox, much more than even this, I will always treasure our time together. And... I'm going to say it..." She swallowed. *"I love you, Fox.* And it doesn't matter if we're together or apart. I know that I always will."

Fox softly said, "You've never said anything like *that* either." He looked at her with a crooked smile and said, "I love you, too, Birdie."

Birdie thought what a sad irony it was that, after all these years, neither of them had ever uttered those precious words until they were parting ways.

Fox put his hands on her shoulders. "That *sounded* like a *Yes."* He looked at her earnestly. "Yes?"

Birdie stared at him, confounded.

Fox realized that his departure from deeply ingrained tradition had left Birdie clueless.

"A choker of silver and gemstones, instead of old leather and beads for *my girl,*" Fox said, fingering the leather choker around his own neck. "I'm asking you to marry me, Litanni."

Birdie's eyes widened and she just stared at him. Then she put her arms around him and buried her face in his chest. She was speechless with disbelief, trembling as tears started running down her cheeks.

Fox swallowed hard. "Don't you want to marry me, Birdie?"

Birdie slowly pulled back and looked at him, whispering, "Of course I want to marry you! Of course I will!"

Fox beamed and kissed her, lifting her off her feet. When he set her back down, she looked at his face and tremulously said, "I-I thought you were saying *goodbye* to me with this."

"W-w-what?!"

Fox was incredulous and very confused. Replaying their conversation in his head, he figured it out. He smacked his forehead and winced. He took Birdie's hand and pulled her down to the forest floor, stretching out on his side next to her.

"What I'm about to tell you should clear things up." Out of reflex, he looked over his shoulder. "All of these years, I *couldn't* ask you to be my girl, and I couldn't marry you, because... that might have put you in danger."

She stared at him, her mind churning.

"Birdie, like Aspen... I've been a SIGNAL Captain for years – since my teens."

Birdie gaped at him in astonishment.

"*That* is why I had to go away so often, and that is why Aspen and I decided to be Co-Chiefs of the tribe. We were usually not on SIGNAL assignment at the same time, so one of us was here for the tribe while the other was away. I was not supposed to be in a relationship at all over those years, but I was afraid you wouldn't wait for me! Is there even one guy in this tribe who hasn't asked you out? I'm sorry for what you thought when I went away on missions and that I made you keep our 'special time' a secret. That was the only way that we could be together and not put your safety at risk. Amazingly, you seemed not to mind. Tonight is the first time you have ever showed me that you thought I went away to be with other women – and that you were hurting."

"Oh, Fox. I had no way of knowing what you were doing, but I was grateful to have so much with you. It *felt* like love to me."

"It *has* been love. I just couldn't tell you."

He pulled her into his arms and hugged her tenderly.

"And, yes, I *was* drinking tonight. With Aspen. It was a ritual acknowledgment that I fulfilled my commitment as a Captain, ending my abstinence – from alcohol – and from a *whole* relationship. *That* was the change I was telling you I've wanted for a long time."

Birdie closed her eyes, now understanding. Still overwhelmed by the night's emotional upheaval, she caressed the beautiful necklace. "You didn't have to give me something like this!"

Fox smiled. "I designed it for you and had it made by a native artisan out of state." He pointed to the lower triangle. "This triangle, in the female shape, represents you – my rock solid support. The North Carolina emerald symbolizes the greenery of the Earth and of the Seas. The triangle above it, in the male shape, represents me, watching over you always – sheltering, protecting, and providing for you. This sapphire comes from Montana, symbolizing the blue sky above us."

Birdie's eyes welled up with tears. Fox fondled the glistening fringe of flat, silver strands dangling from the lower triangle.

"And these... represent what I hope will result from linking us together in marriage."

Birdie threw her arms around Fox's neck and breathed, "I hope so, too!"

"It was just ready last night, so I went to get it today. Aspen met me on my way back. We stopped off-reservation to drink a toast to our futures. In fact, that's how the cologne got on me. Aspen and I helped relieve a cologne-soaked, drunken foreigner of his car keys. So Aspen smells like this too," he laughed. "And *obviously,* Aspen and I used one of those blood alcohol calculators to check ourselves before driving home."

Birdie nodded appreciatively. Then she asked, "About tonight... Did you *want me* to think that I was being chased by a stranger in the dark? Or did you think that I knew it was you?"

"Didn't you recognize my trademark evil chuckle once I caught you?"

Birdie shook her head.

"I'm sorry, Birdie. I came here to surprise you with the necklace. But when I saw that you had left yourself without a gun for self-defense, I wanted to show you the danger of doing that."

"How did you know?"

"Your jar of gun-cleaning solvent outside has parts from all three of your guns in it. That means that you didn't have a usable one while you were here alone. Promise me you won't do that again?"

"I promise. I knew it wasn't a smart thing to do. Will *you* promise to never again let me think that you're a stranger chasing me?"

"I'll promise that when I see that your self-defense skills are top-notch again."

Birdie chafed at that unsatisfactory answer.

"There was no one nearby if you needed help. I know you didn't have cell phone service to call for help since I have the signal-jammer on and electronics in my pockets to monitor it. That was so no ASO jockey or anyone else could eavesdrop while I talked to you about SIGNAL. There's often poor cell service here anyway. It was like a perfect storm for someone to victimize you, and you did not have a gun to defend yourself. I came to your cottage with a gun and a knife, and you had what? Your pillows and blankets wouldn't be much help. You had your knife, and you're a fast runner; but I caught you, and I'm not even a tall man—"

"*No,* but you're like... like... *Superman!*" Birdie blurted out with exasperation. "I could not believe that you caught up to me when I'd had such a head start! One moment you were in back of my cottage, and the next moment you were right behind me in the woods!"

"Well, I'm a Special Forces Warrior, so that's how I train. If I didn't, it could cost me my life."

Birdie shuddered. Then she thought of something.

"Fox! What is your Captain's alias?!"

Fox looked away. Then he said, "You're going to have to marry me to find out."

Birdie glowed at hearing those unexpected words again but pulled a mock moue. They heard the rumble of motorcycles, and in the distance they saw Birdie's neighbors returning home.

Birdie was starting to feel like her old self again and was thinking naughty thoughts.

"So... let's see this Special Forces Warrior bod," she cajoled, tugging on his shirt.

Fox raised an eyebrow and smiled at the possibilities. Birdie's doctors had placed *all* activities off-limits for some time now while she healed from her brutalization in Mexico. He reached over his shoulder, grasped his shirt, and pulled it over his head.

Birdie took it and nodded at his lower half. "Now the rest," she commanded. *"All* the rest."

Fox hesitated, craning his neck towards the neighbors' place. He confirmed that the moon was not illuminating him. Birdie stood in the only remaining patch of moonlight. He unhooked his inside-the-waistband holster, checked that the pistol's safety was on, and placed the holstered gun on the ground, pointed in a safe direction. He stepped out of his shorts and boxers, reached to place them in Birdie's extended hand, and stepped further back into the darkness again.

Because it was so dark, Fox was pretty sure that she really couldn't see him. However, she smiled and leaned back, looking him over and nodding approvingly. She twirled her index finger, indicating for him to slowly turn 360°. He complied, shaking his head and laughing.

Just as he turned away... Birdie pivoted and fled the forest, taking his clothing with her! She looked back and saw his face lean into the moonlight. It transformed from realization to horror and then to anger. "B-ir-r-di-ie!" he bellowed – but not too loudly.

Birdie threw her head back, chiming peals of melodious laughter.

Yes, Foxie, it's payback time! That'll teach you to scare me! She smiled, noting that lights were still on in her neighbors' trailer home. *He's really mad right now, but he has such a great sense of humor, I know he'll be laughing soon. I'll just wait a few minutes before I take his clothes back to him.*

Birdie giggled merrily. She was almost to her cottage when she heard it. It was the unmistakable sound of running footsteps, tearing up the ground behind her at very high speed. Birdie's smirk vanished.

Uh-oh...

COUNTERPOINT XII
RELEASE

"Our partner needs their funds RIGHT NOW to complete the catastrophic weapons project and to fund our highly trained and well-armed Vicious Vipers gang. With the weapon and the Vicious Vipers, the world will be at our feet!"

"The money is no problem. Our partner nation publicly swore that it will only develop the project for human welfare purposes. Our associates in America declared that, since that nation has given its word, America must show good faith cooperation and dispense our partner's funds. We are keeping all other officials with any power too consumed by other troubles to interfere with the release of the funds. So, the money will be disbursed forthwith."

"Good. We must also effect the release of our masterminds in order to complete the final phase of The Plan – and – to get them out of harm's way."

"Over time, our associates have been enabling the liberation of lower-level detainees 'for humanitarian reasons.' We have now set up a gambit to get the masterminds back."

"How is it possible that there will be no resistance to these actions?"

"There are only two nations aggressively fighting the development of the catastrophic weapon, and we are completely distracting both of them. We are bombarding one of them with missiles and the other with human invaders. While the human invaders are preoccupying government officials of *that* nation, our associates there have delayed shipping the tools of defense that would aid the *other* nation that is under attack by our missiles! Who knows, those shipments may even get *sabotaged* during the delay."

"So... our associates have caused delays in aid to America's ally and expedited the release of funds and prisoners to America's enemies? We all believed that The Master Business Plan would succeed – but not this easily! We never dreamed that individuals in a democratic nation could exercise this much power!"

CHAPTER EIGHTY-THREE
Naked Angry Man

Birdie rushed into her cottage, leaving the door open and turning out the lights. She ran across her living area to the other side of her dining table. She was unsure if she needed a buffer between her and the naked, angry man who was racing after her. Seconds later, Fox ran in and slammed the door shut. He stayed there for a few moments before placing his pistol on the bench beside him and locking the door. He and Birdie stood in the dark in silence.

"Um... are you... mad at me, Fox?"

Fox walked around the table towards her. Birdie felt her heart beating faster despite Fox's perennially easygoing disposition. He rarely expressed anger and had never directed any at her. Maybe she was nervous because she had just learned that he was a Special Forces Warrior.

"Fox...?"

As he approached, her trust in him outweighed her uncertainty, and she did not move away. He took his clothing from her and grasped her wrist, leading her over to her bed. He sat on the edge and drew her down next to him. Placing his clothes on his lap, he lit the candle on her bedside table.

"I guess you thought that was funny," he said, uncharacteristically not smiling.

Birdie bit her lip, nodding. "It was just a prank. I was going to bring your clothes to you in a few minutes." She paused, then asked softly, "Not funny?"

"I entrusted you with my clothing which has important electronics in the pockets. I need to be monitoring those, remember?" He patted the shorts on his lap.

"Oh, Fox, I'm sorry. I forgot. Are you *ever* off-duty and able to feel carefree?"

He tilted his head. "Sometimes. It comes with assuming responsibility. I chose this, and I accept the terms. I have no complaints."

He looked away, picturing the scene of Birdie's prank, visualizing it from her point of view. After a few moments, his expression lightened, and he chuckled.

"All right, that *was* funny – *and* humiliating that I was so easily duped! Of course, I trust *you.* Despite what you previously thought, no other woman could have talked me out of my clothes like that."

She smiled uncertainly, not sure she was completely out of the woods with him.

He said, "I guess you also needed to give me a little payback for chasing you in the dark when you didn't know it was me."

Birdie sighed, grateful for his understanding and relieved that he was not actually nettled by her mischief.

"By the way, thank you for leaving the door open and thinking to turn out the lights. I really did prefer that the Ronopo Chief not be seen *mooning* his tribe out there! Before I saw the lights go out, I thought I was going to have to come in through your rear window shutters. *Whether you opened them or not,"* he added menacingly.

"I'm sorry that I upset you," Birdie said, moving onto his lap. His pile of clothes slid to the floor. Sitting facing him, she put her arms around his neck.

He grinned. "You certainly keep things interesting."

"Speaking of interesting..." she said, "I am sitting on the lap... of a naked man..."

Fox raised an eyebrow. "And the woman on my lap has *nothing* on underneath her dress."

He lifted the dangling silver triangles of her necklace.

"You know, when I designed this for you, this was not the backdrop I envisioned.

"No?" Birdie replied gamely.

"No. I imagined seeing it more like... *this."*

Fox slowly peeled her strapless dress down to her waist, uncovering her small, bare breasts. He nodded, smiling, "Yeah.... that's more like it..."

He held the necklace with both hands, allowing his fingers to fan out and brush lightly against her breasts in slow, continuous waves. He knew how arousing that erogenous zone was for her. She closed her eyes and inhaled deeply, letting her head loll backwards. Fox then couldn't resist kissing the sweet and salty-tasting skin along the length of her neck. She sighed blissfully, arching her back and shifting in his lap.

Fox was enjoying how much pleasure his touch always gave her, not to mention what her scooching around on his lap was doing to *him.*

Birdie softly sang into his ear, *"Oh Captain...* have you done your weightlifting reps today?"

He shook his head. "From dawn until dusk I was on the road, to secure a gift for my lady-love."

Birdie kissed him softly on the lips and reached over to the bedside table, taking a foil packet from the drawer. She tore it open and coquettishly whispered,

"Will 92 pounds work for you, Captain? Can you do your lifting reps with 92 pounds?"

Fox looked at her with sparkling eyes.

"That would be... just perfect, you little vixen."

As Birdie reached for him with the condom, Fox tipped her chin up and kissed her hungrily. While kissing her, he helped her to quickly put the condom in place. Birdie placed her arms back around his neck, and he slipped his hands underneath her. Then, with a smile on his face, Fox proceeded to do, by far, his most enjoyable set of lifting reps *ever.*

CHAPTER EIGHTY-FOUR
Gifts

The Ronopo Tribe joyfully celebrated the wedding of their young Chief, Fox Bridgewater... that is, except for the heartbroken girls who had still hoped that Fox might look their way... and the guys who had thought that frisky Birdie Moonsong was still an eligible single female. It was a multi-denominational ceremony since Birdie and Fox followed different religious faiths, though they shared the same values.

A few of their closest friends, who were Washington VIPs, were not in attendance. To the tribe, Hunter implied that their absence was due to important, official obligations. In reality, Sequoia and Breeze were still "off the grid," hiding from what SIGNAL now referred to as: the Cabal. For the Cabal's benefit, Hunter was discreetly, yet frantically, searching for his missing wife. It would have been unrealistic for him to attend a wedding under such circumstances. There were a few people left in the tribe who might spy for Dukon, and SIGNAL leadership expected the Cabal to have eyes at the wedding. The absence of Sequoia, Breeze, and Hunter from an event as significant as the marriage of their friend and Chief of their tribe, was thought to be an opportune indicator to the Cabal that the women were dead.

Birdie scanned the crowd of revelers sharing in the celebratory food and drink. Most people there knew one another. She saw a group of single women whispering, giggling and flirting. She looked to see the object of their fascination – and she almost screamed.

An elegant-looking man approached, carrying himself with an air of total self-assurance. He was trim and fit, and he moved with the power and grace of a wildcat. He noticed the women's attentions, and when he turned his face towards them, they were silenced by the intensity of his expression. The brilliant sunlight momentarily made his gleaming, silver ear ornament appear to be on fire. Then he winked at them, enabling them to breathe and setting off another cascade of giggles and whispers.

Birdie recoiled and clutched at Fox, who was instantly alert. Seeing the man, Fox whispered, "It's okay, he's a SIGNAL Captain." Inhaling sharply, he added, "But I had no idea that he would be here."

Birdie stared at the man in disbelief. It was the head guard from the torture room in Mexico. He had never hurt her – but to her, he had been *one of them*.

"Congratulations, Chief and Mrs. Bridgewater," the man said in his pleasing Mexican accent.

Birdie just stared at him, wide-eyed and speechless. The Mexican Captain turned to Fox with horror, realizing that Birdie had not known who he was. Kneeling down on one knee to be less threatening, and glancing around to be sure no one else was near, he took Birdie's hand. In Spanish, he softly said,

"You have my sincerest apologies. I thought you knew about me. This is a rude surprise on your wedding day. I *know* that I can *never, ever* make up for what happened to you on my watch. I hope you know that the mission required that I not intervene sooner for you or any of the others. You were a most courageous heroine to elicit the information that you did from that monster. That had been my job, and you made it possible for me to accomplish far more than had been hoped for. I did what I could for you without compromising the mission. Fortunately, after reporting the seriousness of your condition, it became possible to exfiltrate you in time. I hope that someday you will be able to forgive me for your suffering. You have my very best wishes for a long and happy life."

The Captain kissed her hand and stood up. He nodded to Fox and departed, trailed by the cluster of intrigued, single women.

Birdie was shaken, and her mind was reeling with questions. She turned to Fox, and he looked back sympathetically. He guided her to a loveseat in a private space away from everyone.

"You have never spoken to me about what happened there. I didn't know if that was because I was not part of the mission, or if you just didn't want to talk about it. Of course, if you ever do want to, I'm here for you."

Birdie nodded, still feeling rattled. Then, she had a thought and was glad to focus on something else.

"This reminds me that you promised that you would tell me your Captain's alias after I married you."

Fox looked away. "Well... I have... an old one... and a new one." He took a deep breath. "I didn't tell you, but... I was... dishonorably discharged from SIGNAL."

Birdie's eyes opened wide.

"I was later reinstated... but with a demotion."

Birdie's face grew sympathetic. "I'll understand if you don't want to talk about it. I don't need to know your alias...es."

Fox hesitated but decided to tell her.

"One of the feats required in order to become a Captain is to climb a sheer-faced cliff. We used one in Yosemite National Park. I happened to beat whatever the world record was at that time for climbing its most difficult face."

"Fox!"

"Of course I could not draw attention to myself by having that record published. But when I made Captain, my comrades decided it would be fitting to *name* me after the rock formation that I had conquered so successfully. It's called... El Capitán."

Birdie stared at him, her mind moiling.

"My full code name became 'Captain Fox' – in Spanish – but my comrades just called me El Capitán."

Birdie was fluent in Spanish and knew that the Spanish word for *fox* was *zorro*.

Fox looked down. "After my... dishonorable discharge... and then my reinstatement, with a demotion from Captain to Brave, I was given a more reproachful name to remind me of my violation of the SIGNAL Captain's Code. So I was given the new alias..." Fox swallowed hard. "My new alias is... it's..."

Birdie nodded with encouragement.

"It's... Brave Desperado."

Birdie's eyes widened. She whispered, "A Mexican word... When I was at death's door... was my rescue... *not* by the Captain on the mission? Was it... someone who had perhaps been... *forbidden* to go for me – so he was like a desperate outlaw – a desperado of old? Fox? Was it you?"

Fox looked up at her with a lopsided smile.

Birdie threw her arms around him. *"Thank you* for coming for me!! Why didn't you tell me?!"

"I did not ever want to bring up your unspeakable ordeal. I also needed to know that you married me because you wanted to share your life with me, not out of gratitude or some... sense of obligation."

Birdie shook her head. "Oh, Fox, I've loved you for so long."

She continued to reconstruct what had happened.

"So... you cut your hair to look more like a man from that region? And speaking of cutting, though I think you've tried to hide it from me, are you now... circumcised?"

Fox dropped his head into his hands.

"Oh Fox, that doesn't make you any less Ronopo... *Wait...* You didn't have that done for my rescue for some reason, did you?"

Fox hesitated then nodded but did not look up.

"So... you needed to be circumcised for some reason? Who would see that and care? Were you trying to blend in with those men from—" Birdie had a lightbulb moment. "Oh! The lady in charge – La Señora?"

Fox did not look up.

"So... for some reason, if you were circumcised, you could pass muster with her, and... you seduced her to secure her help?"

Fox did not look up.

"Where she's from, are the men of her social class circumcised?"

Fox nodded but did not look up.

Birdie could not help imagining Fox seducing the beautiful Señora. She knew how perfect he was for the job. Women were always attracted to him. She thought of what a turn-on his passion and intensity were – and of how much it mattered to him to satisfy his lover. These thoughts conjured up the sensation of his mouth on hers. She felt a flash of heat as she thought of his hands... She smiled. She had previously thought that he was being with many women during a time that, unbeknownst to her, he had personally pledged to be faithful to her. She then had a disturbing thought. She knew that her rescue had been last minute – almost too late, in fact.

"Fox... if you went for me secretly and very suddenly because I was dying... " She paused and then implored, "Please tell me that you didn't... um.. *circumcise yourself?!*"

Fox did not look up.

"Fox!!... Anesthesia?!"

Fox did not look up.

Birdie threw her arms around him and sobbed.

After a bit, Fox reassured Birdie that he was *now* completely fine. He told her that, after performing the procedure on himself, he had used a special American Indian gel referred to as "native magic." He said that all SIGNAL Captains and Braves carried it to instantly, temporarily disinfect and seal a wound. He also told her that, after she was stabilized at the hospital, he received medical attention there himself. *

"It was only by luck that I didn't permanently damage myself. And now that I've been repaired by a doctor and have healed, I can honestly say that I have zero reduction in pleasure due to being circumcised – contrary to claims by anti-cut people – most of whom have not even experienced both. It's healthier, and to be honest, I like myself better this way."

His expression became grave. "It's nothing like the atrocity of *female* genital cutting which actually *creates* health and childbearing risks."

Birdie shuddered, feeling great sympathy for those women and girls.

"How did you even know that circumcision would matter to La Señora?"

"It was in the file I hacked into to learn about the place where you went. Apparently it was a big deal in her segment of society."

"I have to confess that I'm glad that this is what your injury was. When you refused to talk about it, I was afraid that... maybe you had tried to commit suicide."

"Heck, no! Life is short, but being dead is *forever!* I'll be dead later, thank you! If I ever hate my life, *I'll change it* – maybe go someplace new. I plan on getting every minute that I can have being *alive!"*

When Fox and Birdie felt emotionally composed, they returned to the celebration and performed a ritual dance, surrounded by Elders. The tradition was that at the end of the dance, an Elder could ask the bride or groom to perform a task. Fox was worried that Potay Oora, the retired Master Bow-Maker, might ask him to shoot something with the special bow that he had made for Fox as his birth gift. After Fox had returned from the Mexican quest, he had gone to the woods and found that the bow was gone. Of course he had not expected to give it away and then have it back again. He was just curious to see if it was still there. The Great Spirit most certainly had shone upon Birdie and him as they had both returned safely.

Unfortunately, Elder Oora made exactly that request. Fox quietly told him the truth – that he had given the bow as an offering to the Great Spirit, asking for protection for the life of someone he loved whom he had not been in a position to protect himself. He told him that the bow was now gone – and that the protection had been granted. Elder Oora looked down, and Fox felt pained that he had hurt the older man's feelings. The Elder then looked up and nodded at Fox with bright light shining in his rheumy old eyes. He thanked Fox for having given him the *ultimate* honor through a piece of his humble handiwork. Fox bowed deeply to the Elder.

After the wedding guests departed, Birdie and Fox opened their gifts. There were several from their friends, most of them making them laugh. Fox opened one addressed to him from Aspen. Upon seeing its contents, he had to turn his face away. He pushed it towards Birdie. The note on top said:

> *Foxer -*
>
> *I should never have taken this away from you. You are no desperado, my Brother. They don't come any finer than you. I hope I can still call on you when I really need you, ECZ.*
> *Always ~ Aspen*

Fox lifted the note so Birdie could see what was underneath. It was a gleaming, silver ear ornament. Its shape was that of a notable silhouette of the rock formation, El Capitán – with a fox perched on top.

Birdie also had a gift from Aspen. Her note said:

> *May you always be free, dear Bittybird.*
> *With love ~ Aspen*

It was a beautiful little birdcage, just a few inches high, woven from the shoots of an aspen tree. The cage had no door, just an open space.

There was another note in the box that said:

> *Go look in the grove. The ʃℂs left something there for you.*

"The ʃℂs?" Birdie asked.

Smiling with pleasure, Fox whispered, "The SIGNAL Captains. We'll look later."

Another gift addressed to Fox was a handsome, beaded strip blanket. There was a long-standing custom in some tribes for a young man to wrap one around himself and his loved one during courtship. Fox had not had one and was greatly pleased to receive that time-honored, culturally meaningful gift. Unfolding the blanket, Fox found something else inside. A note said:

> *Young Chief Bridgewater ~*
> *When you were born, I made my finest bow for a boy,*
> *the son of a great Chief,*
> *Chief Bridgewater the Elder.*
> *I am now honored to give the big brother of that bow to a man,*
> *a great Chief,*
> *Chief Bridgewater the Younger.*
> *May it always keep you and your loved ones safe.*
> *Potay Oora*

Before departing for their wedding trip, they rode Fox's motorcycle out to the grove of trees in the northwest quadrant. Well away from the old hunting cabin, hidden from view by a cluster of hillocks, Birdie found her amazing gift from the Captains. It was a handmade glider, beautifully painted as a hummingbird.

Birdie saw a silver cross dangling by its chain from a steering control. It was larger than the delicate cross she sometimes wore. The back was engraved with the letters: SFB.

She handed it to Fox. "Those are your initials! This was engraved for you!"

Fox stared at it in his palm. Then he closed his hand over it and looked up at the sky. It was the Mexican Captain's cross. Fox had lifted it from him during their first heated exchange in the torture room and had later returned it to him.

Fox surprised Birdie greatly by kissing the cross and putting the chain around his neck. Seeing her expression, he said, "It's the *same* spirit, Birdie. When I went for you, I prayed for the help and support of both your divine being and mine. Then... I knew that I did have it. It's just that some people pray to the Creator, some pray to a Divine Messenger of the Creator, and others pray to the Creator's Spirit. We all have a spark of the same Spirit energy within us that links us all to one another – no matter what we call it, how we envision it, or how we celebrate it."

Birdie nodded reflectively.

Fox said, "Now we know why 'Captain Carlos' came to our wedding. He brought the glider for you from all of the Captains, and he had a very special gift for me, too."

---

* READER: DO NOT TRY THIS!! *Permanent damage* and loss of sensation is *likely* if done improperly; and some young men have DIED from infections after group, ritual circumcisions without proper medical involvement! (Remember, this book is FICTION!)

CHAPTER EIGHTY-FIVE
Morals of the Story

Aspen's earlier decision to slam Fox with a dishonorable discharge from SIGNAL had *not* been a difficult one. He was stunned that Fox had willfully disobeyed his order to stay clear of Birdie's mission. He could have undermined it, possibly exposing or otherwise endangering other operatives – especially since he had no details about the mission. Aspen learned, however, that he had underestimated his friend. He had not told Fox where the operation was taking place yet he found it. Not only that, but Fox had devised and implemented a successful strategy – extraordinarily quickly, under great stress, and alone.

As it turned out, Fox's involvement helped the mission. La Señora became an ally and invaluable asset, providing information to "Captain Carlos," the Mexican SIGNAL Captain on the mission. Aspen also could not help but be impressed by Fox's brilliantly conceived and executed disposal of the torturer. During a debriefing, "Captain Carlos" told Aspen that, prior to the torturer's demise, Fox, who was going by the name, Capitán Rodrigo Morales, discreetly asked if El Médico was important to the mission.

What amazed Aspen most of all, however, was that Fox had successfully kept from him the depth of his feelings for Birdie over all those years. Of course, Aspen had prided himself in having kept, even from Fox, how crazy *he* had been about Sequoia for just as long. Aspen now knew that Fox had fabricated the roving playboy persona to hide his feelings for Birdie, thus keeping her safe from adversaries while being a Captain. Although Aspen knew that Fox was often off-reservation for SIGNAL missions, even he had been fooled by Fox's artifice. He knew that Fox sometimes chose to spend "special time" with Birdie and that they were very close friends; but Aspen had actually believed that Fox was quite the "tomcat." So, Fox had complied with the *spirit* of the SIGNAL Captain law, while skirting the *letter* of the law.

Meanwhile, Aspen had paid doubly for his adherence to the Captain's Code. Exercising extreme self-restraint, he had refrained from dating Sequoia. Then, just as he fulfilled his commitment as a SIGNAL Captain and was free to do so, Golden Hawk stole her away.

Aspen had been hoping to sweep Sequoia off her feet when she returned after her first year of grad school. He left her messages to come see him as soon as she got back. He did not say more in his messages so as not to distract her before her final exams. Over time, Aspen had been composing a long letter to her, expressing his feelings. He included many pages of excerpts from his diaries from over the years. He planned to give it to her in person. However, when Sequoia came home, Golden Hawk completely monopolized her time. So, Aspen gave Granny Katiri an envelope containing that special missive. He knew he could count on her to deliver it to her granddaughter. When Sequoia did not even *acknowledge* that baring of his soul and spent all of her time with Golden Hawk, Aspen faced the painful fact that she did not love him as he loved her. When Sequoia's engagement to Chief Golden Hawk was announced, Aspen was devastated and decided to stay on as a SIGNAL Captain.

Some years later, after the Cabal's assassination attempt, Sequoia had the shaman quietly dissolve her Ronopo bond of marriage. Once again, Aspen offered Sequoia his love. He was in for a shocking revelation as she accompanied him to check out a place where he might relocate.

"You know, you were my first love, Aspen."

Aspen almost swerved off the road. "What did you say?"

"I was just a young teen, and you were the most sought after guy on the reservation. I understood why you thought of me as just a kid. But I didn't stop having feelings for you... all the way through high school and even college. I had hoped that maybe after college..."

Aspen pulled over and stopped the truck, staring at her.

"To be a SIGNAL Captain, I had to swear an oath to not be in a relationship until I fulfilled my multi-year commitment. It took me every ounce of self-control to not ask you out. I stayed in touch with you through your college years. When you returned for the election, I tried hard to reach you. You didn't even stop by on Election Day, despite my request to come see me as soon as you got home. Then, when you spent all of your time with Golden Hawk and didn't even reply to that... *very* long letter I left with Granny K. for you, I concluded that you had no interest in me."

"Letter? What letter?"

"What letter? You don't even remember my love letter to you?"

"Love letter?! Aspen, I never... Oh no... Aspen! I thought that thick envelope held the summer recreation schedules! I never even opened it! I slipped it into my favorite children's book. It must still be there! I *certainly* would have..."

Aspen closed his eyes and banged his forehead against the steering wheel.

Regarding his disciplinary action against Fox, Aspen ultimately felt anguish over the dishonor to his friend and the loss of a master SIGNAL operative. Sequoia, now working in her new SIGNAL role, knew what had happened. She suggested that perhaps Aspen bore some responsibility for Fox's violation. She pointed out that Aspen undoubtedly breached protocol, himself, by telling an operative of the perilous condition of a friend on a mission. It was then off *his* chest, but Fox was left holding the bag. Fox then had the choice to either violate the Code and try to save Birdie's life or adhere to the Code and let Birdie die. She said that maybe Aspen subconsciously hoped Fox would save Birdie. Aspen would not then have jeopardized the mission by *sending* Fox for her; but by telling him, he provided him the opportunity to save the friend – *and then for Fox to pay the price.*

Aspen took Sequoia's analysis to heart, feeling appalled at the role he had unwittingly played. He expunged the dishonorable discharge from Fox's record, changing it to a demotion for violating the Code. Ultimately, he restored Fox's status as a Captain. Per Fox's wishes, he was made a Reserve Captain, now only on call in times of emergency. Aspen humbly apologized to Fox for his own role in the violation. The two men then felt that the air had been cleared, and their deep bond of friendship was fully restored.

CHAPTER EIGHTY-SIX
Bombshells

In contrast to his usual polish, Vice President Hunter Wolf was in complete disarray. Agents of the Cabal observed him investigating the disappearance of the First and Second Ladies while complying with Dukon's mandate to keep it from the public. Hunter stayed in his office for even longer hours, fervently working at his computer, looking at maps, or pacing. He looked like he hadn't slept in weeks.

He confronted Dukon angrily. "Have you forgotten that I have highly compromising recordings of you? I told you that they are in the hands of people who will distribute them worldwide if anything happens to me or people I care about!"

"I have done nothing!" Dukon snarled.

"Really, Dukon? Then where are our wives?! They left to visit Sequoia's grandmother in the hospital but never got there! I've discreetly checked the reservation myself. No one has been in touch with them. You said you were on top of this, but their whereabouts are still unknown! I believe this is your doing. Maybe you never really loved Sequoia, but I want Breeze back *now!"*

Dukon hissed, "Do not presume to know my feelings. I have made every effort to find them!"

"I don't believe you! I demand a meeting with someone at a high level in your organization! If not, my recordings of you will be broadcast immediately!"

"Organization? I know many people who support my vision, but there is no *organization."*

You're a liar! It took me awhile, but I figured out that you have deceived me at every turn! I've already set in motion the release of my recordings of you. If you do not tell me where Breeze is, they will automatically be uploaded to the Internet and sent to the media!"

"All right, all right!" Dukon said, making placating motions with his hands and looking over his shoulder. "I know a... *fixer.* I'll set up a meeting with him and the two of us. *Do not tell anyone.* You can bring bodyguards, but you'll have to... *dispose* of them afterward. Agreed?"

The Master Business Plan had been meticulously devised over a period of decades. The Cabal believed that they had a team of the highest caliber and that no significant mistakes were possible. Thus, Cabal leaders were incensed that there was doubt about the deaths of the First and Second Ladies. Since the assassinations had been orchestrated on short notice, audio and video monitoring of the event could only be hastily attempted and had not been successful. The Cabal ultimately did conclude that the Executive Ladies must have died in the limo. Agents had recovered a small amount of their fresh DNA, along with DNA of all three suicide bombers. It was clear that the secondary explosion of the jet fuel tank was the reason that so little of the wreckage remained for confirmation purposes. Also, since then, there had been no sightings of the women by Cabal agents, satellites, drones, or reporters. And the Vice President was either a very good actor or he truly did not know what had happened to his wife.

The Cabal only decided to comply with Hunter's demand, because they needed to "persuade" him to destroy his incriminating recordings of the President. If they simply killed Hunter, the recordings might be automatically broadcast, as threatened. They could not risk compromising The Master Business Plan. A successful outcome was in its final phase.

The Cabal would not send a high-level person. They selected a mid-level conspirator for "the negotiation." For the meeting place, they chose the city of New Rootbay. It was once a thriving U.S. metropolis that declined and decayed, and was now conspicuously characterized as a violent wasteland. Police were quoted in the news, warning people to stay away. It did seem to be keeping Americans out, but it had become a rather central place of settlement for foreigners.

Rather than letting New Rootbay or its state work on its problems, the Administration was suggesting a large infusion of federal money – money to which the Administration seemed to have unlimited access. There were multiple American cities in financial trouble, and people were concerned about the Administration choosing any one city for a bailout. Some huge corporations with whom the Administration had ties were also suddenly investing in that city. Government watchdog groups were investigating allegations that foreigners and supporters of certain politicians had previously snapped up property in that city at pennies on the dollar due to its widely publicized deterioration. If the federal government (or corporations bailed out by the government) infused money to restore that city, property owners there stood to enjoy huge profits from the resulting, higher property values – all at the expense of American taxpayers. These allegations were not so different from some of the little-known, murky land deals in which Dukon had previously been involved with American Indian tribes and others.

Public bailouts had not been very effective in the past. In contrast, whole states had successfully recovered under the firm management of new Governors with relevant knowledge, experience, and integrity. Those Governors implemented viable budgets with rational, targeted spending cuts. Instead of raising taxes on their already overburdened constituents, they identified waste, inefficiency, and corruption. They reduced existing budget allocations to the amounts actually needed and used some of the excess funds to augment much-needed public services.

Some prior politicians had boosted their own interests by making generous promises based on unsound financial practices. They had offered extravagant no-bid contracts to past or potential supporters and compensation packages to public employees that no private or public sector entities could possibly afford long-term. In addition to securing the votes of those employees, the politicians then also got to enjoy the gold-plated benefit packages themselves. They were elected on their promises but were not then held accountable for the financial ruin that ensued. The public was hoodwinked by corrupt or unqualified officials who had created a house of cards, benefiting themselves and select supporters. Such officials then moved on to an enviable retirement before the house of cards collapsed... on everyone else.

Golden Hawk told Hunter that he and his associate would each bring no more than two bodyguards to the meeting. Hunter insisted on bringing four to be on an equal footing with them. He arrived early in front of the mostly empty skyscraper that only had a few business tenants left in it. It stood on the corner of a once-bustling intersection. As he and his guards approached the building, Hunter's cell phone rang. Golden Hawk apprised him that the meeting location had been changed – to the thirtieth story of a completely abandoned skyscraper diagonally across the intersection. He said that the switch was for reasons of greater privacy.

The impromptu change of plan made Hunter uneasy. He had honored the limit on bodyguards, bringing only four who were well-armed and attired in body armor suits and helmets. There had been no discussion of a limit on additional protective resources in the surrounding area. Thus, Hunter had undercover security personnel in and around the originally scheduled building. His counterparts were likely doing the same.

This unexpected change of venue meant that Hunter and his four guards were now going to be separated from a backup security team in the originally scheduled building. Hunter wondered if they were walking into an ambush. He believed that his threat of automatic broadcasting of the recordings of President Golden Hawk still gave him some security but might not protect his guards. He suggested that they stay outside and watch for signs of trouble instead of entering a possible death trap with him. All of his guards refused to leave his side.

On the thirtieth floor, they found Golden Hawk, his contact, and four bodyguards in a vacant office. One guard stood by the entrance to the office, two guards flanked the President and his contact, and the fourth guard stood at the window, scanning the urban landscape.

Golden Hawk said, "This is Al Kharuf. Kharuf, Vice President Hunter Wolf."

The two men nodded coldly. They agreed that their guards would keep their weapons slung, holstered and sheathed during the meeting. Kharuf informed Hunter that they had raised an electromagnetic field (EMF) inside the building. That meant that no cell phone or radio communication would be possible with any "extra personnel." It would also prevent any electronic recording of the meeting.

Hunter hid his dismay. He and his team were all wearing audio/video microelectronics precisely for the purpose of recording the meeting. Now, he had no way to let SIGNAL know that was not going to happen.

All four guards with Kharuf and Golden Hawk were well over six feet tall. They wore body armor suits like that of Hunter's guards and sported the same, sinister-looking helmets with opaque visors. Kharuf sneered at Hunter because only two of his four guards were extra-large men.

"Is that the best the American *Vice* President can get?"

The gigantic guards with Kharuf and the President chuckled. One of Golden Hawk's guards displayed aggression by making a fist and punching his other palm a few times. His other guard tapped his fingers, exhibiting both nonchalance and eagerness to engage.

Ignoring the juvenile jab, Hunter thundered,

"WHERE IS MY WIFE?!"

Startled by Hunter's booming voice, Kharuf jerked backwards.

Flustered, he squeaked, "First we'll talk about those broadcasts you keep threatening to use as blackmail—"

"It isn't blackmail!" Hunter interrupted forcefully. "It's insurance that I have been *compelled* to use. It is to protect myself and others from physical harm by your people – including President Golden Hawk. Who the hell are you people, anyway?"

Regaining his composure, Kharuf smiled tightly.

"We are an elite, multinational alliance into which I am authorized to offer you membership. We are men of great power."

"Power to do what?" Hunter asked disdainfully. "I am already Vice President of a powerful nation."

"You mean a once-powerful nation!" Kharuf snorted. "Soon, our alliance will have the power and control of *all* nations!"

Hunter raised his eyebrows. "Another multinational committee? We know how well *that* works. No infighting or jockeying for position? Sounds like a group who will use one another and then kill each other off to gain total power. Sure. Sounds great. Sign me up."

Kharuf scowled, "You mock me? Then so be it! Are you willing to sacrifice your only wife in order to keep those broadcasts to protect yourself and others?"

Hunter frowned. "What do you mean?"

Kharuf paused for effect.

"We snatched your wife, and if you do not call off your broadcasts permanently, we will begin to..." Kharuf smiled wickedly.

Hunter faltered. Hearing his worst fear vocalized, he momentarily wondered if they actually could have abducted Breeze. He swallowed, forcing himself to stay focused.

Kharuf added snidely, "But wait! There is no way for us to ensure that you actually call off the broadcasts permanently, so we need to take you with us. You see, we have *ways* to make you comply. Believe me, you *will* be telling your cohorts to destroy those recordings!"

Kharuf whipped out a scimitar. The sharp edge of the curved dagger gleamed in the light. Hunter's two largest guards stepped between him and Kharuf. Hunter folded his arms across his chest.

Kharuf laughed at Hunter's bravado.

"I see that you are not worried. You are right that we will not *waterboard* you or your wife. We do not believe in that! We do... other things."

Kharuf grinned and made sawing motions with his knife. "I have done a few myself, but I would especially enjoy doing an American!"

Hunter looked at President Golden Hawk.

"Really, Dukon? You're allied with people like this?"

Golden Hawk regarded him contemptuously. "There was a time when I thought you might become one of us – the men who will rule the world! Instead, you became a thorn in my side whom I could not trust. We need to take down America first; and Americans of this era are making that easy to do. The rest of the world will fall even more effortlessly without the military might America *used to have* to help its allies. I did not want to sacrifice Sequoia, but you have outlived your usefulness."

One of Hunter's guards, who was standing near President Golden Hawk, removed her helmet and shook out her hair.

"Sequoia!" Dukon exclaimed, grabbing her. Not realizing he was speaking in a foreign language, he said, "Thanks be to—!" Then in English, he croaked, "I thought you were dead!"

"Why did you think that, Dukon?"

He whispered, "They found your DNA at the site of the bombed limo!"

"Bombed limo?" Sequoia exclaimed. "The news report said that a limo crashed into a fuel tank, causing an explosion. It was actually bombed?!"

"I tried to stop them," he whispered.

Dukon's mind started to recover from its emotional, knee-jerk reaction. "How did you...?" He looked at Sequoia's attire. "Why are you..." He trailed off, realizing his mistake.

Alarmed that Sequoia was alive, Kharuf sent one of his guards to ensure that the path was clear to the helicopter on the roof. He ordered one of Golden Hawk's guards to "check on things downstairs." Now, just one guard stood by President Golden Hawk and one by Kharuf.

Hunter's smallest guard removed her helmet. It was Breeze. She emphatically declared to Kharuf, "A Wolf doesn't need *large* guards when dealing with a sheep!"

She took one step and kicked hard with her other leg. Kharuf's scimitar flew out of his hand. It sailed across the room in perfect parallel with the follow-through of Breeze's roundhouse kick.

Kharuf froze. To his great relief, he saw the two guards he had sent on errands re-enter the room. He commanded his men, "Take the Vice President and the women!"

The guard still next to Kharuf clashed with one of Hunter's men. One of the guards who had just entered the room made what looked like a rude gesture at another guard and then looked down at Kharuf. This tall guard slipped a hand under Kharuf's jaw, gripping it tightly and lifting him into the air. Kharuf flailed, knocking off the guard's helmet. A long, black braid dropped below the guard's hip. A silver ornament gleamed in one earlobe. It was a slanted lightning bolt with a lynx ascending it. The towering SIGNAL officer, Captain Thunderstrike, smiled down at the man frantically squirming in her hand.

The guard at whom Captain Thunderstrike had rudely gestured now rushed at her. She lowered Kharuf back to the floor, and that guard pulled Kharuf protectively behind him. Not otherwise able to tell which of the similarly attired men were his, Kharuf beckoned to this protective guard as he stumbled out of the office. The guard accompanied him up the stairwell to the roof. Another guard who was still up there, climbed into the helicopter with them.

Kharuf turned around in his seat, rubbing his painful jaw.

"What about the President?" he screeched at the guards who were conferring in respectfully hushed tones.

"A chopper with heavily-geared reinforcements is arriving momentarily, sir. I was able to call for a backup extraction team when I got up to the roof – outside the EMF interference. They will secure the President and prisoners – unless you want to wait and have us go back to get them?"

"What about the fire?" Kharuf shrieked at the other guard. "Was it set to prevent their escape to the street?"

"Yes, sir, on the first floor. It's a fast-moving inferno!"

"Then get us out of here!" Kharuf yelled to the pilot, jerking on his seatbelt as the chopper lifted off the roof and sped away.

Having recently seen unexpected faces appear from beneath helmets, Kharuf warily turned back around for a better look at the guards. Their helmets were now in their laps. One man spoke quietly while dabbing at oozing burns on the face of the other guard who was wincing with pain.

"Injuries while checking on the fire, sir."

Kharuf was relieved that these guards were not more *women* in body armor but was annoyed that, in the confusion, he had left with the President's guards. He realized, however, that it was likely better for him if his own men secured the Americans. Kharuf showed no concern for the burned guard. He was concerned for *himself* when reporting back to his superior. Of course, the unforeseen circumstances with the women was someone else's failure. Thankfully, a backup squad was securing the President, the Vice President, and their wives. All would be well as long as his assignment ended well.

Kharuf asked, "Are the diversions in place to prevent fire department intervention?"

"Yes, sir. The Occupy protest across town drew all first responders and has them blocked in."

Kharuf bleated, "Are you *sure* that the President and Vice President are not in danger from the fire?"

The guard tapped some keys on his phone. "The backup chopper already landed. Our team is securing them now, and the fire is not yet an issue."

Satisfied, Kharuf wiped his brow.

"Where did that... *Amazon* come from?" he whined, still rattled by his encounter with Captain Thunderstrike.

"We believe that she and the guard with her were scouts posted there by the VP when he thought you were meeting in the other building, sir. We don't think that there are any more though. We hear that the American President makes sure that his Vice President has very few resources at his disposal."

"Well, that would certainly explain the presence of so many *females* instead of male guards!" Kharuf groused.

Captain Trueheart and Captain Moonbow dutifully nodded in agreement.

CHAPTER EIGHTY-SEVEN
Sky High

Back when Hunter first arrived at the originally scheduled building, and Golden Hawk apprised him that he had changed the meeting location, Hunter's head guard notified their backup squad. That squad, led by Captain Thunderstrike, had moved into position much earlier and were monitoring the area. Her team sprang back into action to adjust for the change of venue.

Captain Thunderstrike had previously posted operatives both outdoors and in vacant offices in surrounding buildings. Thus, she already had two agents inside the abandoned building where the meeting was now to take place. Her team had seen a helicopter land on that roof. An operative inside then reported that the President, his associate, and four guards had entered the building from the rooftop. Shortly afterward, Captain Thunderstrike lost contact with her operatives in that building. She later learned that it was due to the Cabal's EMF.

Captain Thunderstrike had some operatives direct their focus to the thirtieth story of the abandoned skyscraper – the new meeting place. They were to visually locate a reflector worn by Captain Moonbow who was a guard at the meeting. They had planned that he would look out of a window to help them locate the meeting room when they thought it was taking place in the other building. It was a good thing they included "low-tech" tactics such as this in their plan, since the EMF was preventing any electronic tracking or communication between them and Hunter's group.

Captain Moonbow strolled to the window. He surveyed the panorama until he saw a bright semaphore signal, indicating that the flank security team had located his reflector. He turned around and scanned the office. Exactly three minutes later, he again looked out the window, waiting for the signal to recommence. When it did, he coughed a few times, blocking both the sight and sound of the small putty ball that smash-landed in a lower corner of the window's exterior. It had been shot from another building by a SIGNAL operative nicknamed Meticulous Nicholas for his exceptional shooting accuracy.

The audio/video capture of this meeting was an essential component of SIGNAL's strategy to identify the Cabal and document Dukon's involvement with them. Fox Bridgewater, a.k.a El Capitán, was leading that initiative from inside the original skyscraper across the intersection. Before the meeting started, Fox had a little fun jamming the Cabal helicopter's radio with a children's program being broadcast on the airwaves.

True to form, Fox had prepared *two* means of accomplishing the main objective, as he always did with any important undertaking. He was operating a small drone equipped with electronics and laser technology outside the building to record the meeting. Having this backup proved to be pivotal since the transmitters on Hunter's team had been rendered useless by the Cabal's EMF inside the building.

Fox's drone captured clear video and audio boosted by the chip in the putty ball flattened against the window.

"Yesss!" he quietly exclaimed, pumping his fist when he even captured Golden Hawk's whispers to Sequoia.

One of Captain Thunderstrike's operatives had reported when an unidentified person entered the abandoned skyscraper through the only unlocked door at street level. They later noticed smoke coming from there. Since the EMF inside was blocking communications, they could not warn Hunter's team that there appeared to be a fire in the building.

One of Captain Thunderstrike's agents, disguised as a homeless person, found that all first floor steel doors were now locked. She shook the door handles which were already hot, confirming the presence of fire. She also heard the rattle of chains securing the doors from the inside. She shuffled away, muttering to herself and then covertly reported in.

Earlier, one of Captain Thunderstrike's scouts had informed her of a disruptive Occupy demonstration across town. The Captain now surmised that any fire department help for them would be either delayed by that disturbance or non-existent.

Anyway, it would undoubtedly be preferable if firefighters did not find the U.S. President and Vice President together in an abandoned building in a dangerous city. That could be awkward to explain.

Captain Thunderstrike called the SIGNAL helicopter pilot involved in the mission. She asked if the pilot was in a position to evacuate Hunter's team from the building.

The pilot replied, "Brave Bird, here. If I pick up your clients, I will likely strand others who already have a reservation."

"Understood," the Captain said. "Proceed as scheduled but remain on standby."

Fox heard all that on his headset. Despite the gravity of the situation, he asked, "Did you say *Brave* Bird?"

Birdie burbled, "You heard that right! That honorary title was served to me while you were in the field. Private ceremony to follow."

"Congratulations, Brave!" Fox said, not losing focus on his task at hand.

Captain Thunderstrike needed to come up with an alternative rescue plan for Hunter's team – and fast. Standing outside in the shadows, she looked skyward – and she had her plan. She huddled with three particular Braves from her flank team: Darrik, Christopher, and Sheldon. *They* looked skyward – and grinned. The Captain led them and four more operatives, all loaded with gear, into the originally scheduled skyscraper. She tasked each of them along the way.

The Captain dispatched two snipers to the roof as lookouts. The others accompanied her to the thirty-sixth floor. They headed to the side of the building facing the abandoned skyscraper across the intersection. Hunter's meeting was taking place on the opposite side of the abandoned building, so it was unlikely that they would witness Captain Thunderstrike's audacious maneuver. Cabal scouts might spot them, but the rest of the SIGNAL flank team was scouring the environs, ready to alert their snipers to protect Captain Thunderstrike's squad.

The thirty-sixth floor was mostly vacant. An operative with Captain Thunderstrike picked the lock of a utility room, and the team entered. The Captain then used a tool from her pack to open a panel in an exterior wall. The panel opened to a service crawl space inside the thick wall – with an access door to the open air outside the building.

Wind was a frequent issue in this downtown area. Thus, some of the skyscrapers had been buttressed to one another with architecturally attractive steel beams or cables. This building had two, offset, sloping beams dramatically anchoring it to the once-bustling but now abandoned skyscraper where Hunter was trapped with his team. The two beams connected the buildings between their thirty-second and thirty-sixth floors.

The Captain and her three operatives skillfully anchored heavy-duty carabiners with sturdy lines attached, to sound structural supports inside the exterior wall. Captain Thunderstrike then pulled a long ribbon from her pack. She stepped outside onto the buttressing beam and held the ribbon aloft. It fluttered lightly, indicating the wind's direction and intensity. The Captain looked at her operatives. They nodded, and all of them donned helmets.

These four were members of a tribe like one from Canada and the northern U.S., famously known as "Sky Walkers." They were credited with fearlessness, or courage in the face of fear, as they worked construction jobs at dizzying heights. They were tribal heroes, securing high-paying work back at a time when that was especially difficult for American Indians to do. Those in Captain Thunderstrike's tribe had routinely turned over part of their earnings in accordance with that tribe's system of revenue-sharing or taxation. The U.S. Government was supposed to provide the tribal U.S. citizens with additional support as promised in the treaties made in exchange for American Indian lands long ago. This promise was not being kept, however, because federal officials spent all available money, giving preferential treatment to the most *politically useful* minority groups, pet projects, select individuals, and even *non-citizens* instead.

These descendants of Sky Walkers were proudly carrying on the tradition of their ancestors – this time in the hope of saving lives. All four of them regularly engaged in rock climbing and related sports and always had the required equipment with them.

There was no railing whatsoever along the length of this descending beam that was never intended to be a bridge. Captain Thunderstrike went first across the eight-inch-wide, naked beam while the other three waited inside the building. Like the Captain, they each had strong cable line that would issue from the underside of their special body-packs as they advanced. It was this cable line that they had securely attached to the building's girders and struts. The fire in the abandoned skyscraper had become noticeable, and a crowd was forming to watch it.

If the Great Spirit is with me, Captain Thunderstrike thought, *any Cabal scouts will be distracted by the fire and the crowd and will not even notice me up here. Otherwise... well, that's what my awesome snipers are for.*

When she was most of the way across, a terrible groan emanated from the beam. The end in front of her shimmied and started migrating downward. The Captain dropped to a crouch, grabbing for the beam as she started to slide down the steepening slope. A cascade of detritus plummeted to the street below, and people in the crowd screamed and ran. The moving beam ground to a jarring halt, settling atop a concrete ledge. The Captain maintained her balance and raised her hand so no one behind her would follow.

So much for arriving unnoticed, she thought.

The crowd was hushed as they watched the Captain pull cable from a second spool in her body-pack. She quickly wrapped a length of it around and around the beam, nimbly knotting and crisscrossing it. If she made it across, she would anchor this cable tightly to the building in front of her in an attempt to prevent further shifting of the beam. She gave more hand signals. From inside the building behind her, the SIGNAL operatives also reinforced the support of their end of the beam, further securing it to that building. The Captain slowly stood up and cautiously continued across, firmly grasping a carabiner that would release her from being tied to the beam if it were to break away from the buildings and fall.

The beam did not shift further, and when she reached the end, the crowd cheered. The beam had not dropped too far, so Captain Thunderstrike was still able to reach the exterior access panel into the abandoned skyscraper. She pried it open and climbed up into the wall of the thirty-second floor. She fully expected an armed, Cabal "welcoming party" considering her noisy arrival. So, while her snipers continued to cover her from across the street, she performed rapid reconnaissance inside but found no threat. Staying vigilant, she slipped out of her body-pack and secured the spools inside it to the framework of the building. The Great Spirit did seem to be with her, as there was still no sign of danger from inside the building. She signaled to her team, and they proceeded, one by one, safely across.

Once inside, they split up. Two Braves quietly hustled up the fire stairwell to the thirty-sixth floor while the other Brave rapidly headed down the stairs to assess the fire. Captain Thunderstrike stood watch for a few moments then stealthily stole down the stairs towards the meeting room.

The second buttressing beam sloped downwards from the thirty-sixth floor of this building – just under the rooftop – back over to the thirty-second floor of the building across the intersection. After skillfully anchoring two kinds of cable to this building, one of the operatives walked across the second beam. This trip was uneventful and the walker was met back at the original building by the remaining two operatives. They had opened the exterior access door of another utility room where this beam connected in. The operatives then followed their instructions in accordance with Captain Thunderstrike's plan.

CHAPTER EIGHTY-EIGHT
Over the Edge

The Brave that Captain Thunderstrike sent downstairs found the Cabal's fire-setter as well as one of the two SIGNAL operatives that Captain Thunderstrike had originally posted in that building. That SIG-Op, Tamara Cullen Wing, had succeeded in partially extinguishing and slowing down the fire. Then, during a confrontation with the Cabal's fire-setter further up the stairwell, the two adversaries had clashed and fallen down the stairs.

The fire-setter died in the fall of a broken neck. Operative Wing had four broken limbs and a bleeding knife wound. Her broken arms had prevented her from stanching her wound, so she was weak from blood loss. The Brave forcefully pressed a "native magic" sponge against her wound, stopping the bleeding. He could not carry her up the stairs on his shoulders due to her broken limbs. So he stripped off the fire-setter's body armor and rifle, using it along with his own rifle, to quickly fashion a makeshift travois – not unlike ones his own nomadic ancestors had used. He could use it to haul the wounded SIG-Op up the many flights of stairs. Before doing so, he completed his assignment, cautiously heading down to evaluate the fire.

Captain Thunderstrike heard someone running up the stairwell. She ducked into the thirty-first floor, quietly closing the stairwell door behind her. Through the window in the door, she saw someone in body armor pass by. She could not tell if it was a SIGNAL operative.

Playing the part of a trapped civilian in distress, Captain Thunderstrike removed her helmet and loudly rapped a non-rhythmic SIGNAL code on the window of the stairwell door. The guard cautiously came back down the stairs, approaching with gun in hand. He did *not* respond with a SIGNAL counter-code. Captain Thunderstrike frantically gestured for the man to open the door for her. He complied, pointing his gun at her. As he opened the door, she grasped the wrist of his shooting hand and yanked him out of the stairwell. Her other hand gave him a Bear Claw Greeting, and he slumped, unconscious, to the floor. She took some of his gear so as to be attired more like him. Then she gagged and trussed him and pulled him out of sight.

Captain Thunderstrike re-entered the stairwell. She sensed that she was not alone. She quietly drummed part of the SIGNAL salute. The next segment was tapped back from *two* points below her. Captain Moonbow and the second operative that Captain Thunderstrike had originally posted in that building ascended the stairs. They all exited the stairwell, raised their dark visors, and compared notes.

Captain Thunderstrike told Captain Moonbow about the fire downstairs and that a *conveniently* timed Occupy protest across town was likely preventing fire department help. She shared her escape plan.

Captain Moonbow said that the President's associate, Kharuf, had ordered him to go downstairs and "check on things," which he now realized must have meant the fire. He said that, instead, he had been quietly following the other guard towards the roof, and that he had heard Captain Thunderstrike's scuffle with the guard, saving him the trouble of taking him out. He explained the meeting situation and that an EMF was blocking communications.

They agreed that Moonbow would continue up to the roof while Thunderstrike and her operative would "report back" to Kharuf. Captain Thunderstrike said that she would signal to Captain Trueheart to stick with Kharuf. She also said that she was going to try to plant a tracer on Kharuf that they could use to track him once he left the building. The two Captains then went their separate ways.

After the skirmish, when Kharuf fled from his run-in with Captain Thunderstrike, President Golden Hawk realized that he no longer had a guard protecting him. The guard that had been by his side had apparently *defected* and was restraining the only remaining Cabal guard! Golden Hawk tried to follow Kharuf out, but Hunter's head guard smoothly handcuffed and detained him.

Captain Thunderstrike instructed her operative to help Kiwi (the guard who had *defected*) to take President Golden Hawk and the Cabal guard up to the roof. Both captives were now tightly bound at the wrists and loosely shackled at the ankles.

As soon as no more members of the Cabal were present, Captain Thunderstrike strode over to Hunter's head guard. She placed her right hand on his left shoulder. He responded in kind and lifted his visor.

"Lynx," he said warmly.

"Aspen," she replied, smiling.

Captain Thunderstrike informed him and the others of the fire below and of her escape plan. Accordingly, she led them straightaway towards the roof. She told Aspen that she had tagged Kharuf with an invisible tracer like those she had previously used to track smuggled rifles.

"Excellent," Aspen said. "Up on the roof I should be able to contact Fox. I'll let him know so he can acquire the tracer's signal."

Aspen then accounted for everyone who had entered the building to be sure that all were safely getting out.

"Breeze, Sequoia, Captain Trueheart and I came with Hunter as his guards. Captain Moonbow and Brave Kiwi re-infiltrated the Secret Service in D.C. and accompanied President Golden Hawk here, taking the place of his bodyguards at the last minute. Captain Moonbow and Captain Trueheart are hopefully now with Kharuf. We should be able to confirm that up on the roof. Kiwi and *one* of Captain

Thunderstrike's operatives just took President Golden Hawk and *one* Cabal guard up to the roof."

Captain Thunderstrike filled in who was missing. Accordingly, Aspen went to help the Brave who was painstakingly hauling the wounded SIG-Op up the fire stairwell. Captain Thunderstrike retrieved the second Cabal guard whom she had left tied up on the thirty-first floor.

Hunter's group led President Golden Hawk and one of Kharuf's guards across the rooftop towards the edge where a Brave had already taken Kharuf's other guard. There was now smoke curling around them from the fire below.

A gunshot rang out.

A Cabal gunman fell on the rooftop right next to the abandoned skyscraper. The drop was the work of Captain Thunderstrike's snipers from atop the original building across the intersection.

At the sound of the gunshot, Sequoia had dropped to one knee, taking partial cover behind a large climate control unit. The others had taken cover as well.

There was a second Cabal gunman near the first. He was hidden from the SIGNAL snipers but not from Hunter's group who were close-by. The man fired his gun, just missing the Brave who had Kharuf's tightly bound guard at the roof's edge. The gunman was about to fire again, but Sequoia had already steadied her revolver on the A/C unit, acquired the man in her sights, and pressed the trigger. Less than a second later, she pressed the trigger again. Her double-tap shots were on target, and the gunman fell. Golden Hawk gaped at her in astonishment. Sequoia could not resist. As she stood up, she blew the non-existent smoke from the muzzle of her gun and re-holstered it.

The Brave whose life she had saved gave her a thumbs up. He then turned and callously shoved the Cabal guard next to him backwards off the roof of the skyscraper. He screamed as he fell, and they heard the roar of the crowd from the street below.

Golden Hawk's eyes widened as they led him in that direction.

"You're next!" Sequoia said, smiling at the man she had married.

Before reaching the roof's edge, she pulled a hood over Golden Hawk's head so the crowd would not recognize him. He babbled that he was her husband *and the President.* He begged them not to push him off, saying that he could get all of them *anything in the world* that they wanted.

Golden Hawk felt them pull a cord up through his ankle restraints and then wrap it around his body. *They are trussing me like a goat!* Sightless under the dark hood, he heard the urgings and cheers of the crowd on the street far below. In his mind's eye, he imagined the throng clamoring with blood-lust to watch the people be thrown from the roof, thirty-six stories down to the ground.

Then, he realized that those were not imaginings. They were *memories* of a scene long ago in which he had taken part. Back then, he had been one of the "righteous" executioners of political moderates, not one of the victims robbed of their lives.

Sequoia's voice interrupted his dark flashbacks.

"During the meeting, Dukon, I heard you say that you had not wanted to 'sacrifice me.' I cannot honestly say that I feel the same way about you."

With that, Sequoia kicked him in the ass, sending him over the edge of the skyscraper. He screamed as his fettered feet flew from the rooftop, frantically pedaling only air. He felt his bladder empty; and his colon discharged its contents as he fell.

Then, his triple-secured harness tether tautened, and he zoomed along the sturdy zip line that Captain Thunderstrike's team had expertly installed. The crowd roared again, having no idea that they were now watching the President of the United States zip-lining behind the other guy.

The "zippers" were received at the building across the intersection by waiting SIGNAL operatives. Honorable leader that she was, Captain Thunderstrike went last, after Hunter's group and everyone else had used her team's apparatus to zip across the street to safety.

CHAPTER EIGHTY-NINE
Off With His Head

Kharuf's helicopter landed on the roof of the Cabal's satellite headquarters building. He could see that the burned guard was nearly passed out from the pain and trauma of his injuries.

The other guard said, "I'll get him medical assistance."

Kharuf petulantly waved them off, striding ahead through the rooftop doors.

Captain Moonbow helped his "weak and debilitated" comrade inside and looked for a restroom. After passing doors with nameplates in different languages, he found a single-person restroom designated for the handicapped. Perfect. They were about to enter it when an armed guard rounded the corner.

"Who are you?" he demanded.

"We accompanied Mr. Kharuf back from his meeting. He posted his guards there until the others arrive. This man needs medical aid."

The guard looked dubious. Captain Moonbow appeared to lose his hold on Captain Trueheart who slid down. Moonbow's arm shot out, and he gave the guard a Bear Claw Greeting. The two Captains dragged the limp man into the restroom, locking the door behind them.

Moonbow stabbed the unconscious guard with his pen-syringe to keep him knocked out. They bound and gagged him and took his I.D. pass-card and weapons.

The Captains shed their armored suits, revealing rather wrinkled, business casual clothing underneath. They packed their armor into messenger bags that had been folded inside their tactical packs.

Moonbow pulled out his renowned "conversion kit." He rapidly removed the greasy gel that he had dabbed onto Lance Trueheart's old, well-healed electrocution burns to make them look fresh and oozing. He had conceived of the idea after Captain Thunderstrike told him that a Cabal agent had set a fire in the skyscraper. Moonbow then expertly applied makeup to Lance's face, quickly covering his scarred skin to make him less identifiable.

"Hey!" Lance whispered, checking out his face in the mirror. "I gotta get me some of that stuff!"

Moonbow grinned and bumped Lance from in front of the mirror. Lance watched as Moonbow looked from the filched employee I.D. card to the guard on the floor and then to the mirror. Using his kit, Moonbow quickly transformed his own face and hair until he could pass as the man pictured on the I.D. card. Then he stowed his kit in his bag while Lance checked the hall.

They emerged from the bathroom with their messenger bags slung across their bodies. Lance disabled the door in the locked position to buy time before someone would find the guard inside. He pulled out his phone and sent a *Smoke Signals* message to Fox, asking him to now network-in the two Captains' devices so they could stream video directly to him. Fox informed them that Captain Thunderstrike had successfully planted a tracer on Kharuf; so, they could home in on his location there.

Following the tracer, Lance navigated, and Moonbow used the employee pass-card to open security doors. They passed people of various ethnicities as they converged on Kharuf's location. They passed more doors with nameplates in different languages and discreetly captured video of it all.

Kharuf was stalling in his office. He had a message to see his boss, but he did not want to report to him until the backup team had successfully completed his assignment. However, without the guard who had been interfacing with that squad, he had no way of knowing when that would be. He finally decided that enough time had passed. The SIGNAL Captains saw Kharuf leave his office and followed at a safe distance. When they reached his office, Moonbow peeked inside and slipped into the unoccupied room.

Lance continued to follow Kharuf. When Kharuf entered a conference room at the end of the hall, Lance stopped short. He stepped out of view, leaning against a wall. He looked busy, typing on his notepad-like device. He positioned it to video-record Kharuf's debriefing with his boss through the window in the door. Lance increased the power on the long-distance microphone and listened to the encounter with an ear-bud while watching it on his device. There was another person in the room who was very expensively dressed and clearly of higher rank than Kharuf's boss. The boss responded to Kharuf's somewhat embellished account of what had happened.

"Backup extraction team? You mean backup security. There was no backup extraction team. Our satellite view was blurry, but we captured a high-wire stunt taking place during your meeting. Then, we saw you and the two others leave in the helicopter. Where are they? We have been waiting for the American... *dignitaries.*"

Kharuf's eyes were saucers and he wasn't breathing. His mind had gone into horrified paralysis when he heard that there had been no backup extraction team.

"Well?" the boss prodded. "*Wa-a-a-it...* you asked about a backup *extraction* team...? Don't tell me that the two people with you... were *not* the President and VP?!"

Kharuf finally gulped and just barely shook his head.

"*What?!*" his boss screamed. "After you left, we saw people evacuate the burning building on a zip line! Were the President and VP with *them?!* You incompetent FOOL!! You lost our chance to eliminate the Vice President's recordings! And you may have caused the capture of the President now that they know of his complicity! Your failures could thwart the consummation of The Master Business Plan!!"

The boss drew an evil-looking blade from a sheath on his belt. Kharuf automatically reached for his own knife. Remembering that he had left it behind in the burning building, he mindlessly wailed,

"My scimitar! I lost my scimitar back there!"

His boss's eyes bulged from their sockets.

"Your knife?? You lost your *knife?* You simpleton! You've lost your *head!"*

As a SIGNAL Captain, Lance Trueheart had seen some terrible things; but he had to stifle his rising gorge at the scene before him. The boss had launched himself at Kharuf, pinning him against a table. When the boss was done, Kharuf's severed head fell with a thump to the floor.

Meanwhile, back in Kharuf's office, Captain Moonbow plugged one of Fox's specially modified flash drive gadgets into Kharuf's computer. It vibrated and started downloading the entire contents of the computer. Fox's gizmo not only eliminated the need to sign onto a computer with passwords, but the computer did not even have to be on. Moonbow kept glancing up at the office door while watching the screen on the device display names of files being copied.

Without warning, the office door flew open. Moonbow's gun was pointed directly at the head of the man as he came through the door.

"Master Business Plan!" Lance whispered wildly – his Southern drawl always more pronounced when he was amped up. "I don't know what language it would be in, but that might actually be the name of the plot! Let's do a search, but hurry! Kharuf's lost his head... literally." He closed the door behind him.

For this, the computer did need to be on. Moonbow laid down his gun, punched the computer's power button and grabbed the keyboard. He pressed a control key and entered a code. The screen on the device turned green, for *Go.* He typed: Master Business Plan. The device started vibrating again.

"This thing does translate, but if the name is in code, we may be SOL," Moonbow pointed out.

The screen on the flash drive turned red – for *Fail.*

Lance bumped Moonbow from in front of the desk. He pointed to the screen of the now booted-up computer.

"It's not connected to any network. Let's see if we can get in. Kharuf may have been too lowly to have the plan on his computer or to even have access to it, but this device should circumvent any firewalls or network lockouts. Let's see if this plan is out there somewhere..."

While Moonbow kept his eyes and his gun aimed at the door, Lance got the computer to list available networks. He held down a control key and entered another code. He retyped: Master Business Plan. The device vibrated again as it now searched the networks. It stopped, and the screen turned blue – for *Success.*

"Hiawatha!" Lance whispered jubilantly. He verified that a large file had been downloaded, and he scanned some snippets of it on the flash drive's screen. Satisfied that they had what they had come for, he shut down Kharuf's computer and handed Moonbow the flash drive. Carefully eliminating any evidence that they had been in the office, Lance said, "We gotta get outta here. We may have triggered an intruder alert while accessing their data networks. How 'bout you crack the door and check the hall while I whistle for our horses?" He sent a *Smoke Signals* message.

Brave Bird had tailed them into the vicinity, so she was there within seconds to extract the Captains. The Cabal's helicopter was already on the roof, so Birdie could not land. She released the flexible ladder instead. Moonbow grabbed on and started climbing up. He glanced at Lance who was on the roof below.

A Cabal guard was racing towards Lance, gun aimed, finger on the trigger. Moonbow bellowed and gestured to Lance. Lance dove to his right, rolling behind the parked Cabal helicopter. Another armed guard charged from the building, trying to decide whether to shoot at Moonbow and the hovering chopper – which might then crash into him and the building – or to help the other guard to corner Lance.

Birdie initiated auto-retraction of the flexible ladder and shouted fiercely to Moonbow, "Climb up NOW!"

Moonbow took only seconds to weigh if doing otherwise might save Lance. He knew that he would then be putting the flash drive in his possession at risk. This flash drive likely contained the most critical acquisition of the highest stakes SIGNAL operation ever. This mission's success could save the lives or the freedom of millions or even billions of people around the world. Any SIGNAL Captain would sacrifice his life for this cause.

Moonbow also realized that a *Brave* would not issue a command to a *Captain* without good reason. So he scrambled up.

In the blink of an eye, there was a bright flash. The two Cabal guards were knocked down like bowling pins and their rifles skittered across the rooftop. The bright flash whirled about the parked Cabal chopper, and Lance found himself rocketing into the air.

"Ya'haiii!" Lance yelped as he catapulted into Birdie's helicopter, bounced against the ceiling, and tumbled to the floor, securely clasped in the arms and legs of Captain Grant Broadwings. Grant let go of Lance and laughed at his wide-eyed comrade as he detached his bungee cord and unzipped his reflective, metallic jump-suit.

Lance gaped first at Grant, then at Moonbow, and then at Birdie as he caught his breath. Then, in his Southern drawl, he quipped,

"Now *that* gives an all new meaning to the term *Emergency Extraction!*"

They all laughed as Birdie zigzagged the chopper away.

Grinning, and elbowing Grant, Lance entreated,

"Can we do that again?!"

CHAPTER NINETY
Indian Summer

For the first time in SIGNAL history, there was an "All Hands Operation." Every SIGNAL operative across the United States, Canada, and Mexico, including island regions, was on duty. This was SIGNAL's most critical assignment ever.

With The Master Business Plan (The Plan) in hand, SIGNAL teamed up with the independent intelligence assets of their covert partners in Congress. They had to operate under the assumption that the Cabal knew that the intruders at their satellite headquarters had made off with the "keys to the kingdom." That meant that the collaborating intelligence teams had to work fast. They rapidly compiled a plethora of high-quality intel, putting them hot on the trail of the invaders and their armaments.

It appeared that SIGNAL had come upon the plan of attack just shortly before its intended commencement. Thanks to longstanding preparedness by SIGNAL's Congressional partners, a central command for an all new U.S. Defense Team (D-Team) efficiently assembled. This nationwide brigade, led by State Marshal Joe Pontiac Thorpe, was completely independent of the National Protection Agency which was heavily infiltrated with hostile operators. Marshal Joe very quickly and quietly set in motion a colossal interior defense initiative.

Birdie's discovery of the Occupy America plot while undercover in Mexico had previously enabled SIGNAL's Congressional contacts to warn the Governors of border states. Those Governors had discreetly prepared their National Guard, Coast Guard, and State Trooper units. When the U.S. Foreign Relations Agency suddenly started new, cooperative initiatives in countries right outside U.S. borders, those Governors went on high alert.

Mexican and Canadian SIGNAL personnel obtained concrete evidence that some U.S. officials were collaborating with foreign governments to organize hordes of people to flow into the U.S. en masse. The media reported that President Golden Hawk (like a President before him) was proposing citizenship for people inside the U.S. by a certain date. Thus, swarms of people from around the globe descended like locusts upon the U.S. – as planned by the Cabal. According to The Plan, the hordes would not only enter the U.S. across its northern and southern borders but would also travel on airline and boat tickets supplied by the Cabal. The foreigners would be able to bypass U.S. Customs using a prior Administration's controversial program to streamline entry into the U.S. for certain foreigners – including some hostile ones! The Cabal had also arranged transportation for aliens involved in The Plan from all points of entry to many destinations across America. The Plan insidiously schemed to have some foreigners enter the U.S. infected with terrible diseases, including an incurable "Super Bug" developed by a Cabal nation. The chaos of a human invasion, compounded by epidemic health crises, would ensue nationwide.

Terrorists were going to use the hordes as camouflage to enter the U.S. like Odysseus's men of myth who eluded detection by traveling hidden amongst a flock of sheep. Once the Cabal's insurgents were all inside and in place, the President might only offer amnesty or citizenship if it looked like his party needed more votes to maintain their stranglehold of power over the American people. Some states did not require voter I.D. and might unwittingly even allow non-citizens to vote.

Thanks to the early warning from SIGNAL, the border states were prepared. Those Governors secured the confidential support of their most trustworthy Congressmen and Judges. Then, just as the Administration had bypassed laws enacted by Congress, the states halted the human invasion by ignoring the Administration's edicts and threats, using powers granted to the states by the Constitution. The Sheriffs and State Marshals protected the courageous, proactive Governors from the federal thugs attempting to arrest them.

Fortunately, there were many Governors who had successfully turned around their states' budget deficits. They had financial and material surpluses to use in this historic endeavor to stop the invasion (and they would later learn – overthrow) of the USA. They replaced federal personnel at official border crossings with locals carefully prescreened by the state. These residents had a personal stake in protecting their communities, did not answer to federal authority and had no conflicting loyalties. Border states also hired people to patrol the rest of their borders on-site or by use of drones – with strict oversight. Where possible, they would assist neighboring states. America was coming under siege – from without and from within.

Bold members of Congress initiated a highly visible blitz that the mainstream media simply could not ignore. They declared that the President had overstepped his power and that Congress had been close to implementing a streamlined, *legal* process which had been in the works for a long time. They said that illegal newcomers would be immediately deported. And resident aliens claiming to be relatives of the illegal aliens would not receive those alleged relatives in the U.S. but would be given the opportunity to return to their home countries and be reunited with them there. (When people tried to gain citizenship in *other* countries, they found themselves up against requirements even tougher than those of the United States.)

The result: the flow of unidentified aliens into the U.S. stopped cold. This ended the humanitarian crisis of people being lured by false promises – actually for the nefarious purposes of conspirators – and then being victimized during the journey. It also ended the unsupportable influx of foreigners and the terrorists hidden amongst them. Much damage had already been done, however, since many enemies of America had already crossed the border and had been shuttled around the country by Administration employees.

Marshal Joe coordinated the network of trusted leaders in deploying only their most trusted personnel. Governors now quietly tasked their National Guard and Coast Guard commanders as well as their Sheriffs. The American Indian Chiefs discreetly assembled their Chieftains responsible for law enforcement and security. Certain Mayors were brought into the initiative, and they involved select Police Chiefs.

In a major coup, D-Team technical specialists preempted the Cabal and took down *their* communications network being provided by the Cabal's Eurinatian telecom partner. Thus, the invaders' command stream was replaced *with silence*.

While briefly having the element of surprise, D-Team forces used The Plan to locate the Cabal's hidden armies bivouacked on closed-off federal lands. D-Team units ambushed and subdued them. Stashes of weapons, munitions, and toxins were discovered across America and were confiscated. To the great relief of many, it was determined that the botched government sting rifles that had ended up on Native American reservations had been hidden in remote areas without any knowledge, participation, or consent of the tribes.

Wherever invaders found that they had been discovered, there was a chaotic flee-for-all. With their communications system now offline, the warlords could not issue commands. Some terrorists scattered like chickens without heads. Some bolted from the U.S. Others, living amongst unsuspecting Americans, initiated violence unilaterally with weapons hidden in advance. They killed everyone they encountered – mostly in states that had disarmed their unfortunate citizens. Now, other than Law Enforcement Officers (LEOs), *only the bad guys* there had guns. Just like prior mass shootings – virtually all of which had taken place *in gun-free zones* – the assailants knew that there would be no armed resistance there. Law-abiding citizens who no longer had firearms were unable to stop the assailants or to protect themselves or loved ones from the large-scale slaughter.

LEOs did the best they could in those states, which were also the states with budget deficits and maxed-out credit. Those Governors declared the right to seize goods for the state, but firearm and ammo producers had left those anti-gun states. Thus, there was no longer a local source to provide LEOs with what they needed. Also, some guns that those states had previously confiscated from the residents somehow found their way into the hands of the terrorists...

Needless to say, the citizens of those states suffered the most casualties – because of the choices that they and their elected officials had made to disallow personal defense. People there were left to rely upon the limited LEO resources, which can never be a substitute for people being able to defend themselves. Law enforcement officers are called that because that is their job – to enforce laws. They are not bodyguards and cannot be everywhere. They cannot be expected to protect individuals, let alone whole towns or cities, from scores of armed assailants – especially assailants armed with true assault weapons – fully automatic ones like machine guns.

None of the attackers would have passed any background check, but *that* didn't stop them. Like gang members and other domestic criminals, none of the assailants purchased any weapons at a U.S. gun shop, gun show, or any other place where background checks could possibly be performed! So, despite lawmakers' actions that were *supposed to* reduce gun violence, the new laws had no effect – either on violent crime – or on the Indian Summer attack. The laws and bureaucracy of creating new, universal background check databases – instead of increasing the entry of relevant data into the existing system – did more harm than good. It disenfranchised upstanding citizens, making it more difficult for many to acquire weapons to defend themselves. This, of course, played right into the hands of the Anti-West Cabal.

Hostile parties can always obtain weapons on the black market, domestically or via smugglers. Laws will never affect law-*breakers*. Nor do laws stop assailants. *People with weapons and the training to use them do.* The impotence of gun laws was clear; they did nothing to protect Americans. They had, however, turned millions of Americans into sitting ducks.

The Plan led the D-Team to stop Cabal cohorts from sheltering in the updated, invincible bunker beneath the White House – which now had *armed* drones on its roof pointed in all directions including ones aimed at the Capitol where Congress meets. The drones would stop any attempt to unseat the new *rulers* from their White House command center. From there, the Cabal intended to shut down communications across the U.S. to isolate everyone, preventing any coordinated, defensive response. This was possible since the federal government had previously required all telephone and Internet providers to turn over their system blueprints.

Per The Plan, the President would shelter only briefly in the bunker. The Cabal would then fake his death (with no identifiable remains) and take him off-continent to a site beyond U.S. reach. The Plan provided for any children he had with the First Lady to be sent ahead with her "on vacation." Since SIGNAL had already captured the President, the D-Team took him to a location on the continent instead.

Vice President Wolf, who was now America's senior leader, consulted with top-notch military and national security advisors whom he had recommended to Dukon for his Cabinet. Dukon had, instead, mostly chosen people who were rookies, duds, puppets, or buffoons. Hunter and his advisors quickly drew up a redeployment plan for U.S. military personnel.

The Cabal had air, water, missile, satellite, and land forces poised to imminently invade – first the U.S. and a smaller nation, and then – the rest of the free world. The evil intentions of the Cabal, along with its conspiring nations, splinter groups, and arrogant billionaires were now globally exposed. Once it was out in the open, all allied countries joined together to repulse the now-visible legions of hostile conspirators.

In America, all kinds of Chiefs led their people: Governors, American Indian Chiefs, Sheriffs, State Marshals, National Guard Chiefs, Coast Guard Chiefs, Mayors, Police Chiefs, and Fire Chiefs. Local LEOs supplemented their manpower with trustworthy citizens who had firearms training and clean criminal records.

Religious leaders organized their congregations to report threats to local LEOs. Courageous women of a faith whose extremists had participated in instigating the assault on the freest nation in the world were prominently active in safeguarding it. They knew better than anyone the price of oppression – especially when religion distorted to justify enslaving or killing some people in order to serve the comforts, convenience, and desires of others.

And so, it was a motley alliance of Americans who provided: experienced leadership, "Native Know-How," "Yankee Ingenuity," material resources from businesses large and small, and millions of civilian "boots on the ground." There was a unifying camaraderie amongst this extremely diverse group – all citizens of that "melting-pot" nation – the once again *United* States of America.

CHAPTER NINETY-ONE
Takedown

Thanks to the intrepid initiatives of the SIGNAL organization, the Indian Summer massacre and world conquest was thwarted and contained. There were tens of thousands of American casualties – but there would have been many millions had The Master Business Plan not been discovered and disrupted.

Now, government efforts to ban U.S. citizens from gun ownership, as well as the downsizing of the U.S. Military were unmasked for their true, insidious purpose – to facilitate the takedown of America. The facts were linked together into a bruising indictment of Dukon Chatan, a.k.a. President Golden Hawk, and his participation in a global conspiracy. The deluge of evidence was clearly chronicled by members of a nonpartisan think tank. Those scholars laid out legal procedures to follow, and the Governors and Congress were galvanized into action. They brought charges, officially removed the President from office, and made his current detention indefinite, pending judicial review. Besides conspiracy, some of the charges were: political malfeasance, state-created danger, dereliction of duty, and misappropriation of funds. The panel had to determine if Treason applied if the President was not actually a U.S. citizen.

Dukon was also charged with conspiring to murder Kogan Kichoba, Breeze, Sequoia, and Hunter. Kogan was killed because, as the longstanding Official Keeper of the Register, he would have known that Dukon belonged to no Ronopo clan. Like Kogan, the first attempt on Breeze's life was at Rattlesnake Canyon. Breeze now realized that when Dukon appeared to be looking up at her from the canyon floor, he was likely focused on the drone positioning to kill her. When intelligence analysts magnified the images recorded by her electronic binoculars, another person besides Dukon was visible in the canyon along with high-tech equipment and crates with foreign lettering. An earpiece was even visible in Dukon's ear, suggesting that he had been in constant contact with his trainers and was probably warned to move away as the drone took aim at Breeze. Dukon later ordered Hunter to kill Breeze. Then Dukon was party to the Cabal plan to blow up Sequoia and Breeze's limo. He had targeted Hunter for death, as well, by urging him to accompany the women in that limo.

The Administration was also held responsible for the deaths of the aid workers in Central America during the operation that was intended to validate military cuts. In addition, there was abundant testimony linking members of the Administration and their cronies to the deaths of brave military personnel, investigative journalists, and others who had opposed them or whose knowledge presented a threat to that coterie's further acquisition of money or power.

Back when Sequoia had the shaman put her in a hypnotic trance, she transcribed foreign characters that she had seen on a book and on papers sticking out from under Dukon's bed. A SIGNAL analyst recognized the foreign language. That pivotal clue had triggered dogged research by SIGNAL analysts in cooperation with the intel team of their Congressional partners. That collaboration led to the unearthing of video footage of Dukon as a teenager in a foreign country, speaking in both a foreign language – and in English. In the video, he and other young disciples of a violent, extremist ringleader denounced the free world. This explained how he had mastered the English language so quickly on the Ronopo Reservation. *He had already been fluent in it* when he was prematurely "rescued" from Rattlesnake Canyon – where he had been undergoing training for his role in the Cabal's plot.

For his safety, the D-Team had transported the President to an empty compound that his Administration had purchased with federal funds from a financially floundering state that supported him politically. The President had said that it was for a rehabilitation community for veterans. Some of his opponents expressed fear that it might actually be made into a prison for his political foes. Others worried that it might be linked to the recent, massive purchases of weapons, ammo, and protective gear by many federal agencies. Administration spokesmen stated that those purchases were to prepare for civil unrest as a prior Administration had done.

People asked, "Is this Administration *predicting* civil unrest – *or planning it?* Why are they purchasing *lethal* ammunition instead of rubber bullets? Why are the Feds not involving the Governors in these protective preparations? Surely there is no good reason for that to be done at the federal level – especially by officials who seem more interested in serving *non*-Americans."

Stunning revelations emerged upon the President's arrival at the compound. It was found to be anything but empty. There was evidence that a multitude of residents had only just hurriedly evacuated. In their haste to flee, they had been unable to take with them the astounding inventory of armaments, toxic chemicals, unknown biological substances in working laboratories, and an extensive fleet of drones and militarized vehicles. It was clear from what was left behind that the occupants were mostly foreigners from hostile nations.

Later investigations unearthed purchases of land *surrounding* that compound made by certain investors *before* the complex was built. Its construction was then funded by the state – which more than recouped its outlay when the federal government purchased it *at a premium* from the state. That arrangement yielded a windfall increase in the surrounding property values to the benefit of the original, insider investors – at U.S. taxpayer expense. This cast a new light on politicians' attempts to attract a World Fair to that area – which would have increased the value of the surrounding land astronomically! Certain officials had a pattern of involvement in such ventures with other investors, including foreigners and "charities" with questionable objectives. These disclosures ultimately revealed that many grants of monetary aid that the U.S.

had given to foreign nations in recent years had been used by them *to buy U.S. real estate and businesses* – and so much that America was now mostly owned by non-Americans!

It was recognized that, early in Dukon's presidency, he had structured the multiple intelligence services to compete with one another for funding and pay-scale. This led them to not share intelligence with one another – each agency jealously guarding its findings. It was clearly a deliberate segregation of intelligence, such that, if the agencies had been working together, they would have perceived the threatening activities brewing by groups hostile to the free world.

High level Presidential appointees had been resigning over the course of Golden Hawk's Presidency. Most migrated away from D.C. and other major cities, to new homes or "extended vacations" with their families *off the continent.* The Plan clarified the actual, insidious reason for the staggered exodus of most of them: *It was so they could get out of harm's way.* These former officials were detained and returned, under extreme protest, to detention centers in major U.S. cities. When told that their families were also being kept nearby for their safety... the ex-officials quickly started to "sing." The people who had been appointed to replace these powerful officials were also detained. Many were revealed to have ties to the Vicious Vipers terror network.

The Plan also called for *removal* of the VP at a propitious time. He would be replaced by a cabinet member, a Presidential candidate, a Cabal leader, or even the President's wife, to ensure the consummation of The Master Business Plan. The President might then step down (or his death might be faked), allowing that VP to become President. Depending on who it was... their succession might mean facing the cataclysmic invasion with the former President safely away...

With blessings from the highest courts, a bipartisan committee of Congressional Representatives delved further and unsealed all of Dukon Chatan's previously sealed records. They opened an investigation into his involvement with anti-Democracy radicals from around the world. The newly available evidence chronicled how these militants had developed The Master Business Plan for the conquest, terrorization, and plundering of the United States and the rest of the free world. (Allegations of this sort made against prior elected officials had been determined to be nothing more than the paranoid musings of conspiracy theorists.)

Dukon's gang, who had nothing to offer to make the world a *better* place, did the easy thing that hate-filled, bitter and cowardly people do. Like bullies who smash sandcastles built by others on the beach, they strove to destroy what was conceived and built by the blood, sweat and tears of the good, the willing, and the risk-taking brave.

A popular news service published the headline:

The Lone Stranger! Who is that Moscked Man?

Hunter was quickly sworn in as President of the United States. America now jubilantly celebrated its first, true Native American Indian Commander-in-Chief. Following countless years of tradition, the military band played: *Hail to the Chief.*

CHAPTER NINETY-TWO
Life, Liberty, and the Pursuit of Happiness

Hunter's first acts as Commander-in-Chief were to appoint a Vice President and a Chief Advisor. For Vice President he chose Margaret Ramsey, a white woman who had been exceptionally successful in both business and government. As a guest professor at his college, she had taught his favorite economics course: *Commonsensenomics.* For his Chief Advisor, he chose a brilliant, dynamic, young black woman who had come closest to being what he could call a friend at college. Her name was Candace West. No one at college had called her "Candy." They had all privately referred to her as *"Can Do."*

With a full, not handpicked, media presence, President Wya-Wolf addressed the Congress, then the nation and the world. He extolled VP Ramsey's many achievements and impeccable qualifications for leadership. He asserted that she knew how, and would, reignite a vibrant economy in America. She actually had a record of such accomplishments.

President Wya-Wolf predicted that many worldwide woes would start to improve once the American free-market economy was responsibly unconstrained and strong again – and partnering with other recovering economies. He said that the United States and other nations willing to work together would provide a foundation for a peaceful, global synergy for the benefit of all.

He said that while he finished out the former President's term, America would have an Administration with a centrist ideology and that Congress should be able to find middle ground and work together. He charged them to represent the concerns of their constituents – only on matters that belong at the federal level. He exhorted them to abolish all earmarks of federal money going to states or special interests. He promised to provide a "check and balance" from the Executive Branch if the majority leader in either house of Congress, without clear justification, prevented bills important to America from being brought to the floor for a vote by the elected representatives of the American People. He said,

"The President takes an oath to uphold the Constitution, which means serving the citizens of the United States and not serving *others* to the detriment of American citizens. Likewise, you members of Congress were elected by the people of your respective states to be their ears and voices to understand and participate in matters of *national concern.* Americans are tired of hearing that their legislators write and pass bills named for one issue but that actually include hidden, unrelated ones. That you then haggle and cut deals behind closed doors, promising to vote for one another's bills in exchange for federal funds being allocated to your home states or other beneficiaries. Your constituents expect you to vote in their best interests on each issue based on its merits. Your legislation should be targeted, its language clear, and the process transparent to all. And you are meant to be working collaboratively within and between the Houses of Congress to *arrive at solutions* instead of stonewalling one another. Importantly, make no mistake: *it is an unacceptable abuse of your position or mine to provide benefits and exceptions for ourselves and select others which are paid for by the general population but are not available to them as well.*

Vice President Ramsey and I will be designing a significantly reduced and streamlined federal government. Both power and responsibility for many issues will be returned to the states where they belong. There, issues can be handled in a manner that fits each state's unique population and the needs and *choices* of the people who live there.

Congress has been vigorously manipulated to prioritize topics that are not of consequence to the survival or basic quality of life of *all* people of this nation. I have a charge for us. It is to give the nation's critical priorities the precedence that they demand. Let us attend first to issues of urgency to the nation as a whole instead of focusing on matters propelled to the forefront by vocal special interest groups and their sympathizers in the media.

That means that we will focus *immediately* on all aspects of sustained national security, and we will fix our broken economy. No other issues come even close to affecting more people of this country or of having the potential to make or break America's future. Other issues will be much more easily solved once we have dealt with those two moral imperatives.

Much foul play has been allowed to progress unnoticed or camouflaged inside and outside of America. The actions of our former President, in concert with powerful individuals in Congress – and the myopic eye of the mainstream media – drew all attention away from that foul play. They did this by focusing on myriad issues which should have been handled by the individual states or attended to *after* addressing the nation's most critical issues.

The safety of American citizens and nationwide economic health are indispensable conditions to permit *life, liberty, and the pursuit of happiness.* It is our sworn duty to the people who elected us to defend those rights for them. Others who follow the appropriate legal process for U.S. citizenship, or who are born here to U.S. citizen parents, will *then* be entitled to the enjoyment of those same rights, protections, and privileges.

It is said that charity begins at home. We are a compassionate nation that will always reach out to help others to achieve freedom and prosperity. To be able to do that, however, we must *first* get our own house in order. It is tempting to do personally aggrandizing, benevolent-*looking* deeds using *other people's money.* But no elected official has the right to put the welfare of others before the welfare of his or her own constituents. To do otherwise is an abuse of power and of access to the money *taken* from the American people by their government or borrowed by the government at the people's risk. The basic well-being of all Americans, including our American Indian and other minority citizens, must be prioritized ahead of the interests of those who wish to become citizens and nations who desire U.S. economic aid.

Recent leadership and vocal activists have asserted that allowing free entry to this country, along with all of its benefits, is a humane and righteous thing to do. In reality, this leadership fomented chaos for pernicious purposes, harming many unsuspecting pawns. The instigating politicians also sought new votes and more dependents to increase the population over which they would have control. They already counted on the votes of American citizens whose problems they previously promised to address – such as those of Native Americans – problems which they have, instead, neglected. Since nationwide poverty increased under recent leadership, how can it possibly benefit U.S. citizens to admit more needy people who will obviously also not be well-served? Only the politicians involved would gain.

America is a nation of immigrants, possibly including some 'First Americans' who are thought to have come here from elsewhere long ago. America will always invite new immigrants. There must be a limit, however, on how many – as *no nation* can support all of the world's people. Everyone benefits if new immigrants bring needed skills or new contributions rather than unneeded skills or only demands for support. The rule of law and fairness dictate that all must follow the process to legally become a citizen here, *just as is required by other nations.*

Americans and others around the world are best served when America is strong. Recently, economic growth has stagnated, and government policies have poisoned the efforts of businesses and institutions to keep workers employed full-time, let alone to expand and provide jobs for more people. Ignoring America's security, weakening its sovereignty, removing incentives for people to work, and strangling businesses with regulations has been killing the golden goose that makes possible the American Dream – in all its many forms for this nation's diverse people.

America's storied military power and our courageous warriors, sympathetic to the plight of others and willing to risk life and limb to help them, have long discouraged greater violence in the world. Solid military might *can* foster peace, act as a deterrent, and be only judiciously used. Our military must not be diminished, and our warriors and veterans deserve first-class support.

Together we can get this country back on track. Let us ascertain that people already inside our borders and those crossing them are not a threat to us. Let us stop dividing or redistributing rations of a shrinking economy. Let us *add* to the nation's wealth, providing opportunities for all citizens to prosper. Our Elders, who worked their whole lives, deserve to now have the money that was taken from their paychecks as promise of support in their later years.

America is not perfect. Many people choose the word 'exceptional' to describe America – while some do not. All nations and their cultures, including the U.S., should be able to hold onto the positive features that make them unique. Around the world we see globalization, migration, and sometimes dictators, intruding upon the cultures and traditions of other nations or of their own. The traditional character of many cultural groups is being diluted beyond recognition – nudging some towards extinction. Societies are being homogenized due to the influx of immigrants or foreign businesses or the demands of radical politicians.

I, Hunter Wya-Wolf, am an American – of Native American Indian heritage. I understand, firsthand, how important it is for an ethnic or religious group to be able to maintain its unique and precious, traditional culture and way of life – while upholding the *natural rights* of the individual as affirmed and protected here by the U.S. Constitution.

In recent years there has been an assault on the freedoms and values that have made the United States unique. There has been a movement away from the power and freedom of all individuals – towards centralized power for a few. That is a dangerous trend.

An absolute and indisputable *natural right* is the right to protect oneself and others from harm – *and to be free to possess the means to do so.*

Contemplate this:

How different might the outcome have been, long ago, when immigrants *with guns* invaded and overwhelmed the American Indians here – *who were without guns?*

The strangers also had *biological* threats – diseases to which the native populations had no immunity. Whole tribes were wiped out that way.

The threat of invaders and their weapons, be they firearms, tanks, bombs, drones, or nuclear or biological weapons, is a real and perpetual threat everywhere in the world.

Today's democracies could be in jeopardy by the very same vulnerabilities of my ancestors if we allow *unidentified strangers* into our land – *as my ancestors did.*

Will we – or will we not – learn from history?

During my tenure as President, all American citizens who are able to work will be given that opportunity with the *real* jobs that result from a healthy economy. Those citizens who truly cannot work and have no means will receive help. Those of you who *can* work but don't *like* the work that is available and want *other* taxpayers or employers to support you instead – or to pay for costly choices that *you* make... well, you are in the wrong country. The United States of America is a land of *opportunity.* That means opportunity for each person *to make something of themselves* – and – *to work* to fulfill their dreams. There are other countries perfectly willing to take care – *and control* – of their citizens. If that is what you want, all U.S. exits are open. Others who would like to become U.S. citizens, we welcome you – *to apply.* We look forward to finding out who you are and what you have to contribute.

All nations need their best and brightest to make life better at home. Some people come here for higher education. Some may want to stay, while others will make greater contributions by adding to what they have learned here and incorporating it into the richness of their own cultures. By learning from one another we can raise the quality of life across the globe.

I challenge us all to IMAGINE. Imagine a world in which *every* person is free to live *as he or she chooses to live* – in peace, without harming others, and without fear of harm by others; with privacy; and with the opportunity to acquire, by legitimate means, that which one needs to live. *These* are our natural rights.

It is *people* who rob others of these natural rights. It is *people* who seek power over others – through violence or political positions or by exploiting religion to force some people to live – or die – in accordance with the desires or beliefs of *other people*. Everyone should be free to live the one life that they have been given – *as they choose.*

I said IMAGINE, but it need not be just a dream. Together, *We the People,* an unbroken circle of diverse, committed, fellow Americans – can partner with our brothers and sisters around the globe – and make it a reality.

So let's do it."

COUNTERPOINT XIII
RESET

"Our primary asset must not be interrogated! Break him out and take him to Location 5."

"Location 5? I thought he was going to the luxury enclave in the territory that was now to be given total sovereignty, a wide buffer zone around it, and no extradition treaty with the U.S."

"The puppet didn't earn it. He sought to be the hero of his kind, focusing too much on conquering the small nation. Its former, multicultural peace and prosperity irks and embarrasses his blood-spilling, bickering brethren. And his errors exposed us. He supplied us much Classified U.S. intel by various means, but we need the rest. Fake his death at sea and spirit him away."

"Will his wives and children relocate there too?"

"No. He doesn't want his wives nor his children, who are all female. His brothers will take any of his wives or daughters that they want to marry and will dispose of the rest. He thinks he will be acquiring a new wife. He said that the only one he would have kept was his ex, the American Indian woman. He said that she had been allowed to develop into someone more complete – and when he was alone, it was that wife that he missed. He said that he thinks he understands why some men only want one wife at a time, and – maybe – why some only ever have one. Frankly, I think he was just glad to not be dealing with the problems of multiple wives! In any case, Alternate #7 of The Master Business Plan is a new approach. It builds on our first venture. It may take a few more years to implement, but our remaining global partners are in agreement, so proceed. ...Why are you looking at me like that? Are you still worried that the ex-President will do something of concern?"

"Well... I guess he has no real power without our backing..."

"That is correct. The only power he ever had was the power that we gave him."

***

Acknowledgments

I want to thank my draft critics who gave me *mountains* of criticism – some diplomatic and some... uh... painfully direct. I appreciated your ideas and wording suggestions. It all made a difference. But most of all, *infinite thanks* to those who gave me the encouragement and support to write this novel. You know who you are. I could *not* have written it without you.

Author's Pledge

A portion of the proceeds from sales of this book will be donated to a Native American Indian organization and also to a fund that assists American Military Service men and women, veterans, and their families.

39154459R00172

Made in the USA
San Bernardino, CA
20 September 2016